THE ADAMANT I

An Anti-University University Novel

By S. Stiles, Ph.D.

© 2020

To Judi Stiles (1957 – 2016)

Serum auxilium post praelium.

Ye see yon birkie, ca'd a lord,
Wha struts, an' stares, an' a' that?
Tho' hundreds worship at his word,
He's but a cuif for a' that.
For a' that, an' a' that,
His ribband, star, an' a' that,
The man o' independent mind,
He looks and laughs at a' that.

Robert Burns, "A Man's a Man for a' That"

CONTENTS

Prologue: A Fascist on a Friday Afternoon...........................1

Chapter One: Downward-Facing Dogs.............................12

Chapter Two: Sentimental Occasions.............................31

Chapter Three: Circus of the Damned...........................44

Chapter Four: Blessed be the Name of the Lard....................51

Chapter Five: Enter Boudicca...................................67

Chapter Six: Mochaccino Marxists..............................91

Chapter Seven: The Fruit of Her Hands........................106

Chapter Eight: Little Bits of Knowledge........................121

Chapter Nine: Tits on a Bullhorn..............................140

Chapter Ten: Good and Not Evil................................159

Chapter Eleven: Mothers and Other Crosses to Bear..............178

Chapter Twelve: A Gentle Inquisition..........................196

Chapter Thirteen: Sentimental Occasions: Reprise................211

Chapter Fourteen: What You Sow...............................229

Chapter Fifteen: Oblivion is Seafoam Green....................242

Chapter Sixteen: Cubic Zirconia Cut Cubic Zirconia.............249

Chapter Seventeen: Fiddleheading..............................264

Chapter Eighteen: Enter (and Exit) Athena.....................276

Chapter Nineteen: So Long, Deborahann.........................291

Chapter Twenty: The Queen is Dead; Long Live the Queen.........296

Chapter Twenty-One: Happy Hour at The Ranch Hand..............309

Epilogue: Tomorrow (Starting Over)............................319

Prologue: A Fascist on a Friday Afternoon

Fr: Deborahann Stevens—deborahannstevens@hotmail.com

To: Tessa Stevens—te.stevens@svu.edu

Subject: WE LOVE YOU TESSIE!!!

Date: August 27, 2016, 11:48 a.m.

TESSIE-BEAR

WE ARE SO PROUD OF OUR TESSIE-BEAR FOR COMPLETING HER PHD, YOU WORKED VERY HARD, NOW ENJOY. (DON'T ENJOY TOO MUCH THOUGH! HAHA.) NOW THAT YOU ARE A P-H-D YOUR DAD SAYS YOU NEED TO FIND A J-O-B. HAVE YOU STARTED APPLYING ANYWHERE??

LOVE YOU!!!

MUM

P.S. TRIXIE HAD A SEIZURE ON WEDNESDAY BUT SHE IS BETTER NOW…$250 LATER AFTER VET APPOINTMENT IN WEYBURN. SHE MUST THINK WE ARE MADE OF MONEY.

Tessa groaned and screwed shut one bleary eye so the other could make out her mother's email message on the phone screen. Her head radiated pain. Her mouth was a foul pit. Memories of the night before filtered into her consciousness, making their unwanted appearance like so many pervert uncles at a wake. She had been at the pub with friends for hours last night, celebrating her successful defense.

How many whisky sours did I drink, on top of all the beer? she wondered. *5? 6? 7? No, that's alcohol-poisoning level. Impossible.*

From upstairs, a cacophony sounded. Apparently Adrian and Mark were conducting a 50-piece orchestra in the kitchen.

Individual features of the subterranean bedroom came into resolution: mismatched taupe and gray dressers; brown venetian blinds; a laptop bag made of something synthetic and shiny; and a stack of literary theory texts, one featuring Foucault's severe domed profile. A pair of pleather tights and a purple tunic lay crumpled beside the bed. Through the partly-drawn blinds, a few rays of light from The Outside World penetrated Tessa's lair.

Today is the first day of the rest of your life, Dr. Stevens, ran the ironic ticker-tape of her thoughts. *Defense completed and no revisions. Not so shabby, old girl.*

Only nothing had changed. The day was like all the previous ones that summer: she felt discomfort in the present, anxiety for the future—and this morning, a magnificent hangover, to boot. Tessa did not feel any more professional or accomplished today, post-dissertation defense, than she had the day before, although she did feel a sense of pride for gutting out the task.

And all she had to do was follow her mother's advice.

Tessa lay in bed, her mother Deborahann's voice, unbidden, reverberating in her head: *Don't be a shit-disturber, Tessie.* Tessa had winced at the crudeness of the phrase, but she retained its meaning. For women like her and Deborahann—women who came from nothing coffand had no fall-back money—it was prudent not to stand out. You kept your opinions to yourself if you wanted to get along in this world. Both parents often told her that bosses don't like smart-asses.

Back in Beaconsbridge, New Brunswick, Deborahann herself had employed the classic ambitious working man's strategy of shutting-the-fuck-up to rise from poor to less-poor. She had made it into her small town's home-owning lower-middle class. This was no small feat, and

Deborahann knew her hold on it was tenuous. A single critical remark to Elinor Crossman her boss, the owner of the town's only flower shop, might generate enough ill will to jeopardize her position there. Elinor was worth putting up with, despite her airs and graces, because she paid $16 an hour. As Deborahann's husband Victor often reminded her, "Where else in Madawaaksis County are you going to make that kind of money? Keep your mouth shut for once."

For Tessa, the point of the Ph.D. was to leave the realm of the silent. Professors had a platform and their opinions were taken seriously, she thought back then. Tessa was willing to make compromises to succeed in academia, but she was troubled by the growing question of how much shutting-up she had to do now in order to speak freely later. Over time, the discipline of silence grew onerous.

The one time she dared speak her mind, two years into the Ph.D., she almost lost everything. It was the day her supervisor called her a fascist. No one expects to be called a fascist on a Friday afternoon by her doctoral supervisor. Summer-time Friday afternoons in academia should be languid and beery. As Tessa rose from bed and showered in super-slow motion, she replayed the incident in her mind. It was characteristic of Tessa that instead of enjoying a present triumph, she chose to brood on past trauma. But trauma always seemed more real. More vivid and pressing. Triumph was asinine.

* * *

Tessa was the one who had arranged the meeting that day, albeit sheepishly, for sheepishness is the appropriate default emotional state of Ph.D. students in all communications with their supervisors. As her friend and housemate Adrian said, a graduate student is a supplicant, like a medieval peasant. This was as true in her department, English, as it was in his, Commerce. One approaches one's lord with diffidence, and kisses the ring. In the case of Dr.

Elizabeth Wagband, Tessa's supervisor at the time, the ring in question was a conspicuously simple golden band, marking her recent union with Dr. Terrence Stout. They had agreed that using the terms "husband" and "wife" was sexist and outdated, though marriage, as Elizabeth noted, was "still important for social and legal reasons"—at least, Elizabeth agreed, and Terry agreed to agree with Elizabeth.

Tessa was compelled to call the meeting after Wagband rejected three consecutive versions of her fourth dissertation chapter. They returned via email, damned with faint praise and calls for further revision, and littered with staccato-style red track change notes. (*But what does Steward say? Patriarchal structure!!? WOC perspective??*) Wagband would often take months just to review a chapter. Tessa would wait as long as she could, until she could bear it no longer, and then send the gentlest possible email reminder. (*I was wondering if perhaps you had a chance to look at my chapter yet, maybe? Thank you!*) She had noticed a correlation between Wagband's chapter-returns and her supervisor's cat-sitting requests. Mimi was a geriatric Persian who needed to be assisted outdoors to perform certain necessary bodily functions. To reward Tessa for this service, Mimi held her body rigid and hissed. Tessa calculated that she had about a 10 second window for carrying Mimi before the cat would resent her lack of agency and attack. At least one knew where one stood with Mimi. Wagband, with her enormous, blinking frog-eyes, was a mystery. She was vague, distracted, more or less amenable, and then she would make a sudden imperious demand by email that slowed down Tessa's progress by months, if not years.

The current set of chapter revisions, for instance, was deemed unacceptable by Wagband until Tessa first read "the important early work of Helen Kay Steward," a Gender Studies theorist and sometime literary critic. Obediently, Tessa read the works in question, muddling her way through a jargon, style, and line of thinking foreign to her temperament and upbringing. Steward wrote her "theory" in a flowing, free-form poetic style she called "Womynspeak," though Tessa detected traces of Eliot and Ginsberg. Wagband had strongly recommended Steward's early essay, "Discourse and the Vaginal," saying that it "totally transformed my thinking as a graduate student." Anticipating it would become a foundational text for her research as well, Tessa splurged and purchased the heavily annotated thirtieth anniversary edition of *Discourse and the Vaginal, and Other Essays*. It was $75. She ate ramen for lunch for a week to work it into her budget. One afternoon, green tea at the ready, she dove in:

Discourse and the Vaginal:

Repression, Subversion, and the Eternal Feminine

I cried out for another tongue, another discourse, another bloody hole, another insatiable, starving, blackened, beseeching irrelevancy, in a Marlboro Man world.

Who will speak for me? Who will speak for the wounded ones?

They call me Atalanta, the fleet-footed huntress. I am the beloved of Artemis. I am the virgin with eyes aflame. Mother, daughter, saint. Whore of Whores and Queen of Queens.

Kotex and archaeopteryx. Mucinex and tuberoses. Do you hear the children? They are sweetly singing. Born of my bosomed-bloody-bearing.

But all the children are CORPSES. Prattling putrescencies. The teat that nourished them stinks sulphur and leaks lysergic acid...

Tessa was dismayed.

Further exploration of the text yielded similar discoveries. It was Kotex and archaeopteryx clean through. Tessa wondered how, in good conscience, she could incorporate this rubbish into her dissertation, a pedestrian (she did not know this yet) single author study on an obscure male American literary realist and Henry James contemporary, E. Lyle Picayoon. Was the trick to find anything remotely sexist in his novels (by today's standards, naturally), fixate on it, and complain at length, shoe-horning in quotations from Steward whenever possible?

Reviewing Wagband's publications, Tessa discovered this was her supervisor's method. Wagband's most recent article, published in an actual peer-reviewed journal, was entitled, "Dick[ens] Pics: Phallic Imagery in Victorian Novels." It was 20 pages of feminist theory grafted on to four Victorian novels of which Wagband appeared to have only the most rudimentary understanding. Tessa guessed that Wagband's process had been to highlight every passage in the novels where anything even vaguely resembling a penis popped up. Astonishing.

But Tessa had never intended her dissertation to be a feminist critique, and she didn't understand why Wagband was determined to turn it into that. Trouble arose when Tessa began analyzing one of Picayoon's novellas, *A Light in the Doorway*, an unusual work, written in the 1890s, but set in the colonial era. It was mostly a theological debate between a Calvinist fishmonger and a Quaker ironsmith. At one point, the ironsmith's wife Delilah appears to serve the famished debaters supper. Otherwise, there were no female characters, and women were only mentioned incidentally in the work. In a previous meeting, Wagband suggested that Tessa devote an entire dissertation chapter to analyzing Delilah. When Tessa protested that Delilah only made one appearance, and did not speak, Wagband shook her head and said, "That only makes the character *more* significant, not less. Don't you find it interesting that Delilah is silenced by the text?"

Tessa did not find this interesting. She nodded and changed the subject, but from that moment on she felt uncomfortable with her supervisor's editorial directions. She began ignoring the nonsensical ones. Her failure to analyze the character did not go unnoticed. On the last revised chapter, Wagband's final comment was ominous: *Still no Delilah in chapter? We must not be COMPLICIT in the silencing of women's voices!*

All of which led to the Friday meeting. It started pleasantly enough, with Tessa inquiring after Terry and Mimi, and trying her best not to look surprised that her 58 year old, formerly brunette supervisor, had stopped dyeing her hair. Her pageboy was suddenly gunmetal. (*Lioness*, thought Wagband. *Charwoman*, thought Tessa.) Screwing her courage to the sticking place, Tessa ventured further.

"So, umm...as I said in the email, I just wanted to talk about the chapter revisions. I had some trouble incorporating Steward."

Wagband looked grave.

"Tessa, I'm afraid you failed to really *engage* with Steward's theory. Yes, I see you did add *some* passing references to *Discourse and the Vaginal*, but as I explained, Steward's *entire* conceptual framework is useful here—in particular, her conceptualization of the 'voiceless nymph,' which, as I recall, you did *not* include in the revisions."

"Yeah. Voiceless nymph....right. I just wasn't sure how it directly applied to *Light in the Doorway*. It's not about women's issues."

Wagband sighed.

"I'm disappointed you would refer to the silencing of The Other as a 'woman's issue.' *Obviously*, these are *human* issues, broadly relevant to any number of texts. You cannot explicate Picaroon without..."

"Pica-YOON."

"What?"

"Pica-YOON. It's Picayoon, not Picaroon."

Wagband sighed several decibels more loudly.

"Yes, yes, Picayoon. You cannot explicate Picayoon—who is so firmly rooted in the phallocentric tradition of American literature—*without* Steward's insights. And besides inadequate reference to Steward, it appears you did not consult Klein-Degrassi-Harper-Schultz *at all*."

"Klein Degrassi Harper…?"

"YES. Mary Klein-Degrassi-Harper-*Schultz*. We covered her—albeit briefly—in Literary Theory II last year. Don't you remember? *Maiden Voyages: Literary Encounters with Female Victorian Travel Writers*?"

"Uhh, I think so, but my chapter is mostly about, you know, the 'priesthood of all believers' idea. It's not about Victorian women writers at all. The character Cox presents the view that…"

Wagband cut her off with an outstretched hand.

"I'm afraid I do *not* have the time this afternoon to discuss the more *arcane* bits of your project. Suffice to say, I would like the next set of revisions to more *fully* incorporate Steward, and at least make *some* reference to Klein-Degrassi-Harper-Schultz. We can't go forward without them."

Tessa's temples began to throb. The office was hot and airless.

"Is there anything else you wanted to discuss today?"

Wagband glanced at her watch. To make it to her pedicure on time, she would have to leave in the next five minutes. Soo-jin was grumpy last time when she showed up late.

Desperate, Tessa tried honesty.

"Dr. Wagband, to be frank, I've been frustrated all year because I don't see why it's necessary to use the Steward theory—or any feminist theory at all. It's not what I wanted to discuss when I chose Picayoon. My research is on the religious themes in his works, how personal conscience can…"

Wagband looked bored. Tessa started to panic.

"…can conflict with religious orthodoxy, which is not just a…you know, a woman's issue."

The second time tore it.

"*You* are a fascist!"

"WHAT?" (Grainy images of marching Blackshirts and Mussolini flashed in Tessa's head.)

"That is a fascist perspective. By definition. If you want to overlook female experiences and female voices in the text, you are implicitly supporting an authoritarian, patriarchal tradition. As women, it is especially important that we support other women by…"

"But there are no female voices in the text!"

"And isn't that omission telling?"

"No?"

Wagband was openly contemptuous. There was no reason not be anymore.

"If that's your attitude, Ms. Stevens, you might want to consider finding a new supervisor."

"I guess so."

Tessa left the office in tears. She covered her eyes with her sunglasses and stood apart from the other students waiting for the bus leaving campus. It was 20 minutes late. Fortunately, Wagband's parking space was close to her office. She made it to the salon on time.

Within a week, Tessa found a new supervisor. A kindly associate professor agreed to take her on. He would not say a word against Wagband. Graduate students come and go, but difficult colleagues are eternal.

The fascist episode might have been the end of her academic career, but Tessa was still too young, stubborn and stupid to quit. She did not yet understand that Wagband was the breed standard, not a cur. Tessa did not understand politics at all. She lived almost entirely in her own head, regulated by her own fluctuating internal emotional climate. She was 25 then, that dangerous age when young people think they are adults.

* * *

Still brooding over her Wagband memories, Tessa stepped out of the shower. Right on cue, another email message from her mother announced itself with a "Ting" on her phone:

Fr: Deborahann Stevens—deborahannstevens@hotmail.com

To: Tessa Stevens— te.stevens@svu.edu

Subject: P.S.

Date: Aug. 27, 2016, 12:20 p.m.

P.S. LIKE I SAID ON THE PHONE, YOU ARE THE FIRST PERSON IN THIS FAMILY TO DO ANY DEGREE LET ALONE THIS SPECIAL LONG ONE THAT TAKES FOREVER TO FINISH. I CAN'T WAIT TO VISIT YOU AT YOUR BIG OFFICE WHEN YOU GET YOUR BIG JOB!! YOU CAN DO IT. YOU ARE MY SMART GIRL!

Tessa looked at her pale face in the mirror. She closed her eyes and breathed in and out. Coffee. Coffee would cure this sickness.

Chapter One: Downward-facing Dogs

Tessa made her way upstairs, blinking in the light of day. She smacked her shins against the coffee table blocking the basement door. It had been pushed out of the way to accommodate her roommate's yoga session. Her eyes were greeted by the stately twin peaks of Adrian Murphy's buttocks in downward-facing dog pose. His 320-pound form was clad in rayon sweatpants, cut off at the knee, and a lime green singlet. The cheery and libidinal sounds of Cookie's Yoga Challenge! ™ blared from the television's DVR.

"Now hold the restorative pose for a few more big, bold breaths. Breathe in: huh… Breathe out: Ahh… In: huh… Out: ahhh… Now slowly, slowly…eeeeease your way up. You got this, friends."

"Adrian, you're blocking the basement door."

"Shhh!"

"Dude, you're blocking the basement door."

"Then move it, grumpy-pants."

"I can't. I'm too transfixed by your ass blocking the sun."

Adrian gave the ass in question a waggle, snorted and paused the DVR.

"What's your problem? Another lonely, lonely, lonely, lonely night?"

Tessa grunted.

"I thought the gay best friend trope was supportive. Where are my plaudits this morning? Bow before Dr. Stevens, for I am YOUR KING."

"I gave you many a plaudit last night in the form of whisky sours, King Stevens. And as for fag tropes, you know I'm neither supportive nor do I have six-pack abs."

He gestured at his majestic avoirdupois: "I'm every woman. They're all in meeeee."

"That makes no fucking sense."

"You're one to talk, My Lady of Perpetual Literary Theory. At least I'm studying something real."

Cookie piped up again, exhorting her invisible audience to "ground yourself into the positive energy of the earth."

"Yes, figuring out how to coerce people into buying things they don't need is man's noblest science," said Tessa.

"Ahh, the humanities student's vision of the business world. Fascinating. A man's gotta make a living, my dear."

"By exploiting the greed and vanity of the masses?"

"Perhaps. But more often than not, by offering them products and services that will make their lives better."

"*Offering* products and services? HA. I bet your MBA's just crawling with wannabe philanthropists."

"Shows what you know. They're a significant minority."

"Uh huh."

"Well, we can't all earn our wages off the backs of taxpayers."

"What are you talking about? Corporate subsidies?"

"HA. Says the woman who once told me that professors do nothing but beg the government for money—or what you call 'applying for federal research grants.'"

"There are worse ways to spend tax dollars than funding the arts and sciences."

"Yeah, all that important arts 'research' on how many angels can dance on the head of a pin."

"Ahh, the commerce student's vision of the arts!"

"Pshh. We both know I'm not far from the truth. Get back to me when Wagband cures cancer with her 'dick pic' research."

Tessa giggled in spite of herself.

"And no, I am not, for your information," continued Adrian, "in favour of crony capitalism. I'm a von Mises man."

He pointed to his singlet, which read, in 150 font size, "LESS MARX. MORE MISES."

"Where the hell do you even get shit like that?" asked Tessa.

"Live-free-or-die-depot.com."

"I see."

She made her way to the kitchen. Brunch options in the fridge included tomato juice, yogurt, three-day old Hawaiian pizza, and a half-empty bottle of low-end chardonnay. She picked the pizza. *I'm a doctor now, damn it. I've earned my carbs.* Tessa rinsed out the grungy French press.

"Where's Mark?"

Adrian could barely hear her over Cookie: "Center yourself and find your place of total awareness and presentness. Own your space with joy and humility. You are a creature of the earth and you belong."

"Mark? I dunno, saving the whales, trying to get laid. Typical Mark business."

Adrian returned to mountain pose. "Can you make me a Bloody Mary?"

"It's noon."

"Yeah, I'm running late."

"Doesn't drinking cancel out your yoga progress?"

"It improves it, dear heart. The tomato juice is organic."

"How 'bout the vodka?"

"Sure," he shrugged.

Tessa returned to the living room with two slices of cold pizza and a cup of coffee. She eased into the Knislinge Ikea sofa, willing herself not to feel its stickiness or smell its earthy odor. The sofa predated their tenure at the townhouse. Their landlord was able to list the rental as "furnished" because of said sofa, three beds, and a '70s floor-lamp with questionable wiring that short-circuited early into their lease. The three grad students, Mark, Adrian, and Tessa—combined annual income: $39,000—jumped at the chance to live there.

Adrian and Tessa had been friends since their undergraduate years back East. They grew up in adjoining counties in New Brunswick, but didn't meet until university when they worked together on the campus paper, *The Odyssean*. They soon discovered they were simpatico, despite their political differences. They made a fine pair: leonine Adrian, with his shock of sandy blonde hair, and Tessa, a slender brunette, half the size of her constant companion. At the time, Adrian was still in the closet: even then it was dangerous to be a libertarian at a small Eastern liberal arts college.

When they first met, Tessa struck Adrian as a conventional, competent sort. Their regard for one another grew over time. They were both pragmatists. They were both hustlers. They both learned, from an early age, how it felt to wait outside a government office with their parents, hat in hand, waiting for a bureaucrat to cut their father a welfare check. ("It's not welfare, honey, it's EI: employment insurance for seasonal workers," Deborahann, a true daughter of the Canadian Maritimes, explained to Tessa.)

Tessa was in the English doctoral program at Sere Valley University for two years before Adrian joined her there to begin his MBA. It had not been his first choice. Or even his fifth.

But as a result of spending every waking hour in *The Odyssean* office during undergrad, his GPA was so lacklustre that only SVU's Brinkerhoff School of Business would accept him. After Adrian arrived, the two acquired Mark through an online roommate search. Mark Pearson was a genial Edmontonian doing his M.Sc. in Computer Science as an alternative to working.

"I suppose Charming Andrew showed up some time after I left?" grunted Adrian, posing in an awkward version of Warrior I.

"No, he had a family thing."

"I bet."

"I don't get why you're so down on him, Adrian. If I didn't know better, I'd swear you were in love with me."

"I'm in love with Lagavulin, my dear. But you, I like, and I don't like you wasting your time on assholes."

"He's not an asshole."

Adrian rolled his eyes.

"Where's my drink?"

"He's actually quite thoughtful. He sent a beautiful early edition of Dickinson poems last week as an early defense present."

"Oooh, I bet Mommy and Daddy's charge card got a work-out."

"Adrian, he was busy. He has a lot on his plate with school and the Legal Society presidency, and all that."

Adrian did not bother replying. Cookie filled the pregnant pause by asking her invisible audience to "embrace the stillness and inhabit the eternal now."

"Ok, I get it. He's a cad and I'm a fool to be interested. Can we stop talking about Andrew now?"

"My pleasure," said Adrian, poking his head out of child's pose.

"Listen to the song of your soul. Listen to your body. Breathe. Just breeeeeeeeathe," moaned Cookie.

"Girlfriend really enjoys her yoga practice," Tessa observed.

"It's the little things, Tess," said Adrian, reaching for a hand-towel.

At that moment, Tessa's cell phone interrupted them with a pulsating alarm sound.

"Ugh, Mum," said Tessa.

Adrian nodded and Tessa wandered back down into the basement with her cell.

"Good morning, Tessie-Bear!" chirped the voice on the line, unnecessarily loudly. Tessa pulled the phone away from her ear.

"Hey."

"Whatcha' doing today?"

"Nothing. Hanging out with Adrian. Need to get back to lesson-planning soon. I'm nowhere near ready for the term."

"This is your last term at SVU, right? You've been there forever!"

Tessa gritted her teeth.

"I doubt it."

"WHAAAT?"

Tessa sighed.

"I'm probably not leaving SVU for a while, Mum. I missed the hiring cycle cut by defending too late in the summer."

"Hiring cycle?"

She tried to explain: "Yes, for most universities. New Ph.D.s apply for jobs in the fall for the *next* fall. So you start applying now. The interview process usually starts in the spring of the next year. You get selected by, say, May. You prep your courses during the summer, and you start the next fall."

Deborahann snorted. Tessa could sense her mother's eyes rolling from three time zones away.

"You've already been there five years making peanuts and paying *them* money in tuition—which I never got to begin with. Why pay them tuition when you're also working for them as an instructor? So now you're telling me you need to do *another* year there, waiting for a job, making the same crappy money you made as a grad student?"

A pause on the line.

"When do you get to be a real prof and make real money?"

"I am a real prof, Mum. You're always so fixated on money. Why can't you just be happy I finally finished the Ph.D.?"

"I am. But now you need to start thinking about paying back your student loans. And Tessa, I'm not fixated on money, I'm fixated on the lack of it. That department is trying to get you to work for cheap, I think. Go talk to that flim-flam person and sort it out."

"This is not the flower shop, Mum. This is academia. It doesn't work like that. Actually, I'm very lucky that they're still coming up with teaching assignments for me. They're not required to give me any funding now that I'm done the Ph.D. and not a student."

"I don't get why you call it funding when you work for them! It isn't, like, free money. You only make $5000 a term. What do real profs make when you break it down? $50,000 a term? That's a good deal for them."

"But they have research duties, and committee duties, and all sorts of other things. That's called 'service.' I just have to teach a few sections."

"And finish your dissertation. Have you ever worked out what you make an hour, including all the prep and marking, and grunt work on campus the real profs don't want to do? Must be under minimum wage."

"I have to get back to work now, Mum."

Tessa cut the conversation short, mentally lamenting, for the millionth time, that neither of her parents had any idea what she was going through. They had never left Beaconsbridge.

Tessa shuddered at the thought of approaching the Department about her financial concerns, as her mother had suggested. It seemed…indelicate, and she did not want to call attention to the chasm of difference she already felt between herself and the full-time tenured and tenure-track professors.

Adjunct professors aren't wage slaves like Mum, she thought. *Preposterous.*

Nonetheless, she felt uneasy all afternoon while she worked on lectures. Her mother, as usual, had gotten under her skin.

***

Two weeks later, the day before the first day of classes, the newly-minted Dr. Stevens rode the #4 bus to campus to meet the English Department Chair, one Dr. Edwin D. Flamm, eminent Restoration scholar and recent divorcé. ("Please call me Edwin," Dr. Flamm had said to her graduate cohort, at an orientation event five years ago. "We don't stand on ceremony here."

No one ever called him Edwin.) Tessa typically avoided Flamm, which was easy because he typically avoided his administrative duties, or whenever possible, delegated them to lackeys or the longsuffering Pearl Coleman, the department admin.

Tessa's heart had sunk yesterday, when scanning her inbox, up popped the subject head: "Meeting tomorrow…" She knew immediately it was from Flamm. Never had she met a man so fond of the ellipsis. If the meeting request had been from most professors in the department, they would have diplomatically used a question mark ("Meeting tomorrow?"), suggesting, falsely, that she had some choice in the matter. Wagband's subject head would have commanded, "Meeting tomorrow," abandoning even the polite pretense that refusal was possible. But Flamm used his trademark ellipsis, which conveyed a mixture of vague sinister intent and deliberate misdirection.

The body of the email was vague. Did he want to meet in person to tell her one or both of her sections was being pulled, the day before classes started? Tessa had heard such tales from her fellow adjuncts. Did he want to personally congratulate her on the defense? Propose marriage? Initiate her into a cult? The ellipsis opened up a world of fantastic possibilities.

On the way to campus, she considered her position, post-defense, and what she had to do to advance in her career. Nothing had changed. She was still an adjunct instructor at SVU. Status-wise, in the university hierarchy that placed her somewhere above the custodian and below the secretary. As she had tried to explain to her mother, because she had defended so late in the summer, two weeks before fall classes, it was out of the question that she would find a tenure-track position for that term. Just in case, she'd sent out a few CVs listing her defense date as "Forthcoming: summer 2016." No bites.

The Powers That Be in the English Department had obviously assumed it would take her longer than the summer to wrap up the degree, because they assigned her two courses to teach for September. If they hadn't, Tessa would have had no way to support herself in Sere Valley, population 30,502—that is, outside of dealing, stripping, or hooking. ("Can't sell what you can't give away," Adrian said.) Infinitely merciful, the Department spared her this fate by assigning two sections of the usual: dreary ENGL 190: Introductory Composition, or "Intro Comp" as everyone referred to it. She had been teaching it, off and on, throughout her Ph.D.

Intro Comp was the gulag of Sere Valley University's English Department, and SVU in general was considered the school of last resort by locals. It had an acceptance rate of over 96%. ("If you can hold a beer, you can go to Sere," they said.) Intro Comp was taught by graduate students and adjuncts, often one and the same. Occasionally newly hired assistant professors were forced to teach it, which they did with all the enthusiasm of a man tucking into a shit sandwich. The course was a prerequisite for many programs at the university. Most of the freshmen taking it were abysmal English students. Tessa's ranged in expertise from poor to functional illiterates.

In addition to her course assignments, The Most Benevolent Department promised Tessa a few shifts a week at the campus Writing, Research, Professional Development and Student Achievement Center, otherwise known as the WRPDSAC (or Adrian's charming alphabetism: "the ripped sack"). Between her two sections and Writing Center-tutoring, Tessa figured she could cobble together enough money to pay her bills until Christmas, while applying for any better full-time academic jobs that came up in Canada or the United States.

She mused on these things and worried about money as the bus putted along behind pick-up trucks all the way to SVU. She had once read that due to its urban density, in Japan people were skilled at erecting mental privacy barriers between themselves and others in public. They could be packed cheek-by-jowl on a subway and still feign the illusion of distance. To the same end, she maintained an air of abstraction on public transit around Sere Valley: all the better in case she ran into a student, which she often did. She could not afford a vehicle on her graduate student stipend. In fact, most of her students had access to more ready cash than she did. She also had more debt than the average student she taught. Yet she was also their professor. Professional distance, if not strict hierarchy, must be maintained. She daily exerted energy maintaining her fragile dignity. She rode the bus with her mental blinders on, her eyes never leaving the book on her lap.

As the #4 bus pulled into campus, Tessa winced once again at the ugliness of the university's '70s brutalist architecture. It looked like a high school from the wrong side of the tracks. (Her own high school, in Beaconsbridge's neighbouring town of Weyburn, was less offensive to the eyes.) SVU was just outside town, on a plain above the "valley" part of Sere Valley, plopped down on to the prairie in the midst of sprawling housing tracts. Yellow prairie-grass rippled in every direction. When Tessa moved to Sere Valley from the East Coast, she had anticipated pastoral scenes from *My Antonia* or *Little House on the Prairie*—a different type of beauty from the Acadian forest-lands of New Brunswick, but beauty nonetheless. The prairies disappointed her; after a few weeks, they filled her with existential dread. With scarcely a tree or a hill to break the eternal wind, they made Tessa long for apocalypse: lightning, fire, sweet death—anything to break the monotony.

The town itself displeased her. It looked hastily erected, and compared to the Eastern cities and villages she knew, it was. Nothing in town was older than 100 years, and most buildings were from the '60s and '70s. In comparison to the Maritimes provinces—poor as they were—there was a deficit of charm. The efforts of the town council to beautify and modernize the place struck her as unbearably poignant. ("Have you seen the new 'Welcome to Sere Valley: Sugar Beet Capital of the World' sign?" Adrian asked her recently. "It's in Bank-fucking-Gothic.")

The local university's campus culture oscillated between boosterism and apologetic self-consciousness. Ensconced in the academic bubble of Sere Valley U were two different types of faculty and staff. Type One were mostly administrators and support-staff. They were often graduates of SVU themselves: unadventurous, sensible folk, electing to stay put in the land of their birth. They were usually content with their comfortable fate of working in the educational sphere, in their hometown. There was some prestige in that. Not so with Type Two, who were chiefly academics. They were drawn from other parts of the country, places more urban and sophisticated (by Canadian standards). They were not thrilled about being marooned on the prairies for work, in a town with no good restaurants, one semi-literate newspaper, and a culture derived from the harvesting of sugar beets. Some tried to make the best of it, but most eventually felt that fate had dealt them a bad hand when they landed a tenure-track position in an obscure prairie town. Sere Valley U floated on a gentle wave of resentment.

The bus rolled to a stop. Tessa felt the pervasive anxiety in the air as she hopped off with the others, and entered a looming concrete structure, the Carson Center. She passed through the food court area, just barely registering a poster on the wall: "STRUGGLING WITH ORIENTATION ANXIETY? WE HAVE TWO WORDS FOR YOU: PUPPY ROOM! SEE COUNSELLING SERVICES, ROOM 116, STUDENT CENTER, FRIDAY, 1:00 TO 5:00."

Tessa kept going, making her way through the building link to Suzeman, the Arts building. She passed through the Classics Department, slowing her pace to ensure she would be exactly on time for the appointment with Flamm. Classics consisted of three full professors: two octogenarians and a spritely 68 year old, none of whom could be convinced to retire, as their class enrollments dwindled to single digits. (The 68 year old was still referred to as "the new hire," and made to fetch coffee.) The Dean's Office's plan for the department was to wait for them to die, but they clung on heroically, liver spots, cataracts, coughing fits and all. At the very top of the pay scale, it was rumoured that old Christiansen the Chair made as much as even a VP of Student Affairs.

Tessa opened the heavy double-doors marking the border between Classics and English, scanning for any sight of Wagband or other threats. The pass was clear. Wagband usually rolled in five minutes before her afternoon classes anyway. It was highly unlikely she would be in at the uncivilized hour of 9:00 a.m. Tessa popped into the admin's office to pick up her mail. As always, Pearl manned her post. There was an age gap of 30 years between the two women. One was from the East, and one was from the West. One was nominally Catholic, and the other nominally Protestant. But they were both of the Sisterhood of Common Sense. Tessa preferred Pearl to the department's female professors of a similar age—in theory her mentors—whom she found neurotic and precious.

"Another day, another dollar, another cliché?"

"Oh, hi honey." Pearl looked cute, if tired, in her French bulldog-patterned yellow cardigan.

"Is Flamm in yet?"

"He called to say he was running a few minutes late. Something about waiting on a contractor."

They rolled their eyes in unison, and dropped the volume of their speech a few decibels. At 9:00 a.m. on the day before the first day of classes, the safety level for indiscreet conversation was a 9 out of 10. Later in the term, at that time of day, it would dip to about 6, and by 2:00 p.m. it would reach its lowest level: about a 2. By 2:00, most professors who needed to be on campus were present and accounted for, and buzzing like flies in the office with clerical requests for Pearl. But by 4:45, unless there was a departmental meeting, the coast would again be clear. At 5:00 on the dot, even Pearl would be gone, and by 6:00 Tessa could do cartwheels naked down the corridor if she pleased.

"You buy that?" asked Tessa, *sotto voce*.

Pearl raised an eyebrow and cleared her throat. Her eyes darted down the corridor.

"Honey, just a warning: Edwin's been absolutely ridiculous since he got back in last week."

"Whaddya mean? How was he all summer?"

"All summer? I saw him *once* since June."

"Was Wagband Acting Chair then?"

"Nope. Still Edwin, he just went dark after Nicole moved out. He still answered emails sometimes—otherwise I would've guessed he'd dropped off the earth. One sentence responses, stuff like, 'Tell the office I'm devoting my full attention to the matter. Dot, dot, dot…' 'I will reply presently. Dot, dot, dot…' 'Considering all options at the moment. Dot, dot, dot…'"

"God. You must've wanted to murder him. Was he even *in* town all summer?"

"Who knows? Vague as usual. At some point mid-summer he was in Victoria, visiting his parents, but that's all he would say."

"I take it that's why we got our course assignments so late."

"Bingo. And even then"—Pearl's voice dropped another decibel—"I had to ride him just to get those out weeks late."

"Ugh."

"The Dean's Office doesn't even bother emailing him anymore about these things. They bug me instead."

"That sucks, Pearl."

"Mmhmm. Good thing he gets all those course waivers."

"Yes, 'cause he's so busy delegating all his work to you."

Pearl's eyes suddenly widened and her tone became briskly professional: "So I hope the move to the Carson Building isn't a problem, but if it is, I think there's still C15 free in the library."

"No, Carson's great," Tessa replied, straightening up from her hunched posture over Pearl's desk. She turned to see, as she knew she would, Dr. Flamm entering the office. As always, he looked like a grumpy beatnik hobbit.

"Good afternoon, ladies," said Flamm, his air changing from moroseness to expansiveness. He side-eyed the figure of the erstwhile graduate student. *Nice ass.* He cleared his throat.

"Or perhaps I should say, Dr. Stevens? My congratulations once again."

Tessa made humble noises and they made their way to his adjoining office.

Flamm's office was 8 degrees colder than Pearl's sunny antechamber. The venetian blinds were drawn. Instead of switching on the main light upon entry, he turned on his desk lamp, which emitted a feeble light. Tessa stepped around a stack of books and a duffel-bag that smelled of briny cheese, and sat across from Flamm at his desk. She could just barely make out the Chair's lugubrious expression in the near-darkness.

"And what can I do for you today, Ms.—I mean, Dr. Stevens."

"Uhh, you called me in, Dr. Flamm."

"Oh. Right. I was wondering…is your teaching load particularly heavy this term?"

"Uhh, no? I have the two Intro Comps and two four-hour shifts a week at the WRPDSAC. Didn't you assign them?"

"Err, yes. I have quite a few irons in the fire this term."

"Oh?"

"Yes, I'm on two hiring committees, and working on a course proposal, *and* toiling away on some grant apps."

"Right. Are you teaching Restoration Lit this term?"

"No, not this term. Dr. Mincing is. Marvelously adaptable, that Mincing! I'm tied up with administrative work, alas."

Flamm activated his rueful face.

"Right."

Tessa activated her poker-face.

"Well, you mentioned wanting more service work for your CV, correct?"

"Yes…"

"Have you started applying anywhere?" asked Flamm.

"Kind of…Well, not so seriously before the defense, but now…"

"Marvelous! You'll soon be off to great things, leaving us behind in the provinces!"

"Umm…"

"No, no! There's nothing I'd like better than to see a fellow inmate freed from the asylum."

"Sere Valley's not so…"

"You've more than done your time. If only we were all so lucky!"

Flamm's chuckle evolved into a smoker's hack, which evolved into a three-second silence.

Tessa tried to get him back on track.

"So, you wanted to talk about service?

"Service. Yes. Service."

Flamm took the plunge: "How would you like to represent the Department at the New Student Orientation Circus?"

"Circus?"

"Yes, Circus. I was a little skeptical of the idea myself when it came down from the Dean's Office, but really, it's just your garden variety student orientation fair, gussied up a bit. Just the usual: booths, posters, department reps…clowns, popcorn, knife-throwers…"

"Knife-throwers?"

"They're all plastic blades, I was told. For liability reasons."

"Oh. But why aren't we just doing a regular student fair, like every year?"

"All part and parcel of the new promotional campaign. Haven't you been keeping up on the Comm and Strat Dev memos this summer?"

Tessa blinked and Flamm chuckled with ersatz gusto once again.

"I must admit, I've been skimming some of those emails myself, ha. We've been instructed to take to heart the new promo slogan."

Flamm handed her a banner in the school colors of puce and yellow. Tessa read, "Sere Valley U: Where Serious Learning Equals Serious Fun."

"I see."

"A bit asinine, I agree, but the VP of Student Retention has reported that many departing students have been complaining that SVU is really lacking in the 'fun' metric."

"The fun metric?"

"Yes. Too many assignments. Too many readings. That sort of thing."

"And you agree?"

"Well, Tess…Dr. Stevens, I agree that the world is changing: 'Be not the first by whom the new are tried, nor yet last to lay the old aside.' With the Smartphone Generation, the name of the game is engagement. It's quite the challenge."

"Right…uhh, is it okay that I'll be representing the Department when I'm just a temp?"

"Of course. Adjunct instructors are valued members of the Department," Flamm said, nodding for emphasis.

"Right."

"So it's settled then! You can sub in for Mincing at noon on Saturday. She's taking the morning shift."

"Great."

"Marvelous!" said Flamm, forcing the muscles of his face into a cadaver's grin.

"Marvelous," Tessa back-channelled.

Silence.

"Pearl can fill you in on the rest of the details. Thanks for dropping by."

"Thank *you*."

Tessa backed out of the office, nearly stumbling over the stinky duffel-bag.

"Oh, and Tessa, one more thing."

Flamm handed her a large, SVU-branded plastic bag.

"What's this?"

Tessa pulled out a crimson and gold-banded ringmaster's jacket, with matching tights.

"Don't worry," smiled Flamm. "It's one-size-fits-all."

Tessa smiled back and left the freezing office.

Chapter Two: Sentimental Occasions

A few days later, three time zones away in the southeastern corner of the province of New Brunswick, Tessa's mother Deborahann was running late for work at Sentimental Occasions. The flower shop was the only one in Beaconsbridge's single-street downtown, which also boasted a grocery store, a small department store, one bank and one credit union, a drugstore, a post office, a liquor store, a gas station, and four restaurants: pizza, Chinese, subs, and "Canadian home-style." (Home-style cuisine consisted mostly of boiled veg and meat, mustard pickles, chicken pot pies, hot beef sandwiches, poutine, and sugar and shortening-based baked goods).

Deborahann and Victor lived just outside of Beaconsbridge; Deborahnn's drive to work was only 10 minutes. Nonetheless, she was often flustered and behind schedule. Deborahann's elderly blue Civic usually pulled in at 8:35 a.m. when she was supposed to be there at 8:30 to prep before the shop's official opening of 9:00. When she deigned to make an appearance at all, Elinor Crossman, the shop-owner, flounced in around 10:00, immaculate in her sweater-set and rose-gold diamond jewelry. A few days a year, however—just often enough to instill fear—Elinor would arrive as early as 8:15. On those days, when Deborahann pulled up and saw the long slate-grey Lincoln Continental waiting, her blood curdled. She couldn't risk losing Elinor's favor and her job. She and Victor needed what little her shop assistant position brought in. When Deborahann was late, Elinor responded with a subtle derision more ominous than open censure. Last time it was a single raised eyebrow, and the remark, "Busy morning, Deb'rann?"

That crisp fall morning Vic kept Deborahann home an extra 15 minutes. First crisis: his favorite overalls were dirty. He would not wear the proffered clean ones: "They're bunchy, Deb. Too friggin' bunchy." The second crisis, even more distressing, was that the homemade pot pie in his lunch-pail was beef. He preferred chicken. "What is wrong with you, woman?" he asked (presumably rhetorically), his temper in the dangerous border-country between annoyance and real anger. Deborahann, attuned as always to every slight variation in her husband's mood, was quick to respond: "Don't worry, honey, I made chicken too!"

She was almost always cheerful with Vic. It was dangerous not to be. A raised voice could quickly escalate to a slammed door, a slammed door to a thrown plate…and worse. Deborahann was relieved the girls were out of the house now. This took some of the strain off, though she could never be at ease when Vic was home. Half-clothed, hair wrapped in a towel, she exchanged pies from the freezer and placated her husband on the matter of the overalls, but there wasn't enough time before work to resolve both of Vic's problems *and* let the dog out *and* iron her blouse. (Elinor had made a passing remark just last week about "the importance of not looking slovenly in front of customers, Deb'rann.")

As a result, it was 10 to 9:00 by the time Deborahann pulled into her usual parking spot, gulping back some black coffee from the Thomas Kinkade thermos Tessa had given her for Christmas. Sure enough, today of all days, the Continental was parked in its customary spot, waiting like a patient crocodile for its prey. Deborahann glanced in the vanity mirror, quickly smoothing her obstinate frizzy blonde curls (Glam Gals Blend #45: "Sophisticated Ash Blonde"). She winced again at the bags under her eyes, the crowsfeet, and her double-chin. ("Where's the tea, bag?" was Vic's long-time favorite joke.) She hopped out of the Civic, smoothed her blouse and scurried to the shop-door.

"Helloooooo."

No response. The door was unlocked and Elinor had the 9:00 a.m. "OPEN" sign out already.

Deborahann eyed Elinor's office door, in the right-hand corner of the shop, behind the till. It was open a crack. Instead of poking her head in, she booted up the computer and drew back the blinds. Danny the deliveryman wouldn't be in until until 9:30. From the office, Elinor's schoolmarmish hiss broke the silence.

"Deb'rann. May I speak to you?"

"Coming," she said with a smile in her voice.

Damn it.

Deborahann entered the lion's den.

"Good morning, Elinor."

Elinor looked up from her computer screen, lowering her mother-of-pearl reading glasses.

"Deb'rann. Good morning. How are you doing today? Robert and I noticed you weren't in church yesterday."

"Oh, I'm fine! Just a little headache Sunday. But I'm fit as a fiddle today!"

"Mmhmm."

Elinor scanned her employee's face. It was fixed into a mask of oblique cheerfulness.

"How are Tessa and Lilly doing? Tessa's still in school, isn't she? That one's a professional student."

Deborahann ignored the backhanded compliment, and smiled her first authentic smile of the day as she thought about her girls. 22 year old Lilly was the baby of the family. She favored her mother: blonde, petite and feminine. Tessa, the elder at 28, was tall, dark-haired and angular, like her father. Gentle and kind, Lilly was protected by everyone, even Vic, who usually moderated his behavior around her. Tessa, on the other hand, he actively disliked, viewing her, correctly, as a fifth column.

"Haha, yes," she replied to Elinor. "We thought she'd never get done, but Tessa just finished her…whatchamacallit. Her defense. Said it was real tricky. The profs were all over her, but she's a tough girl. She's applying for jobs right now and teaching at SVU."

"Oh. So she's a real professor now?"

"Think so. I don't know exactly how it works. She says the new ones don't get paid much at first. And Lilly just has one year to go in Education. She's thinking about doing her Master's too. Higher on the pay-scale that way, she says."

Elinor smiled. She was irritated that her own two daughters, a decade older than Deborahann's, had never gone on to a four-year university, despite encouragement from her and Robert. They would have been among the minority of students in the province who did not have to take out student loans. *But more importantly,* thought Elinor, *they married well, and Laurie even finished her Business Admin program at the community college in Moncton last year— while watching Brayden and Eli too.*

"That's great. They're such clever girls. You must be so thrilled for them."

"Yes. Vic and I are some proud."

Niceties completed, Elinor switched gears.

"On another topic, Deb'rann, I've noticed you've been tardy lately. I don't want to be a stickler, but you do know that your working hours begin at 8:30, right?"

"Yes, I'm sorry. I was running a little late today."

"I'm afraid it's not just today. I've been told you often pull in a 'little late' to the shop."

Deborahann wondered if that bitch Edith was reporting back. Edith Murray was Elinor's first cousin. She worked across the street at the Madawaaksis Credit Union. Deborahann knew Edith's little piggy eyes watched all the comings and goings at Sentimental Occasions.

"It's absolutely essential, Deb'rann, that you finish your prep-work and print the New Order Report before the shop opens. We've discussed this. Start the day right, and everything else falls into place. It's just common sense."

"Sorry."

"I know we're just a little small-town florist, but we try to maintain professionalism around here. I trust professionalism is important to you as well? Right, Deb'rann?"

"Yes, Elinor."

Never content with partial victories, Elinor gave her samurai sword one final twist to the gut of her victim.

"There haven't been many weddings this summer. Everyone lives together now—what d'you expect? We just haven't had the business we do most years…"

"I thought it was an ok summer. July was pretty busy, I think."

"No. Absolutely not. It's been our worst summer since I opened in '99. Make no mistake about that. We've been struggling mightily, Deb'rann."

Elinor played with one of her six rings. She liked the way her new anniversary diamond-and-ruby from Robert glistened in the track-lights.

"I didn't want to mention it before, but I think you should know I've been considering reducing shop hours and taking you down to part-time."

"Oh."

"I haven't decided yet. Might be within a month or two—or maybe not at all. But it's possible. I just wanted to let you know so you could plan."

Deborahann wondered how she was supposed to plan for maybes and possiblies. Or what would happen if she couldn't find another job in Beaconsbridge. They would have to go down to one vehicle. But then how would she drive around to look for work? The Civic was on its last legs and Vic's old Chev pick-up wasn't much better. At least he could fix them himself. But parts cost money.

"Thanks for letting me know, Elinor."

The entry bells tinkled and Deborahann had an excuse to flee. It was Danny with the flower delivery. Elinor hung around until lunch, making a show of sighing over her spreadsheets, but mostly messing about on Pinterest. Hyper-conscious of her mistress's presence, Deborahann elevated her customer service helpfulness level from her usual 9 to 10. She was a conscientious employee anyway, other than habitual slight lateness. She prided herself on her work ethic.

I might not be smart or cute, but I'm sure as hell a good worker.

Deborahann had lied to Elinor about her church absence, or at least fibbed. It was not a "little headache." She had suffered through a blinding migraine for the better part of Sunday. It was so bad she threw up twice, and was still feeling its effects today. Deborahann had migraines about twice a month, almost always on weekends and in the evenings. She was too busy to look into them properly and when she mentioned the problem to their GP, Dr. Hall just shrugged and told her it was probably stress. Vic had no patience for them. He was convinced his wife used her migraines to "get out of work." By that Vic meant work for him.

In reality, Deborahann did nothing but work. On top of her 40-hour a week job at Sentimental Occasions, she did all of the accounting and clerical work for her husband's small business, Stevens Auto Repair. She also did all the housework and most of the yard-work at home. At Beaconsbridge Baptist, she was an active member of the Benevolence Committee, and she headed the Special Music Committee. The first position mainly involved delivering food and other charitable gifts to people in need in the community; the second involved finding musical acts to perform in church every week. (If she couldn't find anyone, in cases of dire necessity, she played piano herself, badly.) "I like to keep busy," she told everyone.

The migraines scared Deborahann, but she avoided talking about them. She dealt with them the same way she dealt with every other major problem she encountered in her 52 years on earth: she pushed them to the back of her mind to think about later, when she had more time. But somehow that time never came. Instead of discussing her actual problems, she complained endlessly about trifles to anyone who would listen. Vic would ignore her. "Bla bla bla," he'd say, his right hand forming a quacking duck's bill.

As Deborahann's plump, deft fingers cut and arranged flowers all afternoon, unwelcome thoughts churned below the surface of her calm exterior. What would they do if Elinor cut back her hours, or God forbid, if she lost her job entirely? They were barely in the black last month as it was. What else could she cut? She had already pared the grocery bills down to the bone. She bought the generic versions of cereal and other products whenever possible. She purchased inexpensive cuts of meat, and hid them in casseroles, or stretched them out in soups and stews. Potatoes, cheap and plentiful, often filled in gaps—they ate them at least three times a week.

Lilly was coming home from college that weekend with two of her school-friends. How were they going to afford the extra expense? She couldn't very well tell poor Lilly to take back her invitations because they couldn't afford the extra bread and milk. She didn't want to embarrass her daughter. *I'll stop buying lunch at work*, Deborahann vowed, though she almost always brought leftovers to work to begin with, except on days like today, when she was running late. *And I don't need so much milk*, thought Deborahann, resolving to cut down on what she, a teetotaller, regarded as an indulgence: her nightly tumbler of whole milk, sometimes consumed with a cookie. *It's just making me fatter anyway.* Last night while she was putting away his snack dishes, Vic had reached over the recliner, grabbed a roll of his wife's tummy flesh, and tugged. "A little porky here, Ms. Piggie?" He chuckled.

Deborahann felt guilty about buying that new burgundy skirt in Moncton last weekend. It was $30 on sale, but had she really needed it? She justified the purchase by telling herself she could wear it to church and to work on days when she wanted to be "dressier," like Elinor always encouraged her to be. When she told Tessa about her new purchase on the phone, her daughter shot her down: "Why do you need to be 'dressy,' when you're just behind a cash register, or sweeping up carnation stems all day? You don't get paid enough to be 'dressy,' Mum." Deborahann replied that she hoped Tessa got a good job someday, so she could wear whatever she wanted to work. Tessa said, pertly, that profs *could* dress however they wanted, and as a result, many could pass for homeless people. "Why don't they look nice if they can afford it?" Deborahann asked. "If you're not under a car all day, like your father is, why not look nice?"

Deborahann fretted over money matters all afternoon, between customers. She wished she could convince Vic to decrease their monthly tithe to the church—at least on months when they struggled to make ends meet. They could really use that 10%. But the last time she proposed such a thing, it led to a fight, with Vic reminding her of Pastor Fudge's recent sermon theme: "The Lord loveth a cheerful giver." Deborahann bit her tongue. Vic always responded poorly to criticisms of the pastor. Deborahann didn't trust Pastor Fudge, with his faux-folksy glibness. The pastor had a hold over Vic and other members of the congregation, she told Tessa, and she didn't like it.

By the time 5:00 o'clock rolled around, Deborahann had come up with a few more ways to economize, and some inexpensive meal ideas for Lilly's visit that weekend. Her "Tuscan" chicken soup was the ticket. Tasty and cheap. She calculated the cost per serving on the oversized calculator Elinor kept by her computer: 90 cents a bowl. *Not bad.* Her stomach growled in response. Eager to show Elinor what a good worker she was, she had worked through lunch, only eating a granola bar at the till, instead of leaving for a few minutes to pick up a cheap sub down the street, as planned.

Better hurry home before Vic gets in, thought Deborahann. *No need to tell him what Elinor said. It'll only rile him up. I'll start the honey-garlic drumsticks as soon as I get home.*

The blue Civic pulled out at exactly 5:05 p.m. Across the street at the bank, Edith Murray watched it go and noted the time on her watch.

***

Earlier that same day, in Sere Valley, Tessa awoke to the beeping sound of her cell phone alarm. She taught in a few hours and needed to be up, dressed, and on her way to campus. She rolled over, expecting a warm body. Nothing. The pillow was creased, but she was alone.

Odd. I thought he said he didn't have any classes today.

Tessa draped a towel around herself and made her way to the tiny bathroom down the basement hallway. It was empty. Andrew's clothing and messenger bag were also gone.

Is he upstairs?

Audio of a temple gong sounded from her room. Andrew's text! She was across the hall in one leap. The text was brief:

Duty calls, Tessa Fair! Until we meet again?

She texted back, too grumpy and hungry to play along this time:

I thought you were staying for breakfast and driving me to campus? I don't teach for another two hours.

Tessa stared at the phone's screen for the longest two minutes of her life, before giving up and jumping in the shower. She did not hear the gong over the water. When she returned, another brief message awaited her:

Crossed wires? Driving, dear. A plutôt!

Tessa tried to focus on her class notes. *Thank God it's only Sentence Structure Review today.* She could teach dangling and misplaced modifiers in her sleep. At the kitchen table, she brooded over her oatmeal. She usually devoured her food, but today every mouthful went down like straw.

"Good morning!" chirruped Adrian, poking his head into the kitchen.

Tessa grunted a reply, "What are you doing up this early?"

"Places to go and people to see!" Adrian sing-songed. He had a meeting with his Leadership Strategies group at 9:00 on campus.

"Soooo, where's Andrew?" he asked, unable to contain himself a second longer.

She had this coming, he thought. They had kept him up with thumps and giggles all night. Disgusted, Adrian had resorted to Ambien and ear-plugs.

"You know perfectly well. Don't be coy."

Her best friend tried not to look too pleased with himself. He had been monitoring the comings and goings of the second-hand silver Lexus at the townhouse.

"Your interest in my affairs is a touch unseemly, Adrian."

"No, sweetheart. It's not of a prurient nature at all. I just love being right. He cut and ran?"

"I teach this morning. We're both busy."

"Not too busy for a booty call on a Sunday night, I see."

"Adrian!"

He placed one hand on a generous hip and tilted his chin.

"You know I'm right."

Tessa pushed the oat lumps around in her violet-patterned bowl. It was part of an antique set Grammy Ada had given her before she went off to college.

Adrian persisted.

"So are you dating *officially* yet or what?"

"Of course we're dating."

"Riiiiight. So it's the kind of dating where no one introduces the other one to their friends, and where the entire relationship consists of whisky and post-whisky banging."

"Adrian!"

"What?"

"We drink coffee sometimes too."

Tessa giggled. Adrian maintained a poker-face.

"It's still early days," she said.

Adrian rolled his eyes—theatrically, thought Tessa.

"Has *Sex and the City* completely rotted your brain?" he asked. "How many people do you know—people of above-average intelligence, of actual emotional depth, let's say—who are content very long with meaningless flings? Especially women. The unfair sex is *biologically programmed* to become emotionally attached. You're just setting yourself up for a fall."

"What a bunch of gender-essentialist garbage. I don't take my cues from *Sex and the City*, but I can also tell you that not every woman is desperate for a monogamous relationship."

Adrian cocked a shaggy eyebrow.

"Uh-huh. You're not every woman though. Let's not lie to ourselves."

Tessa made a face.

"Have you been listening to Gad Saad again?"

"Better Gad Saad than *Sex and the City* reruns. Science is our friend."

"Can we talk about something else now, Mom?"

Tessa checked her phone.

"I have to catch the bus anyway. I'm going to be late."

"Whatever, Slutty Spice."

"Slutty Spice? Isn't that your Grindr name?"

"That was for research!"

This time they both giggled.

Tessa and Adrian walked to the bus-stop together, chatting about safer topics all the way to campus. It was a beautiful Indian summer day, warm already in the early morning light. Tessa kept her corduroy jacket unbuttoned. Adrian, in flannel, sweated more than usual.

They parted company outside the campus library.

"Bros before hoes?" asked Adrian.

"Always," Tessa replied.

Chapter Three: Circus of the Damned

Five days later, Tessa was on her way to campus for the New Student Orientation Circus. It was the last place on earth she wanted to be on a Saturday morning. She had left with plenty of time to spare, but hadn't counted on the #4 being so late. She should have known better. Transit in Sere Valley was abysmal. It was only used by transients, students, and academics imported from urban centers who were surprised to learn that not every town on earth had proper public transportation. Most local students had at their disposal one battered family pick-up truck, sometimes two. Plump, prosperous, potato-fed burghers all, the Town Council thought of public transit as a frill, like the new window boxes at City Hall. They themselves were not a bus-riding class; they were an SUV-riding class.

Tessa hoped her ringmaster's costume wasn't visible beneath her coat. The material was scratchy. She wouldn't have time to change on campus. She thought about how she'd reached this place in her life: 10 years studying her way out of Beaconsbridge, now off to play the clown for a bunch of teenagers. ("Oh how you suffer!" Adrian laughed in the kitchen that morning, eyeing her polyester attire.)

Looking out the bus window, Tessa cast a grim eye on the waving sweet-grass of the coulees: a study in anomie. She had been tethered to this prairie town for too many years. *Sere Valley. The land God gave Cain. Home of Mormons, driven from the East. The site of one of Canada's largest indigenous reservations.* Tessa remembered what Lesley Two-Bear, her favorite writing center student, had once told her: "If they thought this land was worth stealing, the government would have already." It was a valid point.

The bus arrived at its destination and Tessa marched to the gymnasium, shedding layers as she walked. She wore the ringmaster's coat but had balked at the matching striped tights. The university radiated excitement. Freshmen scurried over campus like ants, many accompanied by their parents. Most were small town kids from the region. For them, a trip to Sere Valley meant "going to town." Attending university there was an adventure. Their eyes were bright. Their mall-clothes were pristine. In a few short years, many would be drop-outs, their experiment in higher education concluded. They would become realtors and homemakers and liquor store clerks and daycare workers and farmers and carpenters and insurance salespeople and contractors and welders and construction workers and receptionists, and all sorts of practical, small town occupations, and they would be just as happy and just as miserable as their fellows who had finished university.

Tessa looked down on them from the lofty pinnacle of her ten-year head start. They made her feel tired. The weight of their dreams was palpable. They still believed in things. They had not yet come up against the limitations of life. Their faces were unlined, their bodies were slender and taut. They were beautiful with the transient beauty of youth, every imperfection and asymmetry softened by youth's freshness. Tessa observed one dewy blonde with an upturned pixie nose and a voluptuous figure—already a trifle plump, but still appealingly so. A woman who was obviously her mother was a step or two behind her, reading a brochure. She looked like the version of the daughter left out in the sun. The upturned nose was more brood sow than pixie now, the barrel-like body with its heavy, sagging teats evoked the same.

"Small-town pretty has a short shelf-life," Tessa recalled Adrian once remarking at The Ranch Hand, their favorite local pub, as they observed an undergraduate flirtation. "Get 'em while the getting's good, girl."

Dodging a sweaty red-headed boy, Tessa stepped to one side and scanned the gym for the English Department's table. It was still 15 minutes shy of noon. The scene before her was Boschian, the gym packed with excited undergrads, bored junior faculty, and self-consciously professional junior admin with smiles plastered to their faces. Keeping true to its circus theme, the New Student Orientation Circus roiled with activity. Most of the faculty and support-staff were wearing circus attire, though Tessa noticed a few hold-outs. In one corner of the gym, gymnasts in cut-rate Cirque de Soleil costumes gyrated to a pulsating mid-'90s dance beat. Free cotton candy and popcorn circulated from parts unknown. Clowns roamed freely. Everywhere, banners were festooned, bearing the words, "SERE VALLEY U: SERIOUS LEARNING = SERIOUS FUN!"

Tessa passed a face-painting booth where a robust 18 year old freshman was being made up to look like a tiger, while his friends looked on and cheered. She dimly recalled her first—and last—face-painting adventure, age five, at the Madawaaksis County Agricultural Fair. Her tiny face had been a smoother canvas than the undergrad's, which was partly covered by a scraggly moustache.

Tessa walked on, slowly. She was not looking forward to seeing Mincing again, even briefly. Dr. Jessica Mincing was a very green assistant professor, well-known as a Wagband protégé. She was born and raised not far from Sere Valley, in another small Canadian prairie town, Fort MacNally, and took great pains to hide the fact. Her father was the town's high school custodian. Small and plain, Mincing was the walking human embodiment of Academic Imposter Syndrome.

Tessa and Mincing had had a few awkward interactions in American Literature I, during Tessa's first year in the Ph.D. program, and had been cordially suspicious of each other ever since. Regurgitating the poisonous pap she herself had ingested as a graduate student, Mincing had taught Tessa's class that there was no such thing as "good" and "bad" literature, only officially sanctioned and officially rejected literature, and that many of the "supposedly canonical" male writers only owed their success to the "patriarchal framework" in which all were embedded, like hapless spiders in amber. Secretly aghast, Tessa had offered a few mild objections to these ideas, only to be shot down instantly by Mincing, whose self-esteem was far too fragile to brook dissent.

Tessa frowned as she recalled the incident. She continued her unhurried loop of the gym. Out of her peripheral vision, she spied a tub of Tootsie Rolls with the sign, "HELP YOURSELF." She swooped in for the kill, before discovering, too late, that she was at the WRPDSAC table. It was manned by a frenemy, Emily Payne, an English doctoral candidate who had begun the program a year before her. They often crossed paths tutoring at the Writing Center.

Now Emily Payne of Deer Park, Toronto, was not a bad person. She weighed 105 pounds, sported a tiny stud nose-ring and dyed her pale blonde hair purple, to signal her bona fide radical credentials. Her father was an investment banker, her MFA mother a sculptress who taught, very occasionally, at a genteel art college. Emily had attended the Rossmount School as a high school student. There Emily and her peers were developed as "leaders for a diverse and inclusive world," as per the Rossmount Mission Statement. (The students were drawn exclusively from Toronto's doctor-lawyer-banker class. One of the scholarship students had a mother who worked for the CBC.)

Emily was engaged in conversation with Stephen Bartolli, an earnest third-year student who was a frequent Writing Center visitor. Tessa always sighed with relief when his name came up on the schedule: an easy appointment. Stephen was conscientious and pedantic—a rarity among typically bottom-of-the-barrel SVU students. Emily and Stephen were chatting about how he had spent his summer.

Emily smiled and motioned in Tessa's direction.

"Hi Tessa. Stephen was just telling me that he did the SVU Malawi 'Helping Hand' program this summer. Isn't that fantastic? I did something very similar when I was his age, only in Haiti."

"I've heard it's a good program," said Tessa.

"It's an *amazing* program," said Stephen. He paused, looking solemn. "Our society is so materialistic in comparison to Malawi's. We surround ourselves with all of this capitalist garbage we don't even need! There's a simplicity and beauty about life in Malawi that many Westerners just don't understand."

Emily nodded vigorously and recounted a related anecdote about her Haiti experiences. It involved happening upon two Haitian children playing joyfully with a discarded gasoline drum. Her eyes glistened with emotion. Tessa tuned out.

"Tessa, did you do any international volunteering in undergrad?" asked Emily, ever-polite, attempting to bring her into the conversation.

Tessa recalled her undergraduate summer jobs. Volunteering abroad was out of the question, of course. She needed to work to earn money to pay her tuition, and she needed to live at home to save money on rent. Invariably, every summer she and Lilly would take the only paid employment available for students in rural Madawaaksis County: working on the dairy farms or in the blueberry fields. They usually ended up raking blueberries, a dirty, laborious job, for which they were paid $5.25 a crate. They worked from sunrise to sunset in the cultivated low-bush blueberry fields covering the thin-soiled, rocky hillsides of the county. They pissed in the woods. They saw bears. They rode in the back of pick-up trucks from field to field. They stained their hands and arms blue. Fair-skinned Lilly burnt a patch on her lower-back that stayed brown for 12 months.

Tessa recalled that, unlike the other laborers, she never developed calluses on her raking-hand. For weeks her right hand blossomed with blood blisters; one set would pop, and another would grow in its place. Her father found this hilarious: "Harder than holding a book, ain't it, Tess?"

"Umm, I mostly worked at home back then, in the blueberry fields. There aren't a lot of options in rural New Brunswick," she said.

"What a privilege to do honest, vigorous work, out in the fresh air!" Stephen enthused. He had been reading a lot of Hemingway of late.

"If you're really interested, I have contacts back in New Brunswick," said Tessa.

"Next summer I'm interning at the office, I think," replied Stephen, referring to his father's law practice. "But otherwise, I'd love to."

Tessa allowed herself a faint smile. She checked her watch. It was noon. Mincing must be looking for her. She took her leave of Emily and Stephen, and continued her course around the gym, finally spying her department's table in the distance. The porcine mother-daughter pair had landed there, their bodies blocking her sight-line. Tessa could just make out the top of Mincing's severe brunette bob from behind them. She took a deep breath and made her way over.

"I'm a very practical person," the mother was saying to Mincing. "Her father and I wanted her to take something useful like Nursing, but her heart's set on English. Kaylee just loves reading, don't you, honey? We both loved the *50 Shades* books. Have you read them?"

Mincing flushed.

"Well no, I…"

"I know, you're a prof and prob'ly think they're trashy, but anything that gets 'em reading, right?"

"Tessa!" exclaimed Mincing, from somewhere behind her visitors.

"Excuse me, but I have to go now," she said to the pair. "Tessa—err, Dr. Stevens—will be taking over. She just finished her Ph.D. here in English, and teaches in the Department. In fact, you did your M.A. *and* your Ph.D. here, didn't you? Dr. Stevens would be more than happy to answer any of your questions."

Laptop bag and coat at the ready, Mincing fled.

Tessa arranged her facial muscles into a smile.

"So, do you have any other questions?"

The pretty daughter had long lost interest. She was drifting in the direction of the juggling act a few booths away, but Mom was settled in for the long haul. She was even taking notes in a SVU-branded notebook.

"Yes. So, what's the point of an English degree? Like, what can you really do with it when you're done?"

Tessa braced herself for the next four hours.

Chapter Four: Blessed Be the Name of the Lard

Deborahann sat in church, trying not to cry, as Pastor Fudge led the congregation in singing the Doxology:

"Praise God from whom all blessings flow.

Praise him all creatures here below.

Praise him above ye heavenly hosts.

Praise Father, Son, and Holy Ghost.

Aaaaaaaaaaah...mennnnnnnnnnnn."

As he led them in singing the Doxology, Pastor Thomas Archibald Fudge of the First Beaconsbridge United Baptist Church surveyed his congregation of assorted farmers, laborers, and housewives, most of whom were within five degrees of consanguinity. They were typical southern New Brunswick Anglophone stock: most were of British Isles origin, with the odd anglicized German descendant among them, as well as a lone Francophone woman married (unhappily) to a local man.

Fudge himself was a migratory Newfoundlander, not a New Brunswicker. Ten generations of intermarriage in Newfoundland had only reinforced the essential Irishness of the pastor and his kin, though in isolation their accent had evolved into something strange and beautiful, like the ring-tailed lemurs of Madagascar. Pastor Fudge had moved to New Brunswick in his early teens, along with his large family. He was not overburdened by brains, but possessed something far more useful: the sensitive nervous system of a jellyfish when it came to survival in his chosen profession, the ministry. Outside of his natal province, Fudge's accent conveyed the becoming artlessness of a peasant. In New Brunswick, Fudge leveraged his Newfie accent as Brits do in America. Throughout his career, it rarely failed to charm his congregations.

What an ass, thought Deborahann, fighting to keep her expression neutral. Like her cousin Yule, who was also in church that day, she was one of the few parishioners who disliked the pastor and his accent.

So put-on. He's been here for ages. Gimme a break, she thought.

Deborahann and Vic sat in their usual spot, two pews from the front, on Pastor Fudge's right. Vic chanted the Doxology loudly, enunciating every word. This was the best time of the week for him. It was a relief to be perfectly correct, to all appearances, the righteous patriarch in church with his family. During these times, he often thought of the verse from Joshua: "As for me and my house, we will serve the Lord." When Lilly and Tessa were home, and sitting with them, he felt especially pious. With just Deborahann by his side, not the full complement, he felt less so, but still fine. He looked up at Pastor Fudge, eyes wide with admiration. *Truly a man of the Lord*, he thought.

Deborahann had found the sermon trying. It felt like a thousand small, sharp needles pricking her: a little sting here, a little sting there, a crimson droplet piercing the surface of her thin skin. Pastor Fudge's sermon was entitled, "Our True Family," focussing on the passages in Matthew 12 where Jesus, preaching to a large crowd, is told that his mother and brothers are outside, wanting to see him. Jesus brushes the request aside, pointing to his disciples, and saying that whosoever does the will of the Father is his brother, sister, and mother. Pastor Fudge interpreted this less than filial passage to mean that other believers in Christ are "our true family, our true community," and that "other worldly bonds should be as nothing to us." His explanation was an orthodox one, but that wasn't what bothered Deborahann. She paid little attention to the content of sermons anyway. Her mind was always running ahead of her, to the next chore she had to complete. Today something pierced her bubble. Her problem was with the pastor repeatedly saying, "true family," "our real family," "our beloved family in Christ," and so on.

Deborahann had been taken in by Ada and Jack Case as a foster child, and eventually adopted. The couple had begun fostering children once it became clear, after several years of marriage, that they were not going to have any biological children. Deborahann's background was mysterious. She was born in Saint John, New Brunswick to an anonymous teenage mother. As a baby, she was shifted from one foster home to another, finally ending up in a province-run group home. She was a sullen toddler by then, with a round face, straw-colored hair and dark blue eyes. At three and a half years of age, she could not—or would not talk. Instead, she screamed like an infant when she was hungry or wanted something. What Ada remembered most about the day they picked her up from the home, was that toddler Deborahann had a large, scabbed-over burn on her foot. When Ada made inquiries, the greasy-haired woman tending the children just shrugged, "Musta happened a-fore she got here."

Deborahann's left heel was still discolored by the burn scar, almost 50 years later. It was a permanent reminder of her origins. During the sermon, every time Pastor Fudge mouthed some commonplace like, "We look to our families as a sarce of love and support," she felt a twinge. She remembered being told, aged 7, by her cousin Connie, "You're not a *real* Blakeney you know. You're adopted." Deborahann had always known this, in an abstract kind of way, though it hadn't really registered before. "Your parents aren't your *real* parents. They just found you somewheres," Connie elaborated. "They are too my real parents!" Deborahann said, eyes filling with tears. Yule ended the conversation by yelling, "Shut up, Pig Nose!" to Connie, who wilted under the accurate descriptor. "Never mind, Sissy," he said to Deborahann.

(Sisterless Yule and his little brother Jim often called their cousin "Sissy.") But the damage was done.

Doxology concluded, the pastor cleared his throat, and began the Benediction:

"Dear Lard our God. Bless all our dear brothers and sisters in Christ, gathered here today. Lighten our burdens. Strengthen our hearts. Guide us as we travel o'er the treacherous highways and byways of life.

"And Lard, guard us all from the evils in the world today. For we live in a world of wickedness and lies. Guard us, Lard, from the lies of the world, for as Your Son has said, Lard, we are not of the world…"

Jesus H. Christ, is he saying a prayer or baking a fucking cake? thought Yule. He was seated beside his wife Abby, four rows back, to Pastor Fudge's left. His parents sat in the pew behind them. Yule was a smallish, wiry man, with a salt-and-pepper beard. His name was short for "Ulysses," an idiosyncratic choice on the part of his mother Moira. Yule's father, Lew Blakeney, was one of the brothers of Ada Case, née Blakeney, so Yule and the adopted Deborahann were cousins by custom, if not by blood. Lew and Ada were two of nine children. The Blakeneys were a well-known Madawaaksis County clan. They descended from opportunistic New England planters who had made their way north from the American Thirteen Colonies before the War of Independence, settling on the lands the French Acadians had been expelled from by the British.

Nearly every Blakeney and Blakeney-adjacent person in the county, including Ada, displayed a distinctive commemorative plate in their home, with a stylized homestead on it, emblazoned with the family immigration date to the British colonies that would become Canada: "1762." Ada's was given pride of place above the kitchen table. The plate was ringed with the names of the so-called "original seven" Blakeney sons: John, Thomas, Enoch, Edward, Samuel, Benjamin, and Zebulon. Every Blakeney in Madawaaksis was descended from one of the seven. One of Deborahann's earliest memories was asking her mother which one was her ancestor, and being told Samuel. Then she asked, "And which one's Daddy's?" The answer was Zebulon. Jack Case's great-grandmother had been a Blakeney. But as Deborahann grew up, and understood more clearly what adoption meant, looking up at the plate on the wall began to hurt her.

As Deborahann ruminated on the other side of the church, Yule cracked his knuckles, a sign of impatience recognized by Abby, whose high heel grazed her husband's ankle in warning. Abby had long tuned out the pastor. Instead, she occupied herself by examining the backs of little Katie and Misty Waller, sitting in front of her. Some well-meaning soul had taken them to church. Their mother Tammy was nowhere to be seen, but that was to be expected, and they had no fathers, for all intents and purposes. It was October and chilly, but the girls were still wearing thin summer dresses from Walmart. Warm-hearted Abby resisted the urge to take off her own cardigan and place it over Misty's skinny shoulders.

Aunt Ada sat ramrod-straight, just ahead of Yule and Abby in the next pew. At five foot eleven inches in her pantyhose, she was significantly taller than her nephew, who took after his mother's people: the diminutive Caldwells, not the gangly Blakeneys. Even at 85, Ada was a fine figure of a woman; she looked quite capable, if called upon, of delivering a beating. She had wed late in life for a Madawaaksis woman of her era: she was pushing 30 when she married Jack Case, who owned the only grocery store in town. Ada was tall and religious, while Jack was short, spunky, essentially pagan, and possessed of a sense of humor still legendary in

Beaconsbridge, though the man had been dead and gone for decades now. Deborahann's father had died of lung cancer when she was still a girl.

Pastor Fudge carried on with the Benediction, his red eyes sewn up like quilt patches:

"And Lard—oh blessed Lard—give us dis-sarning hearts, that we might reject that which is evil and cling to that which is good. For we remember the words the great prophet Daniel proclaimed to the wicked King Belshazzar: *'Mene, Mene, Tekel, Parsin'*—for you have been weighed in the balance and found wanting.' Oh, Lard, we know that this world is found wanting in Your eyes. We must stand firm against it, united with our brothers and sisters in Christ, like Gideon's army: 'For where two or three are gathered together in My name, there am I with them.' We know You are with us, Oh Lard. And if the Lard is with us, who then—truly!—who then can truly be against us?"

Elinor Crossman enjoyed this snippet of Bible verse. Like most of the matrons present, she'd been thinking about what she would make for lunch after church, Fudge's accent filling her professionally curled-and-dyed head with images of delicious baked goods. This last Fudge line diverted her attention back to the service. *It's a great comfort to know the Lord is with you against all opposition*, she mused, thinking about last year's tax audit. The Lord—and a skillful accountant—had served her and her husband Robert well. Robert sat beside her, a stout man with a baby's innocent face. He stared straight ahead, his mind untroubled by even a ripple of thought.

Pastor Fudge concluded, "Let us depart this place of fellowship today in renewed faith and love, trusting in You, oh Lard, to lead us through the trials and tribulations that lie ahead.

"In Jesus' name, Ah-men."

The congregation softly echoed, "Ah-men."

"Please turn to our closing hymn, 'Power in the Blood,' hymnal number 256," directed the pastor. "Today we will be singing verses one, two, and four, omitting verse three."

The congregation began verse one earnestly: "Would you be free from the burden of sin?/ There's pow'r in the blood, pow'r in the blood!/ Would you o'er evil a victory win?/ There's wonderful pow'r in the blood!"

Sitting near the back of the church, Les Richardson, a farm laborer and long-time bachelor, reflected that that being free from one's "burden of sin" was easier said than done. He shifted in the hard pew.

The congregation started in, with vigor, on the second verse: "Would you be free from your passion and pride?/ There's pow'r in the blood, pow'r in the blood!/ Come for a cleansing to Calvary's tide;/ There's wonderful pow'r in the blood!"

Yule and Deborahann's younger second cousin, Jenna Blakeney, up in the balcony with the other naughty teenagers, reflected that she absolutely did *not* want to be free from her "passion and pride." Passion and pride, she believed, made her what she was. Wiggling in her seat, she discreetly adjusted her push-up bra.

Verse three was obediently omitted by the congregation. Verse four inquired, rather obsequiously, thought Yule (though he would not have used the word "obsequiously"), "Would you do service for Jesus your King?/ There's pow'r in the blood, pow'r in the blood!/ Would you live daily His praises to sing?/ There's wonderful pow'r in the blood!"

By the final repetition of the chorus, Deborahann was in control of herself again. During the song, she had successfully pushed the intrusive feelings down into the subterranean level of her consciousness. The congregation ended with a flourish, despite their plummeting blood sugar levels: "There is pow'r, pow'r, wonder-working pow'r/ In the blood/ Of the Lamb!/ "There is pow'r, pow'r, wonder-working pow'r/ In the precious blood of the Lamb!"

The pianist played out the crowd, which drifted out of the sanctuary, to the coat-racks, and then to the parking lot. The pleasant buzz of neighborly conversation filled the church. The Les Richardsons made good their escapes, while the Elinor Crossman-types made slow, regal processions to the exits, stopping to chat, see, and be seen by their neighbors.

Down in the church basement, in one of the meeting rooms, Pastor and Mrs. Fudge were waiting for the other 20 or so members of the Finance Committee to arrive. Margaret Fudge was shaped like her husband: tallish, solid and doughy, her once nubile form long gone to fat. But while the pastor maintained calm behind his affected folksiness, Margaret emanated anxiety. She rarely spoke, and when she did, the effect was like a popped balloon: out came a rush of high-pitched squeals. The couple were childless.

Margaret was known in Beaconsbridge as "nervous," which translated most closely from Madawaaksisish to English as "clinically depressed." Her speech and behavior, which hugged the line of normal at the best of times, was dismissed as "typical Margaret," by most of Beaconsbridge Baptist's parishioners. Ada often told her daughter, "She's poor Pastor Fudge's cross to bear"—"cross to bear" being, incidentally, one of Ada's favorite expressions, applied to misfortunes ranging from the common cold to cancer.

Today Margaret seemed calm, Deborahann noticed. She and Vic were among the last of the Finance Committee members to file in to the meeting room downstairs, behind Yule and Abby. Their progress from the sanctuary to the basement was a slow one because of their escorting duties: they supported 97 year old Aunt Beulah step by agonizing step. Beulah Blakeney was the oldest of the Finance Committee members by some margin. Due to her advanced age—and the fact that she was related to half of Beaconsbridge—she was universally known in the village as "Aunt" Beulah. Unlike most, Deborahann had some legitimate claim to using the honorific: Beulah was the widow of Ada's long-deceased oldest brother, Clayton Blakeney. A cushioned chair materialized magically as 4 foot 11 inch Beulah entered the room, supported on either side by her retainers, Vic and Deborahann.

"Last but sir-tane-ley not least!" said Pastor Fudge. Vic chuckled. Deborahann smiled wanly. Beulah, serenely deaf, said nothing.

As anxious as any of them to get home to his lunch, Fudge dispensed with further niceties.

"An unfore-sane event has led me to call an emergency meeting."

He paused for dramatic effect.

"I don't need to tell you," the pastor told the room, "that everything I'm about to say must remain com-plate-ley confidential."

A frisson of excitement circulated around the room, jolting everyone but Aunt Beulah.

"As you all know, our youth minister recently left under…less than ideal circumstances."

The Finance Committee members maintained their professionalism despite the images dancing in their heads.

"Luckily, the girl's mother understood that nothing would be gained by pursuing the matter further, but it turns out, unfortunately, that the Chairch will not be emairging from the tenure of Pastor Jonathan totally unscathed."

Tension mounted in the room. Aunt Beulah leaned back in her chair, resting her eyes and easing into a mid-day nap.

"As you know, Pastor Jonathan was residing in Parsonage Two," Fudge continued. "The cost of readying the building for occupation after five years sitting empty was considerable."

"Tell me about it," interjected Jim MacBride. A carpenter and committee member, he often provided labor and renovation materials free of charge to his church.

Fudge smiled a crooked smile.

"Pastor Jonathan let us down tare-ibly. But what we did *not* expect, I can tell you, is what we found in Parsonage Two after he left."

The committee leaned forward. Fudge lowered his voice:

"I am less than familiar with the term, but what we found in the attic was…it was…"

"Speak up!" croaked Aunt Beulah from the back of the room, suddenly awake. "If it's worth sayin', it's worth hearin.'"

Fudge cleared his throat.

"We found a grow-op."

The room went silent. Yule let out a guffaw. Abby poked him in the ribs.

"The deacons and I elected not to involve the authorities. It was a very small operation. We removed the, uhh…plant matter and other equipment. It has been destroyed. However, a significant amount of water damage has occurred. We also smell mold. We'll need to get a professional in to be sure—a *discreet* professional, if anyone here can suggest one."

The room turned to Jim. He shrugged.

"What's all this going to cost?" asked Yule.

"The million dollar question, Mr. Blakeney," said Fudge. "That remains to be seen. Pastor Jonathan and company also appear to have done some rewiring and added some new vents…The parsonage is in quite a state."

Aunt Beulah interrupted with a soft snore. She was out again.

"I can take a look at it," said Jim. "But I can't promise I can fix it."

"Have you seen this type of thing before, Jim?" asked the pastor.

"Yup."

"What were the reno costs?"

"Well, it depends. If there's mold, we've got problems."

A gentle fart wafted across the room from the general direction of Aunt Beulah. Pastor Fudge sped up the proceedings.

"Jim, could you take a look at it, and we'll go from there?"

Jim nodded assent.

"Vic? Yule?" Fudge nodded in the direction of the other two men in the room generally considered the most "handy." Vic agreed. Yule sighed and agreed. They would meet Jim at the parsonage after lunch.

"After these gentlemen have taken a look, and after we get some professional repair estimates in, we will need to immediately begin planning on how to absorb these unfore-sane costs," said Fudge. He turned his gaze to the women in the room.

"My better half has some fundraising ideas…" He smiled in Margaret's direction.

Margaret stood bolt up-right, taking her cue: "We can do another pancake breakfast. Or a crafts fair. Or a bake fair. Or a quilt raffle."

Abby and Deborahann smiled encouragingly at her. Margaret rarely spoke in meetings, despite her elevated position in the church hierarchy as minister's wife.

"Who would like to lend Margaret a hand?" the pastor asked.

"Deb can help," said Vic. "She's not busy."

Deborahann nodded.

Abby and a few other matrons in the room committed to the fundraising efforts as well. Pastor Fudge brought up a few more logistical matters, and wrapped up the meeting. Aunt Beulah was awakened and escorted home by another one of her many dutiful distant relatives.

In the car to Abby, Yule said, "That Pastor Jonathan sure got around. The ministers weren't so fun when I was a lad."

"Oh I bet they were," replied Abby.

***

Fr: Deborahann Stevens—deborahannstevens@hotmail.com

To: Tessa Stevens—te.stevens@svu.edu

Subject: ARE YOU STILL ALIVE??

Date: October 23, 2016, 2:30 p.m.

TESSIE-BEAR

SOMEONE ISN'T PICKING UP HER PHONE. DO YOU KNOW WHO, TESSIE??!! CHURCH WAS VERY BORING TODAY AS USUAL. THE FINANCE COMMITTEE MET AFTER WARDS AND BY THE TIME THAT WAS OVER I WAS STARVING. BIG NEW COSTS AND NO MONEY IN THE BANK. (STORY OF MY LIFE!) SO GUESS WHO GOT ROPED IN TO MORE FUNDRAISING? THAT'S RIGHT. YOURS TRULY. I NEED TO LEARN HOW TO SAY "NO." YOU ARE VERY GOOD AT THAT TESSIE. ARE YOU GIVING LESSONS? HA.

YOUR FATHER HAS A BAD COLD. HE THINKS I PICKED SOMETHING UP AT SENTIMENTAL OCCASIONS. HE SAYS I AM A "CARRIER" BUT NEVER GET SICK MYSELF. JUST LUCKY I GUESS.

HOW ARE THE COMPOSITION CLASSES GOING? THE ONES FOR "SPECIAL" STUDENTS, HAHA.

DID YOU HEAR BACK ABOUT A REAL JOB YET? WHAT HAPPENED ABOUT THE FULLTIME ONE IN YOUR DEPT??

TRIXIE SAYS "I MISS YOU!"

LOVE YOU.

MUM

P.S. PICK UP YOUR PHONE.

Fr: Tessa Stevens—te.stevens@svu.edu

To: Deborahann Stevens—deborahannstevens@hotmail.com

Subject: RE: ARE YOU STILL ALIVE??

Date: October 23, 2016, 3:35 p.m.

    Mum, could you please stop writing in all-caps? We've been through this. It's the equivalent of shouting into the phone.

    Yes, I am still alive. :P Just busy. When is Madawaaksis County getting some cell towers or something, so we can text updates like normal human beings? Rural New Brunswick and Outer Mongolia must be the only places on earth right now without decent cell coverage.

    Intro Comp is sapping me of the will to live. Did I tell you I teach my sections back-to-back? It's awful.

    I submitted my application for the TT position here last week, just before the deadline. Pearl told me they received 85 (!) applications for it. I can't believe so many people want to teach at a cow college like SVU. I still think I have a chance though, because they know me and it's basically the full-time version of what I've been teaching for four years here already: Intro Comp and Intro to the Novel. I've also put in a lot of service, including, for example, representing the Department at a godawful New Student Orientation "Circus" last week. (Will explain later on phone.) Should hear back in a few weeks about first-round interviews, if I'm going to.

Other than that one, I also submitted four other job applications: three in Canada, and one in the States. They're all TT English jobs, except the American one, which is also TT, but in some unusual interdisciplinary arts program at a hippie college in Oregon—looks interesting.

More later,

Tessa

Fr: Deborahann Stevens—deborahannstevens@hotmail.com

To: Tessa Stevens—te.stevens@svu.edu

Subject: RE: RE: ARE YOU STILL ALIVE??

October 23, 2016, 3:37 p.m.

WHAT DOES TT MEAN??

MUM

Fr: Tessa Stevens—te.stevens@svu.edu

To: Deborahann Stevens—deborahannstevens@hotmail.com

Subject: RE: RE: RE: ARE YOU STILL ALIVE??

Date: October 23, 2016, 3:40 p.m.

"Tenure-track." I've explained this before. They hire you full-time from the beginning, but you go up for a review after about five years to decide if they want to keep you permanently.

Why are you still writing in all caps? Seriously, stop. Annoying.

Fr: Deborahann Stevens—deborahannstevens@hotmail.com

To: Tessa Stevens—te.stevens@svu.edu

Subject: RE: RE: RE: RE: ARE YOU STILL ALIVE??

October 23, 2016, 3:43 p.m.

OOOH, THEN THEY CAN'T GET RID OF YOU EVER AND YOU'RE ALL SET, RIGHT? CHA-CHING CHA-CHING! WISH I HAD TENURE AT WORK. ELINOR WOULD LOVE THAT. HAHA.

LOOOOOOOOVE YOU.

MUM

Fr: Tessa Stevens—te.stevens@svu.edu

To: Deborahann Stevens—deborahannstevens@hotmail.com

Subject: RE: RE: RE: RE: RE: ARE YOU STILL ALIVE??

Date: October 23, 2016, 3:45 p.m.ce

Basically.

Fr: Tessa Stevens—te.stevens@svu.edu

To: Deborahann Stevens—deborahannstevens@hotmail.com

Subject: Re: Re: Re: Re: Re: Re: ARE YOU STILL ALIVE??

Date: October 23, 2016, 3:48 p.m.

P.S. And btw, it's not your fault Dad has a cold. He's being a jerk, Mum. As usual. Love you too.

Chapter Five: Enter Boudicca

It was 4:30 on a Friday, nearing the end of Tessa's work-day on campus. She was huddled over her laptop in the tiny office she shared with two other sessionals, Myron and Pamela, both of whom had already headed home for the weekend. They had begun the Ph.D. at the same time as her, only both of them were still completing their dissertations. Pamela was on Year Six, with an upcoming defense, while Myron, amazingly, was on Year Ten—he was probably a lifer, one of those Ph.D. students who made a career of writing the dissertation, clinging to the hulk of academia like a barnacle through any storm. Tessa both liked Myron and held him in contempt. He was a good person to discuss Fitzgerald with, but she wondered what kind of grown man was content to live 10 years plus on ramen and 22k per annum.

For hours that afternoon, Tessa had been diligently composing a letter of application for yet another assistant professorship she would never get, willing herself to avoid all internet distractions. Letter completed, she rewarded herself by checking her email. There was nothing from Andrew, but her inbox was clogged with dozens of other emails since she had last checked it that morning, all from the Womyn's listserv. She held her nose and dove in, starting at the beginning:

Fr: Amy Mephistos—a.mephistos@svu.edu

To: Womyn's Scholars Group Listserv

Subject: Organizing Protests of Paulson Talk

Date: Oct. 14, 2016, 10:40 a.m.

Dear Colleagues,

As you may have heard, the (ahem...) "Students for Free Inquiry" have invited Bernard Paulson to speak on the last day of classes. That's November 29th, in Suzeman. It should come as no surprise to you, that given the unfavorable publicity generated by the University of Toronto protests in September, the administration has been unreceptive to our concerns that Paulson's speech will embolden alt-right elements in the university and town. His very presence endangers the lives of SVU's most vulnerable communities: women, queer people, non-binary people, people of color, and others. Frankly, we are shocked that SVU—an institution that claims to offer a safe and welcoming space for marginalized individuals—would open its doors to Paulson, who has been linked to far-right hate groups, and whose message is completely inimical to the university's mission.

We understand that a number of student groups, led by Postmodernists for Peace (with whom we continue to maintain warm ties of solidarity) will be forming a "Diversity Wall" to block Paulson and his entourage from entering the auditorium and speaking. We have heard reports that the administration has been made aware of PFP's strategy, and intends to FORCIBLY remove them by security if they attempt to block the speech.

Given the disturbing authoritarian bent of the administration, what can we do as a group to show our support for the PFP and other anti-fascist groups protesting Paulson? As discussed at the last meeting, the Executive is hesitant to join the Diversity Wall for a number of reasons: for one, our members have expressed reasonable concerns that we will be subjected to unfavorable attention from the public. Some fear we will be targeted for abuse by regressive elements if we are identified in any pictures or video of the event. (Note: I've heard that the PFP has advised all its members to protest dressed in black and to obscure their faces with scarves or masks. We fear that even this measure may not prevent identification.)

Any suggestions for supporting the PFP and stopping Paulson in his tracks, ladies?

In the spirit of peace and solidarity,

Amy

--Amy Mephistos

President, Womyn's Scholars Group

Associate Professor, Department of Women and Gender Studies

Sere Valley University

Fr: Linda Galavant—l.galavant@svu.edu

To: Womyn's Scholars Group Listserv

Subject: RE: Organizing Protests of Paulson Talk

Date: Oct. 14, 2016, 10:52 a.m.

Firstly, I completely agree that we need to act to stop Paulson from polluting our campus with his racist, misogynistic drivel. No platform for hate! I will certainly be in attendance at the talk to lend my support to the PFP and any other anti-fascist groups protesting Paulson.

Secondly, apologies for being a trifle pedantic, Amy, but I thought we agreed that "ladies," even utilized in jest, is problematic because it has also been used by the patriarchy, historically, to demean and belittle women? (Please see our esteemed colleague Elizabeth Wagband's excellent article on the subject. The title escapes me at the moment, but I believe it was published in *Subversive Encounters* last year. Any help anyone?)

Cheers,

Linda

--Linda Galavant

Professor, Department of English Literature

Sere Valley University

Fr: Margaret Truffle—m.truffle@svu.edu

To: Womyn's Scholars Group Listserv

Subject: RE: RE: Organizing Protests of Paulson Talk

Date: Oct. 14, 2016, 10:55 a.m.

    Linda is entirely correct. Although I am sure it was not Amy's intent, "ladies" is a suspect term. In addition to its use by the patriarchy, it conveys a sense of being "lady-like," which my online dictionary defines as "showing undue concern for elegance or propriety," as well as "lacking in strength or force" (!). Far from being a neutral term, "ladies" conveys a number of harmful stereotypes about women.

-M

--Margaret Truffle

Professor, Department of Sociology

Sere Valley University

Fr: Ophelia Cross—o.cross@svu.edu

To: Womyn's Scholars Group Listserv

Subject: RE: RE: RE: Organizing Protests of Paulson Talk

Date: Oct. 14, 2016, 10:58 a.m.

…Not to mention its close etymological connection to "ladle," a kitchen utensil. Eeek!

Best,

Ophelia

--Ophelia Cross

Assistant Professor, Department of Women and Gender Studies

Sere Valley University

Fr: Tilly Tippaloo-Montmorency—t.tippaloo@svu.edu

To: Womyn's Scholars Group Listserv

Subject: RE: RE: RE: RE: Organizing Protests of Paulson Talk

Date: Oct. 14, 2016, 11:01 a.m.

    This is not my area of expertise (Dr. Claremont?), but hasn't "ladies" been reclaimed by women of color as a term? See: the popular Beyoncé anthem, "All the Swingin' Ladies."

    Tilly

--Tilly Tippaloo-Montmorency

Associate Professor, Department of Women and Gender Studies

Sere Valley University

Fr: Angelika Franco—a.franco@svu.edu

To: Womyn's Scholars Group Listserv

Subject: RE: RE: RE: RE: RE: Organizing Protests of Paulson Talk

Date: Oct. 14, 2016, 11:10 a.m.

    Does anyone know if "All the Swinging Ladies" has also been used subversively by the queer or differently-abled communities to reclaim discursive space?

    Cheers,

Angie

--Angelika Franco

Lecturer, Faculty of Education

Sere Valley University

Fr: Amy Mephistos—a.mephistos@svu.edu

To: Womyn's Scholars Group Listserv

Subject: RE: RE: RE: RE: RE: RE: Organizing Protests of Paulson Talk

Date: Oct. 14, 2016, 11:18 a.m.

Colleagues,

"All the Swingin' Ladies" is undoubtedly an empowering example of pop culture being used by women of color (and re: Angie: possibly other marginalized groups?) to challenge an oppressive linguistic paradigm. Nonetheless, I'm afraid we are getting off-course here. Can we return to strategizing vis-à-vis the Paulson talk?

Best,

Amy

--Amy Mephistos

President, Womyn's Scholars Group

Associate Professor, Department of Women and Gender Studies

Sere Valley University

Fr: Marilyn Hampton-Cho—m.hamptoncho@svu.edu

To: Womyn's Scholars Group Listserv

Subject: RE: RE: RE: RE: RE: RE: RE: Organizing Protests of Paulson Talk

Date: Oct. 14, 2016, 11:32 a.m.

 A quick comment before we return to Paulson…I just listened to "All the Swingin' Ladies" on the YouTube, and I'm sorry to say that this song is unlikely to serve as an empowering anthem for our friends in the differently-abled community. The lyrics repeatedly demand of the listener: "Now put your hands up!" Sadly, many members of this community are unable to follow such a command.

 Regards,

 Marilyn

--Marilyn Hampton-Cho

Professor, Department of Cultural Studies

Sere Valley University

Fr: Destiny Claremont—d.claremont@svu.edu

To: Womyn's Scholars Group Listserv

Subject: RE: RE: RE: RE: RE: RE: RE: Organizing Protests of Paulson Talk

Date: Oct. 14, 2016, 11:42 a.m.

The song is called "Single Ladies" not "All the Swingin' Ladies."

 Destiny

--Destiny Claremont

Assistant Professor, Department of Theatre Arts

Sere Valley University

***

An additional 19 reply-alls were generated (elapsed time: approximately three hours), further discussing issues related to the etymology of "lady," and Beyoncé's oeuvre.

***

Fr: Ophelia Cross—o.cross@svu.edu

To: Womyn's Scholars Group Listserv

Subject: RE: RE: RE: RE: RE: RE: RE: RE: RE: RE: RE: RE: RE: RE: RE: RE: RE: RE…

Date: Oct. 14, 2016, 2:45 p.m.

    What if we all wore pins to the Paulson talk, similar to the ones we wore for International Women's Day? I still have my in-town printer contacts. They're inexpensive. I think a simple image would have the most impact. Perhaps a rainbow? Or a rainbow-hued uterus? A raised fist superimposed over the female gender sign? Or the outline of a Rosie the Riveter in hijab?

    Ophelia

--Ophelia Cross

Assistant Professor, Department of Women and Gender Studies

Sere Valley University

Fr: Elizabeth Wagband—e.wagband@svu.edu

To: Womyn's Scholars Group Listserv

Subject: RE: RE: RE: RE: RE: RE: RE: RE: RE: RE: RE: RE: RE: RE: RE: RE: RE: RE…

Date: Oct. 14, 2016, 3:23 p.m.

    Ophelia's pin idea is a good one. I think a raised fist over a female gender sign WITH a rainbow behind it would be very effective indeed—though I do worry that a raised fist may suggest an ableist bias. Not everyone, of course (as Marilyn noted) can elevate one's arm, particularly in such an aggressive, forceful manner. On second thought, can anyone suggest a symbol along these lines that better includes our differently-abled sisters?

A further thought: my PFP contacts tell me that in addition to the proposed Diversity Wall, at least one of their members plans on disrupting the talk by bringing in a concealed bullhorn. I know in the past some of you have opposed such strategies as extreme, but desperate times call for desperate measures. What do we think about our group bringing in some type of noisemakers, at the very least? Perhaps whistles? Drums from our First Nations colleagues? (Particularly meaningful!) How can we drown him out?

Another thought for our consideration: we must be BOLD in the face of any opposition from the administration or negative responses from locals. We all remember the blowback two years ago, during my tenure as president of this organization, when we successfully lobbied to have Laura Bouldheart's invitation to campus rescinded. My name was dragged through the mud in the editorial pages of the local daily rag. Nonetheless, we achieved our goal of protecting the rights of women and other marginalized groups on campus by having Bouldheart's hateful talk cancelled.

We know that regressive elements will always be out there, particularly among the uneducated. Sere Valley in particular—outside of the university community, of course—is a hotbed for the alt-right. Be strong and ever-vigilant, friends.

In solidarity,

Elizabeth

p.s. As I write this email, the inspiring face of Rosa Parks smiles down radiantly upon me. Don't forget, dear colleagues: we stand on the shoulders of giants!

--Elizabeth Wagband

Professor, Department of English Literature

Sere Valley University

Fr: Jessica Mincing—jd.mincing@svu.edu

To: Womyn's Scholars Group Listserv

Subject: RE: RE: RE: RE: RE: RE: RE: RE: RE: RE: RE: RE: RE: RE: RE: RE…

Date: Oct. 14, 2016, 3:45 p.m.

    Elizabeth is right. Our group can expect a negative response from the town once our opposition is known. (I'm a member of the PFP as well, and they're also preparing for this.) We should mentally prepare ourselves. Sadly, we can also expect criticism from some of our less progressive colleagues. As I was telling Elizabeth yesterday, I had a disheartening conversation with an older, cisgendered white male colleague on this topic (a historian, if you can believe it). I expressed shock that SVU was allowing Paulson to speak, and he responded by saying something along the lines of "free speech means some people will be offended." I patiently tried to explain to him the link between hate speech and violence toward marginalized communities, and he rolled his eyes, cut me off, and said, and I quote, "The threat of violence has long been invoked by tyrants to silence subversives." (!!!) He then launched into some tangent about Augustus and the Roman Empire, etc., etc… I must admit I tuned out at that point. Can you believe that?

    In solidarity,

    Jessica

p.s. And further to what Elizabeth said about Rosa Parks: Elizabeth, mentors like you and Linda inspire ME! Thank you for your sage advice and friendship!

--Jessica Mincing

Assistant Professor, Department of English Literature

Sere Valley University

Fr: Angelika Franco—a.franco@svu.edu

To: Womyn's Scholars Group Listserv

Subject: Subject: RE: RE: RE: RE: RE: RE: RE: RE: RE: RE: RE: RE: RE: RE: RE: RE…

Date: Oct. 14, 2016, 3:52 p.m.

That sounds like rampant mansplaining to me, Jessica!

Angie

--Angelika Franco

Lecturer, Faculty of Education

Sere Valley University

Fr: Monique Cormier-Shafer—m.cormiershafer@svu.edu

To: Womyn's Scholars Group Listserv

Subject: Subject: RE: RE: RE: RE: RE: RE: RE: RE: RE: RE: RE: RE: RE: RE: RE: RE…

Date: Oct. 14, 2016, 4:02 p.m.

    Indeed it does. And I think I can guess the perpetrator. Let's just say he's been less than a force for positive change in the History Department for some time now. If it's who I think it is, we've done committee work together. He suggested that we do a job search "blind," with all names and identifying information blacked out, so we could pick a candidate "based solely on merit." Sigh.

Monique

--Monique Cormier-Shafer

Associate Professor, Department of History

Sere Valley University

***

An additional 35 reply-alls were generated (elapsed time: approximately seven hours), discussing major topics ranging from the injustice of "mansplaining," to the selection of appropriate images for the Paulson protest, to the use of free speech to justify bigotry. Other topics discussed included the importance of female role models, the relative cuteness of Persians versus Scottish Folds, and the ethically suspect use of terms like "merit" and "talent" by the patriarchy to maintain the status quo when selecting job candidates.

***

"Rosa Parks. Rosa fucking Parks," said Adrian to Tessa later that night, holding up two fingers, and gesturing to their grim-faced waitress.

The Ranch Hand was busy as usual on a Friday night. It was a townie bar, but the odd academic sometimes wandered in, especially if the usual haunts of the university crowd were full. The Ranch Hand was a large, airy, wood-beamed space, utilitarian save for its collection of old country music concert posters tacked up everywhere.

"I was done at that point," said Tessa, pausing to drain her third cider. She was starting to feel it.

"Ahh, that lesser-known tale of courage and humanity: *Liz Wagband's Long Walk to Freedom*. I must've missed that one."

"Long walk across the parking lot to her SUV, more like."

"Thought you said she drove a Tesla?"

"Correction. She *wanted* to drive a Tesla. But Sere Valley, backwater that it is, has nary a charging station, so she told me she was forced to go with an Acura MDX Hybrid."

"Heartbreaking! But I'm sure that's what Rosa would drive today. You know, either that or take a motherfucking bus."

"Honestly, Adrian, for that elitist bitch to compare herself to Rosa Parks makes me sick. She had a total breakdown when Pearl booked her at a Holiday Inn for Victoriana last year. The conference hotel was full, which was her own damn fault for not booking in time. No boutique hotels available either. She made Pearl drop everything and find her 'suitable' accommodations. 'Even Indianapolis must have a charming bed-and-breakfast or two,' she said."

The waitress deposited another IPA and a cider on the table. Tessa nodded at her.

"Where'd she end up?" asked Adrian.

"A fucking bed-and-breakfast, just like she wanted. People like her don't have problems. They have inconveniences."

"People like her, Dr. Stevens dear? Do I detect a soupçon of class rage?"

"You detect a whole ladle-full of it, Mr. Murphy. No one in that department, or the goddamn 'ladies' listserv,' knows jack-shit about working people, and yet they natter around the clock—'marginalized' this, 'disenfranchised' that. I don't know how much more of it I can take."

"Not true, my dear! You read a reply-all from one 'Destiny' in Theatre Arts. My spidey-senses tell me that a 'Destiny' may not have had as easy of a ride in life as an 'Emily.'"

"Ha. Paging Malcolm Gladwell circa *Freakonomics*. Is that one of his top '80s white trash names? Like Stephanie or Amanda? This Destiny is a new hire. Presumably around my age. I've seen her around but we've never met. She's biracial. I only know that because someone kept pestering her once on the Womyn's Scholars listserv for her opinion on something as a 'woman of color,' and she replied with 'Actually, I'm biracial.' I got the idea she wasn't crazy about being made a token."

"And did the questioner find a way to pin down what kind of biracial?"

"She tried…obliquely, as I recall. But to no avail. Destiny didn't even bother to reply. She's unpigeon-hole-able."

"Ahh, mysterious Destiny—only appropriate. Good for her."

Adrian drained half of his IPA with a mighty gulp.

"I feel bad for her. I heard Flamm in his office on the phone making a snide remark about the 'dubious qualifications' of a new hire in Theatre Arts. Could only have been her. Now I don't know how she got the job, but I do know she gets to fight a fun battle from now on. On one side she's dealing with the deluded lefty profs fawning all over her to prove that no, *they* are the least racist in the land, and on the other she's got the closet-righties like Flamm who think she's a diversity hire who couldn't get here on her own steam. Hard to say which is the most annoying."

"Oh, totes the left," said Adrian. "The right are just being suspicious dicks. Sucks for her, but she can still prove them wrong. The left thinks she's their pet. I've seen it before. They smile and nod at every precious syllable that comes out of her mouth. What's that Johnson quote?"

"A woman preaching is like a dog walking on its hind legs. It doesn't do it well, but you are pleasantly surprised to find it does it at all—something like that."

"Yeah, that's the leftist prof's patronizing opinion of the Destinys who've made it this far."

Adrian raised his voice to a falsetto: "A Ph.D.? How extraordinary for your kind! Have a biscuit!"

Tessa grimaced.

"*Are* there right-wing profs at SVU? I sure haven't come across any. Flamm presents Left. He's a skirt-chaser, but he's a socially democratic skirt-chaser."

"Oh, there's a strong 10%, dwelling in the shadows. They keep their heads down. Come to the Business School. Or Econ. And the hard sciences. We even have centrists!" said Adrian.

"But not the Humanities."

"No, you're in Crazy Town, dear. You're left of Stalin."

Adrian crammed a gummy nacho into his mouth.

"I would also point out," he continued, "that Wagband's go-to mentor is Rosa Parks, and not, let's say Ayaan Hirsi Ali. Safe."

Tessa was pretty sure she knew where that was coming from. She considered diving into the issue of Islamophobia versus Islamic fundamentalism concerns with Adrian, but thought better of it. A few weeks back, Adrian had confessed to a crush on a very cute, very repressed Lebanese-Canadian guy in his program. She guessed the affair had not ended well; there had been an abrupt and total cessation of talk of Samir of late. She paused then headed in a safer direction.

"And the sheer suck-up-itude of Mincing! It's like she has no mind of her own. She's just a junior version of Wagband and Galavant. The thing is: I think she's a decent person. She's just absolutely terrified of losing the approval of the herd."

"Can't say I blame her. A girl's gotta' make tenure. I can guarantee she has student loans to pay."

"And something to prove."

"And something to prove," agreed Adrian.

"You know, when I started the Ph.D., five years ago, and joined the Womyn's Scholars, it didn't seem so bad: women helping other women. What's wrong with that? We need to look out for each other. But it's changed over the years. Or maybe I have. There's this knee-jerk assumption now that every time someone disagrees with you, it's because they're a racist or a misogynist. It's such a cheap way to discredit your opponent's arguments."

"Oh, it's a classic ad hominem attack. A rhetorical trick as old as time."

"And this 'mansplaining' garbage. Why can't we just say, 'This person is patronizing me?' Why do we have to attribute patronizing behavior to one sex only?"

"Preach, sister!" Adrian reached for another nacho.

"I guess men do it more often—maybe?—but as you say, it's a dishonest rhetorical move. Labelling something as 'mansplaining' turns down the volume to mute on those voices. The content of the argument becomes irrelevant. It's just another example of men subjugating women, and therefore must be ignored. How can you have a reasonable debate when one side pulls that shit?"

"Ahh Tessa," smiled Adrian. "You and your beloved 'content.' You haven't changed a lick since *The Odyssean* days. Content doesn't matter anymore in an emoji world."

Tessa looked pained.

"Don't say that! Content does matter. It has to matter! If it doesn't matter anymore, we should all just lay down in the middle of the highway and wait for the eighteen-wheeler."

"We're not going to go down that way, Tess."

Adrian was also far from sober.

He continued, "Then the Communists win…or is it the Nazis?"

"It's the terrorists now," said Tessa, wanly. "Or as Paulson would say, the postmodernists."

"Another one?"

Adrian's pint was empty already.

"I'm not done this one."

Adrian took that as a Yes.

"I'll flag her down again at the bar."

"Ok. Another cider."

"No more fucking cider, woman. What kind of Maritimer are you? At least upgrade to a lager. Do it for Rosa."

Adrian carefully maneuvered his bulk through the crowded bar. Tessa's gaze followed him, noticing a sign over the bar advertising, "The Shameless Contrarians: A Live Music Event. Opener: The Earnest Progressives." Within two minutes Adrian had bagged his prey and returned to the table with two more pints.

"Answer me this. I know why you joined the Womyn's Scholars to begin with: naïveté about the ideology, but also cunning pragmatism—contacts are important. But why haven't you challenged any of their crap? What's stopping you from speaking up? All you do lately is bitch to me about their thought-police horse-shit."

Tessa shifted in her chair.

"I came to SVU to do my M.A. and my Ph.D., not to stir up shit. It made more sense to stay under the radar, until I finished."

"Well, you're finished now. Time to speak up."

"No, it's not. I still need references and peers and…all those things. I don't want to be an adjunct forever. Earning a reputation as a bigot will wreck everything. Petty politics is not worth torpedoing my career over."

"So will you speak up once you've landed a tenure-track job?"

"Maybe. Or maybe after I'm tenured."

"So you'll speak up six years from now?" Adrian laughed. "Wait, let me guess, there'll be a new reason then to be a pussy, just like there's been for the past five years."

Tessa's eyes narrowed.

"You have no idea how far I've come, Adrian. My father is a backwoods evangelical weirdo who thinks we're living in the 'end times.' My mother sweeps flower clippings for a living and thinks university is a great place to catch a man. The first time I tasted cheese that didn't come from a can, I was 16 years old. If you think I'm throwing away the academic life on a matter of fucking principle, you're crazy. I can't afford middle class principles. I'm not going back to Madawaaksis County."

Adrian looked her in the eye.

"I know damn well where you came from—I came from there too. And fuck you for patronizing your mother for working for a living. What have they done to you here?"

Tessa took a breath. She sighed.

"I know, I know. But you know what I mean."

"Look, telling the truth is not being a bigot, Tessa, and you goddamn well know it. Don't play their stupid games."

They drank their beers in silence.

Adrian continued, "You know what it might cost to speak up and question this crap: your career. That's a big price to pay. But what does it cost to stay silent? How much is your integrity worth?"

Before she could respond, Mark ambled over to the table. He was wearing faded skinny jeans, a retro '70s t-shirt, and a furry, oversized novelty cowboy hat. Mark was a regular at The Ranch Hand; his name was carved into one of the bar stools.

"Homies!" he yelled over Alan Jackson's "Chattahoochee." Adrian shifted in his chair. Mark was one of those rare creatures, Adrian had once told Tessa: "a Computer Science student *not* on the autism spectrum." Instead, Mark was on the bro spectrum, somewhere between ironic hipster cowboy and actual cowboy. Adrian resented that despite the bro-speak, Mark wasn't stupid, exactly. In fact, he was a good programmer. And he was good-looking.

"How's it going, dudes?"

Tessa wrinkled her nose at Mark's Brut and Jack Daniel's aroma.

"Not bad, just chit-chatting, as usual," she said.

"Aw yeah? About what?"

Mark didn't look at either of them. He leaned over a chair, scanning the room.

"The Paulson talk," said Tessa.

"Sweet! I'm going! Got hooked on his YouTube videos this summer. Paulson's THE MAN. Are you guys going?"

"Reluctantly. Adrian's roped me in. The Womyn's Scholars Group I'm a part of is protesting it. They're trying to stop him from speaking. I was just reading Adrian the email back-and-forth. They seriously think his presence is a 'danger to marginalized communities.'"

Mark shrugged.

"He's a cool dude. He basically just says everyone's got to get their shit together. I don't get why some people are so worked up about him."

"Because that kind of thinking flies in the face of everything we've been taught here. We've always been taught that the system—the imperialist, cisgendered, white patriarchy—is what keeps women and minorities from being successful. The women scholars I know think Paulson, essentially, is blaming the victim."

Tessa paused. She was too drunk to get into "systemic inequalities" with Mark, who was obviously cruising for chicks and tuning her out.

"It's like, both," Mark said.

"Probably," agreed Tessa. "But I can tell you it's frustrating not to be taken seriously, just because I'm a woman. I've definitely had that happen in my life. That's something you and Adrian don't have to deal with."

Adrian harrumphed.

"Oh yeah? It's also frustrating to be called *fag* every day in high school, but tough shit, that's life. The world is full of assholes. I only have so much energy. Do I want to spend it bitching and moaning about inequalities and discrimination, or do I want to spend it bettering myself, so I can better compete out in the world?"

"Maybe the world's not all about competition, Adrian," said Tessa.

"The hell it's not."

"He's a fringe figure."

"Have you actually *read* any Paulson, Tessa, or just the hot takes from his enemies? Look, he's not fringe. Lots of people like Paulson—centrist, reasonable people—but they're afraid of saying anything for fear of it affecting their livelihoods. Why else would he be on every bestseller list? Neo-nazi white boys living in their mom's basements can only buy so many books."

Mark wasn't listening anymore. His gaze had migrated to a skinny girl in black, a sort of goth Twiggy wearing fishnets and a Peter Pan-collared mini-dress.

"Who's that?" he asked no one in particular.

"Huh? Where?"

"In the corner, between the blonde and the Asian chick."

"Her name's Maia Worthing. Gender Studies grad student. PFP member. I've tutored her at the Writing Center."

"PFP?" asked Mark.

"Postmodernists for Peace," Adrian sneered. "SJW-types. They're protesting Paulson. They protested Spearman last year. Take a piss standing up and they protest it."

Mark's eyes stayed locked on Maia.

"How well do you know her? Can you introduce me?"

"A little bit. I guess. She's also in the Womyn's Scholars...Isn't she jusht a little too SJW for you?"

Tessa was on pint five. The room was starting to fall in on itself like a kaleidoscope.

"She's beautiful," said Mark.

He removed his cowboy hat, all the better to see the vision of loveliness at the back of the bar.

"Are you still working at Computing Services' helpdesk, Mark?" asked Tessa.

Adrian tilted his head.

"Yeah. Why?"

Mark reluctantly tore his gaze away from Maia.

Tessa smiled and patted the chair between her and Adrian.

"Come sit."

***

Fr: BOUDICCA (Boudicca34$#@crypticonicamail.com)

To: Womyn's Scholars Group Listserv

Subject: RE: RE: RE: RE: RE: RE: RE: RE: RE: RE: RE: RE: RE: RE: RE: RE...

Date: Oct. 15, 2016, 1:02 a.m.

Sisters,

For years I have watched the decline of our sisterhood, but I chose to stay silent. I feared speaking my mind and being banished from your midst, sentenced to roam the borderlands forever, a stranger among all peoples. But I can stay silent no longer. The blood in my veins bids me speak. I would rather fix my tent in the wilderness, and keep my soul, than dwell in a community that is no longer righteous, and lose it. I would rather live estranged from my sisters than estranged from my conscience.

When we banded together, generations ago, we did so to protect our kind from the intolerable abuses of the aggressors, who too often used their strength and capacity for cruelty to subordinate us. In those days, women of character and intelligence were treated as slaves: our talents were not developed; our voices were not heard. We toiled and bred and died, like animals. But in union with our sisters we grew strong. We women demanded the rights accorded to our brothers: among them, the right to speak and be heard; the right to own ourselves; the right to educate ourselves; the right to own the fruits of our labor; the right to choose our leaders; and the right to stand as leaders ourselves, if we so desired. Our sisterhood prospered.

We never achieved the Power of the Sword, but over time we achieved the Power of the Tribe. The Elders, our early leaders, used this power to do good for all men and women; they sometimes failed, but their hearts were pure. However, as the Power grew greater and greater, too many of the later generations were corrupted. They used the Power to dominate others, as their mothers and grandmothers were once dominated. They used the Power to humiliate others, as their mothers and grandmothers were once humiliated. And they used the Power to SILENCE others, as their mothers and grandmothers were once silenced. They feared any speech that could possibly diminish the Power of the Tribe that they wielded. The Power meant more to them than Truth or Freedom or Humanity, the very goods the first rebels of our sisterhood had struggled so mightily to acquire.

And now you want to use the strength of our sisterhood and the Power of the Tribe to silence Paulson, who you say does not speak to illuminate the Truth, but uses words with great wickedness against us. You say Paulson wants to return us to the days of our subjugation. You say Paulson is the enemy. And you say that if your sisters do not join with you to silence Paulson, then we too are the enemy.

I tell you this: I do not know this Paulson. I do not yet know if his words are for good or for evil. But I know that Paulson bids EVERYONE speak and be heard, and be judged accordingly by the tribes, while you, my sisters, would have many remain silent. In doing this, you diverge from the ways of the Elders, who first freed us from silence. You take on the cloak and the aspect of the oppressor.

You say words are like swords: some are so sharp they can never be unsheathed. Their very possession is a potential assault on the tribes. But the Elders said words are like lanterns: they show us the path through the dark woods, so we need not wander anymore, cold and cheerless, in the fog of our fears.

I tell you the truth, my sisters: I do not fear words. I fear the silence. Let Paulson speak.

--BOUDICCA R

Queen of the Iceni

Protector of the Orphans

Lover of Freedom

Defender of Truth

Chapter Six: Mochaccino Marxists

As planned, Mark arrived at Green Goddess just after 4:00 that Saturday afternoon. It was two weeks after he'd happened upon his housemates at The Ranch Hand. Green Goddess was a small on-campus coffee shop and pub, run as a cooperative by the Women and Gender Studies Society. It served fair trade coffee, a limited selection of craft beers, some questionable Canadian wines, some hard liquor, and unpalatable vegetarian and vegan food. Tessa generally avoided it, but a promise was a promise. She sat slouched over a stack of papers, drinking Americano after Americano. Pushed to the side were three dirty mugs and a plate with the remains of something resembling a discolored, Plasticine grilled cheese sandwich. Tessa had been at the pub marking since lunch.

"Hola amiga!" said Mark, plopping down across from her. Tessa noticed his voice was a touch louder than usual.

"Are you sure you want to go with a leather jacket?"

"Why not? Oh…"

Mark examined his surroundings more closely. He had never been inside Green Goddess before. He pretended not to do a double-take at the mural behind their table. It featured a scowling Asian woman with a shaved head. She was wearing an apron, and presenting a severed set of enormous breasts on a serving tray.

"You're not in the Computer Science building anymore, Dorothy," said Tessa. "Stay focussed."

Mark removed his jacket, feigning a chuckle. Underneath he was wearing a tight pink t-shirt emblazoned with the slogan, "PUSSY POWER."

Tessa grimaced.

"Too much?"

She shook her head.

"How much longer until they show?"

"No clue."

"But the PFP always come here after meetings, right? That's what you said."

"That's what I heard. But even if they do, there's no guarantee she'll show up with them. Maybe she'll go straight home…For all I know she's not even a member anymore."

Mark noticed her plate.

"What *is* that thing?"

"A vegan Croque Madame."

"A what?"

"A crime against God and man," Tessa explained.

Tessa waved over the waitress. She was uncomfortable with small talk in general, even with her housemate. It was like reciting lines in a banal play she was being forced to act out.

The waitress, "Astra," was straight out of Central Casting: spiky purple hair, nose-ring, pro-choice t-shirt. Tessa didn't object to her politics, just the uniform. *So predictable.* She was unsurprised to glimpse a mandala tattoo on the back of Astra's neck: as conventional and proper to her breed as orthotic shoes were to Grammy Ada's.

Mark ordered a craft beer and flirted with the lesbian waitress. Flirtation was his default mode for all interactions with women, even Tessa. Astra looked at him with disdain. Mark settled in with his beer.

"And now we wait," said Tessa, regretting her promise to Mark already.

***

One floor above Green Goddess, the Postmodernists for Peace meeting was in full-swing. They met in what used to be a custodial supply room; it still smelled faintly of Lysol and industrial-strength cleaning products. It was spacious for a supply room, but cramped for a meeting space. The PFP membership had attempted to spruce it up with Ikea couches and rugs, but that only altered its aesthetic from "dank hole" to "Swedish contemporary dank hole," which was not an improvement.

The membership took turns selecting a picture of a revered progressive cultural icon to tape to the door each week. It had varied widely this term: from Derrida, to Gloria Steinem, to Che Guevera. Sadly, in recent weeks the sanctity of the office door had been violated. That Monday some miscreant had drawn a top-hat and tails on Linda Sarsour, and the week before someone had pasted the face of Milton Friedman on to Marx's body. (They only knew it was Milton Friedman because the vandal had left a sticky-note with the words, "THIS IS MILTON FRIEDMAN." Upon googling, the membership was horrified.) The PFP Executive suspected the Students for Free Inquiry down the hall, but weren't counting out the Econ Society either.

Jessica Mincing slipped in through the back door, red-faced and clutching a paper coffee cup. She was an hour late already and had debated going, but felt it would be better to make an appearance and apologize profusely for tardiness, than not show up. It was, after all, a serious meeting.

"Hi Jess!" chirped Millicent Miles, at sweet 18, the youngest and perkiest PFP member. Millie hadn't picked a major yet, but was seriously considering Women and Gender Studies. As she told her boyfriend, her first two intro courses on the subject had been "life-changing."

"Oh, Jess, you made it. We were worried," said Christa Winstead, President, who hadn't been at all worried.

Christa was an adjunct instructor in the Education faculty, and as such, well below Jessica, an assistant professor, in the academic pecking order. Christa, however, was the daughter of one of the best-known and best-connected trial lawyers in Canada, and Jessica was the daughter of a small town school custodian.

"I am *so* sorry, everyone! I was working on an article and just lost all track of time," sputtered Jessica.

"Time for coffee, I see," Christa said, "*capitalist* coffee." The heavy-handed joke landed with a thud.

Jessica giggled. She felt every eye in the room drawn to the Starbucks logo on her half-fat soy mochaccino. Her cheeks burned redder. She had forgotten her coffee thermos (with its conspicuous green recycling symbol). Knowing that, on principle, the nearby Green Goddess did not provide take-away cups, she'd been forced to caffeinate on the way at the Starbucks outside the library. Late as she was, entering any campus meeting without coffee was unthinkable. It fortified her in all social situations.

Christa carried on, "Anyway, to return to the topic at hand…"

Millie handed Jessica a Meeting Agenda, and pointed to Item Five.

AGENDA

Postmodernists for Peace Meeting

October 29, 2016

1. Call to Order and Roll Call
2. Financial Report from Treasurer
3. Presentation on Costa Rican Youth Ecotourism Initiative—Sara Lallygig

4. Vote on Changes to Mission Statement

5. Struggle for $60: Stay Engaged?

6. Vote on Representative for the Office of Equity and Diversity

7. White Male Imperialist War Day Protests (a.k.a. "Remembrance Day"): Strategizing Session

8. Paulson Talk: Strategizing Session (Diversity Wall??)

9. Other Matters: Open Discussion

10. Conclusion: Petition to Gaia

Jessica tried to focus on the proceedings.

"...So, while I hear and honor Polly's objections, that's why I would *strongly* recommend that we stay affiliated with the Struggle for $60," said Christa, nodding in her fellow PFP member's direction.

Polly Glamorous crossed her arms and glowered. *Don't cross me, Cisbitch.*

Christa was ill at ease but determined to press her case. Polly Glamorous was a pre-op transgender woman with a limp and rumored remote indigenous ancestry. She was a powerful enemy.

Christa continued, summarizing her arguments: "Poverty-level subsistence for North America's most exploited workers is not acceptable! All human beings not only have a right to basic services like clean housing and running water, they also have a right to quality medical care and post-secondary education. Additionally, all humans have a right to fully engage in culture, which means internet access, smart phone ownership, art gallery passes, and more. And it goes without saying that all people have the right to nutritional, sustainable, fair-trade organic foods—at the very least, Whole Foods level or above. For these reasons and more, a basic $60 an hour minimum wage is necessary for workers today. It behooves us to continue to financially contribute to this worthwhile global movement."

Polly Glamorous rolled her electric-blue-lidded eyes. She muttered something under her breath that sounded like, "the real minimum wage is zero."

Christa pointedly ignored her.

"Do we need to put this to a vote, or can I assume everyone's in agreement?" Christa asked.

Polly stewed silently, and the other PFP members refused to make eye contact with their president, so Christa carried on: "I'll take that as a Yes. We will continue to support the Struggle for $60. Next agenda item: voting on a representative for the Office of Equity and Diversity. Allie?"

Allie Wonkus, Vice President of the PFP, nodded, looking up from her IPad. She explained that they had been approached by SVU's newly-created Office of Equity and Diversity about joining their Stakeholder Committee.

"They're looking for input from progressive campus organizations on their initiatives and on disciplinary interventions. They've also asked the LGBTQ2+ Association, the Rainbow Alliance, the Indigenous Students' Association, and End White Supremacy Now."

"What kind of 'disciplinary interventions?'" asked Maia Worthing, long-standing PFP member.

"They said they investigate student and prof complaints on instances of discrimination and hate speech on campus."

"All types of discrimination? Like that hockey coach last term who wouldn't let the transgender woman play on the women's team?" asked Millie. "What was her name?"

"The coach was something Miller, and the woman was…" Allie trailed off.

"Meredith Clarkson," said Emily Payne, who was another PFP member.

"Right. Yeah, I think the Equity Office was involved somehow before Miller was fired," said Allie. "It was a pretty blatant example of bigotry. The coach claimed Meredith had an unfair physical advantage or something like that, just because she was 6'4 and 220 pounds. Women come in all shapes and sizes!"

"Biological determinism at its finest," said Karla Kobayashi, a PFP stalwart. The room murmured its approval.

"What happened to the player Meredith concussed in practice?" whispered a member sitting near the door. "Is she off the ventilator?"

Christa cleared her throat and asked that they let Allie continue. Allie asked if there were any volunteers for the representative position, adding quickly that "members of color" would be most appropriate, "of course," for the role. The flesh colors of the 19 members in the room, for the most part, ranged in color from ivory to egg-shell.

"Sorry, I'm already on three committees," said Karla.

Silence.

"What about you, Annabeth?" asked Christa. "I know I speak for everyone when I say that we would be delighted to have you represent us."

Annabeth Santos, a new member, looked confused. Born and raised in Sydney, Nova Scotia, she was one-quarter Filipina and three-quarters Scottish-Canadian. She'd never met her grandfather, Yanno Santos, and spoke with a Caper accent thick enough to cut with a knife.

"Uhh, I guess I can do it."

Allie looked relieved, and pencilled her in. Christa moved on to the next item before Annabeth could change her mind.

"As you all know, the stat holiday known as 'Remembrance Day' is coming up. Nothing's happening on campus, but Sere Valley is holding an event at Town Hall, with a procession to the Cenotaph to lay wreathes, like they always do. Are we all still on-board with the 'silence protest' idea I put forward last meeting?" asked Christa.

"Wait a sec—we're protesting *Remembrance Day*?" asked Jessica. She still had vivid memories of her grandfather, former Private John Mincing. His left arm had been a stub, ending at the elbow joint.

"As we discussed last meeting—I don't believe you were present—a better name for it would be 'White Male Imperialist War Day,' though of course it's still popularly known as Remembrance Day in this country," said Christa.

"I'm not, umm, questioning the name, Christa. I'm just wondering about the, uhh…optics of such a thing," Jessica explained.

"What do you mean?"

"I mean, there are hardly any World War Two veterans *left*. Is it really going to look good for the PFP to be protesting three 95-year olds being pushed to the Cenotaph in their wheelchairs?"

"I think my great-grandfather was in that war and he can still walk. Kinda," said Millie from the back of the room.

This generated no responses.

"We'll look like assholes," said Polly. "I agree with Jessica. It's a terrible idea."

Christa took a deep breath, as her counsellor had advised. Polly had been a thorn in her side for years now—since that big sustainable farming fight at the Vernal Equinox party. She wished she had followed her instincts then and purged the bitch while she was still Paul Mercer. It was too late now.

"There's no statute of limitations on *war crimes*, I don't believe," said Christa, through gritted teeth.

"But we don't need more bad PR," said Allie. "Especially with the big Paulson protest coming up. It's probably a good idea to just focus on that."

Christa shrugged.

"Let's put it to a vote," said Allie. "Quick show of hands: who thinks we should protest Remembrance Day?"

Christa raised her hand.

"And who thinks we shouldn't protest?"

Seventeen hands went up, including Polly's. Annabeth, who wasn't paying attention, abstained. She was still trying to figure out how to shuffle her schedule to fit her new position as representative.

"Ok, fine," said Christa. "*Whatever.* Let's move on to Item 8. As you know, the Paulson talk is a month from now. That gives us plenty of time to come up with a solid protest strategy."

"One would think…" said Polly, half-under her breath. Christa ignored her.

"Last meeting, Millicent came up with an excellent idea: the 'diversity wall.' Would you like to expand on that, Millie?" asked Christa, nodding in a gesture of *noblesse oblige* to the group's most junior member.

Millicent beamed.

"So, we all know Paulson is against diversity, right? Well, I thought, what better way to protest him than to make a human diversity wall blocking the entry, showing the beauty of unity through diversity!"

Allie frowned.

"But how will we show that our human barrier is a 'diversity' barrier, if you know what I mean?"

"Umm, we can have a big sign saying so. Also, the protesting group can be umm…diverse," explained Millie.

Everyone in the room made an effort not to stare at Karla or Annabeth, including Karla and Annabeth.

"My mom is Syrian," offered Maia.

"Christian or Muslim?" asked another member.

"Christian," said Maia apologetically. The room groaned.

After another moment of silence, Polly cut in, "Let's face it, ladies, we don't have enough members of color for a proper diversity wall."

"What if we just tried to *represent* people of color?" asked Millie. "I'm great with makeup! We just need to buy dark foundation, and we can wear wigs, and…"

"Are you insane?" interjected Polly.

"We're not doing blackface, Millie," said Christa.

Millie looked hurt. "What's blackface?" she whispered to Emily, sitting beside her.

Christa moved on, suggesting they could still form a human wall, and not worry about making a point about its ethnic composition. She pointed out that the Suzeman building would be ideal for this purpose, because its main entry led down a long, narrow hallway that attendees had to pass through to enter the auditorium. The PFP could "set up shop" there, said Allie.

"You mean we're going to block people from attending the talk?" asked Jessica.

"Precisely," said Christa. "The university is providing a platform for hate speech. Paulson's talk could incite violence against the trans-community and other minority groups. Blocking people from attending this is like stopping the Nuremberg Rally."

Jessica looked dubious.

"Christa, Paulson is vile, but I don't know if you can exactly compare him to Hitler."

"True, he's much more subtle," said Allie. "He hides his hate speech behind professions of scholarly objectivity and...*science*." She pronounced this last word like it was *gonorrhea*.

"Dr. Cross says we need to problematize the place of science in the modern university," said Millie, with solemnity, citing her much-adored Women and Gender Studies professor. "'Cause there's a long history of male scientists using 'science' to try and show that women and minorities are inferior."

Other members nodded in agreement.

"That's a big reason why I changed my major from Biology to English. Best decision I ever made," said Karla, whose dentist father had been apoplectic with rage by his only child's decision. Mr. and Mrs. Kobayashi told Karla they were going to cut off her tuition money if she didn't change back, but so far they hadn't made good on the threat.

Basking in the warmth of the group's approval, Millie repeated another of Dr. Cross's greatest hits: "Dr. Cross also said we need to problematize 'facts.'"

"Why?" asked another member, genuinely confused.

"Facts are sexist," said Millie. "Dr. Cross says you can never trust a fact."

Annabeth shifted in her seat. Jessica played with her hair. But neither of them said anything, while the rest of the room murmured assent, agreeing that facts were, in fact, all too often patriarchal, imperialistic, transphobic, and at times, even genocidal.

Christa again tried to right the ship. The meeting was running late. She asked who among them, by show of hands, could commit to protesting the Paulson talk. Most of the room agreed, even Polly, whose long sigh and slowly raised hand showed she was acting under duress. Maia and Millie were tasked with making protest signs, and the group agreed to sort out other details via email over the next few weeks.

"Do we have any other matters to discuss today?" asked Christa.

Karla raised her hand.

"Just a quick question Jessica might know. I'm curious. Did the Womyn's Scholars ever catch that Boudicca troll on their listserv?"

The membership perked up its collective ears. The tale of the anonymous "Boudicca" had made the rounds of all of SVU's progressive organizations. Rumours abounded. Some blamed the Russians, others the pro-Paulsonites. Allie speculated that the PFP's door poster vandal and Boudicca were one and the same.

Jessica shook her head.

"'fraid not. And 'Boudicca'—or whoever it is—sent out another one last night. Computing Services has been useless."

"Is it a hacker?" asked Maia. "Or maybe an inside job?"

"If they have any idea, they're not saying." Jessica shrugged.

"Let's continue with this at Green Goddess," said Christa, who was tired of fighting outside reactionaries, and even more tired of fighting fifth column elements like Polly.

"Let's conclude with the Petition to Gaia," she said.

The PFP membership, with the exception of Polly, who was playing on her phone, fixed their faces into appropriate expressions of solemnity. They stood up. Millie placed a hand over her heart.

"Ok, all together now." Christa began.

"Our Mother, who art in Safe Spaces,

Hallowed be by Thy name.

Thy Queendom come, Thy social justice be done,

On earth as it is in Berkeley.

Give us this day our daily Huffington,

And forgive us our micro-aggressions,

As we forgive those who micro-aggress against us.

Lead us not into unconscious bias,

But deliver us from the patriarchy.

For Thine is the intersectionality, the equity, and the diversity,

Forever and Ever,

Ah-Women."

The membership paused a few respectful seconds before dispersing.

"Oh shit!" exclaimed Polly, the first one out.

During the meeting, the door vandal had struck again. This week was Polly's choice of cultural icon: Josephine Baker. Baker's image was covered with a sticky note.

Polly snatched it off.

"What does it say?" asked Maia.

The note read as follows: "OK. GENUINE BADASS."

The shadow of a smile flickered across Polly's face.

Christa looked grim. "Assholes."

Jessica took her leave, while most of the other PFP members made their way downstairs to Green Goddess. Maia, Millie, and two other junior PFP members settled in near the bar. Mark and Tessa were waiting, the former downing his fourth beer, and the latter nursing another Americano.

"Don't look," said Tessa, under her breath. "They're here."

Mark jumped up, knocking over his over-priced IPA. Tessa sighed and waved over Astra.

"Sorry!" said Mark, eyes fixed on the bar as Astra wordlessly dumped a roll of paper towel on the table.

"Ready?" asked Tessa.

Mark nodded vigorously.

"Jesus, man, you spilled half of it on yourself." Tessa dabbed her roommate's t-shirt. "I can barely make out the pussy."

"You can't?" Mark squeaked.

"Your pussy is practically invisible."

Tessa squinted. Dampened, the purple font letters were indistinct from the dark pink background of the t-shirt.

"Fix it!"

"I'm *trying*."

Tessa continued dabbing at "PUSSY POWER" with a soggy piece of paper towel.

"Kinda looks like 'pissy power' now," she said, cocking her head and eying Mark's torso.

"What?"

"Put your jacket back on."

Mark followed Tessa's command, zipping up the leather jacket over the beer-soaked tee.

"Ok, remember the plan. Follow my lead. Ready?"

Tessa slapped him on the back. Hard.

Mark gulped and nodded. Tessa's eyes narrowed. She steered him toward the bar.

"Maia!" she exclaimed, tapping her erstwhile Writing Center student on the back. "How're you doing?"

Maia turned and smiled. Tessa had been an enormous help with her Master's thesis: clarifying her ideas, bringing out her main arguments, and editing away sloppy grammatical errors. A few times, Tessa even stayed past the Writing Center's closing time, to help her finish rewrites on deadline.

"I'm good! We just got out of the PFP meeting. How's your day going?"

"Oh, that was today? I've been here all afternoon. Marking endless papers. Reconsidering my life choices. You know, the usual."

Maia chuckled.

"This is my roommate, Mark Pearson."

Mark flashed a toothy smile in the direction of Maia, accidentally netting her two companions as well. Unaccustomed to the attentions of a heterosexual male, even a damp and disheveled one, they blushed deepest scarlet. Maia smiled back.

"What would you like, ladies? I've got this round," Mark said.

Chapter Seven: The Fruit of Her Hands

A week later, Deborahann, like her daughter, was fulfilling an obligation, only hers was of a social, not a personal nature. Across the country in New Brunswick, Deborahann was up at 5:00 a.m. on a Saturday baking pies for the Beaconsbridge Baptist Church Bake Sale. For the occasion, she had agreed to contribute two blueberry pies (from her copious stores of frozen berries). Because Vic resented any outside baking, she was compelled to bake a third pie for his personal consumption as well. He helped himself to a piece with breakfast, grumbling when Deborahann informed him that his pie was the ugly one with the cratered crust.

"Second-fiddle, as always!"

"The good ones are for the sale!"

"Vanity."

Vic shook his head and stalked off to the living room with his plate. Deborahann felt guilty for being unable to produce three pristine pies, only two.

Squeamish as always about "turning a house of prayer into a house of commerce," ("Like the Catholics!" clucked one devout Baptist matron), the church's Finance Committee decreed that the bake sale would be held at the Women's Institute Hall, not the church. Besides baking, Deborahann promised to mind the cash-box from noon to the end of the sale at 4:00. Between the baking and the table-minding, the bake sale would take up her entire, precious Saturday.

Officially, the bake sale money was going toward parsonage two maintenance, though everyone in the village now knew some version of the truth. It was leaked by a half-dozen sources within hours of Pastor Fudge's revelations at the Finance Committee meeting, now a month ago. In the telling, the original, accurate "water-damage-from-a-grow-op" story—already a juicy morsel of gossip—mutated into a fantastical tale of meth lab explosions and mob drug debts. Some parishioners speculated that Pastor Jonathan had been involved with the Roaring Lobsters, a notorious Shediac-area biker gang.

"'Magine!" exclaimed 68 year-old Brenda Collings on the phone with 70 year-old Janet Blakeney, her second cousin. Brenda lived two houses down from Deborahann.

"I'd believe anything of that young feller. Came here lookin' like butter wouldn't melt in his mouth. I told Donnie I trusted him 'bout as far as I could throw him, and I was right."

Janet nodded, pointlessly, over the landline.

"Bill and I never liked him from the get-go. We voted for that quiet feller from Tatamagouche. With the Indian-looking wife. His mother was a Weyburn Crossman."

"Them Crossmans are crooked, but at least you *know* them," said Brenda.

The village was awash with conversations like these.

Meth lab or grow-op, the fact remained that substantial damage had been done to parsonage two. Jim MacBride, Yule, Vic, and a few other Beaconsbridge Baptist congregants contributed their labour *gratis*, but the water and mold damage was beyond what they could fix. Professionals were called in from Moncton. When all was said and done, repair costs came to over $20,000—a fortune for a small town Maritimes church, where the average parishioner was an elderly pensioner on a fixed income. As that merry sinner Jack Case would've put it, had he been alive, *Even Baptists can't tithe blood from a stone.*

The women of the congregation stepped up, as they usually did, to save the day. The burden of fundraising to make up the financial gap fell to them, after the men did their part. It was the usual gendered division of labor at the church, and in Madawaaksis County as a whole, even in 2016. There were always exceptions: Norm and Lydia Dixon's disabled adult son Tommy had a knack for cross-stitch and knitting. Jim and Audrey MacBride's 40-something daughter, Pam, was as skilled a carpenter as her father. Pam was an openly closeted lesbian, which was unfortunate for Tessa, in her on-going attempts at educating her mother on feminism and gender stereotypes. (Tessa, sighing: "Just because a woman is good at carpentry, it doesn't mean she's a lesbian, Mum." Deborahann: "Abby saw her at the Costco holding hands with a real butchy-type wearing overalls. *Overalls*, Tessie.") Pam, Tommy, and company notwithstanding, the men and women of Beaconsbridge kept to their assigned spheres. Who dominated whom in relationships depended on temperament, not sex. (It was generally accepted, for example, that Elinor Crossman "ran" her husband Robert.)

Not surprisingly, the bake sale fell within the purview of the Beaconsbridge Baptist females. When Deborahann arrived, Margaret Fudge, Abby Blakeney, and Audrey MacBride were holding down the fort. Audrey was taking Margaret's place on the coffee and tea station, and Abby was waiting for Deborahann's arrival so she could head out. The main room of the Women's Institute was dominated by two large tables of baked goods. A few smaller tables were set up nearby to facilitate coffee and conversation. The room was full of locals circulating, chatting, and perusing the wares. No one in town needed more baked goods: every good matron in Beaconsbridge already had a freezer full of cookies and "squares" in case of emergency guest arrivals. The event was well-attended for two reasons: 1.) community spirit; and 2.) gossip potential, and in Madawaaksis County, the two often overlapped.

Abby Blakeney, an overblown peony of a woman, greeted her cousin-by-marriage with a smile. "Sub!" she laughed, raising a hand, as they used to in high school basketball.

Deborahann set her bags down on the table and high-fived her friend: "Sub!" They giggled.

"So, are we rich yet?" Deborahann asked, looking at the cash-box.

"$600 and counting, last time I checked," Abby replied.

"Has it been this busy all day?"

"Since about 11:00. First two hours were dead."

Deborahann nodded and looked across the room at Margaret and Audrey. She lowered her voice.

"How's Margaret?"

Abby moved closer and matched her tone.

"Pretty good today. Only got frazzled once when she got a rush. I gave her a hand."

Deborahann lowered her voice even more.

"What d'you think is going on over there at parsonage one?"

Abby shook her head.

"Hard to say. Yule was over a week ago to drop off clothes for the Drive. He said he heard yelling before he rang the doorbell, and Margaret crying."

"You don't suppose he…?"

"I *do*."

"I've wondered to Vic—but he thinks the sun shines out the pastor's you-know-what," said Deborahann, still whispering.

"Many will say, 'Lord, Lord,' on the final day, and He will say, 'Depart from me, for I never knew you,'" said Abby. (Even Ada, who didn't like her, had to admit that her nephew's wife knew her Scripture.)

"Mum just thinks Margaret's 'peculiar,' of course." Deborahann rolled her eyes.

"Well, she is. But is it any wonder? There've been stories for years. Yule thinks the pastor takes it out on her. He's had a lot of problems from Day One here—not just this parsonage grow-op foolishness…"

"I guess we don't know anything for certain."

"No."

At that moment, Margaret walked by, eyes focussed like lasers on the exit. Her clothes hung loosely off her frame.

Abby called after her, "Callin' it a day, Margaret?"

Margaret nodded, thin lips pursed in the ghost of a smile. Abby and Deborahann waved.

"Margaret's lost a pile of weight," Deborahann observed.

"She told me she's lost 25 pounds this fall," said Abby. "And no dieting."

"How is that possible?"

"Overwrought. The woman's overwrought. She's a bundle of nerves."

"You never know what's going on behind closed doors," said Deborahann, looking down at the table. She fiddled with the cake display, moving a boiled icing chocolate cake from out behind a bouffant coconut layer cake.

"Ain't that the truth," said Abby. She admired Deborahann's pies. In the village Deborahann had a reputation for being "crafty"—in a good way—a perfectionist with a number of wifely talents, including flower-arranging, baking, gardening, and painting.

"I can always tell in a blink which ones are yours, Deb. Those perfect scalloped edges and the blueberry-bunch stencil in the middle. So pretty. You're good at everything you try."

Deborahann blushed.

"You ought to see poor Vic's. The crust all fell-in. These were the only good ones."

Abby suppressed a sarcastic comment about "poor Vic" and filed this exchange away to share with Yule later. They had their own opinion of Victor Stevens.

"Guess I should head out now. Jayson and Matt are home for the weekend."

"Oh, that's nice! How's Jay doing at Law School?"

"Better now than in September. Said he felt like a flounder in a shark tank. He was thinking about dropping out."

"Oh?"

"Yeah, Yule had a talk with him. He said, 'Look at my hands, Jay'—you can imagine. He said, 'Work outside for 40 years in the cold, and your hands'll look like this too. It's your call, bud.'"

"What'd Jayson say?"

"Said he was going back to the shark tank."

"Ha!"

Abby grabbed her purse and the package of rolls she'd picked up for supper, and turned to go, almost colliding with the lumpen form of Pastor Fudge at the door. His fishy eyes read the guilt on her face, and on Deborahann's from across the room.

Gossipy old bags, he thought. But he never broke character in public.

"Good afternoon, Abby. Say hello to that man of yours."

"Will do, just heading out!"

After a polite exchange with a couple departing parishioners, the pastor made his way to Deborahann's table. He greeted her and inquired after Victor and the girls before asking if she'd seen Margaret.

"Margaret? She just left."

"When?"

"About five minutes before you got here. Why?"

Pastor Fudge looked around the room just to be sure. It was almost empty. Audrey was in the kitchen at the back, taking advantage of the break in traffic after lunch to brew fresh coffee.

"I'm sure I can count on your discretion, right, Deborahann? Naturally, I don't mind you speaking with Vic. I've alluded to this…problem on a number of occasions with him."

"Sure."

"Margaret's always been high-strung. Everyone knows that. But I'm afraid her mental condition has deteriorated of late."

"Oh?"

"The troubles with Pastor Jonathan took a lot out of her—and some other personal issues. It's been piling up, unfortunately."

"I'm sorry to hear that."

"She's on quite a lot of medication for her nerves. We've been trying something new since…the incident, and we're still working out the correct dosage. She's been quite confused since she started on it—do keep that in mind when you talk to her."

"Oh I will."

Deborahann wondered what "the incident" was.

The pastor changed the subject.

"To be frank, I'm just here looking for her. She told me she'd be home from the bake sale two hours ago."

"Maybe she confused her hours? I'm pretty sure she was supposed to be on the coffee station 'til noon, then Audrey."

"Mmhmm."

Pastor Fudge looked dubious.

"Well, I should head home and see if she's back yet. It's been necessary, of late, to keep a close eye on her. The lack of cell coverage in this county certainly doesn't help matters."

Before Deborahann could reply, Audrey waddled over, proffering steaming mugs of coffee. It was 10 more minutes before Pastor Fudge could leave. A fresh wave of customers arrived and Audrey returned to her post. The pastor leaned over, patting his parishioner's shoulder for all to see, and lowered his voice.

"Thanks again for keeping this to yourself, Deborahann."

"No problem."

Pastor Fudge nodded and turned to leave.

It'll be all over Beaconsbridge by Sunday.

He smiled. He could count on Deborahann.

***

At the townhouse in Sere Valley that night, Tessa was losing her patience.

"Turn it down!" she yelled from the basement. She could hear every syllable dripping like melted butter from the mouth of Cookie, of Cookie's Yoga Challenge! ™ fame, on the television upstairs.

"Are your legs locked right now, friends? That's a no-no. What you want is a fluid...*silky* bending motion. See? Like this. Take the time to really *enjoy* the practice. There's no one-size-fits all here. You have options. Do what feels right. Right for you."

"Adrian, turn it down!"

"What?"

Cookie continued: "Find that…*fe*-line bend in the knees. A welcoming bend…a *generous* bend…"

Tessa emerged from her basement lair. "Stop generously bending and turn that shit down."

Adrian paused the DVR and observed his friend. Tessa was wearing a ratty terry-cloth housecoat and clutching an old-fashioned glass close to her breast like a long-lost child. Her hair was in a stringy pony-tail. Her eyes were puffy.

"I see you're drinking alone in your room at 8:00 on a Saturday night, Tessa."

"I see you're doing yoga with Cookie at 8:00 o'clock on a Saturday night, Adrian."

"Gotta' maintain my girlish figure."

"Gotta' get more whisky."

Tessa walked to the kitchen, swaying slightly, with conspicuous dignity. Adrian followed her. He watched as Tessa prepared her drink, adding egg whites, lemon juice, sugar, whisky, and ice cubes to the cocktail shaker. She shook it for precisely 20 seconds and poured. The froth pleased her. She added a single, long-stemmed maraschino cherry. It landed with a satisfying "plop" into the drink.

Adrian lifted the nearby bottle: "Gibson's?"

"Ish under-rated," said Tessa.

"I see."

Tessa held her tumbler to the light and moved it to her lips. Adrian coughed. She paused.

"Shall I?"

Adrian smiled. "Please."

Tessa set her drink down and repeated the process with a second old-fashioned glass. She handed it to her friend and raised her own in the air.

"Sociable!"

They clinked their glasses and drank in silence. Adrian waited a civilized minute before speaking.

"Tessa, my love, would you care to explain why you're falling-down drunk at home alone this evening?"

"I would not."

"What did Andrew do?"

"Why d'you suppose ish always Andrew? I have other thoughts in my head besides that arrogant man-child, you know."

"Ahh, now he's an arrogant man-child! I'm enjoying the return of the famed Tessa Stevens' backbone. Just a few days ago you were telling me how misunderstood he was."

Tessa's green eyes flashed.

"You know, if I *was* having problems with Andrew, the last person I would go to for relationship advice is an asexual libertarian."

Adrian blinked a few times and considered his drink.

"There's no need to go so hard, Tess."

She immediately felt guilty and then angry for feeling guilty. *Stupid interfering Adrian.*

"The best defense is a good offence."

"But is there a price to pay for always being on-guard?"

Adrian paused to let that one percolate.

Mark bounded into the kitchen like a gazelle, oblivious to the mounting tension. Instead of his usual going-out uniform of leather jacket and jeans, tonight he was wearing an olive-green Mao jacket paired with low-crotched, tapered grey joggers.

"Are you Communist Bieber now?" asked Adrian. Tessa giggled.

"Dude. Hurtful."

Mark turned to Tessa: "How d'I look? Will Maia dig it?"

Tessa examined her housemate.

"You look like Deng Xiaoping and Justin Timberlake had a baby."

Mark finally noticed the fumes wafting from Tessa's person, and the three-quarters empty bottle of Gibson's on the counter.

"Dude, you're drunk."

"Ding ding ding! Adrian, tell him what he's won!"

"You have won one socially awkward evening at Green Goddess with an attractive female social justice warrior! There you will enjoy endless watery craft beers, quinoa salads, and earnest discussions of white male privilege!"

Mark shrugged. He grabbed his book-bag from the kitchen table.

"Look, we want to be supportive, Mark, but we wonder how mush the two of you haf in common," said Tessa, trying her best not to slur. She rocked back on her heels with her drink, leaning against the cupboard.

"We have loads in common. I'm progressive as shit. I voted Green once. I have a Haida raven tattoo."

"Well, we stand corrected then," said Adrian. He gently assisted Tessa into a chair at the table.

"Whatever dude."

Mark wasn't going to let Adrian and Tessa harsh his vibe.

Tessa raised a glass in Mark's direction.

"Happy huntin', buddy," she said.

"Viva la Revolution!" Adrian shouted to Mark's departing back, clinking his tumbler against Tessa's.

Fucking drunk Maritimers, thought Mark, as he headed out the door.

"That whush mean," said Tessa.

"We're trying to protect the dumbass," said Adrian. "Now will you tell me what Andrew did already? I have to get back to my hot date with Cookie."

Tessa's face fell. She paused.

"The bastard blew me off."

"The Law Ball?"

"The Law Ball. I was supposed to be going with him tonight. Bought the dress months ago. Was going to meet all of his friends. This morning he texts and says it's a no-go."

"What?"

"He texted that his parents pressured him to take one of his classmates instead. The daughter of a family friend. He referred to her as 'the debutante.'"

"Why the hell is he just telling you this now?"

"I dunno. I was so mad I stopped texting back."

"And why the fuck wouldn't he at least call you to cancel? Seriously, he bails on you via *text*? Who pulls that kinda shit?"

"I know."

"Well, I hope this is the end of this Andrew bullshit."

"It is."

"I've heard that before."

"I mean it this time."

"You're better than this."

Tessa put her head in her hands. The room was spinning. She forced herself to stand up.

"One more for the road."

Adrian placed his bear-like paws on his friend's shoulders.

"We're switching to Earl Grey. I suppose you didn't even eat supper."

"Whisky or tea," she joked. "The classic Atlantic Canadian responses to human suffering."

"Don't forget Jesus Christ and child abuse."

Adrian paused and frowned. "Religion is still the best value transmission system ever devised…But I digress. Another day."

Tessa let Adrian brew her some weak tea. She even consented to eat half of a stale blueberry muffin. It came up a few hours later in a recognizable form. Tessa was ill most of the night, and the next day she was useless. But it wasn't as bad as it could've been.

***

While Tessa was bringing up stomach bile in Alberta, in New Brunswick, Deborahann was lying in bed beside the snoring lump of flesh that was her husband. She was a troubled sleeper at the best of times, and tonight she had lain awake for hours pondering the Margaret episode.

He wants everyone to think she's batty. Well, she is *batty, but why?*

When Deborahann finally drifted off into an uneasy slumber, she had her recurring dream. It had haunted her since childhood. She dreamt it at least once a month, sometimes as often as once a week or more during times of particular strain.

In the dream she was her 10-year old self: a pudgy, solemn little girl in pigtails. She was in the basement of Uncle Lew and Aunt Moira's old farmhouse, in the hilly countryside outside Beaconsbridge. As a child, she had many happy memories of playing there with her cousins Yule and Jimmy, while the adults visited upstairs. The basement was officially off-limits to the children: it was where Uncle Lew kept his rifles, hunting knives, animal traps, and other objects regarded with fascination by his eldest son Yule. The cousins found reasons to sneak down there, pinching apples, and on one occasion, a large jar of crab apple jelly, spirited out of the cold-room and eaten surreptitiously in the tool-shed. The property had been sold and torn down decades ago. It was replaced by a charmless, practical modular house.

In the dream, however, the farmhouse was still standing, and the basement was as it had been when Deborahann was a little girl—except it was flooded, the dirt floor covered in murky water. The foundation wasn't visible, only the odd wooden beam. The staircase leading upstairs was gone. Deborahann the child stood in the corner of the basement, balanced on a beam, as the water level rose. She would carefully make her way across the slippery beams, looking for an escape route, but in every dream, no matter what she tried, there was no way out. She was always bitterly cold and trembling. Her desperation level rose with the water; with every second, she felt more panicked. She cried for help and no one ever answered. Her heart, throbbing with fear, felt close to bursting.

As usual, at this point in the dream, as the water reached her chin, Deborahann woke up, coated in sweat, screaming. Vic woke up beside her.

"Damn it, Deborahann! Not again!"

Vic gave her an angry shove. Deborahann had migrated to his side of the bed.

"Not everyone sits on their arse all day and arranges flowers," he said. "Some of us work for a living. Do I need to send you to the guest room?"

Trixie the German Shepherd-cross slept on the saggy guest room bed. Deborahann often shared it with her.

"Sorry Vic."

On her side of the Queen-sized mattress, Deborahann tried her best to calm down. She breathed as quietly as possible. Vic hated it when she "huffed and puffed," as he put it, after her nightmares.

Chapter Eight: Little Bits of Knowledge

It was a Thursday morning. For the past two weeks, Tessa had thrown herself into work to avoid the temptation of contacting Andrew. That morning she sipped her coffee and grimly forecast the long day ahead of her. Thursdays were the worst day of her week: she taught two sections of Intro Comp back-to-back, followed by a quick lunch, and then a four-hour shift in the afternoon at the Writing Center.

Tessa usually escaped campus at 5:00 on the dot on Thursdays, but that day she had to stay for an evening equity and diversity training session. Pearl had informed her that for tenured faculty the training was "recommended only." Tessa noticed very few of them had bothered to sign up for the after-hours session, despite their avowed interest in the topic. ("The Office of Equity and Diversity does such important work," Wagband told Pearl. "Unfortunately, I have some important deadlines coming up.") For graduate student instructors, new, or contract faculty like Tessa and Adrian, however, attendance was mandatory. The two had picked the same time-slot to attend. Adrian was teaching a tutorial in Business Ethics ("HA," said Tessa), and was attending the training session—kicking and screaming—in his capacity as an instructor.

"An ED session. How appropriate," said Adrian at breakfast.

Mark snorted into his muesli.

"Grow up, boys," said Tessa.

"*Flaccid* is precisely the word I would use to describe mandatory university training designed to combat quote-unquote 'institutional racism,'" said Adrian.

Mark giggled again, reflexively, and looked up 'flassid' on Webster.com on his phone.

"It just makes things worse, you know," said Adrian. "Studies show that a.) people resent going; and b.) it just draws attention to perceived differences between racial groups. For group solidarity, you should emphasize similarities instead."

"Uh huh."

"It's true."

"Pam told me her training session was interesting and informative," said Tessa, who took everything her (anorexic, kindly, neurotic) office-mate said with a grain of salt.

"Balls."

"See? No balls at the breakfast table. You micro-aggressed me right there. You clearly need this training."

Adrian grinned.

"Seriously though, it's just a way for colleges and companies to virtue-signal, and that's about it. Oh, and it's a way to employ earnest young humanities grads who would otherwise be waiting tables for a living."

"It's honest work."

"Indeed—waiting tables, that is, not propaganda consulting."

Tessa refused to take the bait, and changed the subject.

"If you make a scene tonight, I'll kill you."

"So I *shouldn't* wear my snazzy new 'What Would Paulson Do?' t-shirt?"

"Adrian…"

"I shouldn't even have to go to their bloody propaganda training," he sulked. "They can't brainwash me. I'm a Maritimer. We're immune to bullshit."

"No we're not, look at our premier," said Tessa.

"You go on. My folks voted for a new call center in Madawaaksis, not a politician. The suits are interchangeable to them."

"Mada…what?" asked Mark. They ignored him.

***

By lunch time at the campus food court, Tessa was already tired. It was 10 to 1:00. She had given up gnawing on her semi-edible chicken pita, and was on her way to the Center, carrying her fresh coffee to-go. She breathed deeply, steadying her nerves for whatever horrors lay ahead.

The Writing, Research, Professional Development and Student Achievement Center was located in a large, featureless room in the Student Center. It contained two sofas; a phone; a small, circular table; two elderly desktop computers; two small desks; a printer; a white-board and markers; and a modular shelving unit full of out-of-date writing manuals. Like all student service offices at SVU, the wall bordering the hall-way was mostly glass: this kept the room rape-free, but it also subjected the tutors and students within to attention from every passing drone. No privacy was afforded the tutors who worked in that fishbowl. Tessa found herself performing for the public like Olivier on-stage: An Acceptable Nose-Blowing, a Diligent Email-Checking, an Efficient Chapstick Application. "You're sitting ducks in here," Pearl chuckled, on the first day she walked Tessa over to try out the new room key.

From down the corridor, Tessa could see the back of her first appointment waiting outside the door. Millie Miles paced, her eyes locked on her phone. Her body language was tense, and Tessa knew as soon as she entered Millie's line of vision, the remedial student would pounce on her like a starving hyena on a rancid baboon carcass. Millie would suck her writing tutor dry of her superior syntax, grammar, and writing style knowledge.

Jesus H. O'Reilly, Tessa mentally cursed. She spun on her heel before Millie saw her, and walked back from whence she came. Millie often showed up early to her appointments, much to the chagrin of the tutor on duty, in hopes of squeezing out still more assistance. As it was, Tessa felt like she had written Millie's last three term papers for her. Editing Millie's illiterate meanderings for an allotted 60 minute session was more than enough—70 minutes constituted cruel and unusual punishment. To avoid this, Tessa did a loop of the building to kill time, before the Center's official opening time of 1:00.

As Tessa walked, she checked her email on her phone. There was a new message from Andrew. She hadn't heard from him since the Law Ball debacle. Her heart leapt up.

Fr: Andrew Moore—aj.moore@svu.edu

To: Tessa Stevens—te.stevens@svu.edu

Subject: Mea culpa

Date: Nov. 24, 2016, 12:40 p.m.

>   Lovely Girl,
>
>   As predicted, the Law Ball was a drag. The debutante dismayed.
>
>   But Dear Tessa delights.
>
>   Is there anything I can do to make amends? Are you busy perchance tomorrow night? I have a hankering for Cucina Stefano's…or failing that, even Ranch Hand tacos will do.
>
>   Aww shucks, what I really have a hankering for is you! Admit it, I must: I miss you.
>
>   What say, Tessa Fair?
>
>   Yours,
>
>   Andrew

It was easy for Tessa to imagine Andrew's face as he asked that last question. His strawberry-blonde head would be tilted, imploringly. In these moments, he looked like an overgrown school-boy. She thought his smile was irresistible, though Adrian disagreed, once calling it "that treacly grin." Despite herself, Tessa felt her heart thaw. She knew she was going to email back.

"As a dog returns to its vomit, so a fool repeats his folly," echoed the Bible verse in her head. It was a Grammy Ada classic, last used with a *tsk-tsk-tsk* in reference to Stewart Tavistock, the town drunk. Tessa tamped it down. A dozen times a day, she ignored the Bible verses from childhood floating to the surface of her consciousness. They didn't play well in this Peoria. At SVU, only secularism was civilized.

Tessa checked her phone: 1:00 exactly. She could dilly-dally no longer. Loins girded, she walked briskly back to the Center. Millie was still waiting. She looked up, saw her tutor, and her troubled face cleared, like sun-beams parting the clouds. So pathetic was Millie's look of relief that Tessa felt guilty for her resentment and resolved to put her heart and soul into helping the student.

"Hi Millie. Sorry, I'm running a bit late today," said Tessa, which wasn't technically a lie.

"That's cool!" said Millie, nervously checking the time yet again. It was 1:02. She wondered if she could tack on those two minutes to the end of her session.

"So what are we looking at today?"

Millie handed her the assignment instructions. Tessa read the header: "WGST 1025: INTERSECTIONALITY-SEXUALITY: An Introduction to Women and Gender Studies—Dr. Ophelia Cross, Women and Gender Studies Department." Tessa suppressed a shudder. Dr. Cross's freshmen were frequent users of the Writing Center. Her instructions were always vague in the extreme, but such was the power of the professor's personality cult that her students were too overawed to ask questions. It fell to the Writing Center tutors to interpret the Dictates of Cross from on High, like Moses reading the tablets.

"Ok, so this looks fairly straightforward," Tessa said. "A Final Response Paper, like the one we looked at earlier this term. You're just applying feminist theory to the discussion question, right? And she still wants personal reflections?"

Millie nodded. Tessa wondered if the student was aware of her habit of chewing on her hair. The blonde tendrils hanging in Millie's face were slimy with saliva.

"So which question did you choose?"

"This one, on fashion."

Tessa read it aloud: "Using terms and concepts covered in class, discuss how the media and/or the fashion industry privileges certain types of female bodies over others (for example: white, blonde, thin). How has this idealization of certain body types negatively impacted your own self-image? Give examples."

Ugh, so Second-Wave it hurts, thought Tessa. *Always with this assumption that fashion is only ever oppressive, not liberatory, not a type of creative expression. Thus Hillary and the pant-suits. And always casting all women as victims. Well, at least the question's coherently fucking articulated for once.*

"...So I finished my draft and showed it to Dr. Cross—she did me a favor because she said she doesn't usually look at drafts. She didn't like it."

Millie's eyes were watery. Like so many of Tessa's millennial students, she did not take criticism well.

"May I see the draft?"

Millie handed it to her. Tessa read the title aloud: "The Kardashian Effect: The Idealization of Women with Substantial Buttocks in the Media."

"Umm…"

"I thought 'buttocks' sounded more professional than 'butt' or 'ass.'"

"Yes…"

"Should I change it to 'posterior?'" asked Millie.

"Let me read a bit more."

The first few sentences were as follows:

Kim Kardashian, Nicki Minaj, Blac Chyna, Iggy Azalea, Jennifer Lopez, Beyonce. What do these celebrities have in common-large buttocks. The media conveys that large buttocks are desirable in all women. Even though some women naturally have flatter behinds, they are treated as second hand citizens. Everyone wants a large buttocks or "big booty" as it is often referred. As a result of the media's generalized stereotypes, women turn to gluteus implants and injections to have that desireable full-bottomed look. But from a Feminist perspective, we know that women come in all shapes and sizes and that the patriarchy and the media use negative images to enforce women into boxes of dominance…"

"Ok, I think I get it. Where are Cross's notes on your draft?"

"She said she doesn't do written notes for drafts. And she cancelled office hours last week because she is very busy with important research. So I only have the notes I took down from after class yesterday, when we talked. She was in a hurry. I didn't really understand them…"

"Ok. What do you have?"

Millie consulted some chicken-scratchings in a notebook.

"Your topic choice is problematic," she read.

"Uh huh."

"She said, 'Beauty standards only come from dominant cultural groups. They are enacted from the top-down."

Tessa sighed.

Millie continued, "Your analysis is in itself…fetishistic of women of color." (Millie stumbled over "fetishistic," pronouncing it "feta-shush-stick.")

"Ok."

"So I looked up feta—that word—and the root was 'fetish,' and so I looked that up and it means, 'a talisman or other inanimate object believed to have supernatural powers.' I don't get it. Is she saying that I think Beyonce's butt has magical powers?"

Tessa glanced up at the clock on the wall. 1:15. It was going to be a long afternoon.

***

Hours later, Tessa met Adrian in the atrium outside the library before the equity and diversity training session. His expression was dark. Tessa greeted her friend.

"Cheer up, buttercup, it'll all be over soon."

"…said the CBC radio host to his guest."

"That's right, get it all out now, so you can be good in there."

"Oh, I'll be good all right."

They made their way into the library to room L-15, where 21 other youngish, junior instructors were seated, in three rows of desks in front of a lectern. The two friends grabbed their name-tags—the only ones remaining in the pile—and sat in the back row. Tessa recognized a few faces, including Jessica Mincing and Destiny Claremont. Presiding over the session was a short-statured man from the Office of Equity and Diversity. He sported a thick chestnut bowl-cut and an efficient little pot-belly. His name-tag read, "Equity Facilitator: John D. Preferred pronoun: he." John D. played with a fountain pen, his eyes darting around the room, from participant to participant, then back to the clock above.

I should never have agreed to the transfer, John D. thought. *I worked normal hours in HR.*

It was his third evening training session that week.

"Welcome to the Faculty Equity and Diversity Training Session," he said. "My name is John D. and I will be your Equity Facilitator this evening."

After briefing them on the format of the session, John D. passed around a sign-in sheet, dimmed the lights and began a "brief introductory video on our topic." The opening credits rolled: "Better Together: Building a Diverse, Safe, and Respectful Workplace—a Dynamic Progressive Production." On-screen, a racially ambiguous woman with unnaturally bright red hair and a calm demeanour smiled at the camera. Her lips moved but no sound came out. John D. fumbled with the controls, and the audio roared to life. The serene woman stared directly at her invisible audience:

"…BOOTY," she said.

Adrian giggled. Tessa kicked him under the desk.

"As this example shows, a word as simple as 'booty,'" she continued, "generated feelings of profound discomfort and anxiety in the classroom. At that moment, what began as a lecture on Sir Francis Drake and English imperialism during the Elizabethan era, metamorphosed into something far more sinister: a micro-aggression."

From Tessa's peripheral vision, she saw Adrian's eyes widen. The rest of the room appeared nonplussed.

"When professors commit micro-aggressions like these, they create an environment that is hostile to students and colleagues alike. Oftentimes people will say, 'But I didn't mean to offend!' or 'But it was just a joke!' No. That is unacceptable. Remember: when it comes to micro-aggressions, intentions are irrelevant. What matters is the hurt *perceived* by the target of the micro-aggression."

Adrian's jaw dropped.

"...to reiterate, a micro-aggression is any comment or action that consciously or unconsciously communicates a negative attitude toward a marginalized group. Here are a few real-life examples, submitted by academics from across the country."

Enormous cue-card graphics flashed across the screen, in an authoritative bold font.

You speak English really well for an immigrant.

You must be the first person in your family to be a professor.

You're the best female scholar in the department.

The cheerful lobotomized ginger reappeared.

"As you can see, even though these comments are framed as compliments, they actually belittle their victims. In the first example, the speaker is implying that immigrants speak poor English and are therefore unintelligent. (Adrian to Tessa, in a pig-whisper, "No correlation.")

"...In the second example, which was directed at a black colleague, the speaker is implying that blacks are less likely to have parents who are academics." (Adrian: "Statistically true. Just like us poor whites.")

"...and in the third, the speaker is implying that female scholars are in a sub-class of scholars inferior to men." (Before Adrian could whisper again, Tessa mouthed, *Shut. Up.*)

The video host droned on, covering other "key concepts in diversity training," such as "white privilege," "implicit bias," "equity versus equality," and "the intersectionality of oppression." It was old hat to Tessa. Normally, she would have tuned out within minutes—she possessed the glorious ability to raise the cognitive drawbridge and retreat into the fortress of her mind—but Adrian's body language was making her tense and alert. He leaned back in his chair with his arms crossed. Every few seconds he breathed heavily and rolled his eyes. Other people in the room were beginning to notice. Mercifully, the video ended after another 30 minutes or so, the camera freezing on the final scene: the red-headed woman shaking hands in slow-motion with a doltish-looking white male colleague. The title reappeared, floating in like a '90s Windows screensaver. "BETTER TOGETHER," it proclaimed.

John D., lost in a reverie, came to as the ending credits played. He paused the video and cleared his throat.

"I know many of the concepts were probably familiar to you, but hopefully everyone learned a few new things as well. I've seen this video about, oh...27 times now, and I seem to learn something new every time."

He paused and continued, "Are there any questions before we move on to the learning activity?"

Adrian's arm popped up.

"Yes? Oh, and please introduce yourself."

"Hello, my name is Adrian. Preferred pronoun: it. I have a few questions about the video content."

Tessa felt her blood pressure rising.

"Ok."

"Great. First question: are fags part of the patriarchy?"

"Excuse me?"

Adrian spoke louder, "I said, are FAGS part of the patriarchy? You know, white male fags like me."

John D.'s mouth formed a fish-like *O*.

Adrian made a show of holding up his notes and reading them.

"Pardon me, but didn't we just learn in the video, and I quote, 'Context and the relationship between communicants is key in determining what speech is appropriate in a university setting. Words that have been used historically to degrade marginalized groups by culturally dominant groups are generally considered inappropriate for use in the classroom by members of said dominant groups, though it is usually acceptable for members of marginalized groups to use them in reference to themselves.'"

"Umm…"

"So anyway, I can say 'fag,' but you can't. Got it. But that's not my question. My question's about the patriarchy. You seem confused, so I'll elaborate. In the video, they said that the university, 'like most institutions in the West' is still a 'patriarchal institution.' Leaving aside the obvious logical objection that many departments, particularly in the humanities, now have a majority of female professors, I was just wondering, if universities are, overall, patriarchal, do I count as being part of that dominant class, or am I part of the subordinated class?"

"Uhhh…"

"Am I victim or oppressor?" persisted Adrian, enjoying himself for the first time that night.

John D. frantically tried to recall material from his Equity Facilitator Handbook.

Destiny Claremont raised her hand.

"I think gay white men count as the patriarchy now. But I haven't taken a Gender Studies course since undergrad, so don't quote me on that."

Albert Huang, an adjunct in the Chemistry Department, raised his hand.

"Are Asian males part of the patriarchy?"

That opened the floodgates.

"What about trans-men?"

"Jewish men?"

"What about Jewish-Asian trans-men?" piped up a voice near the lectern. It belonged to Ari Moscovitch-Tanaka, a graduate student in Physics.

"Ok, ok, please raise your hands first!" said John D. "I don't see how relevant this discussion is to the topic at hand, but let's just say, that…generally speaking, the patriarchy is composed of straight, white males, who traditionally have held positions of power in society…Ok?"

"Any other questions, before we move on?" John D. asked

Adrian raised his hand.

"Ok, so moving on," said John D. "Before we break for the evening, we're going to do a little activity which may shine some light on this topic. Could everyone please get up from your seats and come stand in a line up here? We'll need to push the first few rows back a bit—a little help please?"

The room awkwardly did John D.'s bidding, reconfiguring the space, and forming a shoulder-to-shoulder single line in front of the Equity Facilitator's lectern.

"Ok. So we're going to play the 'Privilege Points' game. Please listen carefully to these questions and follow my instructions."

Adrian side-eyed Tessa. Her eyes implored him. *Be good.*

"If you grew up somewhere where it was easy to find band-aids in your skin-tone, take one step forward."

Everyone in the class stepped forward, except Destiny.

"If one or both of your parents attended a university or college, take one step forward."

Mincing's face fell, as everyone stepped forward but Tessa, Adrian, and her. Promise Olatunji, the only international instructor in the room, also stepped forward. His father was a cardiologist, his mother, an ophthalmologist.

"As a child, if you were ever taken to museums, art galleries, the symphony, or the ballet, take one step forward."

Everyone stepped forward but Tessa and Adrian.

Mincing defiantly stepped forward. *The Fort MacNally Annual Quilting Bee at the Legion totally counts as a museum visit*, she thought.

"If you attended a private school, take one step forward."

One-fifth of the participants stepped forward.

"If your high school offered advanced placement classes or an equivalent, and you took at least one of them, step forward."

Everyone but Tessa, Adrian, and Jessica Mincing stepped forward.

"If your parents read to you frequently when you were a child, take one step forward."

Everyone but Tessa and Adrian stepped forward. (Tessa remembered, in undergrad, her father using her copy of Simone de Beauvoir's *The Second Sex* as a coaster. When she objected, he read the title, scowled, and threw the book across the room. "What are they teaching you up there?" he asked.)

"During high school, if your parents were able to help you with your homework, take one step forward."

Once again, Tessa and Adrian alone were immobile. It would never have occurred to Tessa to seek help from her parents. By custom, Vic was left alone in his recliner after work, to watch television. His supper would be wordlessly delivered to him on a tray by one of the three women of the house, usually Deborahann. Equally improbable was getting help from her mother, who flitted between the kitchen and the living room at night, busily preparing supper and tending to Vic's needs.

"If you had to work to contribute to your family's household expenses while in school, take one step back."

Tessa and Adrian stepped back. Tessa remembered every stick of cord-wood she and Lilly had loaded into the old pick-up, to take to the mill. Vic had always viewed his daughters as readily available child labor. The relative physical weakness of their sex was a pity, but some work could still be extracted from them.

"If you regularly act differently in public than in private, to better fit in with the dominant culture, take one step back."

Five of the 23 participants stepped back, including Tessa and Adrian.

"If you attended a school where your first language was not spoken, take one step back."

No one moved, including Promise, the only one in the room who spoke the Queen's English.

"If either of your parents was involuntarily unemployed, take one step back."

Tessa and Adrian, and two other participants stepped back.

"If you ever felt uncomfortable about a joke or insulting comment made by a colleague, related to your personal background, but felt it was unsafe to confront them about it, take one step back."

One-quarter of the participants in the room stepped back, including Tessa and Adrian. Tessa couldn't remember a single day in grad school when a professor hadn't made some kind of offhand disparaging remark about a group she was a part of while growing up: the working class, social conservatives, rural Canadians, gun owners, country music listeners, hunters—the list went on and on. Christians were patronized as a matter of course. (Unless they were the fancy sort that did not believe in an anthropomorphic, "personal" God.) Tessa soon discovered there was an entire cluster of beliefs and behaviors that were unacceptable in a university environment. Professors didn't outright say these things were forbidden; it was simply assumed that everyone there, by virtue of being there, was part of the same elite and enlightened group.

"If your parents owned the home you lived in when you were growing up, take one step forward."

At last, Tessa and Adrian stepped forward with almost everyone else in the room. Deborahann sometimes had to hide from the Girl Guides selling cookies, but she and Vic had never missed a single mortgage payment on their Madawaaksis County home. (2016 market value: $139,000 CAD.)

John D. asked the class a few more questions, concluding with, "If you live your life without fearing sexual assault on a daily basis, take one step forward."

Tess and Adrian, and most of the male participants, stepped forward. The rest of the room stayed put, including, to Tessa's surprise, all of the other female participants.

All of these female profs live their lives in fear of rape? Really? Am I some weird outlier? In her experience, heterosexual male English graduate students were practically neuter. None of them had ever tried anything with her, and if they did, she was confident she had enough Madawaaksis in her still to make them regret it.

The Equity Facilitator moved on to the "analysis" section of his notes. He'd scarcely looked up once while rattling off all the questions.

"Now stop and look around you at your peers. Who is beside you, in front of you, and behind you? What does this configuration mean? Let's take some time to really consider how certain people are advantaged, and others disadvantaged, by life circumstances beyond their control."

The participants duly looked around. Most of the group stood at the front of the class, including Destiny Claremont and Promise Olatunji. Jessica Mincing had managed to answer the questions so creatively that she now stood in the middle of the room. A large gap separated Tessa and Adrian from the rest of the class. They stood well behind the others, with Adrian furthest away, his back almost touching the wall. Adrian stood with his arms folded. Tessa shifted from one foot to the other, and tried not to look directly at anyone else.

John D. finally looked up from his notes, expecting to see a white male cluster nearby, followed by a white female cluster. Instead he looked into the bored eyes of Destiny Claremont, a toffee-colored woman. His brow furrowed. Clearly, this group hadn't answered the questions correctly. He continued reading from his notes, trying to buy time.

"The, uhh...purpose of this activity is to reveal the many invisible layers of privilege that play a part in our lives. By acknowledging this privilege, we begin the journey of understanding, and start to realize what some of our colleagues have had to overcome..."

"Excuse me!" Adrian called out from the back. John D. grimaced.

"...to achieve what they have in their lives. *Yes*? In the back?"

"I have something to say." Adrian's face was flushed. "This activity is bullshit."

Mincing gasped.

"I am fat. I am gay. I am white. I am rural. I am poor. My mother is a waitress and my father is an alcoholic. That's why I'm standing at the back of the class." Adrian stood with his hands on his hips, enunciating every syllable.

"But I am *not* a victim. I am *not* disadvantaged. I am *not* oppressed. I'm probably the most intelligent and capable person in this classroom—or else I'd still be in backwoods New Brunswick right now. And maybe I'd be better off back there. At least there people treated me like an individual—with *agency*—not a fucking charity case."

John D. remembered his training in time.

"The point of the exercise is merely to note systemic advantages that..."

"The point of the exercise is to reduce complex individuals to caricatures. The point of this exercise is to impose limitations on free people. And the point of this exercise is to stir up hate for political reasons, by emphasizing differences, instead of our common humanity. What you are doing is wrong. *Dead* wrong!"

"Excuse me?"

Adrian's face was beet-red. His voice grew louder and louder.

"How dare you assume anything about me! How dare you categorize and patronize me! To hell with this!"

With that, Adrian threw his name-tag on the floor and stomped out. The room was silent.

There was a pause. The door opened.

"I forgot my briefcase!"

Adrian grabbed it from under a desk and again departed.

There was more silence, followed by a whispered, "White male privilege: Exhibit A!" from someone in the room.

"That will be all for tonight," said John D, rubbing his temples. *Fuck this. I'm going back to HR,* he thought.

Chapter Nine: Tits on a Bullhorn

Tessa blamed the equity and diversity training incident for pushing her best friend over the edge, into full-on resistance mode. The flame of defiance flickering in Adrian's doughy man-boobs grew ever brighter. After the training session, he made a point of confronting any instances of what he called "identity politics horseshit" on campus. For the rest of his time at SVU he fought the good fight: he wrote letters to the student paper; he posted long angry comments online; he asked pointed questions and gave pointed answers in class; he successfully convinced his longsuffering Department Chair to allow him to skip any future diversity training. And he was adamant about publicly defending Bernard Paulson, whom he viewed as a Voice in the Wilderness, Omega Man, and surrogate father, all rolled up in one.

"Not one more inch to these people," Adrian said to Tessa. "Not *one* more."

"Easy for you to say," said Tessa, who had just applied as an internal candidate for a tenure-track position in her department. Such an opportunity was too rare to waste for the sake of political grandstanding, she told him. Besides, he was doing an M.B.A.—almost none of his Baby Boomer-aged Commerce professors bought in to identity politics. She, on the other hand, in the English Department, was knee-deep in the muck of this ideology.

It was now a week after the training session, and they were running late for the Paulson talk. Just before leaving, Adrian showed Tessa the placards he'd made to challenge the protesters. He was going to hand them out at the talk to his friends from the business school. He also expected Tessa to carry one. Tessa, who had hoped to attend incognito, read Adrian's posters with a dubious expression on her face.

Sign One: "FREEDOM OF SPEECH IS A HUMAN RIGHT." (Tessa was of two minds: she liked how it turned the protesters' rhetoric against them, but thought that emphasizing rights rather than responsibilities wasn't exactly a Paulsonian thing to do.)

Sign Two: "IDENTITY POLITICS = RACIAL PROFILING AND DISCRIMINATION." (Tessa largely agreed.)

Sign Three: "'HATE SPEECH' IS WHATEVER THREATENS THE STATUS QUO." (Tessa said it was kind of weak. Adrian disagreed.)

Sign Four: "...ONE OF THE BEGINNINGS OF HUMAN EMANCIPATION IS THE ABILITY TO LAUGH AT AUTHORITY."—CHRISTOPHER HITCHENS (Tessa approved, in principle, of using Hitchens quotes, but reminded Adrian that the protesters saw Paulson and company as the ones with authority in society, and themselves as perennial victims. Adrian sniffed, "If that's true, name one tenured social conservative in your department. One...No, Stanfield doesn't count. He's half-dead.")

Sign Five: "RATIONAL PEOPLE UNITED FOR PAULSON." ("Straightforward enough," Tessa said.)

Sign Six: "MEANING VERSUS NIHILISM." ("Ditto.")

Sign Seven: "THOSE WHO WOULD GIVE UP ESSENTIAL LIBERTY, TO PURCHASE A LITTLE TEMPORARY SAFETY, DESERVE NEITHER LIBERTY NOR SAFETY."—BENJAMIN FRANKLIN ("An oldie but a goodie," said Tessa.)

Sign Eight: "IF YOU WANT TOTAL SECURITY, GO TO PRISON."—DWIGHT D. EISENHOWER ("Succinct.")

Sign Nine: "OBJECTIVITY IS NOT A MICROAGRESSION." (She approved.)

Sign Ten: "MILLENNIALS: THE PRUDE GENERATION" ("They're not even fucking anymore," Adrian said. "I read a survey." The two then argued for five minutes over whether, demographically speaking, they too were millennials. Tessa said they had to accept the bitter truth that they were. Adrian vehemently denied this, insisting they were part of a culturally distinct microgeneration between the Millennials and Generation X, known as "Xennials.")

Sign Eleven: "THE RIGHT TO BLASPHEME IS THE CORNERSTONE OF OUR CIVILIZATION—DON'T TELL ME WHAT TO SAY, YOU AUTHORITARIAN TWATS." (Adrian admitted he was a little drunk by the time he made that last one.)

Tessa agreed to help him carry the signs to campus—covered up in garbage bags—but she refused to be seen passing them out, and she certainly wouldn't hold one at the talk. Adrian asked if she planned on growing a pair after she found out about her SVU job application. "Maybe once I sign the offer," she replied. Adrian said he had his doubts.

By the time the #4 reached campus, they had only 10 minutes to spare, just barely enough time to make it to the auditorium. The very air on campus crackled with nervous electricity. Masses of students and members of the general public roiled about, like hot stew in a cauldron, all headed in the direction of the Suzeman Building. News crews and reporters were everywhere, and every third person had their cell phone camera out, recording the scene. Everyone was eyeing everyone else suspiciously, trying to gauge the potential threat: friend or foe? Tessa assumed that the more conservatively dressed students were in the pro-Paulson camp, while the white-kids-with-dreads crowd were anti-Paulson, but she knew this was an imperfect method of reckoning. To be inconspicuous, she had dressed all in black.

"Hurry up!"

Adrian tugged on her coat like an enormous puppy, steering Tessa toward the auditorium. Angry murmurs wafted out into the night. The auditorium seemed to pulsate.

On the way in, they stepped around a pair of protesters holding aloft a large sign. It read, "SOCIALISM = COOPERATION. CAPITALISM = CONFLICT."

Adrian smirked. In a loud whisper he said, "All this anti-capitalist shit is just unwillingness to accept the reality of human nature."

"Sssh!" Tessa said.

When they stepped through the doors, her heart beat faster. The noise rose to a clamor. A few feet beyond the entry was a long corridor leading to the auditorium's main doors. Anti-Paulsonites were stationed on either side of the corridor, holding up signs, and raising hell with a variety of noisemakers—some regular musical instruments, and some cunning improvisations. One pink-haired fellow shook a bottle full of rocks over his head, legs bowed, half-squatting, like an angry chimpanzee. Other belligerent protesters stood in the middle of the corridor, hands on their hips, attempting to block the stream of foot traffic. They had succeeded in turning back a few of the less hearty souls, while some even more timorous would-be attendees walked inside the building, took one look at the scene, and turned around.

Tessa recognized some of the protesters as PFP members, including Maia Worthing, but others appeared to be another breed entirely: these protesters' faces were obscured by bandanas or ski masks. She saw, for the first time, flashes of red and black "As" on their signs and persons. Tessa felt her adrenaline kick up into a higher gear.

Three or four different protest chants were being screeched by the mob, in and out of unison. Tessa and Adrian could make out one of them above the ruckus. It grew louder with each repetition:

"No platform for hate!/ We ex-ter-minate!/ No platform for hate!/ We ex-ter-minate!/ No platform for HATE!/ WE EX-TER-MINATE!"

Adrian reached for Tessa's shoulder and looked into her eyes. Hers were questioning, his defiant. She knew there was no way he was turning back now, and if she did, he would go on alone. She decided. They would run the gauntlet together.

Eyes trained on the auditorium door in the distance, they marched forward into the mêlée. The scene was latent with violence. Never had Adrian's imposing presence come in so handy; the pink-haired protester saw him coming and stood down. Adrian plowed forward like a dreadnought, towing Tessa along behind him. No one dared touch her, but she could feel the hatred radiating from the protesters, who were determined to intimidate everyone passing by. One angry protester came so close she coated Tessa with a fine spray of spittle. In under 30 seconds the pair had almost cleared them all. There was just one more member of the mob to deal with: a solid, gray hoody-clad female protester was the only thing standing between them and the auditorium double-doors.

"What are you doing here?" she snarled at Tessa, outraged by the sight of a woman attempting to hear the lecture. "Paulson is a misogynist pig!"

Tessa ignored her.

"Did you fucking hear me?"

Gray Hoody stepped in front of her, a few inches from Tessa's face, blocking the corridor.

"Paulson hates women!"

Tessa tried to go around her and was blocked again. Barely audible over the noise, Tessa said, "Let us through."

"Go home!" screamed the banshee, refusing to move.

Tessa's heart pounded. Her body trembled.

"No."

"Go home!"

"No."

"Go home, you stupid fucking bitch!" screamed Gray Hoody.

At the word "bitch," Tessa felt something snap. She grabbed Gray Hoody's hood with both hands, and in one smooth motion, tugged it to the side. Caught off-guard, the woman tripped and fell to the floor, bellowing like a wounded heifer.

"Go!"

Tessa grabbed Adrian's hand and they sprinted the rest of the way to the doors. In the distance, Gray Hoody's screams reverberated, "She hurt me! She hurt me!"

"Holy fuck, Tess," said Adrian as they made their way to their seats.

The auditorium was packed full-to-bursting. They weren't out of the woods yet. Dangers lurked inside as well. Compared to the entry-way, the inside of the auditorium was ominously quiet. Tessa scanned the room, her heart still thudding from the encounter with Gray Hoody. The Postmodernists for Peace contingent was present: a clump of them were seated near the entry. The Womyn's Scholars were also there. It was Tessa's bad luck to pass right by them, resplendent in their identical white t-shirts and rainbow uterus pins. A half-dozen had showed up, including Wagband and her trusted henchwoman, Jessica Mincing. Tessa could feel Wagband's eyes drilling into her back as she took her seat beside Adrian and his business school friends. She prayed Wagband would assume she was there protesting as well. She wondered how all this would affect her job application in the Department.

For such a big event, Tessa noticed that there were few faculty members in attendance. She assumed that most of the Womyn's Scholars members had been scared off by the unexpected (to them) positive public response to Paulson's speaking tour. Paulson's last talk, just two days ago at a Saskatchewan university, was cut short by the efforts of a small group of protesters who chanted over him whenever he tried to speak. The administrators at the event—gormless, craven, like so many of their breed—adopted the Chamberlain approach to dealing with the disruptive students. Their entreaties for "respect please" were ignored. (One was told to "Shut the fuck up" by a student protester, and he obeyed, while the other protesters laughed.) Multiple videos of the event popped up on YouTube, and they spoke for themselves: the public saw a composed man in front of a lectern, being rudely shouted down by a mob. Contrary to what most media sources had told the public, Paulson was saying innocuous, and to them, commonsensical things. They wondered, was this calm, white-haired man in a cardigan the firebrand and bigot they'd been promised?

Online comments, letters to the editor, and alumni emails piled up: *I thought universities were supposed to be places where people discussed new ideas?* they said. *What about free speech?* they said. And finally: *treat Paulson with basic civility or we cut your purse-springs*, they said. Administrators in publicly funded universities and colleges in North America began to take the Paulson issue more seriously. It suddenly behooved them to grow an opinion on the matter.

These faint echoes from the Outside World began reaching the ears of the faculty, and although their bubble wasn't quite breached, like skittish deer sniffing something unsavory on the wind, up flipped their white tails and away they bolted. Best to take cover in the brush while things sorted themselves out. Only the ideologically pure remained, vocal and intransigent, like Wagband and her followers.

Tessa and Adrian had just settled into their seats when the President of the Students for Free Inquiry introduced the speaker, some 30 minutes later than the scheduled start-time. All eyes lasered in on Dr. Bernard Paulson, Professor of Philosophy, a tall, spare figure, emerging from stage left. He was dressed in a shaggy, mud-colored cardigan and grey slacks. His clothing appeared to be borrowed from a man at least two sizes larger. His face was all angles and dark hollows, like driftwood. His expression, as he settled in behind the lectern, was one of infinite weariness. He surveyed the room like a Biblical patriarch, as if to say, *You're a bad lot, and it's a bad job, but I'm here, goddammit.*

Outside in the corridor, the anti-Paulsonites began pounding on the locked main entry doors. The rhythmic pounding reverberated throughout the auditorium. The audience shifted in their seats.

Paulson tapped the mic once, and said, "Good evening Sere Valley University, and a special good evening to the barbarians at the gates."

The audience saluted his brio with applause and cheers. The thumping at the door paused, then continued apace. Paulson ignored it.

Once the applause died down, Paulson began without further preamble, his formerly unprepossessing form now as animated as a lightning rod. He posed a single stark question to the room:

"What is the antidote to pain and suffering?"

The room was silent, save for the *thump, thump, thump* at the doors.

Paulson repeated himself, more loudly, "I'm asking you: what is the antidote to suffering in this life?"

Continued silence.

Thump. Thump. Thump.

"Call out, for God's sakes. You're allowed to speak," said Paulson.

From somewhere in the auditorium, someone ventured a guess: "Love?"

"No. *No.* Love is absolutely not the antidote to suffering."

"Peace," shouted another voice.

"Not peace," said Paulson. "Impossible."

"Equality!" cried a defiant voice coming from the PFP contingent.

Paulson snorted like a mule.

"Ask the Soviets!" piped up one of the members of the Students for Free Inquiry. The largely pro-Paulson audience cheered.

"Any other answers?" asked Paulson.

"Truth," said one of Adrian's Commerce student friends, a sensible Nova Scotian named Eldon Mackenzie. Eldon had listened to hundreds of hours of Paulson's online lectures and had read both of Paulson's best-selling self-help books: *You Better* (2012) and *You Bloody Well Better* (2015).

"That's the best one yet, by some measure," Paulson said. "Tell the truth and you will avoid some of the worst evils in this loathsome and twisted world. Telling the truth, in fact, is the only way you can hope to preserve your integrity—no matter what else happens to you. Remember that. Tell the truth. *However...*"

Thump. Thump. Thump.

Paulson paused and scanned the crowd. He took a long drink of water from a glass. Tessa leaned forward, like everyone in the room.

Thump. Thump. Thump.

"However, even a strict adherence to the truth cannot save you from suffering. As we all know, truth-tellers are often reviled by the wicked. Telling the truth when people aren't ready to hear it is a sure-fire way to make them hate you."

"No kidding!" shouted the same over-enthusiastic member of the Students for Free Inquiry. The room tittered.

"So what is the antidote to suffering, if not even the truth can save us?" Paulson asked. He lowered his voice.

"The answer is this…" He paused again.

Thump. Thump. Thump.

"Nothing."

"Nothing," he repeated. "There is no antidote to suffering."

He stopped to let that percolate. Faces fell in the audience.

"On this earth, there will always be human suffering," said Paulson. "That is what it means to be human: to suffer. That doesn't mean we don't still have a responsibility to act nobly! But seeking the truth and other virtuous behaviors cannot shield us from pain. Just ask our friend Job. Suffering cannot be avoided, and attempting to avoid it, paradoxically, will only lead to new and *monstrous* mutations in the forms of human suffering—I can guarantee you that."

"So what do we do?" cried a voice.

Thump. Thump. Thump.

"What indeed?" said Paulson. "The anguished cry of the ages! Shall we lie down and die? Surrender ourselves to nihilism, hedonism, or some other 'ism?' There's only one answer. There's only one way to *mitigate* suffering."

Tessa was on the edge of her seat, every muscle tensed.

"The answer is…" said Paulson.

At that moment, Paulson's microphone went dead, and six black-clad protesters rushed the stage from the wings. Five of them held a large banner, which read, "PAULSON PROMOTES HATE." The sixth, who had a shaved head, gripped a bullhorn. They stepped in front of Paulson.

"We're shutting this down!" bellowed the protester with the bullhorn.

Tessa was surprised to recognize Olivia Miller, a mild-mannered, rotund adjunct in the English Department. Tessa had met her a few times in passing. Word in the Department was Olivia was transitioning (or gender-fluid, or gender-fluid *and* transitioning). This was by far the most interesting thing about Olivia. But tonight a new Olivia had emerged. She looked like she had Google-imaged "hipster vigilante" and copied the results. She wore black skinny jeans, a black long-sleeved t-shirt, and a vaguely keffiyeh-esque checked scarf that had originated from The Gap. Her head was shaved. Tessa was impressed by the adjunct's surprising agility, as Olivia scrambled across the stage, bullhorn aloft.

"Paulson promotes hate! Paulson promotes hate!" chanted Olivia into the bullhorn, in time with the other five protesters. Paulson at the lectern was half-visible behind the large banner, standing with one hand on his hip, bemused. The crowd roared its disapproval at the interruption.

Where the hell is campus security? wondered Tessa for the hundredth time that evening. They were nowhere to be seen. She recognized a handful of administrators in the audience, including the VP of Student Services. They looked stricken but were making no moves to control the situation. Tessa also noticed that the anti-Paulsonites thumping at the entry had gone silent during the storming of the podium. *Are they all working together?*

"Let him speak!" yelled Adrian, standing up and turning to the crowd. Most of the auditorium took up the chant: "Let him speak! Let him speak!" Simultaneously, Olivia and company continued chanting, "Paulson promotes hate!" But even with the bullhorn, they could not drown out the voices of some 300 angry spectators, there to hear Paulson.

The PFP and Womyn's Scholars' groups, and the other anti-Paulsonites in the audience felt outnumbered and outgunned. Even Wagband was afraid, squirming in her seat. Mincing was checking for alternative exits.

The duelling chants went on for another minute. Then the ear-splitting sound of audio feedback cut through the din, echoing through the auditorium. There was a tussle backstage. Paulson's mic was back on.

"Meaning!" cried Paulson. "Meaning is real! And meaning mitigates suffering!"

The crowd cheered louder than ever.

"Meaning is real! Meaning is real! Meaning is real!" they chanted.

Olivia and her fellows were aghast. Her energy was waning, but she wasn't beaten yet.

"Your meaning is my subordination!" she yelled into the bullhorn. "Meaning is fascism!"

"NOOOO!" cried the crowd.

The balance of power shifted again. The anti-Paulsonites at the entry suddenly broke down the doors and streamed into the room. Screams rippled through the auditorium from the entry. Tessa, processing the situation in slow-motion, realized she was about to experience her very first riot.

If I die, I'll never have to pay back my student loans. It was a comforting thought.

As the protesters flooded in, a voice boomed over the P.A.:

"THIS IS THE POLICE. REMAIN CALM. PROTESTERS: DO NOT MOVE. RAISE YOUR HANDS ABOVE YOUR HEADS. THIS LECTURE IS OVER."

***

Fr: Deborahann Stevens—deborahannstevens@hotmail.com

To: Tessa Stevens—te.stevens@svu.edu

Subject: PAULMAN TALK??

Date: November 30, 2016, 10:10 p.m.

TESSIE-BEAR

PICK UP YOUR PHONE AND CALL YOUR MOTHER!!

WE SAW PART OF THE PAULMAN TALK AT SVU, WHEN THE POLICE ARRIVED. ITS BEEN ALL OVER THE NEWS. THEY SAID EVERYONE WAS OK BUT IT LOOKED SCARY TO ME!

WE LOOKED FOR YOU-WE THINK WE SAW ADRIAN MAYBE BUT NOT YOU IN THE CROWD (??) ARE YOU OK??

THE CBC REPORTER KEPT SAYING PAULMAN IS PART OF THE ALT-RIGHT? WHAT IS THAT? IS THAT LIKE THOSE YAHOOS NANCY MORLEY'S SON GOT ALL MIXED UP WITH IN MONTREAL. THE BIKER GANG PEOPLE??? THAT BOY ONLY HAS HALF A BRAIN ANYWAY.

WHY WAS THE SHAVED HEAD PERSON SO MAD? WAS SHE A BOY OR A GIRL? YOUR FATHER WANTS TO KNOW IF YOUVE JOINED THE "BRA-BURNING CLUB" TOO AT COLLEGE. (HAHA. VERY FUNNY, I TOLD HIM.)

LOVE YOU!!!!

BE SAFE!!!

MUM

Fr: Tessa Stevens—te.stevens@svu.edu

Fr: Deborahann Stevens—deborahannstevens@hotmail.com

Subject: RE: PAULMAN TALK??

Date: November 30, 2016, 10:35 p.m.

Ok, Mum, first of all, it's "Paulson," not "Paulman."

Yes, Adrian and I were there. We're fine. Some irrational people ruined it for everyone. Things were dicey for a few minutes, but luckily the police got a handle on things. They're investigating. Word on the street is that some of the protesters weren't even students. I will explain more later on the phone

Btw, Paulson is not a member of the "alt-right," obviously, or I wouldn't have gone to the talk. He's just an academic who dares talk about morality and personal responsibility, so the CBC and many university intellectuals don't like him.

You need to take the CBC with a grain of salt. They usually get the facts right, but they have their own slant—and that doesn't mean you and Dad should get all your information from crazy email forwards from your Bible group either. :P

Tessa

Fr: Deborahann Stevens—deborahannstevens@hotmail.com

To: Tessa Stevens—te.stevens@svu.edu

Subject: RE: RE: PAULMAN TALK??

Date: November 30, 2016, 10:56 p.m.

SO GLAD YOU ARE OK.

AND YES FANCY-PANTS. ARENT YOU COOL BECAUSE YOU DON'T GO TO CHURCH ANYMORE.

JESUS LOVES YOU WHETHER YOU LIKE IT OR NOT!! HA.

...AND BOY OR GIRL? AFTER PRAYER MEETING YULE SAID HE BETS BOY BECAUSE SHE HAD AN ADAMS APPLE BUT I THINK GIRL BECAUSE SHE HAD BOOBS!!

Fr: Tessa Stevens—te.stevens@svu.edu

To: Deborahann Stevens—deborahannstevens@hotmail.com

Subject: RE: RE: RE: PAULMAN TALK??

Date: November 30, 2016, 11:10 p.m.

    I believe that protester, who happens to be an adjunct faculty member I know, identifies as gender-fluid, Mum. It's complicated, but basically their logic is that gender does not have to be black and white, but exists on a continuum.

    Furthermore, I should note that there is a difference between gender and sex. In a nutshell, sex refers to a person's anatomy, and gender refers to one's social behavior and identity.

Fr: Deborahann Stevens—deborahannstevens@hotmail.com

To: Tessa Stevens—te.stevens@svu.edu

Subject: RE: RE: RE: RE: PAULMAN TALK??

Date: November 30, 2016, 11:15 p.m.

BUT DO THEY HAVE GIRL PARTS OR BOY PARTS??

Fr: Tessa Stevens—te.stevens@svu.edu

To: Deborahann Stevens—deborahannstevens@hotmail.com

Subject: RE: RE: RE: RE: RE: PAULMAN TALK??

Date: November 30, 2016, 11:17 p.m.

> It doesn't matter. How they identify is what matters.

Fr: Deborahann Stevens—deborahannstevens@hotmail.com

To: Tessa Stevens—te.stevens@svu.edu

Subject: RE: RE: RE: RE: RE: RE: PAULMAN TALK??

Date: November 30, 2016, 11:18 p.m.

SO CAN I IDENTIFY AS ELINOR AND BE RICH? BECAUSE THAT WOULD BE NICE!! THEN I WOULDN'T HAVE TO GO TO WORK TOMORROW.

Fr: Tessa Stevens—te.stevens@svu.edu

To: Deborahann Stevens—deborahannstevens@hotmail.com

Subject: RE: RE: RE: RE: RE: RE: RE: PAULMAN TALK??

Date: November 30, 2016, 11:20 p.m.

> Mum, you're trivializing a serious matter. People have lost their lives over these things.

Fr: Deborahann Stevens—deborahannstevens@hotmail.com

To: Tessa Stevens—te.stevens@svu.edu

Subject: RE: RE: RE: RE: RE: RE: PAULMAN TALK??

Date: November 30, 2016, 11:22 p.m.

YES YES, TESSIE. EVERYTHING IS A SERIOUS MATTER WITH YOU SINCE YOUVE GONE TO COLLEGE. YOUR A GRUMPY LITTLE BEAR!

IS ADRIAN GENDER-FLUID NOW TOO?

Fr: Tessa Stevens—te.stevens@svu.edu

To: Deborahann Stevens—deborahannstevens@hotmail.com

Subject: RE: RE: RE: RE: RE: RE: RE: PAULMAN TALK??

Date: November 30, 2016, 11:30 p.m.

    No, Mum. Adrian is gay. But while we're on the topic, sexual attraction also exists on a continuum. People aren't just heterosexual or homosexual. There are many different sexualities, including bisexual, asexual, pansexual, etc.

Fr: Deborahann Stevens—deborahannstevens@hotmail.com

To: Tessa Stevens—te.stevens@svu.edu

Subject: RE: RE: RE: RE: RE: RE: RE: RE: PAULMAN TALK??

Date: November 30, 2016, 11:34 p.m.

PAN-SEXUAL?? THOSE PEOPLE NEED TO GET OUT MORE. HA HA

SO IS ALL THIS STUFF WHY THEY SAID PAULMAN WAS ALT-RIGHT TOO? ARE THEY THAT MAD BECAUSE HE STILL THINKS PEOPLE ARE USUALLY EITHER

BOYS OR GIRLS? EVERYBODY THINKS THAT IN BEACONSBRIDGE. ARE WE ALL ALTRIGHT TOO??

Fr: Tessa Stevens—te.stevens@svu.edu

To: Deborahann Stevens—deborahannstevens@hotmail.com

Subject: RE: RE: RE: RE: RE: RE: RE: RE: RE: PAULMAN TALK??

Date: November 30, 2016, 11:40 p.m.

    No, none of you are alt-right (with the possible exception of Nancy Morley's son...) The truth is, only a very, very small percentage of the population is biologically intersex.

Fr: Deborahann Stevens—deborahannstevens@hotmail.com

To: Tessa Stevens—te.stevens@svu.edu

Subject: RE: RE: RE: RE: RE: RE: RE: RE: RE: RE: PAULMAN TALK??

Date: November 30, 2016, 11:47 p.m.

KODY'S SURE ALT-SOMETHING SINCE HE MOVED TO MONTREAL AND GOT IN WITH THE WRONG CROWD THERE. ALT-STUPID MAYBE. HAHA.

BUT REALLY ITS NOT FUNNY. NANCY'S REALLY WORRIED. ☹

ANYWAYS, TESSIE, IM SO GLAD YOU GOT SO MUCH SCHOOLING AND CAN EXPLAIN THESE THINGS TO YOUR POOR OLD MUM! DO YOU DO ANYTHING OVER THERE BUT TALK ABOUT SEXY THINGS ALL DAY AND DRINK COFFEE? I'M ON MY FEET ALL DAY AT SENTIMENTAL OCCASIONS-I WENT INTO THE WRONG BUSINESS.

Fr: Tessa Stevens—te.stevens@svu.edu

To: Deborahann Stevens—deborahannstevens@hotmail.com

Subject: RE: RE: RE: RE: RE: RE: RE: RE: RE: RE: RE: PAULMAN TALK??

Date: November 30, 2016, 11:50 p.m.

I'm going to bed now, Mum. Goodnight.

Fr: Deborahann Stevens—deborahannstevens@hotmail.com

To: Tessa Stevens—te.stevens@svu.edu

Subject: RE: RE: RE: RE: RE: RE: RE: RE: RE: RE: RE: PAULMAN TALK??

Date: November 30, 2016, 11:51 p.m.

NIGHT NIGHT TESSY-BEAR!! I LOVE YOU!!

Fr: Deborahann Stevens—deborahannstevens@hotmail.com

To: Tessa Stevens—te.stevens@svu.edu

Subject: RE: RE: RE: RE: RE: RE: RE: RE: RE: RE: RE: RE: PAULMAN TALK??

Date: November 30, 2016, 11:52 p.m.

I love you too.

Chapter Ten: Good and Not Evil

A month later, Tessa was home for the holiday break. She'd been in Beaconsbridge for a couple weeks, flying in earlier than planned to attend Great-Uncle Milt's funeral. Milton Blakeney made it to 90, but he'd been ailing for years. A bad flu going around at the Home finally dispatched him. The funeral was a simple social obligation. Great-Uncle Milt was a distant elderly relative Tessa hadn't seen in years. Throughout the brief service, she kept her facial expression appropriately solemn, out of respect for the family. Vic rarely bothered attending functions for his wife's relatives, so Tessa and her mother were at the funeral alone. After making their way, step by decorous step, through the receiving line of family, Deborahann gestured discreetly for them to leave. In the car, she stretched out in the driver's seat, uncoiling her body.

"Another one bites the dust!"

Tesssa frowned. That was callous, even for her no-nonsense mother, though she knew she'd never liked her Uncle Milt.

As they pulled out of the church parking lot, Deborahann began to sing, "Na na,/ Na na na na,/ Hey hey hey,/ Goodbyeeeeee."

"Geez, Mum."

Deborahann shrugged and changed the subject.

"Do you think you're going to get the SVU job? You must be a shoe-in! They know you, after all. They won't have to train a new guy."

"It doesn't work like that in academia, Mum."

"Well, if that falls through, have you looked in to government? There's a new call center opening up in the Miramichi, I hear. Processing disability claims? Something like that. That wouldn't be too bad."

Tessa suppressed a scream. This was approximately the one-millionth time her mother had suggested the public service. Like so many New Brunswickers, Deborahann's fondest dream for her children was for them to land cushy government jobs. In a province with little private industry and low wages, these coveted jobs provided decent money, stability and a degree of status. Young people who knew what side their bread was buttered on aimed at finding a government job, whether that meant working at a call center processing claims or stocking shelves at one of the government-monopoly liquor stores. It made no difference.

"Oh my God, I don't want to be a bureaucrat, Mum. Get it through your head. And you don't need a Ph.D. to work at a provincial call center. You need French and one good connection."

"Is your French still good? They'll pay you to upgrade now, Abby said."

And so on, all the way home. Tessa felt a headache coming on.

She had noted a pattern emerging with these visits home: they plateaued early, then went downhill, and by the end of it, both parents were getting on her nerves so much that she was happy to leave. This visit was the same. The first two days or so after arrival were pleasant. Mum baked all of her favorite things; Tessa's bed was piled high with cozy quilts and comforters; Missy the orange tabby was fatter and more self-satisfied than ever; Trixie the dog was as bouncy and dimwitted; and the house was layered with the old, familiar chintzy Christmas decorations: the porcelain nativity scene, fake holly, Royal Doulton praying angels, and the rest. After a few days, Lilly drove down from Fredericton—a late exam had prevented her from attending Uncle Milt's funeral—and the two sisters settled back into their comfortable teasing rapport.

During these last few visits, Tessa began noticing some problems in Beaconsbridge. It was now difficult to overlook the poverty of the community, especially in comparison to the out-of-province towns and cities where she'd gone to university. Most of her caste, the church-going class of the village, were clinging with both hands to their precarious lower-middle status, and some were really struggling. Many of the villagers who rented or even owned homes in town lived in relative poverty. Even Grammy Ada's house now looked rundown to her—and Tessa had once considered it the height of elegance (before she advanced from Victorian to mid-century modern in her architectural pretensions). Tessa knew that inside what was once the grandest home in the parish, Grammy Ada lived on a government dole of $985 a month.

One Saturday afternoon before Christmas, Tessa saw the worst of the problem in the flesh. Deborahann had work to do as a member of the church Benevolence Committee. Tessa accompanied her mother to drop off a dozen frozen turkeys from the church to needy families. They traveled from one shabby home to another, mostly rented from landlords who were but one rung up from their tenants on the village's stubby social ladder. With every stop, Tessa felt more uncomfortable. The last one was the worst. They pulled up to a trailer outside town, in an area known as Carpenters' Settlement. A dumpy, ginger-haired woman came to the door—to Tessa, the very living embodiment of the word "slattern."

"G'day Deb."

"Hi Tammy. Just dropping off something from the church."

Deborahann handed Tammy Waller the heavy, double-bagged turkey, which she received with alacrity. Other than a quick "thanks" from Tammy, they both politely ignored the fact that Deborahann was there on a mission of charity. They moved on rapidly to other topics, like "the girls." (Tammy had four in total, and at least two were a matching set, the fathers the subject of speculation.) They discussed the weather ("some cold"), and whether or not they were ready for Christmas. (Tammy had "a pile of presents left to get.") Because this was Madawaaksis County, it was impossible for them to leave without a cup of tea. Tessa ignored the layers of brown sludge ringing her teacup. She also tried to ignore how dirty all four of the girls were, ranging in age from five to 11, and the sour smell of spilled beer and cigarette smoke in the crowded trailer kitchen. Tessa admired her mother for keeping up a steady stream of cheerful conversation, though she knew full well she wasn't missing a single detail of the squalor. After a few more minutes of pleasant chit-chat, Deborahann made her excuses, "Well, I better get home and get started on supper or Vic will pitch a fit. Nice seeing you, Tammy."

"You too, Deb. Don't be a stranger."

Deborahann crouched down to the eight year old's level.

"You be good for your Mum, Katie. Santa's coming soon!"

Katie squealed. Her face was dirt-streaked and she had a runny nose. She'd chattered like a songbird throughout the visit, between coughing fits.

Tessa and Deborahann left. In the car Tessa let out a groan.

"I thought we were never going to get out of there. Why did you say yes to tea?"

"She's stuck up there without a vehicle half the time. I thought she could use some company. Who knows if that Terry even lives there with them anymore. Did you see any sign of him? I went to school with Tammy's sister Mary Jean."

"I know, I know. My word, that trailer was disgusting!" (Tessa slipped back into the vernacular when she was home. In Sere Valley, she would've said, "My God, that trailer was disgusting.")

"She's not a bad woman."

"If she cared about those girls' health, why would she smoke in there? It just *reeked*. That's probably why the two little ones were hacking up a lung."

"I think poor Tammy's just trying to get by. She never had a chance, Tessie."

"What do you mean?"

"Tammy, Mary Jean, and the boys grew up with no father in the picture and without two cents to rub together."

"You grew up with no money and no father, and we don't live like that. No one held a gun to her head and told her to have four children on her own, on welfare."

"My my, hard words from my little socialist!" Deborahann teased.

"I'm not a socialist…I don't know what I am…There is such a thing as individual agency, as well as social context, Mum. We can be more than the environment we grew up in."

Deborahann steered carefully downhill, back to the village. The dirt road needed plowing. The government crew was always late getting out to Carpenters' Settlement.

"Well, Tammy and Mary Jean's 'social context' was a drunk mother who took in sewing—and any man with two feet and a heartbeat."

"Ewww. Mum."

"It's true. That's a hard life for kids—men in and out all the time. With all her faults, your grandmother sure didn't raise me that way. I was never allowed to play with the Wallers outside of school. Lord only knows what Tammy's been through."

Tessa tried not to smirk at her mother's airs. Though separated by a hair's breadth financially while growing up in Beaconsbridge, Deborahann knew perfectly well that her family was considered "respectable" and Tammy Waller's was not. Tessa knew now, in the wider world, that they'd all be considered, broadly speaking, Maritimer white trash.

Deborahann and Tessa pulled into their driveway. The house was sided in pale-yellow vinyl, typical of Madawaaksis County residences. It was tidy with window-boxes and shutters. Vic had turned on the Christmas lights. They glittered in the dusk in a secretive fashion. Tessa thought about the cold, dilapidated trailer and felt guilty.

She didn't speak much during supper, which was just as well. Vic was in a particularly foul mood, still brooding over a dispute with a customer at the shop last week. "This slop again?" he said as Deborahann served her homemade clam chowder for the second night in a row. Tessa looked over at Lilly, but her sister's eyes were glued to her soup.

"Where's the damn pepper?" Vic asked.

Deborahann hopped up to get it, almost knocking a plate of dinner rolls onto the floor, in her haste. Vic rolled his eyes at her clumsiness. As usual, Deborahann make a joke of it. "At your service, Your Majesty," she said, handing the shaker to him with a sarcastic little bow. Vic snorted.

Tessa wondered, for the first time, why her parents always framed Vic's imperiousness and Deborahann's eagerness to serve as funny.

Later that night, parked in front of the television, Vic cycled through the channels, never stopping on one for more than two seconds. Lilly and Tessa were sitting on the sofa nearby. Deborahann popped into the living room with a surprise snack of chips and chives dip. She carefully set the tray down on her husband's lap.

"You know I don't like this Sobeys' crap!" said Vic, shoving the tray back against his wife's ample tummy. He laughed as it caught Deborahann by surprise and a gust of air expelled from her mouth.

Debrorahann smiled weakly. Lilly and Tessa didn't smile.

"What? That's funny!"

Silence.

"None of you would know funny if it bit you in the butt!" protested Vic.

Lilly and Tessa got up together and left him to watch television by himself. Vic sulked for a few minutes, but then forgot about the incident, lost in a M.A.S.H. rerun. He was asleep and lightly drooling on himself before it ended. Deborahann wiped his chin and placed an afghan around his shoulders. After she let the dog and cat out, she'd have to wake him up to go to bed.

***

Another night, a few days later, Deborahann and Tessa were home alone. Lilly was out with friends and Vic was at the shop. As always when Vic was away, the atmosphere in the house was relaxed. When Vic was home, the household perpetually cycled through three emotional climates correlating with his moods: tepid, tense, and terrifying. The third stage was bad, but the second, characterized by an electric sub-current of anticipation, was the worst: managing a crisis is often better than waiting in agony for the inevitable. That night, Tessa was taking advantage of her father's absence to get some work done at the kitchen table.

"Whatcha doing, Tessie-Bear?" asked Deborahann, who'd been hanging around, ostensibly making hot chocolate, for the past five minutes.

"Working on a journal article, Mum. *Trying* to work on a journal article," Tessa replied. "I'd like to get this done before Dad gets home and starts bugging us."

"He just called. He thinks he's going to be at the shop *all* night finishing the Taylor job!" gloated Deborahann.

"Good."

Deborahann plopped down beside her daughter at the table and handed her one of two warm mugs. She cleared her throat. Tessa sighed and closed her laptop. She would be getting no more work done tonight.

"So, what's up?"

"I want to talk to you about why I was so mean about Uncle Milt dying. I know you thought I was being nasty about it."

Tessa looked at her closely.

Staring down into the depths of her hot chocolate, Deborahann told her story.

***

It happened when Deborahann was a girl, a few months after her father had died. It was early fall, potato harvest time in that part of New Brunswick. Like all of her cousins, she was pulled out of school for "potato break," to help bring in the large crop on Uncle Lewis and Aunt Moira's farm. Ten kids were helping, including Yule, and even little Jimmy, though he was mostly getting in the way. Deb, Yule, and Jimmy were the youngest of the cousins, at 10, 10, and 7, respectively. Most of the others were in their early teens. Back then, everyone was expected to do their part around the farm. The families were paid in kind for their labor: with sacks of tawny Russet Burbanks. They would keep all fall and winter, stored in burlap sacks in musty basement cold rooms across the province. By the end of the winter, the potatoes would grow long, curious tubercle eyes that would have to be removed before cooking.

It was the last day of harvest. Surveying the field at 4:30, Uncle Lew decided that instead of returning for another half-day, his crew of mostly kids and a few hired-men should put in a few more hours of work "and just finish the damn thing." And so they did, though it took another three hours. They worked through supper and were tired, dirty and hungry. Cold ham, carrots, beans, and the omnipresent boiled potatoes awaited the laborers inside, ably prepared by Aunt Moira, Aunt Ella, and Aunt Ada. Deborahann, typically, had wandered away from her herd of cousins to pop in to the barn. She was ravenous, but she also wanted to see Fluffy the barn-cat's newest litter of kittens before supper. Yule had said they were in the hayloft somewhere.

One pair of eyes watched Deborahann turn off into the barn and make her way up the rickety ladder inside. Uncle Milt followed her up the stairs, and into a corner of the dim, untidy hayloft. In the shadows, he kept his shirt on, but removed his pants and underwear. He whispered his niece's name once, and then a second time. Deborahann froze when she saw him, trouser-less, making his way toward her in the loft. His eyes were vacant and dilated, his lips were parted in a broad smile. Even in the dull light, she could make out one big drop of perspiration glistening on his forehead.

Time slowed down and the encounter took on the hazy feeling of a dream.

Deborahann had never seen an adult man's "thing" before, only her little baby cousins', while changing them. She was afraid. Drawing nearer, Uncle Milt entreated her to touch it. A few more seconds passed. Deborahann couldn't move or talk. Uncle Milt leaned over and firmly gripped her right hand, pulling it toward him. Deborahann's heart beat as quickly as a hummingbird's wings. Something very bad was happening, but she couldn't stop him. Hot tears filled her eyes. She wanted to flee, but was immobile with fear and shock, like she was hypnotized. Instead of looking at Uncle Milt, she kept her eyes fixed on a thin beam of light coming in through a key-hole window.

It felt like hours, but it was only seconds, when suddenly a rock struck the rafter by Uncle Milt's head. He dropped Deborahann's hand and lurched sideways. Another rock landed at his feet. The third was the kill-shot, striking him squarely on the back of the neck. It was a small stone, but it stung like hell.

"Goddamnit!"

Milt turned. At the top of the ladder Deborahann could just make out Yule, a stick-figure in overalls. He was out of rocks and scanning the loft for other potential weapons.

"You little shit!" Milt lunged in his direction, off-balance, and tripped over a rusty bucket.

The spell was broken. Deborahann ran to the ladder. Yule shoved her down and followed close behind. They ran like the devil was at their heels and didn't stop until they made it across the yard to the glowing beacon of the farmhouse. The porch was warm and safe. Inside they could hear the sounds of talk and laughter. The smell of maple-baked beans was in the air.

"Are you okay?" asked Yule.

"Yeah."

"Dawdling again, Mister and Missus Slowpokes," teased Aunt Moira, as they walked into the kitchen. "We were going to send out a search party."

***

Deborahann sat and cried. Tessa was speechless. She gave her mother a hug.

"Did you tell Grammy?"

Deborahann blew her nose.

"I told her, and she told me, 'You promise me: don't you ever tell anyone about this! You promise!'"

"What? That's it?"

"She was…embarrassed."

Tessa took a few moments to let this sink in. Her grandmother had only ever been good to her and Lilly.

"She was dead-wrong to do that. That must've made you feel like you were the one in the wrong—that wasn't right."

"I don't know...Telling wouldn't've helped anyway. No one would've believed me."

"You don't know that. Yule would've backed you up. Did you ever talk to him about it again?"

"No."

"It's all crazy...I can't believe Grammy did nothing."

"I think maybe she went to Uncle Milt privately and told him to leave me alone."

"How do you know that?"

"I don't know...I just think maybe."

"But wasn't he and Aunt Ella over at the house all the time?"

Deborahann sniffled.

"All the time! I had to give that big...PERVERT hugs! Mum made me! 'Come down and give your uncle a hug!'" Deborahann dissolved into tears again.

Tessa breathed out a heavy sigh.

"Listen to me, Mum: Grammy was wrong to act like that. Wrong, wrong, WRONG! She made you feel like you did a bad thing, and you did nothing wrong! You were just a kid! At the very least, she should've told him off, and she should've had nothing to do with him ever again. I can't believe she hung you out to dry like that!"

"But Tessie, we needed him. He paid half the bills at the house. We owed him money. Mum was under so much pressure after Dad died. I remember hearing her on the phone, talking to the bank. She'd act fancy, and tell them 'the funds are coming.' Then she'd get off the phone and cry. She didn't know I saw her. She'd pull herself together in front of people. She couldn't piss off Uncle Milt, Tessie. He and Aunt Ella were the only ones in the family who had any money."

"I can't believe you're defending her. She should've told Milt to fuck off! She should've protected you!"

Deborahann ignored the obscenity.

"It's not always that easy, Tessie-Bear. Life's not always that easy."

"But isn't this why you've been mad at her all these years? She didn't protect you."

"She might've...I don't know what she said to Uncle Milt."

"She didn't say a fucking word to him, Mum. You know she didn't."

They were both crying now.

Tessa tried to swallow, but her throat was dry. She had to convince her mother now. She might never bring it up again.

"It wasn't your fault."

More crying.

"Mum, please tell me...did anything else ever happen with Uncle Milt?"

"No," Deborahann said quickly.

Tessa paused.

"I'm so sorry that happened to you."

"It's okay, Tessie. I'm okay!"

Deborahann wiped her face with her hand and stood up. She smiled a horrible smile. The truck pulled into the driveway. Dad was home.

"I bet he'll be hungry and grumpy! No one wants a hungry, grumpy man!" Deborahann attempted a chuckle, and trotted out to the kitchen to make up Vic's plate.

***

Tessa didn't sleep much that night, piecing together the puzzle of her family's dysfunction. She and Lilly had never understood why their mother held Grammy Ada in such contempt. Deborahann did everything that was expected of her as the dutiful only daughter of an aging mother, running her to doctors' appointments and the like, but she never had anything positive to say about her mother, and would roll her eyes if anyone else did. Tessa and Lilly's working theory for explaining their mother's rudeness to her own mother was resentment over growing up poor and beholden to extended family. They were partly right.

To Lilly and Tessa, Grammy Ada could be annoying—and preachy—but her heart was in the right place. As kids, they had always fled to their grandmother's house just down the road when Vic and Deborahann had serious rows, about three times a week. The crumbling old house her mother had married at 20 to escape from, became the place the sisters escaped to. Grammy Ada had never asked questions when her granddaughters showed up in tears, though she did distract the girls with cookies, dolls and books. She was of the generation that looked the other way.

Tessa decided not to tell Lilly their mother's story; her younger sister was too sensitive and too enamoured of her vision of the Stevens family as wholesome, inviolate, and good, to process negative information about it. Tessa imagined the gears in Lilly's blonde head grinding to a halt, and smoke pouring out of her ears. She remembered Lilly's response whenever she broached the subject of their father's "issues." Lilly would remind Tessa of her own stubborn personality ("just like Dad"), and change the subject. The conspiracy of silence continued.

Tessa reflected that this was why she was drawn to academia: there was something civilized about discussing even unpleasant truths in a calm, objective way. She believed that all men and women of reason should be this way. She had once underlined a passage in Sinclair Lewis's *Main Street*, copying it on to the flyleaf: "…they saw no reason why anything which exists cannot also be acknowledged." What a contrast that idea was from those that proliferated in small towns like Beaconsbridge, places where people prided themselves on being plain-spoken, but where too many ignored abuse going on before their very eyes. They acted as if it was impolite, or crude, to draw attention to these things, as if the person who did so was the one responsible for bringing them into being. This was an ersatz gentility, a sham morality.

Over Christmas, Tessa took breaks from obsessing over her mother's story to obsess over the Andrew situation. Much to her dismay, he kept popping up in her mind, preventing her from concentrating on anything for very long, even her mother's revelation. Despite what she'd told Adrian, she had relented, of course, and had seen Andrew a few times before the Christmas break. He blew hot and cold. Their encounters were always semi-secretive and no longer satisfying. She knew she should've given up on him months ago, but she still clung to the forlorn hope that he would eventually come to his senses and realize he was in love with her. Over the break there had been radio silence on his end, and she was determined not to message him first. She refreshed her inbox constantly, but nothing. Finally, the day before she was scheduled to fly back to Sere Valley, she heard from him. The corny subject-head vanquished her completely.

Fr: Andrew Moore—aj.moore@svu.edu

To: Tessa Stevens—te.stevens@svu.edu

Subject: Tessa Fair...

Date: Dec. 30, 2016, 3:32 p.m.

Tessa Fair,

I have but one question for you, lithesome lady of light and laughter:

Can you pronounce "Proust" correctly yet?

Your faithful knight,

Andrew

p.s. When will I see you next? There's no one I'd rather trip the light fantastic with...

If Tessa could have blushed, she would have. She had mispronounced Proust as "prowst" once in a conversation and he had never let her live it down. His upbringing always gave him the advantage over her. She read constantly but her roots showed. She had a wide vocabulary of words she could write but not pronounce because she had never heard them spoken aloud. Embarrassed, Tessa marched downstairs and purposely distracted herself with a few rounds of Chinese checkers with Lilly, to kill time before responding.

Fr: Tessa Stevens—te.stevens@svu.edu

To: Andrew Moore—aj.moore@svu.edu

Subject: RE: Tessa Fair...

Date: Dec. 30, 2016, 4:45 p.m.

Faithful knight,

I can pronounce Proust, but can you pronounce Solzhenitsyn? All break, I've read nothing but *The Gulag Archipelago* and that dreadful Milford textbook Flamm insists all the

Comp instructors use this term. Rough going. I could badly use a diversion. Will you be back in town for New Year's Eve? I get back tomorrow afternoon.

Ever and Always,

Tessa the Quite Unfair

p.s. Text me. Sometimes I can get a signal out here.

She had tried to match his off-hand tone. Tessa deleted and re-typed the p.s. a half-dozen times. *Too desperate? Too obvious?* she wondered.

"Tessa! Tessa!" Vic bellowed from downstairs. He was having trouble with the computer.

"Can't Lilly help? I'm busy!"

A pause. Evidently, Lilly was out.

"Get your arse down here! Now!"

Tessa winced. "Arse" was a bad sign. Normally he would've been content with yelling, "Get down here now!"

Tessa slowly made her way downstairs, and placed herself at her father's disposal, daring to show some annoyance. As always, Mum hovered nearby, nervously giggling, to provide a buffer.

"Yer the Ph.D. Can you fix this? SHE'S useless"—he pointed at Deborahann. Vic explained the problem. He couldn't figure out how to attach picture files to emails with his new email service provider.

Tessa leaned in and gingerly touched the resting mouse, careful not to get too close to her father. He reclaimed his space, pushing out his elbows to carve more out.

"Move!"

Tessa tensed but held her ground.

"Do you want me to help you or not? I can't stand here and explain it to you, step by step." she said, through gritted teeth. "Just let me do it."

"Just explain it!"

"It's kind of tricky, isn't it, honey?" said Deborahann, popping her head in from the kitchen.

Vic forced Tessa to spend 20 agonizing minutes at his side, slowly and repeatedly explaining how to do this simple task, before he would allow her to leave. ("No, just click once…Once. No, you highlighted the wrong one. Click anywhere in the black to un-highlight it. No. No. Try again.") She knew if she attempted to leave, he would have no qualms about physically dragging her back downstairs to help him, as one would a recalcitrant toddler. He'd done it before. Emails with picture files finally sent, Vic waved her off with a grunt, without looking up.

That evening before bed, Tessa was packing and still stewing over the incident as her mother dropped off fresh laundry.

"That's not normal, Mum, the way he makes us do things like that."

"Oh hon-bun, helping your Dad on the computer is no big deal."

"It's not, and I wouldn't mind if he didn't force us to and act so angry when I'm the one doing *him* a favor."

"He's embarrassed he can't do it himself, but I'm sure he's grateful. Your father's just not good at showing his emotions."

"That's because he doesn't have any," observed Tessa.

"Tessa…"

"He's a hamster, Mum, an angry hamster."

"Anger's an emotion," Deborahann replied, with a wry smile.

"Yes, the most primitive one."

Deborahann set the laundry basket down on the bed. She sat beside it, her bottom cratering the mattress.

"He doesn't have any empathy," Tessa said. "He doesn't see what other people do for him. Ever."

Her mother sighed. Deborahann began rolling up each garment tightly, and packing them in Tessa's already full-to-the-brim suitcase. It was after midnight.

"Mum, leave it. I'll finish tomorrow."

"You won't have time before the flight. It'll be rush-and-tear as it is."

Deborahann finished the packing. She was pleased that she'd managed to cram in every last item—and with a little extra space left over for the cookies and the new knitted socks she planned on adding tomorrow as a surprise.

"Did you have a nice Christmas break?"

"Yes, Mum."

"Good! I missed my girls. I love having you home."

"'Night, Mum."

"'Night 'night, Tessie-Bear!"

Deborahann kissed her grown daughter on the head.

Tessa watched her mother pad out of the room. Deborahann's face suddenly creased with a frown, and she sped up. Tessa knew she was trying to make it to bed before he yelled at her to hurry up.

Chapter Eleven: Mothers and Other Crosses to Bear

Deborahann steeled herself for the drop-off at her mother's. It was a Saturday afternoon. As usual, she had given herself many more "urgent" errands to run that day than it was physically possible to do, leaving her in a state of low-level anxiety. She was always running an hour behind. Deborahann was late for life. She'd progressed to Errand #5 of the day, the most tedious on her list. She drove down the gravel driveway to the drafty, vaguely Gothic Revival-style house she had grown up in, the house her octogenarian mother had lived in for over 50 years, most of those as an increasingly poor widow (as the insurance money and the scanty savings Jack left them trickled away to naught). The old house was the picture of respectable New Brunswick poverty: the sagging pitched roof, the chipped white paint, the scabrous gingerbread trim. Deborahann, who lived just down the road, was there at least once a week, every week, and every time she stepped inside she felt her blood pressure rise.

She knocked once, then let herself in through the unfinished area of the house Ada called the "outside kitchen." It was full of random rusted things; plastic bags; wicker baskets; mousetraps; an aloe vera plant, a yellowed fern, snowshoes that hadn't been worn in a half-century; Tupperware; a faded poster celebrating the 1967 Canadian centennial; a World War Two-era army helmet; an enormous crock-pot; a one-eyed porcelain doll in Victorian dress named Wilhelmina; a tin wash-tub; a loudly humming freezer; and a washer and dryer set of advanced years. Deborahann threaded her way through the familiar chaos. She planned on being in and out in five minutes.

"Deborahann? Is that you?" her mother hollered from the kitchen. "Shut the front door! Yer letting the heat out!"

Ada feigned deafness when convenient, but she never failed to hear the arrival of a visitor.

Deborahann entered the orange and brown 1960s era kitchen, greeting her mother with an "I only have five minutes, Mum."

Ada made a sour face. She was sipping orange pekoe tea at her kitchen table, a faux-wood Formica affair.

"Luckily, they did have an Extra-Large," said Deborahann, setting her purse and a Sears bag down on the table.

The bag contained a peach-colored sweater, her Christmas gift to her mother from a week ago. She had exchanged a Large for it that morning in Moncton. Her mother didn't own a car or even drive—had never driven—and lived an hour away from the nearest mall, doctor, or major grocery store. Since Jack died in '74, Ada had relied on family and friends to drive her to appointments, and do most of her errands for her. "Look to the Lord," was Ada's motto. Deborahann's motto was "the Lord helps those who help themselves." They were both always right.

Ada didn't look inside the bag.

"I s'pose that'll be too big."

"Let me know, I can get the money for it."

"Never mind money...I don't s'pose you have time for a cup of tea?" asked Ada, knowing the answer.

"I told you, I'm busy today, Mum," said Deborahann. "I have two more stops before home, and then I need to do some invoices for Vic."

Ada carried on as if she'd heard nothing.

"I've had a busy morning. Well sir! Heard a knock on my door around 9:00—was just nicely finishing up the dishes—and who do you think it was? Pastor and Mrs. Fudge! They dropped off a fruit basket someone left them at the church. Pastor Fudge gets indigestion something terr'ble. Can't touch acidic things. They stayed for a cup of tea and some date squares."

Deborahan grunted. Instead of sitting at the table with her mother, she was up picking dead-heads off the begonia.

"The pastor always says the same thing: that I remind him of his Mum. She passed away a few years ago, back in Gander."

"Uh huh."

That suckhole, Fudge, thought Deborahhann. Aloud, she said, "Did he let Margaret get a word in edgewise today?"

"She's an awful queer woman," said Ada lugubriously. "Poor man."

Deborahann grunted again.

"Idella's poorly, you know. They say she's not coming home from the hospital this time," said Ada. "Are you going to get out to see her? She was yer father's favorite cousin."

"I know, Mum."

"Don't put it off until it's too late. Soon I'll be the last of my generation still with us…"

"You've been saying that for 10 years, Mum," said Deborahann (adding, in her head, "and you're still with us").

Ada had already moved on.

"Are you going out to the benefit Monday at the church?" (Ada, like all elderly New Brunswickers of her class, pronounced it "Mun-dee.")

"Hadn't planned on it."

"Sue Pickering's singing. She was some good at the jamboree last year. You remember her, don't you? Her mother was a Porter Brook Blakeney."

Deborahann grabbed her purse.

"Well, I gotta' go."

"Don't forget your slacks!"

Ada scurried to the sewing machine. At 85, she was still hemming her daughter's clothes for her.

"Thanks Mum," said Deborahann, retreating with the slacks.

"Wait! I've got peanut butter balls for Victor in the fridge," said Ada.

"He doesn't need more sweets," called out Deborahann. She'd made it as far as the outside kitchen.

"You wait!" yelled Ada

"Here," Ada panted, catching her daughter in time. She triumphantly shoved the Tupperware into Deborahann's hands.

"Thank *you*," said Deborahann, 52, as sarcastically as a teenager.

"Yer welcome!" puffed Ada.

As she made the quick drive back to the house, Deborahann tried her best to push aside the riotous thoughts. Her mother irritated her at the best of times, but since confiding in Tessa, she felt more than resentment. She felt rage. Keeping it under control was exhausting. She wasn't sure how she'd managed it over Christmas; the presence of other family members had perhaps provided a buffer. Deborahann still couldn't believe she'd told Tessa. She hadn't allowed herself to tell anyone that story, or even articulate it in her head, for over 40 years. She certainly hadn't told Vic. Like everyone in Beaconsbridge, he was well aware of Milton

Blakeney's reputation as an old lech, but he never thought to ask his wife why she despised her uncle, or why she avoided all Blakeney family reunions, despite her mother's repeated proddings.

Uncle Milt's death, and Deborahann's subsequent revelations to Tessa, began an excavation. As a child, Deborahann had buried the memories deep underground. They were something to think about some day in the far-off future when she finally had the time and the strength to do so. Today there were too many bills, too many responsibilities, too many appointments, too many commands from Vic demanding her immediate attention. If she allowed herself to think about the past, it could destroy her. And so there were layers upon layers of repressed memories, a Pompeii of dangerous thoughts and emotions. Things she didn't dare remember. It was safer to just pile the dirt high above them.

But rotten things grew out of the soil where the bodies lay buried. Clammy tentacles pushed their way out of the dirt, and arose, blinking, into the light. One day at work that November, Elinor politely said, "So sorry to hear about your uncle," referring to the circulating news of old Milt Blakeney's palliative state. "Only the good die young," Deborahann replied. Elinor looked shocked. For the rest of the day, Deborahann kicked herself for being indiscreet.

Turning the corner home, Deborahann remembered other uncomfortable moments. One Sunday at Beaconsbridge Baptist, a special speaker gave a presentation to raise money for Lockland House, a Fredericton charity that provided support for the adult survivors of child sexual and physical abuse. Deborahann had struggled so mightily to control her emotions in church that she had to call in sick on Monday with a migraine.

Even then, a few years back, just to say the words "sexual abuse" in Beaconsbridge was a breakthrough, sending a shockwave through the congregation. So remote was the village from changes in The Outside World, so stalled in the 1950s (for good and for ill), that people still used euphemisms. Pedophiles who abused male minors might be referred to, with a nervous giggle, as "too fond of the little boys." The digital penetration of a six-year old girl by an older cousin might be described thusly: "Well, he lifted her skirt and just went to town." Deborahann recalled hearing her mother recently tell Tessa and Lilly that Cousin Billy, Ada's adored nephew, was "away for a while right now." Dear Billy was "away," Deborahann knew, doing time for rape.

Deborahann reflected that the ruling faith of Beaconsbridge protected the Billies and the Miltons. First of all, more often than not the victim was blamed for bringing up the unseemly matter of his or her own victimhood. Deborahann still remembered the look of disgust on her mother's face when she told her what Uncle Milt did in the barn. That look told her that these things—these *sinful* things—were too vile to discuss. Despite her unwilling part in it all, child Deborahann was made to feel that she was to blame, not her adult uncle. He maintained a dignified silence, Ada's words to her implied, while Deborahann had the temerity to tell, making her mother uncomfortable, and possibly threatening the unity of the extended family structure.

Second of all, there was the Christian duty of love and forgiveness: "Love the sinner, hate the sin," Deborahann was always told by her mother. And there were other favored Bible verses:

"Turn the other cheek."

"Love thy enemies; pray for those who persecute you."

These prescriptions placed the burden of emotional labor on the victim, not the perpetrator. The victim was expected to "suck it up, buttercup," and to "forgive and forget." And behind the benign guise of forgiveness, the community enabled abusers.

Deborahann parked the car and walked inside the house in a brown study. Vic greeted her from his usual spot in the living room. Over the blaring television, he called out, "Yer late!"

Deborahann absentmindedly moved Vic's work boots from the welcome mat to the shoe rack and hung up his coat, which he'd tossed on the table.

"Mum wouldn't let me get away."

"Yap yap yap," said Vic. He was still wearing his grease-splattered work overalls.

"I'm starving. You knew I'd be working all afternoon and hungry, and you still dawdled. And I bet you didn't even start the invoices this morning."

Deborahann dabbed at a grease spot on the recliner.

"Bloody inconsiderate," said Vic.

"How did it go with Marshall's Ford?" she asked.

"The whole damn transmission's blown," he replied, without looking up from *The Highlander* rerun. "Where's supper?"

"Nice to see you too, honey." She attempted a joke.

"Don't be smart."

Deborahann tried again to soothe him, "Mum sent over your favorite! Peanut butter balls."

She held up the Tupperware in a propitiatory gesture.

Vic looked up, eyes blazing. His right hand shot out and grabbed the plastic container from her. He whipped it across the room. The top popped off as it hit the wall, sending sweets ricocheting everywhere.

"I told you I was on a diet after Christmas! I don't want this crap in the house!"

Deborahann ran to clean up the mess.

"Get outta' the road!"

Deborahann was crouched in front of him, picking up peanut butter balls, and blocking the television screen.

"Sorry."

She moved faster, completing the task, and retreated to the kitchen. She then quickly made a Caesar salad with the artificial bacon bits Vic loved, and popped some breaded chicken strips into the oven.

The sooner he's fed, the sooner he'll calm down, Deborahann thought. *He's so tired. He probably can't help it. I wish we could still afford Darren part-time to help. Vic's behind at the garage all the time now.*

Deborahann understood Vic like no one else did. She'd observed his origin family dynamics for decades. Vic was the youngest of three sons, a caboose child born almost a decade later than the others. His father, Winthrop Stevens, now deceased, was a local contractor who had provided a comfortable living for his family. He had also been a war hero, and was thus beyond reproach in Beaconsbridge. Ruby Stevens, née Forsythe, was Vic's mother. Once vivacious, she was now a well-to-do, querulous elderly widow. Vic's two older brothers, David and Richard—an accountant and an office manager, respectively—could do no wrong in the eyes of Winthrop and Ruby. Vic had struggled academically, unlike his older brothers, to whom he was often unfavorably compared.

Winthrop had paid little attention to Victor. Early on, he sized up his youngest son as a dullard, and his opinion never changed. His other two sons were of above-average intelligence, with a poise to their stolidity, while Victor was thick as a plank, and panicky as a rabbit when pushed out of his intellectual comfort zone, which was often. Victor told his wife that as a boy he "caught hell" from his father for bringing home report cards full of Cs and Ds. Dave and Rich often teased their younger brother. At family get-togethers they liked to gang up on him, repeating the line: "Hi, my name is Victor and I am slooooooooow." Victor held his tongue but exploded with anger to Deborahann when they got home.

Publicly, Vic honored his late father as a war veteran. Every Remembrance Day, he solemnly placed a wreath on the Beaconsbridge cenotaph monument, thus checking the boxes for "filial" and "patriotic" all in one go. Vic puffed up with dignity before the approving eyes of the crowd. But back at home he would slam doors and rage at Deborahann about a bank teller: "That idiot Shayna at the Credit Union, talking down to me again! Who the hell does she think she is?"

Deborahann understood that Vic's sensitivity to perceived slights was rooted in his childhood. When she tried to explain these things to an exasperated Tessa, usually after Vic had "acted up"—Deborahann's favorite euphemism for behaviors ranging from shouting to throwing an entire pot roast in the garbage—her oldest daughter fumed. "I don't care about the pathogenesis!" she once yelled at her mother, after yet another of Vic's out-of-control episodes. Deborahann didn't know what a pathogenesis was, but she did know Tessa's patience with her father's "quirks" (another Deborahann term) decreased with every visit home.

Deborahann brooded over these things while she cleaned the grubby kitchen until it was once again pristine. Then she threw a ball around with Trixie in the frozen backyard. (After two minutes, Vic yelled out the backdoor: "The invoices!" Scanning for neighbors, Deborahann hurried back in.) Vic demanded tea and cookies after supper; he could not or would not prepare them himself. ("I've been working all day while you've been out gadding.") It was after 8:00 by the time Deborahann finally settled into the tiny, closet-like room upstairs which served as Vic's office, and started on the pile of paperwork he'd left for her.

She was distracted by the blare of the television downstairs. She knew Vic wasn't listening to it. As he did every night after supper, served to him in his recliner, Vic entered into a semi-catatonic state in front of the television. There he lay for hours, half-awake and half-asleep, like a lizard in the sun. He would eventually doze with the television volume on maximum, a wet patch of drool spreading down his shirt. During this time, no one else was allowed to use the television, even if he was sound asleep, and no one dared suggest he turn the volume down or the tv off—this would surely lead to a complete Victor meltdown. After four hours or so of this, he would go to bed. This routine was one of the many "quirks" to which Tessa now objected, though Lilly always brushed it off as "typical Dad."

Victor's nightly television stupor was the natural result of both physical exhaustion and a paucity of mental resources. Unlike Deborahann, who gardened in the summer, and painted in the winter, or his daughters, both of whom read voraciously, Victor had no intellectual pursuits or hobbies. He depleted his animal energy through his work as a mechanic, and then he came home and didn't so much watch television as camp out in front of it, letting his grey matter go on auto-pilot. A near-illiterate, with the zeal of an Aztec appeasing his Gods, every Sunday morning Vic stumbled through his King James Version Bible reading, in preparation for Sunday school. He would solemnly remove his Walmart reading glasses from their pleather case, place them below the bridge of his nose, and read, tracing the passage, word by word, with a work-roughened index finger. He understood about 25 per cent of what he read, which he interpreted literally, and within a modern context. Other than the Bible, Vic hadn't read a book since high school.

But he was an excellent mechanic, and like many of the Beaconsbridge Baptists at that time, a teetotaller. His ill temper couldn't be blamed on drink.

He works hard and he's a good provider, thought Deborahann, as she flipped through the stack of paperwork. *The mortgage is almost paid off. We'll get there.*

She rubbed her eyes. Downstairs the television boomed. The lovable, paunchy patriarch on the sitcom delivered his punchline: "...but don't ask me. Ask my better half!" An even louder laugh-track followed. Deborahann sipped her cold tea and tried to focus. She had hours of work ahead of her.

***

That night in Sere Valley, Tessa was reading in bed. She took a break and refreshed the email on her phone. That was a mistake. There were 35 new messages, all from the Womyn's Scholars Group. The oldest email in the thread began with some surprising announcements.

Fr: Yvonne Addams—y.addams@svu.edu

To: Womyn's Scholars Group Listserv

Subject: Introducing Your New Co-President: Me!

Date: Jan. 9, 2017, 8:30 p.m.

Dear Colleagues,

Allow me to officially introduce myself: my name is Dr. Yvonne Addams, and I will be your new Co-President, and the new Administrator of this listserv! I will be taking over the latter from Amy, who's done a fantastic job and deserves a break.

For those who don't know me already (or who didn't attend the last meeting before the holidays), I was hired in fall 2015 in the Department of Women and Gender Studies. I am currently teaching WGST 1020: Introduction to Women and Gender Studies and WGST 2050:

Diverse Femininities: An Intersectional Journey. I'm delighted to bring a new sensibility and awareness to SVU, and to this group.

In addition to our usual discussions on publishing, teaching, and supporting other women in academia, in the months to come I will be emailing articles, opinion-pieces, and other news of note specifically related to women of color, in and out of the academy. As discussed at the last meeting, it is critical that the Womyn's Scholars Group more actively engage with the most important issues of the day. Remember: IGNORANCE IS NOT AN OPTION! WE ARE ALL INVOLVED!

As such, as administrator, I am implementing a new rule, approved by the membership last meeting: only women of color are invited to respond to this type of email, which will be identified in the subject-head by the acronym "WOCO" (Women of Color Only). This policy will allow other members of this group the unique opportunity to LISTEN and LEARN. (If you have any questions on this new policy, please don't hesitate to drop me a line!)

When I'm not consciousness-raising or conducting research, I enjoy knitting and playing the piano. I also make a mean paella. (Stay tuned for the next potluck!)

In Solidarity,

Yvonne

p.s. Come say Hi any time! I'm in Anderson 405.

--Yvonne Addams

Co-President, Womyn's Scholars Group

Assistant Professor, Department of Women and Gender Studies

Sere Valley University

Fr: Amy Mephistos— a.mephistos@svu.edu

To: Womyn's Scholars Group Listserv

Subject: RE: Introducing Your New Co-President: Me!

Date: Jan. 9, 2017, 8:34 p.m.

Dear Colleagues,

    Let me be the first to welcome our new Co-President to the fold: welcome Yvonne! I look forward to learning more about these important political issues in the months to come.

    Stay woke, ladies!

    Amy

--Amy Mephistos

Co-President, Womyn's Scholars Group

Associate Professor, Department of Women and Gender Studies

Sere Valley University

Fr: Jessica Mincing—jd.mincing@svu.edu

To: Womyn's Scholars Group Listserv

Subject: RE: RE: Introducing Your New Co-President: Me!

Date: Jan. 9, 2017, 8:39 p.m.

Another big welcome to Yvonne!

    The educational "WOCO" emails are a great idea. Just a quick question, re: the new rule: is it acceptable for non-WOC to reply-all to these email discussion links with a thumbs-up or other emoji, to show solidarity?

--Jessica Mincing

Assistant Professor, Department of English Literature

Sere Valley University

Fr: Yvonne Addams—y.addams@svu.edu

To: Womyn's Scholars Group Listserv

Subject: RE: RE: RE: Introducing Your New Co-President: Me!

Date: Jan. 9, 2017, 8:43 p.m.

Hi Jessica—Thanks for asking, but I'm afraid that's a No. Thin end of the wedge, as they say. I'm sure you understand. ☺

--Yvonne Addams

Co-President, Womyn's Scholars Group

Assistant Professor, Department of Women and Gender Studies

Sere Valley University

Fr: Jessica Mincing—jd.mincing@svu.edu

To: Womyn's Scholars' Group Listserv

Subject: RE: RE: RE: RE: Introducing Your New Co-President: Me!

Date: Jan. 9, 2017, 8:45 p.m.

Absolutely! That's fine by me!

--Jessica Mincing

Assistant Professor, Department of English Literature

Sere Valley University

Fr: Destiny Claremont—d.claremont@svu.edu

To: Womyn's Scholars Group Listserv

Subject: RE: RE: RE: RE: RE: Introducing Your New Co-President: Me!

Date: Jan. 9, 2017, 8:50 p.m.

Hello Yvonne,

I also have a question: how will you, as administrator, be able to determine whether or not someone replying to an email thread is a "woman of color"?

Thank you,

Destiny

--Destiny Claremont

Assistant Professor, Department of Theatre Arts

Sere Valley University

Fr: Yvonne Addams—y.addams@svu.edu

To: Womyn's Scholars Group Listserv

Subject: RE: RE: RE: RE: RE: RE: Introducing Your New Co-President: Me!

Date: Jan. 9, 2017, 9:04 p.m.

Hi Destiny—That's simple. If I am unfamiliar with the member in question, I will look her up in the SVU faculty directory and find her profile photo. Although it is true that some women of color can "pass" as non-WOC and much more infrequently, vice-versa, and racial identification can be rather difficult, I am confident that I will be able to make this determination, based on the profile pic. And if not, I will just email the person and ask that she racially identify herself. Hope that helps! ☺

--Yvonne Addams

Co-President, Womyn's Scholars Group

Assistant Professor, Department of Women and Gender Studies

Sere Valley University

Fr: Destiny Claremont—d.claremont@svu.edu

To: Womyn's Scholars Group Listserv

Subject: RE: RE: RE: RE: RE: RE: Introducing Your New Co-President: Me!

Date: Jan. 9, 2017, 9:22 p.m.

    Racial identification is indeed difficult, Yvonne, as administrators throughout history could tell you. Would it be easier for you if either the "women of color" like me or the white members of this group updated their profile pictures to include a clear mark of identification on their person? Maybe a yellow star?

--Destiny Claremont

Assistant Professor, Department of Theatre Arts

Sere Valley University

    Adrian let out a low whistle as Tessa read aloud the Destiny email over breakfast the next morning.

    "Oooh, the nuclear option. Quick, get Mum on the phone. I'm switching teams. I think I'm in love with Destiny."

    "You'll have to fight me for her," said Tessa. "She went there. I was impressed."

    "Then what happened?"

"All hell broke loose on the listserv. Most of the group sided with Yvonne, but a few sided with Destiny. The Destiny-ites basically said it was racist to bar group members from discussions based on their skin color. The Yvonne-ites said—among other things—that people can only be racist if they have power, so clearly women of color cannot be racist."

"But Yvonne is the fucking co-president of the group! She makes the rules! How does she not have the power in this instance?"

"They mean *historically*, Adrian."

"Well *historically* the Romans led the Brits around by the nose, but that doesn't mean I can't be racist toward Italians today, if I feel like it. Can and *will*. Kiss my pale Celtic ass, Caesar, you colonizing son of a bitch."

Tessa didn't bother looking up from her toast and marmalade.

"I suppose Destiny confuses the essentializing Yvonne-and-Amy-types," Adrian continued. "She's biracial, right? So she's both oppressor and oppressed—depends on whether or not she's hit the tanning salon that day."

"She *is* a paradox for them," Tessa admitted.

"What else did Destiny say?" asked Adrian, sipping his coffee.

"Nothing. She mysteriously disappeared. Then this morning Yvonne sent out an email notification saying some members were being disciplined for 'uncollegial' remarks."

"Yeah, calling the new administrator a Nazi probably counts as uncollegial. Even more uncollegial when you're absolutely right," said Adrian. "I can just imagine Yvonne, getting out a ruler and measuring the width of noses on profile pics. What an idiot."

"Why would Destiny care so much?" asked Tessa, who was also wondering if the marmalade had expired. "She's a woman of color. So she still gets to comment on Yvonne's stupid political emails."

"This may come as a shock to you, my dear true believer in identity politics, but not everyone makes decisions based on their skin color or genitalia. Some people have principles."

"I make decisions based on my genitalia!" shouted Mark from upstairs.

Tessa gulped down the dregs of her coffee.

Adrian's insufferable when he's right, she thought.

She's still grumpy Andrew ditched her at New Years', Adrian thought, as he loaded his Adam Smith mug into the dishwasher.

Chapter Twelve: A Gentle Inquisition

Tessa was alone that afternoon in her office on campus, pacing back and forth in the cramped space. She had an hour to kill until the Search Committee interview, followed by what would surely be an equally awkward dinner out at the only venue in Sere Valley deemed formal enough for such occasions, Cucina Stefano.

She had made it through the first few sets of flaming hoops without searing her ass—only a light browning, like a gently toasted marshmallow. In early January, she was finally informed by Flamm she'd been selected for the short-list of four candidates for the position of tenure-track Assistant Professor of English at SVU. As an internal candidate, she bypassed much of the tedious getting-to-know-you academic interview routine, other than the teaching talk component, which she had completed the day before. Flamm told her she was the only internal candidate, and ominously, that she should be pleased that the Search Committee was considering a "known quantity"—whatever that meant. Pearl, Tessa's man on the inside, was professional and didn't pass on any information about the candidate search, but she did let slip that the other three were all very junior, new Ph.D.s, like Tessa.

Tessa had no way of sizing up the competition, though she was pretty sure she'd seen one of the candidates. Through the departmental rumor mill, she had learned that one of them was an American being flown in for her interview. A week before her own interview, while picking up her campus mail, Tessa spied a thin, youngish blonde woman backing out of Flamm's office. Something told her it was the American. Overdressed by the standards of the English Department (best described as Cautious Frump Chic), the blonde carried a briefcase and was giggling in the self-conscious way straight female supplicants are obliged to giggle at the (bad) jokes of their straight male potential bosses. She looked young, cute and pliable. *Just what Flamm likes*, Tessa had worried at the time.

She wasn't any more confident today about her chances. While she waited for her interview, she tried to psych herself up, mentally reviewing everything in her CV that made her a strong candidate. She had given her heart and soul to the Department as a graduate student and sessional instructor, never turning down a difficult teaching assignment, taking on Writing Center work other instructors loathed, and representing the Department at events no one else wanted to attend. She often volunteered before she was voluntold. On the academic side of things, she was in the middle of the pack, with a few good publications. She had done well in her graduate courses, area exams, and the dissertation defense. She had finished her dissertation in four and a half years, which was almost unheard of in her field; among her peers who had actually completed the degree, the average was more like eight.

The X-factor, she knew, was departmental politics. *Obviously, Wagband's out to get me*, thought Tessa, eyes narrowing as she remembered her ex-supervisor. Wagband wasn't on the Search Committee, but Jessica Mincing, her running dog, was. How much power, if any, was wielded by the two of them, remained unclear.

The job ad hadn't been helpful. It was a jumble of politically correct buzz-words and academic jibber-jabber, obviously the half-assed result of multiple political compromises. As customary for all faculty jobs, the applicants were required to submit a packet of application documents thicker than a Gutenberg Bible—this despite the fact that the new hire would be selected primarily based on the Committee's gut feelings (and in some cases, level of sexual arousal). Besides a letter of application, references, transcripts, curriculum vitae, teaching evaluations (for ballast), samples of scholarly work, and a Statement of Teaching Philosophy, this year, under the influence of the Office of Equity and Diversity, a new and curious document was also required: a "Statement of Commitment to Multiculturalism." As per the job ad: "Sere Valley University's student body is reflective of the multicultural nature of Canada as a whole. In the Statement of Commitment to Multiculturalism, the candidate should address how the value of multiculturalism is supported in their teaching…"

Tessa had wracked her brain over this one. In the end, her completed Statement had zero substance, but was rich in words and phrases that would elicit Pavlovian responses from the Search Committee. She wrote some poppycock about "transactional and Freirian" exchanges she had had at the Writing Center with members of "traditionally underrepresented" groups, specifically, indigenous students. She felt ill as she wrote; Lesley Two-Bear was her friend.

As usual, Adrian hadn't helped matters. As Tessa paced her office, her mind wandered back to the disconcerting conversation she had had with him in November, while she was working on the Statement.

"What the fuck does multiculturalism have to do with teaching academic writing anyway?" Adrian had asked.

"Well, as the ad says, SVU is multicultural, so…"

"No it's not. Let's get real here: SVU is a cow college on the Canadian prairies. It's 95% potato-eating whiteys like us, along with a tiny percentage of international students—ones who probably couldn't afford better schools in the U.S. or the U.K. Oh, and a handful of local indigenous students the admin endlessly panders to but doesn't really give a shit about."

"That's cynical of you, Adrian. Many of my colleagues care a great deal about indigenous students."

He'd shrugged.

"Sure they do. The drum circles look great in the brochures—I'll give them that. But if you think it's a coincidence that all the SVU promo materials star that one indigenous guy on campus everyone knows, you're daft."

Adrian had glanced down at the job ad up on Tessa's laptop and frowned.

"And how do you 'develop pedagogies' for 'multicultural' students? Do you patronize black students by dropping a little Kendrick Lamar for rhetorical analysis? Just what they want to discuss with their little white female prof, I'm sure...As if they can't handle Shakespeare—that's the implication of such pedagogy. Why not just treat everyone the same?"

Tessa looked sheepish. She *had* incorporated Jay-Z lyrics for rhetorical analysis in class last term, in an attempt to be topical and relevant.

"That's the old way of doing things. It doesn't recognize that different groups of people face different challenges. A good instructor should try to accommodate the needs of a diverse student body."

"Yeah, yeah, I attended that bullshit diversity training with you, remember? Only I spat out the Kool-aid. Of course, what that kind of talk boils down to in real life is applying a shit-ton of racist stereotypes. You assume, for example, that indigenous students are going to be poor and under-educated, and need hand-holding. It's insulting. They're individuals, not 'examples of their race.'"

"This is not helping me with my Statement."

"Side-note," continued Adrian, barely looking up from his well-worn copy of *The Road to Serfdom*, "The people who blather on and on about the virtues of multiculturalism are probably secretly extremely racist, and overcompensating. Just like the politicians who yammer on and on about the sanctity of marriage, then get caught with boys in bathroom stalls. Normal people don't fixate on race, and aren't constantly patting themselves on the back for having this many black friends, or this many indigenous students, or whatever."

"We're very lucky that we don't have to 'fixate on race,' Adrian. Some people don't have that luxury."

"Ahh, more of the Party line. Don't tell me that 'people of color'—or queers like me, or transgender people, or fill-in-your-victim-group-here—are *systematically* mistreated today in the places where the North American elite are processed. Like universities. Or Big Tech. If anything, we're treated very carefully in such places, because everyone is so fucking terrified of being accused of bigotry or racism. Nothing kills a career deader than that. You're better off being accused of pedophilia."

"There are still bigots and racists, even here. Even now. Professor Stanfield?" Tessa said, referring to an elderly professor in the English Department notorious for talking down to women and students of color.

"That old geezer has one foot in the grave and the other on a banana peel," said Adrian. "He's irrelevant. The power brokers of today aren't Stanfields. They're Zuckerbergs."

Tessa wondered if any of the professors in the Department knew she questioned the orthodoxy of "social justice," "equity," and all the other misleading Orwellian terms bandied about at SVU. She also wondered how many of them were true believers themselves, and how many were simply pragmatists with careers to advance and bills to pay.

Tessa tried to clear her head of these troublesome thoughts, and focus on the trial ahead. She checked her watch. It was time. She straightened her new navy blazer, a magical garment that made her feel like she knew what she was talking about, and walked a few doors down to Pearl's office.

"Go get 'em, girl!" Pearl whispered, before Flamm appeared as planned to escort Tessa to the interview room down the hall. As they entered the room, all chit-chat halted.

"There's the hot seat," said Flamm, with a forced chuckle. Tessa took the proffered seat, and smiled shyly. To her left and right sat Search Committee members. Tessa's mind instantly ranked them according to their official status and place in the academic hierarchy: Conrad Christiansen, Classics Department Chair and Professor; Edwin Flamm, Committee Chair, English Department Chair, and Associate Professor; Thomas Mills, Associate Professor, Kinesiology Department; Jessica Mincing, Assistant Professor, English Department; and Angelika Franco, Lecturer, Limited Term Appointment (one year), Faculty of Education. Tessa knew Flamm, Mincing, and Franco personally, and the other two vaguely by reputation.

Ever a font of useful gossip, Pearl had filled in the gaps for her. Mills was a hail-fellow-well-met, sailing along happily to retirement. Christiansen was a harmless relic, still stubbornly holding out in Classics, having repeatedly refused the Dean's offers of a gold-plated retirement package.

Flamm, oily as a diner dishrag, cleared his throat and launched into his opening remarks on how pleased the Committee was to have the opportunity to learn more about Tessa as "a scholar and a potential colleague." He was in what Pearl sarcastically referred to, to Tessa, as "maximum charm mode." Tessa mirrored back his smile. Flamm continued, explaining the format of the interview: each committee member would pose two questions to Tessa on topics of his or her choice. Following the panel interview, they would adjourn and meet later for dinner.

"We'll begin with Dr. Mincing and work our way around the table," said Flamm, turning to his colleague. His face took on a serious cast as he briefly wondered whether or not Mincing was wearing a push-up bra. *They look bigger.*

Mincing noticed her Chair's expression and blushed. *I knew he wasn't happy I turned down repping the Student Success Committee. But I'm already busy with the Innovations Committee!* She clutched her trusty Montblanc, unconsciously drawing strength from a pen that cost more than her father made in two weeks of work.

Mincing made appropriate noises about enjoying Tessa's teaching talk from the day before, then began, "My two questions are related. *As a member of the Innovations in Teaching Committee*, these questions are of particular interest to me. You touched on this in your cover letter, but I was wondering how you specifically incorporate appropriate technologies into the classroom, and what technological changes do you foresee having the greatest impact on the university in the near future?"

There, thought Mincing, who had changed her questions on the spot. *See, Edwin. I'm doing my share!*

Fuck, thought Tessa. Despite her age, she rivalled only Christiansen as contender for Top Luddite in the room.

Tessa hated using new technologies for teaching. For one thing, "new technology" in most Canadian universities actually translated to "MySpace era technology." She used SVU's "learning management" software only because she had to, posting her lecture PowerPoints and course hand-outs there. It was a pointless duplication of effort and a positive pedagogical ill, in her opinion, because students who knew their lectures would be posted online were less likely to a.) show up for class, and b.) pay attention if they did bother showing up. She remembered in graduate school the utter pointlessness of Flamm's attempts at incorporating technology into his Milton course. Students were required to post comments to an online discussion board every week, on questions from the readings. The resulting "powerful online dialogue" (Flamm's words) was as stilted as it was artificial.

In her cover letter, Tessa's rote two sentences on technology in the classroom were Grade A bullshitting. *If I had my way, I'd throw all the iPads out the window and go straight-up Peripatetic School with my students*, she thought.

Aloud, Tessa said, "Integrating technologies into the classroom is important to me. To elaborate a bit on my cover letter…"

She then repeated verbatim what she'd said in her cover letter, but slowly, in Mincing's direction. Mincing nodded, still wondering if Flamm realized how much service work she was doing. The other four committee members tuned out once they realized Mincing was asking a question about technology. Christiansen even snorted dismissively.

Next to ask questions was Dr. Mills. Genial as always, he lobbed two softballs: the first, "Describe a difficult situation you faced with either a colleague or a student. How did you resolve this problem?" and the second, "Where do you see yourself in 10 years?"

These were typical Search Committee questions, and Tessa had practiced them both at home with Adrian. For the first, she alluded to a misunderstanding with a fellow graduate student instructor, overcome through the magic of "one-on-one communication." (*Close enough*, she thought.) For the second question, she wanted to reply, "safely tenured at a different university, far from this dismal cow-town," but instead opted for a response emphasizing massive departmental service combined with massive research output, at SVU.

Mills nodded approval, his mind wandering to menu options at Cucina Stefano. *The sirloin was rubbery last time. Maybe I should give the beef medallions a try.*

·

Dr. Christiansen was next up to the plate. Tessa looked straight into his bifocals, and awaited her fate.

"Young lady..." he began, his voice unnecessarily loud.

Angelika Franco looked pained.

"Young lady..." the antediluvian professor continued, losing his place in his notes.

Angelika looked pained and annoyed. The rest of the Committee, and Tessa herself, maintained neutral expressions.

"Young lady, as you no doubt know, the ancients believed that the greatest human good was *eudaimonia*: broadly defined as human happiness or flourishing—the ultimate human good, that which cannot be instrumental, but is good in and of itself."

Tessa made a serious face and nodded, as if *eudaimonia* was her constant concern. Her brain desperately tried to retrieve information from an Intro Philosophy course she'd taken a decade ago. The other committee members looked bored. Franco looked increasingly aggrieved. *Aristotle was a misogynist!* flashed in red across her lizard brain. *Or was it Plato? No matter. All the Greeks were!*

"Aristotle believed that virtues are the character traits necessary to achieve *eudaimonia*. In developing virtue—or *aretē*, in the Greek—we also exercise our reason, mature, and become fully human. That is what it means to live 'the good life.'"

The Committee members shifted in their seats.

"And so, young lady," said Christiansen, for a fourth time, "bearing all these things in mind, which virtue do you believe is the most important to encourage among your students?"

A pause.

"Feel free to select a virtue from among any tradition you like: Roman, Greek, Christian—even from an Oriental tradition," he said, looking pleased with himself.

Flamm winced.

Tessa's brain froze. She couldn't think of a single virtue. Not one. The second-hand on the clock in the corner of the room ticked.

"Prudence!" she said, her mind latching on to a buried memory from Philosophy 1000. She expanded: "Prudence is the most important virtue for students. Prudence is key, meaning wisdom, but also foresight and discernment. We are living in an age where information is abundant, but the ability to discern the wheat from the chaff, and then use that information toward good ends…that ability is lacking in most. As educators, we must encourage the development of prudence in our students."

Christiansen beamed.

"Thank you, young lady."

"Ahem…and your second question, Dr. Christiansen?" asked Flamm.

"What?" said Christiansen.

"Your second question please," said Flamm, hoping this would be his last candidate search for some time.

"There will be only one," said Christiansen, with dignity.

A pause.

"Ok, thank you Dr. Christiansen. Let's move on to Dr. Franco," Flamm said, suddenly noticing her seat was empty. She had sneaked out for a bathroom break during Christiansen's discourse on The Good Life.

"She would appear to be away at present," said Flamm, reflecting that pregnant coworkers were tedious. "I'll go ahead and ask my questions."

Flamm asked two research-related questions, designed to present no challenge whatsoever to Tessa, who was his second-favorite candidate, after the youngish blonde (who was, according to Pearl, single…). Tessa's responses were glibly competent.

And clear! thought Tessa. She relaxed a bit. *One more hurdle to jump.*

Franco had returned from the washroom in the middle of Flamm's final question. It was now her turn. She'd never sat on a university committee of any kind before and she intended on making the most of it. As a contract employee, Franco had been a desperation pick by Flamm, selected at the last minute after an associate prof in Sociology bailed on him. Of course, he hadn't told Franco that.

"Here at Sere Valley, we are dedicated to equity for all," said Franco, redundantly, her eyes serious behind her oversized hipster glasses. Tessa was immediately annoyed that Angelika, whom she had known for years as a fellow SVU doctoral student and Womyn's Scholars group member, was talking to her like a subordinate.

Franco continued, "In your previous work, please discuss some specific instances in which you acted in a way that promoted equity."

Tessa blinked in Franco's direction. She tried to remember the gobbledygook she had written in her Statement of Commitment to Multiculturalism.

"Do you mean equity in the modern sense: as in equality of outcome, as opposed to equality of opportunity?" she asked.

"Yes, that's right," said Franco.

All Tessa could hear in her head was Adrian's voice on-loop asking, "Why not just treat everyone the same?" The words tumbled out without a filter:

"Contemporary progressive thinkers are quite right in noting that not everyone starts out at the same place in life. Women, people of color, low-income people, transgendered people, differently-abled people, and other minority groups, often face major challenges that other people do not."

Franco and Mincing smiled. Flamm and Mills activated their "concerned ally" faces. *Aequitas, Roman Goddess of Fair Measurement?* thought Christiansen, looking puzzled.

"According to this line of thinking, it's not enough to just 'treat everyone equally,' to ensure equal outcomes. Some people need special assistance: a few seconds head-start at the gate, if you will, is needed for slower runners."

Clouds of concern drifted across Franco's face.

"Among my colleagues, the way this manifests itself, practically, is by providing more assistance, or extra inputs, for students of color. Here at Sere Valley, for instance, we have a special first-year program for indigenous students, many of whom enter university under-prepared. This seems reasonable to me. It also seems reasonable to offer increased assistance to students—*any* students—who are struggling, perhaps in the form of one-on-one office hours."

"More concerning to me," continued Tessa, "is what I've heard from several colleagues: that they are more lenient when marking the work of indigenous students and other students of color. One colleague even told me it was appropriate to, I quote, 'mark them up to make up for past injustices.'"

"To me, this is unconscionable, as well as unfair to the other students. We must strive for impartiality when grading. We do no favors to students from minority groups when we lower the bar for them—when they get out into the work world, a poorly-written memo won't help them get a raise or be taken seriously by management. And that's not what a good education is about: dragging everyone down to a lower level. It's about helping people rise to a higher level. It's about believing that many of them can, if they put the work in."

Flamm cleared his throat twice in succession, but Tessa was too focused to hear him.

"Who am I, to look at a student with more melanin in his skin than me, and make a series of assumptions about his ability, or about his background? But that's what the equity believers do: they look at darker-skinned people and assume they're poor and under-educated, and need to be held to a lower standard. How patronizing and racist is that?" asked Tessa, her voice rising with indignation.

"We professors are not here to play social engineers. Or Gods. We are here to educate. And the best way to do that is to treat students like individuals—individuals with great potential—instead of members of an impoverished class, that we, out of our great 'benevolence,' are here to bestow charity upon."

Flamm was now openly gesturing at her to stop.

"The doctrine of equity sounds good—and maybe the hearts of some of those who profess it are in the right place. But in reality, it's immoral, unfair, harmful to academic standards, and deeply paternalistic. So in response to your question, Dr. Franco, I do *not* promote equity in the classroom. I promote education instead."

Tessa took a breath and smiled, a real smile. She could breathe freely again.

Franco and Mincing looked at the job candidate like she'd just taken a shit in the middle of the table.

"Ok…thank you, Dr. Stevens. Your second question, Dr. Franco?" said Flamm.

"Like Dr. Christiansen, I only have one," said Franco, arms crossed.

"Very well! So that concludes our panel interview today. Thanks everyone for your, umm...thoughtful questions. Let's all take a little breather and reconvene at Cucina Stefano at 7:00, ok?"

Tessa's smile was already fading as she looked around the room.

Poor kid, thought Flamm. *You're toast.*

Fr: Deborahann Stevens—deborahannstevens@hotmail.com

To: Tessa Stevens—te.stevens@svu.edu; l.stevens@usm.edu

Subject: UPDATES

Date: January 25, 2017, 10:49 p.m.

TESSIE-BEAR AND LILLY-WILLY

HOW DID THE JOB INTERVIEW GO TESSIE?? I BET YOU KICKED BUTT!

DID YOU GET THE PEDAGODGICAL (SPELLING??) REVIEW THING IN, IN-TIME LILLY?

WE ARE FINE HERE. WORK IS BUSY NOW BECAUSE OF ALL THE FUNERALS. GRAMMY SAYS "SOON I WILL BE THE LAST ONE OF MY FRIENDS ALIVE." BOOHOO.

ELINOR HIRED HER NEICE AMBER TO WORK PART-TIME AT THE SHOP. DID YOU GO TO SCHOOL WITH HER LILLY? SHE IS SLOW AS COLD MOLASSES RUNNING UPHILL ON A SUNDAY. DRIVING ME CRAZY. BUT I GUESS SHE'S A "FRESH FACE FOR CUSTOMERS" LIKE ELINOR SAYS. SHES FRESH ALRIGHT. WHATS WRONG WITH MY FRESH FACE? HAHA.

OH WELL.

WE HAVE INVENTORY THIS WEEKEND SO YOUR DAD IS MAD I WILL BE BUSY. TOUGH BISCUITS!

COUSIN IDELLA DIED ON TUESDAY FINALLY. 86 YEARS OLD. SHE SURE HUNG IN THERE AFTER THE STROKE. DADDY USED TO SAY THAT COUSIN IDELLA WAS TOUGH AS NAILS. "HAD A BABY IN THE MORNING AND WAS OUT CHOPPING WOOD BY LUNCH-TIME." HAHA. SEND A CARD TO LAWRENCE. CAN'T IMAGINE HE'LL BE AT THE HOUSE MUCH LONGER BY HIMSELF. I DON'T REMEMBER THE ADDRESS BUT IF YOU PUT "LAWRENCE ARMSTRONG, BREWSTER MTN ROAD, BEACONSBRIDGE" IT WILL GET TO HIM.

SEND IT RIGHT AWAY-ESPECIALLY YOU TESSA, BECAUSE IT WILL TAKE AWHILE TO GET HERE FROM OUT WEST.

YOUR FATHER HAS BEEN UNDER THE WEATHER LATELY AND GRUMPY. LAST NIGHT HE KICKED ME OUT OF BED BECAUSE I BREATH TOO LOUD AND KEEP HIM UP ALL NIGHT, SO I SLEPT ON THE SPAREROOM BED WITH TRIXIE. THE JOKE IS ON HIM. I SLEEP BETTER THAT WAY ANYWAY! HA.

LOVE TO MY TWO SMART GIRLS!!

MUM

Chapter Thirteen: Sentimental Occasions: Reprise

POP.

Deborahann winced and willed herself not to look up. She continued making floral arrangements at the messy work-table behind the counter, trimming a sprig of Baby's Breath another half-inch. She poked it into the vase with its mates, alongside some blush-pink roses, and observed the effect with an artist's critical eye. The increased fullness was good.

Pop. Pop. POP.

Deborahann suppressed a sigh. Amber, her young co-worker, was supposedly working on the display window, swapping out the old Valentine's Day display for a non-holiday specific teddy-bear-and-carnations motif. She'd been camped out there all morning, periodically cracking bubbles, and sucking them back behind her sticky, coral-colored lips. Sometimes her fluid back-suck failed, and the gum splattered on her lips and face. This bothered her not a jot, as she methodically picked the gum off with her chipped purple talons. Always conscious herself of maintaining a tidy appearance in public, Deborahann was horrified. When she objected to the gum chewing earlier that morning—politely, she thought, shrewishly, Amber thought—her co-worker shrugged. "Gum or smokes?" she asked, presumably rhetorically. Deborahann didn't know how to counter this logic.

Twenty-one year old Amber Crossman was a nepotism hire. She was the daughter of Robert Crossman's black sheep younger sister, and therefore Elinor's niece-by-marriage. She'd been a year behind Lilly at Weyburn High, and the two were aware of each other's existence. Amber had dropped out of high school in Grade 11 to have her daughter, "Starry." ("And so the cycle continues," said Tessa to her mother on the phone. "It certainly didn't help matters,"

Deborahann replied to the older of her two products of matrimony, over the sound of Vic roaring for his supper.)

"She'll be a big help!" Elinor had said with a smile, when she told Deborahann about her new co-worker. One month in, the prophecy was unfulfilled. Though Deborahann was nominally her supervisor, Amber quickly made it known that she viewed Aunt Elinor and Aunt Elinor alone as her boss. Amber invested no authority whatsoever in Deborahann, despite her age and years of experience in the floral industry. Indeed, Amber often thought some variation of *that old bag doesn't know jack-shit.*

After another loud *POP* from Amber's direction, Deborahann could bear it no longer. It was almost lunch time. She'd consumed nothing but coffee all morning and her blood sugar was low.

"Amber, are you done up there?"

Deborahann stalked to the front of the store, where Amber was crouched on the floor, texting furiously. Deborahann noticed once again, the peculiar shellacked quality of Amber's bleached and dyed neon blue hair.

"Justasecond."

Amber didn't look up from her phone.

Beside her a pile of debris blocked the shop-door: flower clippings, bits of cardboard, glitter, ribbon, and twine. There was also a half-emptied bag of craft supplies, and three boxes of assorted teddy bears, figurines, and other bric-a-brac used to make displays; the boxes' contents were strewn everywhere. Deborahann noticed, with annoyance, that Amber had crumpled up her laboriously constructed red tinsel hearts, tossing them in the pile of garbage. It had taken

Deborahann a week to make the hearts, working in between customers, and she'd planned on using them for years of Valentine's Day displays. No longer, it would seem.

Deborahann checked out Amber's display. Big Tan Teddy and Big White Teddy were posed conventionally, seated in front of a large white vase of pink and yellow carnations. Smaller vases of carnations surrounded the large one, each accompanied by small white teddy bears, wearing tuxedos. Pink ribbons were tied into bows around each vase. The entire tableau was liberally dusted with glitter and confetti stars. Deborahann judged Amber's work uninspired but acceptable. *Not sure how that took three hours*, she thought.

But there was more. Further down in the display window were another two of the shop's teddy bears: Medium Grey Teddy and Medium White Teddy. Amber had started a second, smaller display. Deborahann looked more closely. Medium White Teddy was posed on his hands and knees. He was being mounted from behind by Medium Grey Teddy, whose arms were raised above his head with exuberance. Below him, Medium White Teddy's button-eyes were glassy with horror. His face was turned toward the street, as if imploring passers-by to stop and come to his aid.

"Amber Lynn Crossman!"

Amber looked up. Deborahann was already taking down the display.

"Are you crazy? How long has this been like this?"

Amber rolled her eyes. *Bitch.*

Aloud, she said, "Uhh…all morning. It's just a joke."

"Not funny! Who knows how many people saw this! I thought I could trust you with this display!"

Amber was more interested in the incoming text messages on her phone than Deborahann's lecturing. A new one from Dustin flashed across the screen. It read, "Tbh, you are the hottest grrl in Beaconsbridge, I dont say that to evry1 btw lol."

"I'm going to lunch now."

"You're just going to leave me with this big mess to clean up?" Deborahann had taken down the offending teddy bears, but Amber's other display debris was everywhere.

"Later!"

Amber was out of there. She was meeting Dustin at the Dairy Queen in 10 minutes.

Deborahann shook her head and went back to cleaning up the display. In a few minutes, the entry and display area were once again pristine for customers.

Deborahann was just putting on her coat to nip out and grab a sandwich, when Elinor arrived, making one of her surprise visits to the shop. Deborahann hadn't expected her in today. She was supposed to be in Moncton at a doctor's appointment, and then, presumably, out shopping all afternoon. That was her usual Moncton-day pattern. But sometimes Elinor liked to throw her off.

Elinor swept in looking flawless, as always, in the burgundy suede jacket Deborahann had long admired as the epitome of chic. ("I bet she paid five hundred dollars for it!" she said to Tessa on the phone.) Elinor's helmet of curls was as piss-yellow, tidy, and immobile as ever. But underneath it her eyes blazed. She ran to the display, tottering in her block-heeled leather boots.

"Deb'rann! Get up here, Deb'rann!"

Deborahann scurried back to the front of the shop. Elinor viewed the display, relief flooding her face.

"Oh, thank goodness."

Her expression darkened again, as she saw Deborahann.

"What is this I heard about an *obscene* display in the window this morning?"

Deborahann's eyes widened, but she bore up under pressure.

"Amber did something silly with the teddies while I was working on arrangements at the cash. But it wasn't up very long."

"Not up very long! You go on! Edith said she walked by four times from 9:30 to 12:15, and every time it was still up!"

Then why didn't she tell me? thought Deborahann, mentally cursing Elinor's busybody cousin.

"I took it down as soon as I saw it."

"It never should've been up in the first place! You're supposed to be watching her!"

She's not a two-year old.

"I'm sorry, we had so many orders this morning. I didn't have a chance…"

Elinor held up a perfectly manicured hand, cutting her off.

"This is unacceptable, Deb'rann. Absolutely unacceptable! Day in, day out, what do I tell you we strive for at Sentimental Occasions?"

Deborahann hung her head like a child. Across the street, four bank tellers at the Madawaaksis Credit Union watched the scene unfold. ("Up one side and down the other," said Edith with relish to a younger teller.)

"Professionalism," said Deborahann.

"Speak up!

"Professionalism."

"And would you describe that display as professional?"

"No." Deborahann's voice was barely audible.

"It certainly was not. I expected more from you, Deb'rann. Amber is just a girl—a young, naïve girl."

At that precise moment, at the Weyburn Dairy Queen, Amber's tongue was jammed down Dustin's throat.

"If you can't do something simple like supervise a young girl, what *can* you do?"

Deborahann said nothing.

A new thought made Elinor's face fall. She was very fond of the shop's teddy bears, accumulated over the years. There were some 50 of them, in varying sizes, shapes, and colors.

"Was it Seymour? It was Seymour, wasn't it?" Elinor looked distraught.

"Uhh…"

Elinor breathed in and out, making an effort to control her emotions. She noticed Deborahann had her coat on.

"I think you should go take your lunch now, Deb'rann. I'll mind the cash."

"I was just going to run down to the bakery and get…"

"Go take your lunch, Deb'rann. A *long* lunch. We'll discuss this more when you get back."

Deborahann left for lunch. She was only able to eat a few bites of her turkey BLT. She made polite small talk with Cindy at the bakery, asking her how Randall's back was doing after the surgery. Below the surface, her mind raced.

She wrapped up the remaining two-thirds of the sandwich to bring home to Trixie.

Those bakery sandwiches aren't cheap, thought Deborahann. *Shouldn't waste it.*

***

A few days later in Sere Valley, at The Ranch Hand, Adrian and Tessa were draining their pints and preparing to call it an (early) night. Tessa had been dragged out by Adrian, who was bored and procrastinating on an assignment. She rarely went out on Sunday nights, preferring to spend them at home tweaking her Monday morning lesson-plans instead.

Since the panel interview, Tessa was being even more conscientious than usual. She threw herself into teaching and writing center-tutoring with renewed vigor. It was three weeks now, and she still hadn't heard a peep back from the Department. She knew the Committee was making its final deliberations. She wondered if she had imagined the guilty frown on Flamm's face when she ran into him last week in the mail-room. She wasn't sure. As for Pearl, if she knew anything, she was hiding it well. While she waited to hear back, Tessa tried her best to keep her mind off things. Her only other bite on the full-time academic employment front was a Skype interview for a community college job in the Yukon. "Can you go half a year without sunlight?" was the first question. Tessa withdrew her application.

At The Ranch Hand that evening, Adrian complained about the pub's music, "I swear to God, if I hear any more Chilliwack, I'm going to walk out into traffic. Are they subject to fucking Canadian Content requirements in here or what?"

Adrian paused. His shaggy ginger brows suddenly shot skyward. In a split-second his expression changed from surprise to craftiness.

Tessa laughed. "Never play poker, buddy. I see you're in stealth-mode. What is it?"

"Upstairs. Behind you—my 6 o'clock. Andrew and some chick."

Tessa felt a twinge and battled to control her expression. She reached for her glass, and slowly made the motion of drinking. It was empty, save for the bitter foam.

"So what? Maybe he's out with a friend."

"A very special friend, by the looks of things."

Tessa abandoned what remained of her dignity and spun around in her seat. It was Andrew all right. He was seated, and the lighting was dim, but the reedy silhouette and jaunty tilt of the head were unmistakable. He was tête-à-tête with a young Mia Farrow-type; they were tucked into the corner of a booth, seated almost on top of each other. Even at a distance, Tessa could make out the characteristic conspiratorial grin playing across his face—the same smile he'd flashed at her a thousand times. This was the first time it failed to thaw her heart. He playfully tapped the tip of the blonde's nose with a forefinger. Tessa recognized this as another classic move from the Andrew Moore Playbook. She was beginning to see why Adrian called him, "Too cute by half."

As she watched, her pulse began to race. The room spun. The contents of her stomach—two craft beers and a half-serving of loaded nachos—began shifting.

"D'you know her?" asked Adrian.

"Yes."

"Who…?"

"It's Emily Payne."

"The prep school proletarian in your program? Say that three times fast. What happened to her Sandinista costume?"

"She's defending soon. Professionalism?"

"Ahh, a J. Crew Che Guevera. I love it."

Tessa and Emily were acquaintances. Around the Department of late, Tessa noticed that Emily had ditched the nose-ring and purple hair in favor of a more conservative look. She no longer looked like a patrician in costume as a modern-day Rosie the Riveter.

"Hmm."

"Well, as Grammy McGinty would've said, 'Ain't he bold as brass?' Going after one of your peers. And making out with her in *our* bar," said Adrian. The latter offence was a personal affront.

"Shut up, Adrian. They're not making out."

They watched as Andrew leaned in, cupped Emily's chin, and kissed her full on the mouth.

Tessa groaned.

"You go outside. I'll settle up."

Tessa was paralyzed, eyes darting back and forth between Adrian and the scene on the upper level.

"You're torturing yourself, Tess. Go, go. I'll meet you out there."

She nodded and left.

Out in the parking lot, Tessa waited and paced midst the discarded cigarette butts. She checked the time on her phone. Adrian was taking ages, but the servers at The Ranch Hand were notoriously difficult to flag down. A nearby dumpster stank of sour beer and rotten citrus fruit.

Tessa reflected. She and Andrew had been a couple, off and on, since meeting last summer at a house party. She had never met his parents, though they lived in town and Andrew still lived at home. Adrian had pointed out this fact several times, much to her annoyance. He had also observed that Andrew had never introduced her to his friends. When she worked up the courage to question him about this, Andrew had only shrugged, "Why put a label on it?" *Respect*, thought Tessa, but she said nothing. It was an old-fashioned response.

Now she wondered how she could've been so stupid. She could feel the blood pulsing through her brain, and every cell of her body vibrating at a high frequency. Chaos swirled all around.

Fuck this.

Tessa spun on her heel and marched back into the building. On the other side of the pub, Adrian was still waiting in line to swipe his Visa. In Tessa's Terminator-like state, the room consisted of glowing organic and inorganic blobs of matter. Eyes locked on the upper level, Tessa maneuvered her way around the pub, and up the stairs, circumnavigating a waitress with a tray full of drinks, and a pair of oafish locals in ball-caps, obstructing her path. Andrew and Emily were still in their corner booth. Emily was seated with her back towards her, while Andrew's face was now in Tessa's direct sight-line. As he saw Tessa approach the booth, his flirtatious smile dissolved. He pulled back from Emily with a jolt, guilty as a dog caught pissing on the rug. Tessa noted, with satisfaction, the look of terror in his eyes.

"Hello Andrew…Emily. How's your evening going?"

Tessa spoke so loudly her question was audible three tables down, over the music.

Emily looked back and forth between them. Her eyes widened. A becoming pink flush spread across her cheeks. Andrew smiled but his voice wavered as he replied.

"We're fine, Tessa. How are you?"

"Fine and dandy! Adrian and I were just leaving when we saw you. I didn't know you two were acquainted. What a surprise!"

"Indeed."

Andrew was unusually tongue-tied.

"Did you meet at the departmental holiday party? Maybe while I was out of the room? You remember, don't you, Andrew? Right before the break. *You were my plus-one.*"

Andrew's smile stayed pasted on. He exchanged a glance with Emily, who looked grim. Emily reached for her coat and purse. The two stood to leave.

"We're going to head out now, Tessa," said Andrew.

"Oh, don't leave on my account! Sit! Sit! How 'bout a round on me?"

Tessa stood in front of him. The other side of the booth was blocked by another patron's chair. Andrew and Emily were trapped.

Andrew peered around her. Tessa didn't budge.

"No really, a round on me," Tessa repeated, her voice shrill. "One more round at my expense!" Half of the upper level of the pub was watching now.

Andrew swayed in either direction, eyes panicky. He stepped backwards, trampling on Emily's shoes. She let out a yelp. He hopped forward again. Tessa remained immobile, blocking their escape-route. Andrew was helpless.

Stand-off.

Andrew's face darkened as he saw the amused expressions of his fellow pub-goers. Three seconds passed. When he spoke, his voice was low.

"You're making a fool of yourself."

"Correction: you're making a fool of me."

Tessa's gaze shifted from Andrew to the tiny blonde standing behind him. She looked Emily in the eye.

"He's making a fool of both of us."

"Get out. Of. The way," Emily said through gritted teeth. Her face was now scarlet with commingled shame and rage.

The entire upper level was watching now. A fourth voice suddenly sounded above the music.

"Oh shut up, Hanoi Jane!"

The insult emanated from the direction of a bear-like arm. It reached in and pulled Tessa like a doll, out of Andrew and Emily's way. Andrew didn't waste any time. He squeezed by, dragging Emily behind him. They were down the stairs and out of the pub in seconds.

"You better run, bitch!" called out Tessa, eyes wild, to Andrew's departing back. She wrenched herself free from Adrian's grasp.

"Tessa..."

It was a few seconds more before she calmed down enough to register the details of the scene. She recognized Adrian, and noticed the dozens of curious eyes watching them. She was conscious of her chest rising and falling with each breath, and the perspiration running down her back. Overlooking the scene like a grim deity was a poster of Johnny Cash at Folsom Prison. He looked disgusted with them all.

Adrian and Tessa left, following the same route as Andrew and Emily. The tension dissipated within seconds, and the pub's usual air of conviviality returned. It was as if nothing had happened.

***

The next day, Tessa was still processing the Andrew drama. Adrian had wisely said nothing on the way home the night before or at breakfast, though it was killing him not to say, "I told you so." Tessa knew she should feel embarrassed for acting out the humiliating role of scorned woman. She was sure the story was already making the rounds of the Department, but she was too stunned to care. Beyond the numbness, the only emotion she felt was spite, a spiteful pleasure that she had caused Andrew some discomfort. She had always resented his way of sauntering through life, availing himself of all the ripe, overhanging fruit along his path.

Choke on it, she thought.

She wondered what nonsense he would feed Emily. She guessed he would tell her she was a crazy ex-girlfriend. Her behavior certainly supported such a claim. She knew he would admit to no overlap, no ambiguities. She supposed Emily would stay with him, full of reservations she was unable to express, lest she, like Tessa, come across as unfashionably interested in monogamy.

Tessa brooded all day. She felt fragmented, but she hadn't the luxury of time to recover: she had classes to teach and office hours to attend. She could have come up with an excuse to cancel the latter, but the habit of reliability, instilled in childhood, was too strong. (Life with a father like hers was unstable enough—she never dared add the x-factor of personal irresponsibility to the mix.)

By 3:50 Tessa had made it to the last 10 minutes of her office hours. None of her students had showed up, allowing her the better part of two hours to mark assignments in peace. The room was blessedly silent without the fidgety presence of her office-mates. Myron was away and Pamela had left by mid-afternoon.

A knock at the door interrupted the stillness. Edwin Flamm poked his head in and entered before she could say a word.

"Do you have a minute? I wanted to catch you during your office hours."

"Sure."

Flamm shut the door behind himself, first looking both ways down the hallway, eyes only, no neck movement, like a CIA agent. He took a seat.

"This won't take up much time, Tessa."

Tessa nodded. She noticed, as usual, how much Flamm resembled a courtly hobbit. She wondered how it was possible for anyone outside the homeless population to be so rumpled, so consistently.

"I'm sure you've been wondering about the outcome of the candidate search."

Tessa nodded some more.

"I thought it would be…respectful if you heard from me first, before you receive the official letter in your mailbox. Pearl is sending them out tomorrow."

Tessa smiled through a clenched jaw.

"You've been an absolute credit to the Department, Tessa. Your service and teaching record has not gone unnoticed around here. And you were an excellent student. You should be so proud of everything you've achieved."

Achieved?

Flamm paused a beat, and continued, "And in such a short span of time! The average Ph.D. completion-time in the Department is something like eight years—among those who even finish, that is…" His eyes flickered over to Myron's desk.

"And you finished in…five, right?

"Four and a half."

"Right."

Flamm's smile was strained. Like a hobbit with hemorrhoids.

"So, regarding the candidate search...it pains me to say this, but unfortunately, the Committee decided to head in another direction."

Tessa felt nothing.

"You were a very strong candidate, but there were some concerns about your teaching specializations, which, given the needs of the Department at this time, as you know..."

Tessa watched his mouth move. Her eyes floated up to the second-hand on the clock above the door.

"...and I think we can agree, academic credentials like those are very impressive indeed, wouldn't you say? There's no shame in coming in second to such a strong candidate, especially when..."

Tessa interjected, "But I've been teaching here for years. You've sat in on my classes. You wrote positive teaching evaluations—said I was the 'most engaging' student instructor you've seen in years. Wasn't that considered?"

"Certainly, but teaching is only one consideration. One of many."

"I've also published."

"Well, all four of the candidates we interviewed have publications, Tessa."

"Did *you* have any publications before you were hired for your first post-Ph.D. position?"

Flamm frowned.

"Well, no."

Crickets.

"But that was a different time, I guess?" Tessa cocked a quizzical brow.

"Precisely."

Flamm's forehead was clammy. He shifted in his seat.

"I'm sure Pearl can find you a term or two of adjuncting while you look for a permanent position. And I would be absolutely delighted to write a reference for you, Tessa, so don't hesitate to ask."

She said nothing.

Flamm rose to leave. He regretted not delegating this task to Pearl. *She was so good with Anthony*, he thought, dimly recalling the last internal candidate the Department had rejected, three years ago. *He had all of his things cleared out by the last day of classes. So amenable. Tessa, on the other hand...*

"I have a few questions before you go."

"By all means."

"Did my politics play a part in the Committee's decision?"

"What?"

Flamm was silent, unaccustomed to direct questions from subordinates. Tessa repeated herself.

"My politics—my answer to the equity question."

"No...No! Absolutely not. No."

Tessa and Flamm sat in silence, listening to the clock tick.

"Will another position be coming up soon in the Department?"

Another pause.

"I'm afraid not. The Dean's Office said we were lucky to free up funds for this one. I don't expect another one coming along for quite some time. Of course, if I hear otherwise, I'll let you know. Again, we typically *do* have a couple spare adjuncting spots available every term...so there's that."

"Are you concerned that the Department relies so heavily on part-timers?"

"Oh yes. We all are. But that's just the way it is now, you know."

"I see."

"And English does better than most. I would say a good, oh, probably 50 percent of our courses are taught by tenured faculty. That's far better than the SVU average. It's well under half now, I believe."

"Right."

Flamm had been backing up while he was talking. He was at the door.

"Don't forget about the reference—again, my pleasure!"

Tessa nodded. Flamm escaped to the hallway.

Acting aggrieved, he thought, *and with that performance in the interview! And did she really think an SVU candidate could compete with an American Ivy League one? Not in this market. Ridiculous.*

Edwin's Ph.D., circa 1993, was from the University of Northern Saskatchewan.

Tessa sat in silence in her office a few minutes, before gathering up her marking to leave. It all made sense. She had never belonged here, among these officious little men and women, these conventional radicals, marooned and dissatisfied on their university island-fortress, in a sea of plain prairie people. The faculty of Sere Valley University fancied themselves the elite of this small town. They were drawn from the same tier of reasonable, moderately intelligent, and thoroughly middle class citizenry who also staffed Canada's vast government bureaucracy.

They're not bad people, thought Tessa, *just common, everyday cowards.*

These people weren't her people; their God was not her God. She had skated on the surface of this life. Her kernel of Maritimer common-sense and humor was inviolate. She had thought hard work and intellectual rigor would win the day. It always had in the past, as she climbed up each rung of the academic ladder, from kindergarten to the Ph.D. So many hours of study, of writing, of diligent pen-scratchings. Was she really living or just killing time? What was it all in preparation for, if not an academic career? Maybe it was a cosmic joke on her. Maybe it was nothing.

On the way out, Tessa observed her reflection in the display case outside Pearl's office. The eyes in the reflection mocked her.

Maybe, maybe not, sweetheart.

Chapter Fourteen: What You Sow

Fr: Andrew Moore—aj.moore@svu.edu

To: Tessa Stevens—te.stevens@svu.edu

Subject: A Final Communication

Date: February 27, 2017, 7:15 p.m.

"Tessa Fair looked up with lovely grace. But there was no smile on Tessa Fair's face..."

Tessa Fair,

I'm sorry that I've caused you pain, but to be fair, I always made it abundantly clear that we had no exclusive understanding. Your response is honestly quite confusing to me.

Your anger is quite misplaced, my dear.

I think it's best that we discontinue communications, given the animosity you harbor toward me. This will be my last response to any of your communications. With all due respect, I think your unhappiness has little to do with me, and more to do with past personal trauma. You may want to consider seeking professional help to resolve these issues.

I wish you all the best, as you work toward a happier and healthier Tessa!

Cordially,

Andrew

***

Bastard, thought Tessa.

The email was in response to an angry voicemail she had left on his phone a few days after the nasty scene at The Ranch Hand. She had called against her better judgement.

It would take some time before Tessa could honestly respond to the question the psychologist asked her, about a month later. The woman was blunt: "Sure he was dishonest.

Sure he was emotionally abusive. There's no doubt about that. But the bigger question is this: why did you tolerate it for so long?"

Why indeed? It was a question that put Tessa back in the driver's seat. As Paulo Coelho put it, "A mistake repeated more than once is a decision."

Tessa should have spent her Reading Week processing—in private—the dual rejections of Andrew and the SVU Search Committee, and deciding what they meant for her future. Instead she flew half-way across Canada, using money she didn't have. Tessa always went home on Reading Week. It never occurred to her that she had a choice in the matter. Her family expected her and Lilly to spend every break in Madawaaksis County, known center of the world.

On the plane, Tessa steeled herself to withstand her father's offhand contempt and her mother's cloying sympathy over the SVU job rejection. She had already told her over the phone. Lilly's commiseration would have been tolerable, but she wouldn't be there. Lilly's Reading Week at UNB was scheduled a week later than Tessa's this year.

Tessa landed and made her way to Arrivals, where her mother was standing alone, fiddling with her rings. Deborahann plastered a wide smile on her face when she saw her daughter, a smile that didn't reach her eyes.

"Are you ok?" Tessa asked after they embraced. "Where's Dad?"

Deborahann's eyes darted back and forth before answering in a whisper.

"Before we get to the car, I need to warn you. Your father's been acting peculiar lately."

"Is he being more or less of an asshole than usual?"

"Tessa!"

Deborahann checked again to make sure no one had heard. It was a small airport, with only two gates. Tessa's flight had been late; it was almost midnight and the airport was dead.

Nonetheless, this was a public space in New Brunswick: there was always someone around they might know.

"He's having some religious difficulties," Deborahann said.

The two made their way through the terminal. Flush with government cash, the airport specialized in the transfer of working-aged men to and from the Alberta oil fields. They passed a large provincial tourism poster showing one of New Brunswick's iconic covered bridges. It featured the government's newest tourism slogan: "NEW BRUNSWICK: RICH…IN HISTORY."

Tessa frowned.

"He thinks he's committed…" Deborahann paused, eyes widening, "…the *unforgivable sin!*"

Tessa burst into laughter.

"You've got to be kidding me."

"No, I'm serious. He hasn't been at work for a week. He just lies in bed all day and cries. I was surprised that he got up to drive to the airport, but he said I couldn't be trusted on the icy roads. When I try to talk to him he just yells at me. I don't know what to do."

"What? Is he depressed?"

"I don't know, Tessie-Bear. Pastor Fudge has been at the house a lot, trying to calm him down. I try and stay out of the room. They pray at the kitchen table."

Tessa sighed.

"He doesn't need that imbecile. He needs a clinician. There's something wrong with him. There always has been. I think it just manifests itself as religious mania, because that's all he knows."

"I know there's something wrong with him," replied Deborahann. "But he won't see anyone but Pastor Fudge."

"Right. Pastor Fudge, personal shaman, bringing order to the Cosmos."

"What?"

Tessa held her tongue. She didn't want to further upset her mother, who believed in Jesus Christ as her personal savior, but not in Fudge. They walked out to the near-empty parking lot.

"He keeps saying he's going to go to hell, Tessie. It's very strange."

"I'll bet it's strange."

They approached the Civic, parked in a far corner of the lot.

"Shhh! Don't say anything!" whispered Deborahann.

Vic was visible through the tinted glass, seated in the driver's seat, his head in his hands. He did not get out to help with Tessa's bags. He barely looked up when he heard them approaching. He just popped the trunk.

"Hey Dad," said Tessa, climbing in to the passenger seat. It was Deborahann's custom to sit in the backseat when she and Vic picked up their daughters from college. She thought they'd enjoy the ride home more that way.

Silence.

Vic started the ignition. He didn't look in his daughter's direction. His voice, usually brusque, was tremulous. He had heavy bags under his eyes.

"How are you doing?" she tried.

A pause, and then a great snort as he blew his nose.

"I s'pose your mother told you?"

Deborahann's eyes in the rear-view mirror pleaded with her.

"No."

Victor spoke in the third person, breaking off in the middle with a sob: "I'm afraid your father is travelling...through the Valley of the Shadow of Death!"

Tessa noticed the Civic drifting toward the highway's yellow line. She had no intention of going through that valley with him.

"Oh...I'm sorry to hear that, Dad."

They drove a few minutes in silence.

Deborahann piped up, "Well, we're sorry Sere Valley turned you down for that job, Tessie! But you know what, it's their loss!"

"Thanks Mum."

"They never appreciated you anyway! This is just as well. I'm sure another, *better* university will hire you instead...Did you try Winslow? UNB?"

"There are no English positions at either of those universities right now—well, only LTAs and adjuncts."

"Adjuncts? Are those the crappy part-time ones? Like what you have now?" asked Deborahann.

"Yes, they hire term by term at 5k a class."

"Maybe you could start with one of those and get your foot in the door," suggested Deborahann.

"It doesn't work that way, Mum. I know people who've adjuncted for a decade without getting a full-time job. Experience only hurts you in academia. You get pigeonholed as a journeyman, a 'professional adjunct,' and they don't take you seriously. Besides, I'm not picking up my entire life and moving across the country for four months of work."

Victor was barely aware of them speaking. He was driving the vehicle but he wasn't present. His eyes were glazed, fixed at mid-distance on the road, but not seeing it.

"Where else did you apply in the Maritimes?" asked Deborahann

"Nowhere."

"Then how do you expect to get a job? You're not doing enough!"

"Mum, there are only two tenure-track positions in *all* of Canada right now in English, in my specialty," said Tessa, exasperated.

"Can you apply in another specialty?"

"No! I can't exactly teach 'Postcolonial Theory and the Sri Lankan Novel' at the drop of a hat when I've never studied it before."

Deborahann was nonplussed.

"But why did they let so many people into your program if there are no jobs for them when they come out?"

"Good bloody question," said Tessa.

A black Saturn sped up, passing them as quickly as possible. The driver gave them an angry honk for good measure, startling Deborahann and Tessa. He wasn't happy that he had been stuck for 10 minutes behind an erratically accelerating-and-decelerating Civic.

"Vic…do you want me to drive? You've had a tiring week," said Deborahan slowly.

"I'm fine!" growled Vic.

Deborahann and Tessa exchanged anxious glances in the rear-view mirror. Victor took the off-ramp. The sign read, "Weyburn/Beaconsbridge/Idlewild." They were 15 minutes from home now, on a road that was usually deserted by this time of night. Deborahann's eyes signalled to her daughter: *Almost there, Tessie! It'll be okay.*

"Will other universities post more jobs before the fall term?" asked Deborahann.

"Maybe a few, but the vast majority of job ads are out by now. It's a very slow and specific hiring cycle for good TT jobs."

"T...T?"

"Tenure-track! *God* Mum, I've told you that a million times!"

"*TESSA!*" Victor bellowed.

"*WHAT?*" she yelled back for once, out of patience.

With one sweeping motion, Victor made a hard turn right and pulled off the asphalt on to a dirt logging road. It was now after 1:00 a.m.

"Victor..." said Deborahann.

"You listen to me, you little BITCH." His voice rose on the last word, which was full of hate. Tessa and Deborahann tensed. This was strong, even for Victor.

"You do *not*...take the name...of The Lord...*in vain!*"

Tessa had been away from home for too long, in an environment full of secular dogmas. She had forgotten that her father and some of the other deacons at Beaconsbridge Baptist adhered to a particular fundamentalist reading of the Third Commandment. In their home, "God" as an exclamation had always been forbidden. As children, she and Lilly had instead always substituted the benign New Brunswick-ism, "Oh my word," instead, to avoid a meltdown from their father.

But that day Tessa was tired—tired of living under the domination of one set of fundamentalists after another, first in Madawaaksis County and now in academia.

I can't get away from them, these bloody-minded little tribalists, with their taboo words, their witch hunts, their petty heresies, their obsession with purity and sacredness. How dare they tell me what to do, and what to say, and what to think? How dare they dehumanize me?

It all boiled down, in every case, she thought, to a lust for control. All weak, insecure people crave control over their environment. But no amount of power is ever enough to put them at ease.

"Oh God, God, God, God...*God*!" she cried, deliberately.

It was a mistake.

Victor jumped out of the car and flung open Tessa's passenger-side door. She reached to lock it, but he was too quick. And then too strong. He was a man and she was a woman; she was an academic and he was a laborer; he had 70 pounds on her. In a few seconds he had the seatbelt off, while she struggled, wriggling like a fish in a net. He wrenched it off her, then dragged his daughter out of the car by the hair and threw her down onto the snow. One of her boots fell off. Tessa screamed and the screams seemed to come from someone else.

Everything was happening too quickly to process. Sounds and images came to her in flashes imprinted on the senses for a millisecond, then disappeared. The moon and stars shone hard and cold. The snow-laden trees glistened in the moonlight. Tessa could smell the crisp, piney air, while her boot, a handy weapon, struck her again and again on the torso, the arms, the legs. Even incensed, Victor knew better than to go for the face.

"Victor! Stop it! Stop it!"

Deborahann's screams pierced Tessa's consciousness. She saw her mother grab his arm. She was flung aside.

He stood over Tessa, triumphant, panting.

"Apologize! Apologize for taking the name of the Lord in vain!"

Tessa lay in the mud and the snow, and looked up at the face that was a rough-hewn version of her own. Victor loomed over her, eyes ablaze. Tessa felt no physical pain or cold. She felt fear and hatred, and the hatred was stronger than the fear.

"No!"

Still lying on her side, she managed to kick him as hard as she could in the back of the shins. It didn't hurt, but it surprised Victor, who stumbled forward in the snow, landing on one knee. His jeans were dirtied and that just pissed him off more.

Tessa didn't remember much of the thrashing that followed, only flashes of action: the zipper torn out of her coat and the coat ripped off her body, her own oxblood-colored boot beating down like a cudgel, and the screams of the daughter mixing with the screams of the mother. If anyone had been at the edge of the logging road, they would have seen an undignified tussle, a grown man kicking and beating his grown daughter, who alternately fought back frantically, or tried to crawl away on her hands and knees, out of his reach.

It may only have lasted a few minutes, but in those few minutes, Tessa was severed from her family. She lost her father, for fathers protect. (But maybe she never had him.) She lost her mother, who would cry endless real tears over this. Deborahann would cry and cry, and protect the family unit with her silence and inaction, like her mother before her.

And soon enough, as a result of those few minutes, she would lose her sister, because Lilly wouldn't believe her—couldn't really believe terrible things about the father she loved, who treated her differently from her older sister. *Tessa's exaggerating,* she would think. *She loves a good story.* And Tessa would think, about her mother and sister, *There's a hair's breadth between the peacemakers and the collaborators.* From that night on, Tessa stood alone.

Victor's blind rage eventually receded. His breathing slowed to normal. The heavy sole had detached from the winter boot he'd used to batter her. Disgusted, he threw it in the ditch and walked back to the Civic.

He rolled the window down.

"Get back in the car," he said.

Deborahann tried to help Tessa up from the ground. Tessa pushed her away, and rose unsteadily to her feet. Deborahann tried again to help her to the car, but Tessa wouldn't have it. She looked at her mother with disgust. *You should've left a long time ago. You brought this on us.* She hopped on one foot back to the car and got inside. There was nothing else to do. *What can I do, run along the road and try to hitch a ride back with a neighbour? Make a public spectacle of ourselves?*

Perhaps if no one said or did anything further, they could deny the reality of what had happened. They drove home in silence. Victor even carried Tessa's suitcase in, like he usually did when they picked her up from the airport. Trixie bounded up to them, but sensing the tension, skulked away. Tessa and Victor avoided eye contact with one another.

"Are you hungry, Tessie? There's leftover stew," offered Deborahann. Tessa ignored her and went up to her room to bed. She tried to cry as quietly as possible, but Victor could still hear her. The walls of the house were thin.

"Is that girl going to sook all night? What a baby!" he said aloud into the air, on the way to bed. It was for Tessa to hear. Deborahann didn't reply. She went in to check on her daughter.

"Leave me alone," Tessa said to her, from under the covers.

"He didn't mean it, honey. He's under so much pressure. The garage is failing. We can barely keep the electricity on over there. And now this religious breakdown thing…"

She placed a hand on Tessa's trembling shoulder.

"I know he's sorry, but won't say so. You know your father—he has to save face. It will never happen again."

You're damn right it won't, thought Tessa. *Because I'm never coming home again.*

Aloud she said, "Shut up."

"You know he hardly ever does things like that, honey…"

"Hardly ever?" Tessa popped her head out of the covers, remembered herself, and whispered, "Has he done that to you before?"

She had seen her father mock, humiliate, and scream obscenities at her mother. She had seen him slam doors, punch walls and throw things. She had even seen him push her mother, but she'd never seen him beat her before.

Deborahann paused and chose her next words carefully.

"Almost never."

Tessa's stomach lurched. She felt contemptuous of the entire rotten world.

Quietly, she said, "Maybe you think you deserve to be treated like shit, but I don't."

Deborahann said nothing.

"Get *out*." Tessa spat out the words.

"Turn the lights off and come to bed!" Victor hollered from the master bedroom down the hall.

"I love you, Tessie-Bear," whispered Deborahann, crying, as she shut the door.

In the darkness of her childhood bedroom, Tessa wept under the covers. She stayed up most of the night. Even with the blinds down, the room was never properly dark. She could make out her bookshelf, filled with all of her old friends: *Anne of Green Gables, Emily of New Moon, Jane Eyre, What Katy Did, Little Women*, the Nancy Drews, the Laura Ingalls Wilders. Her old Cabbage Patch kid was there too, on the shelf. Laura Lenora observed the scene with her doleful brown eyes.

Tessa already felt guilty. *It's cowardly of me to go after her, the only parent I can safely go after.* She wanted to tell her mother that it didn't matter how often he crossed over from emotional to physical violence, like he had tonight—or even if he never crossed over at all. It was the subordination of others that mattered. *He's a parasite who feeds on her. On all of us. Why does she put up with this?*

***

Sunday dawned, bright and clear. Deborahann was up early, making Tessa's favorite chocolate chip pancakes. As Tessa entered the kitchen, her mother looked up with a hopeful smile, as if confident that delicious carbs could solve any problem. It was not reciprocated. Deborahann nattered away while Tessa ate. By the time Victor made an appearance at the breakfast table, Tessa was done. As she showered upstairs, she could hear him complaining about breakfast: he preferred blueberry pancakes, not chocolate chip.

The shower stream stung. Tessa's body was covered in bruises, mostly on her torso, where they wouldn't be seen, but also on her arms, where they would be. Luckily, she had packed plenty of long-sleeved sweaters. Tessa didn't want to go to church. She didn't want to leave her room. But she knew that not going wasn't an option when she was home, under her father's regime. She would go to church, smile. Put on a show. She had done it many times before.

Tessa formulated her survival plan for the rest of Reading Week: she would stay out of the house as much as possible, visiting old high school friends and Grammy Ada. When home, she would keep to her room. Above all else, she would avoid being alone with her father, or doing anything to further upset him—he was obviously more dangerous now, while going through this religious breakdown, than ever before. She would make it to the end of the week, and get her drive back to the airport. Once she returned to Sere Valley, she would ask her mother to box and ship all of her precious childhood books to her. She was never going back to that house, not while her father was there, at least. She would never place herself under his control again.

Chapter Fifteen: Oblivion is Seafoam Green

Back in Sere Valley after Reading Week, Tessa kept to herself and ruminated over the meaning of her injuries. She had always been wary in her father's presence. She had no memory of a time when she wasn't afraid of him. As a child, Tessa had grown accustomed to living on the knife-edge of violence all the time, without quite crossing over. When Victor was angry at some childish misdemeanour, he reacted. He did many things to frighten her when she lived in his house: he screamed in her face; he slammed doors; he threw her belongings. But it was as if he knew that the price of violating certain boundaries would be outsider involvement, and the subsequent loss of control over his family. So he walked the line. Until the day he didn't.

Tessa's earliest childhood memory was of being a baby, confined to her crib. Clothes hung overhead on a rack. It had been great fun to pull down every article of clothing, one by one, and play in the pile. Then a face appeared. Her father. The face was mottled with rage. Angry sounds burst forth from the pie-gash mouth in the middle of it. She had done a terrible thing! She was a very bad girl! And he would, rightfully, punish her. Tessa the baby screamed. Another face appeared over the crib: *Mama!* Deborahann swooped in and grabbed her one year old.

"She's just a baby, Vic! Don't yell at her!"

"Why the hell do you keep my good coat in here anyway? What's wrong with your head, woman?"

The baby cried harder.

"Shut it up!"

End scene. Fade to black.

After the Reading Week incident, Tessa forced herself to think about her father's decades of bizarre behavior. He had always carried out rituals, things Tessa didn't begin to understand until she took a few psychology courses in undergrad and learned about obsessive-compulsive disorder. Whenever they left the house as a family, Vic would make everyone wait in the car while he walked around the house by himself doing "The Check." Every light was turned off. Every plug was unplugged. Every water faucet was turned tightly, lest a single drop of water escape. Every burner on the stove needed to be checked: "in the off position," Victor said. And as he walked around the house, from checkpoint to checkpoint, he chanted an incantation: "Off, off, off, off, off, and…OFF." Woe betide anyone who dared interrupt The Check. Victor would yell, forcibly return them to the car, and start over, doubly slow and methodical this time. The entire routine took about 20 minutes, so the family was often late.

Victor was subject to other paranoias. Tessa remembered how he lived in fear of the pump running while they were away from the house. This was the worst of all possibilities in his world, leading to flooding, high bills, and God knows what other Biblical-level catastrophes. As a result of this obsession, his wife and daughters were effectively banned from using the toilet half an hour before they left the house. Once a trip to Maine was almost ruined by Victor refusing to leave until someone admitted to the crime of using the bathroom, thus causing the pump to run. Deborahann ended up confessing just to end the stalemate—she knew Victor was capable of waiting hours to prove a point. He called his wife a "stupid arse," as usual, but the paranoiac demons were momentarily quelled and he was calm enough to drive. The real culprit who had dared urinate before they went on vacation was 12 year old Tessa. She knew her mother had taken the fall for her. It wasn't the first time. She felt gratitude and contempt. In the same psychology course that covered OCD, Tessa also learned the term "enabler."

Reflecting on these things in the wake of what had happened over Reading Week, Tessa became fixated on getting Lilly to admit that their father was pathological. Tessa decided, with sorrow, that their mother was a lost cause. Married at 19, Deborahann had never left Beaconsbridge and was accustomed only to the constraints of life living with a lunatic.

Tessa called Lilly and told her everything. There was a long, pregnant pause on the line. "Are you *sure* that's what happened?" Lilly finally said.

Out of desperation, Tessa played her last card. She brought up something Lilly didn't want to think about anymore. Once, when Tessa was in high school and Lilly was in middle school, Lilly had told her a strange story about being alone with their father after school, and him trying to force her to wash his hair. This was a task he often made his wife do, but that day Deborahann was working late and Tessa was also out. Lilly, a bashful 11 year old, shied away from the forced intimacy of such a thing. At first she laughed at the request, but Victor was determined. He tried pulling her into the bathroom by the arm. At that moment, something shifted in Lilly's brain. She pulled away and ran out of the house. Lilly stayed outside until it was dark and her mother and sister were back. When she returned, her father was at his customary post, the recliner in front of the television. Half-asleep, he grunted at her in greeting, and acted like nothing had happened.

"So, what about that weird hair-washing thing he did to you?" Tessa asked. "You know he's fucked in the head."

"He's just pushy. He's not...*abusive*, if that's what you're trying to say," said Lilly.

She whispered the word "abusive," as if saying it aloud would bring it, Rumpelstiltskin-like, into being. Lilly wanted her sister to stop talking.

Tessa breathed heavily and ended the conversation. Lilly's response was the final betrayal. Tessa was tough, but her family had knocked her to the canvas at last.

After that frustrating phone call, Tessa felt permanently tired. She moved slowly. She walked slowly. She barely had enough energy to get through the day. She maintained her professional duties in a zombified state, teaching her composition courses and tutoring at the Writing Center, but engaging emotionally with no one. Every day she arrived on campus, did her work, and returned home to her basement room. The trick was getting through the day without crying—she was proud of herself for holding it in until she returned home. Tessa ate little and it showed: her already slender frame became gaunt. Her reserves dwindled. She felt weakened and fragile, with no protective barrier between herself and the world.

Tessa was too depressed to even care about Adrian's latest budget of gossip: Maia had broken up with Mark over Reading Week. ("She found his cache of Paulson books under the bed and they had a *colossal* fight. I mean, *huge*. I heard every syllable through the wall...He chased her to her car in his underwear. It was pathetic.") Adrian had bounded up like a puppy to tell her, and Tessa just shrugged, poured the kettle, and returned to the basement with her Lapsang Souchong. Adrian was hurt, but he intuited that whatever had happened to his friend in Beaconsbridge went deeper than her love life and career problems. He decided to wait for Tessa to tell him herself, when and if she ever felt like telling.

The bottom fell out for Tessa one Saturday night, a few weeks after her father had beaten her. Adrian and Mark were both out for the evening. Tessa had decided to take advantage of having the townhouse to herself by enjoying a long, warm bath in the upstairs bathroom. Her basement bathroom only had a shower. Like everything lately, carrying out this basic task was exhausting, but she was determined to do it, as if taking a bath would help her somehow achieve normalcy.

Tessa drew her bath in a daze. The bathroom filled with steam, giving the scene an even more dream-like quality. She lowered herself into the tub and sat there, lumpen, staring at the rusty faucet.

Drip, drip, drip. The world was reduced to that faucet, that slow, interminable *drip, drip, drip.*

Tessa panned back and saw, peaking out above the tub-water, two white pillars of fat and muscle. She recognized her own legs, though they seemed as separate from her and as inanimate as the tub and the faucet and the water. There was no Tessa at that moment. There was only a limited number of things: big, heavy, meaningless things. Tessa observed the things without emotion. It didn't matter what happened to the things. They were only things. She waited what might have been a minute or an hour, and then lay back and submerged herself. She lowered her face under the water, and automatically began blowing air-bubbles. She counted in her head. *One, two, three, four, five, six, seven...*

It was peaceful down there. Everything moved slowly. She could hear her bubbles churning the water, and the steady thudding of her heart. She opened her eyes and stared up at the blurry outlines of the dated bathroom: the white popcorn ceiling; the brass trim on the fixtures; and the seafoam green tub, sink, and flush. From below the water, she gazed at it all as a bored museum-goer would an Impressionist painting.

What if I just kept my head down?

The thought didn't strike her as dangerous. It was the next sensible step. Why not stay underwater forever, where it was quiet, calm and warm? Here she felt safe.

Tessa wondered why the option of opting-out had never occurred to her before. Instead, she had always struggled to make sense of her problems, to confront them head-on. But there was no making sense of what had happened over Reading Week. Not yet. It was one thing to sense enmity inchoate, it was quite another to process fully-realized hatred in the form of physical violence. She couldn't reason her way out of the pain and confusion, the swirling chaos in the world above.

She had been underwater for over a minute now.

What about just hitting the "off" button?

Tessa's body refused to comply. Of its own accord, her head jerked to the surface, gasping for air. She lifted herself up on her spindly arms and coughed, hacking up water. Her lungs convulsed. She rocked back and forth in the water, sobbing and shaking.

Fuck. Tessa, are you really going to do this? Are you going to let the bastards win?

She stepped out of the tub, dripping, and looked at herself in the mirror. The woman in the reflection was flat-chested and pallid. She could count her ribs. Her eyes were twin voids, cigarette burns in a white sheet.

Still detached, but more clear-headed now, Tessa began to enjoy the drama of the scene: in the still of the night, a sordid suicide, alone in a dreary room, in a dreary house, on the edge of the dreary Canadian prairies. Her inner self smirked. *Oh the pathos! Oh the bathos!*

Tessa realized that it would have been almost impossible to kill herself in this idiotic way. *The classic move is cutting your wrists and bleeding out into the water,* she observed, *not trying to hold your breath underwater in a shallow bath like a dumbass. The reflexes will kick in and save you every time.*

Another ghastly thought occurred to her.

What if Mark was the one who found my corpse—my nude corpse?

She could accept the possibility of Adrian finding her, but not Mark. She was horrified by the idea of Mark's prurient little bro-eyes drinking in the scene. She realized then that if she was truly suicidal, she wouldn't be worrying about Mark learning the secrets of her bikini-area shaving regimen.

Tessa toweled dry and made her way to her bedroom. Adrian and Mark were both still out. The house was empty. She was conscious of veering off a dark path. She was intervening now in the flow of events, an agent in her own life. Despite all she'd accomplished since leaving Beaconsbridge, she'd never felt that way before. She'd always felt constrained by circumstances, and the decisions of other people: a fatalist, typical of her Maritimer class. As frustrating as it was, there was also safety in believing that, because then failures could be blamed on factors beyond one's control. There was terror and magnificence in the essential question:

What does it mean to be responsible for your own life?

She admitted to herself that she'd been wounded. She had been wounded by the wicked, but also by the kind and good. She had to go forward without their understanding or assistance if she wanted to save herself. And she had decided to save herself.

That night, Tessa resolved that first thing Monday morning she would find a behavioral psychologist in Sere Valley and book an appointment. She would charge the sessions on her credit card. She needed help putting herself back together. There could be no more Saturday nights flirting with oblivion.

Chapter Sixteen: Cubic Zirconia Cut Cubic Zirconia

Fr: Amy Mephistos— a.mephistos@svu.edu

To: Womyn's Scholars Group Listserv

CC: Darlene Morris—dk.morris@svu.edu

Subject: Surprise Baby Gift for Angelika: Suggestions?

Date: Apr. 10, 2017, 1:40 p.m.

Ladies,

 I'm sure I'm not letting the cat out of the bag by telling you now that our friend and colleague, Angelika Franco, is due in under a month! Naturally, this is a very exciting time for her, and Yvonne and I thought it would be nice if the Womyn's Scholars presented a thoughtful baby gift. Any suggestions?

 Angelika, btw, told me she's expecting a girl: another "nasty woman" is on the way! Haha!

 Please drop off your financial contributions toward the gift with Darlene, administrative assistant for the Dept. of Women and Gender Studies (Swineham 340). Please have them in by the end of the week, so Darlene can pick up a present over the weekend. I suppose if our choice of gift is more expensive than the funds received, Darlene can cover the rest—we will, of course, be happy to reimburse her from petty cash. (Thanks Darlene!)

 In solidarity,

Amy

p.s. I've temporarily removed Angelika from the listserv for this discussion. Please keep this under wraps...

--Amy Mephistos

Co-President, Womyn's Scholars Group

Associate Professor, Department of Women and Gender Studies

Sere Valley University

Fr: Darlene Morris—dk.morris@svu.edu

To: Womyn's Scholars Group Listserv

Subject: RE: Surprise Baby Gift for Angelika: Suggestions?

Date: Apr. 10, 2017, 1:41 p.m.

I will not be purchasing a gift more expensive than funds received.

Darlene

--Darlene Morris

Senior Administrative Assistant, Department of Women and Gender Studies

Sere Valley University

Fr: Jessica Mincing—jd.mincing@svu.edu

To: Womyn's Scholars Group Listserv

Subject: RE: RE: Surprise Baby Gift for Angelika: Suggestions?

Date: Apr. 10, 2017, 1:57 p.m.

    What a great idea!

    I suggest we give Angelika a "Children's Starter Library" of sorts, with all of our favorites: maybe some Dr. Seuss, Babar, Curious George, *Goodnight Moon*, *Where the Wild Things Are*, *The Very Hungry Caterpillar*, etc.

    Best,

Jessica

--Jessica Mincing

Assistant Professor, Department of English Literature

Sere Valley University

Fr: Elizabeth Wagband—e.wagband@svu.edu

To: Womyn's Scholars Group Listserv

Subject: RE: RE: RE: Surprise Baby Gift for Angelika: Suggestions?

Date: Apr. 10, 2017, 2:30 p.m.

Greetings to all,

Jessica's idea is a good one, HOWEVER, I would note that many of the particular books she has suggested are deeply, DEEPLY problematic. As one of the Co-Organizers of the 1994 *PFL* (*Prairie Feminist Literature*) Children's Literature Conference, this happens to be one of my areas of scholarly expertise.

I presume all of you have at least a passing acquaintance with the Flora L. Ingersoll Montague Feminist Literary Analysis Monograph? (I should note it's become all but indispensable today in the field of Oceanian Homosocial Disability Literature.) You may recall seeing the cover of the '70s first edition? It presents Ingersoll Montague herself, magnificently bare-breasted on a cross, head hanging, covered in red welts—a powerful illustration of the monograph's thesis: "YOUR ART IS MY SCOURGE."

I'm afraid Jessica's selections are indeed a scourge. To begin with, Dr. Seuss is racist. Babar is a postcolonial nightmare. (And the relationship between the Old Lady and her under-age protégé, Babar, is, shall we say, unsettling...) The Curious George series encourages the deeply cruel exotic pet trade (as does Babar, come to think of it). *Goodnight Moon* inculcates harmful gender stereotypes (a "quiet old lady...whispering 'hush[!]'"). Sendak's *Where the Wild Things Are* normalizes toxic masculinity. (As I recall, the "Max" boy character dominates the "wild things" through the threat of violence.) Finally, *The Very Hungry Caterpillar* encourages disordered eating and body dysmorphia.

I'm sure we can do better than this, ladies.

Regards,

Elizabeth

--Elizabeth Wagband

Professor, Department of English Literature

Sere Valley University

Fr: Tilly Tippaloo-Montmorency—t.tippaloo@svu.edu

To: Womyn's Scholars Group Listserv

Subject: RE: RE: RE: RE: Surprise Baby Gift for Angelika: Suggestions?

Date: Apr. 10, 2017, 2:46 p.m.

Overall, I agree with Elizabeth, though I would note that at least one scholar has pointed to some subversive feminist elements in the Babar series. Please see Alexandra Crossthwaite's insightful essay, "A Curious Ménage à Trois: Babar, Celeste, and The Old Lady" in the spring issue of *Feminist Transmutations*. (I presume you all keep abreast of *FemTrans*? They've been putting out some truly remarkable work of late. I would say it's the *Feminist Peregrinations* of our time. No, scratch that, the *Feminist Iterations* of our time. It's really that good!) Crossthwaite argues, among other things, that the youthful Babar's relationship with the Old

Lady is clearly that of a gigolo and a mature woman of means—an interesting departure from sexual paradigms established in earlier pachyderm-protagonist children's literature.

Would it perhaps be worthwhile to include the Crossthwaite essay, in addition to one or more of the Babar books, so that Dr. Franco might better explain the complex sexual politics of the series to her infant when it is developmentally ready? (Age 2 or 3? Excuse my ignorance on these matters.)

Tilly

--Tilly Tippaloo-Montmorency

Associate Professor, Department of Women and Gender Studies

Sere Valley University

Fr: Amy Mephistos—a.mephistos@svu.edu

To: Womyn's Scholars Group Listserv

Subject: RE: RE: RE: RE: RE: Surprise Baby Gift for Angelika: Suggestions?

Date: Apr. 10, 2017, 2:59 p.m.

Hmm, perhaps rather than give Angelika problematic texts (with or without proper explication, as per Tilly's helpful suggestion), it might be better to include only those that are wholly positive and progressive. My sister received a cute book last year at her baby shower. I'm sure you've all heard of *Heather Has Two Mommies*? It really broke the heteronormative mold in the '80s. Well, this is sort of an updated version of that: *Lennon Has Four Mommies*. It's adorable. It discusses the IVF and surrogacy process in simple terms that are easy for a young child to understand. In the book, Lennon's four mommies are "Mommy," "Mama," "Egg-Mommy" (the egg donor, natch) and "Tummy-Mommy" (the surrogate). I really liked how the author included the egg donor and the surrogate in the list of "mommies." It was so respectful. The underlying message is that families come in all shapes and sizes. Isn't that lovely? And did I mention it rhymes? *And* it teaches legal terms? ("All the Mommies played a part,/ Each one with a loving heart./ Tummy-Mommy did gestation./ She received fair compensation./ Not all Mommies want exposure./ So they sign a non-disclosure.")

What do you think, ladies?

--Amy Mephistos

Co-President, Womyn's Scholars Group

Associate Professor, Department of Women and Gender Studies

Sere Valley University

Fr: Monique Cormier-Shafer—m.cormiershafer@svu.edu

To: Womyn's Scholars Group Listserv

Subject: RE: RE: RE: RE: RE: RE: Surprise Baby Gift for Angelika: Suggestions?

Date: Apr. 10, 2017, 3:14 p.m.

Lennon Has Four Mommies sounds delightful. Put me in the Yes column for that one. Has anyone checked out the *A is for ANTIFA* series? My Allegra is a big fan. It's technically YA fiction, not children's, but I'm sure Angelika would appreciate it for when her daughter is a bit older. I can only personally vouch for the series up to *C is for Cultural Appropriation*, but based on the first three, I'm guessing they're all first-rate. I see here on the publisher's site that the authors have made it as far as *G is for Genocide*. Yay or nay, friends?

It's funny that the topic of children's literature keeps coming up in my world. Last week at Montessori, Allegra staged an in-class demonstration with some of her friends. They were protesting the course's dearth of literature by female/LGBTQ+/writers of color. They chanted over their teacher until their voices were hoarse. I was so proud! You won't believe this, but that deplorable teacher had the gall to send my Allegra to the principal's office for being "disrespectful and disruptive." (It's Montessori, but Montessori Sere Valley, I would note, so he's probably a local...) In the note home, he wrote that Allegra "actively prevented other students from learning by talking over the lecture" (!!!). Don't get me started on the underlying assumptions in that statement—as if students' "right to learn" supersedes Allegra's right to protest injustice! Also, since when do middle school teachers "lecture" in their classes? Cute, no? At any rate, I did not mince words with the principal. I even brought in our psychiatrist's note detailing the magnitude of psychic violence poor Allegra had suffered as a result of this episode. There may be a happy ending after all though: the principal has assured me that the teacher has been disciplined and will be apologizing to Allegra immediately.

  Excuse the digression, ladies. I think I just needed to vent after last week's ordeal!

Monique

--Monique Cormier-Shafer

Associate Professor, Department of History

Sere Valley University

Fr: Jessica Mincing—jd.mincing@svu.edu

To: Womyn's Scholars Group Listserv

Subject: RE: RE: RE: RE: RE: RE: RE: Surprise Baby Gift for Angelika: Suggestions?

Date: Apr. 10, 2017, 3:35 p.m.

Ladies,

I've just returned from teaching to read this email thread. I'd like to apologize to Elizabeth and everyone else. Please believe me when I say it was never my intention to suggest offensive children's literature! Truthfully, I was just making suggestions off the top of my head. I haven't read any of these books since childhood, and I was politically ignorant back then.

I think the two progressive suggestions from Amy and Monique sound marvelous.

Once again, my absolute sincerest apologies to everyone for my earlier suggestions—especially to Elizabeth.

Yours in solidarity,

Jessica

p.s. This dialogue has given me an excuse to dust off my much-treasured first edition of Ingersoll Montague: a perennial delight! Thanks for reminding us, Elizabeth!

p.p.s. Lunch tomorrow, Elizabeth? Will PM.

--Jessica Mincing

Assistant Professor, Department of English Literature

Sere Valley University

Fr: Elizabeth Wagband—e.wagband@svu.edu

To: Womyn's Scholars Group Listserv

Subject: RE: RE: RE: RE: RE: RE: RE: Surprise Baby Gift for Angelika: Suggestions?

Date: Apr. 10, 2017, 3:50 p.m.

Apology accepted, Jessica. This may be, as they say, a "teachable moment" for us all. As I tell my grad students every day, in a patriarchal society like ours, there are no "innocent" texts. When producing works conveying regressive attitudes—or outright hate speech—very often the writer will say, "But it wasn't my intention! You're reading something into it that wasn't there!" Utter nonsense. Ninety percent of the time they're lying; the other ten percent of the time they're subconsciously communicating their TRUE biases through the text. The text, in fact, is really beside the point: white, male, cisgendered authors are in the business of maintaining their privilege. Full stop.

 Best,

Elizabeth

--Elizabeth Wagband

Professor, Department of English Literature

Sere Valley University

Fr: Isla Smythe—i.smythe@svu.edu

To: Womyn's Scholars Group Listserv

Subject: RE: RE: RE: RE: RE: RE: RE: RE: Surprise Baby Gift for Angelika: Suggestions?

Date: Apr. 10, 2017, 3:53 p.m.

Hello ladies,

 Does anyone have any objections to *Ten Little Fingers and Ten Little Toes*? That was one of our favorites with Sadie, back in the day. For those unfamiliar with the book, it presents an international group of babies, emphasizing commonalities across cultures (i.e. they all have "ten little fingers and ten little toes").

 Cheers,

Isla

--Isla Smythe

Lecturer, Department of Psychology

Sere Valley University

Fr: Margaret Truffle—m.truffle@svu.edu

To: Womyn's Scholars Group Listserv

Subject: RE: RE: RE: RE: RE: RE: RE: RE: RE: Surprise Baby Gift for Angelika...

Date: Apr. 10, 2017, 4:10 p.m.

    Without reading the text in question, I have some concerns: firstly, *Ten Little Fingers and Ten Little Toes* sounds alarmingly ableist; and secondly, it excludes one of society's most marginalized and misunderstood groups: the polydactyl community. No Isla, not "all" babies have "ten little fingers and ten little toes," and to exclude this group from the dialogue is to do violence to them.

    In addition, if I understood you correctly, the author is attempting to universalize human experience (in this case, through the claim that certain physical features are universal—which as noted, is a fallacy). If history has taught us anything, it is that in Western societies so-called "universal" human values and behaviors are often code for "white, male, upper-class" values and behaviors. Does a white baby or parent narrate the book, by any chance? And what values, behaviors, and physical characteristics are deemed "universal?"

    Whatever the answers to these queries, it behooves us to question both the *possibility* and the *desirability* of human "universals." Too often, the claim of universality is naught but a tool for cultural imperialism and the patriarchy.

M

--Margaret Truffle

Professor, Department of Film Studies

Sere Valley University

Fr: Isla Smythe—i.smythe@svu.edu

To: Womyn's Scholars Group Listserv

Subject: RE: RE: RE: RE: RE: RE: RE: RE: RE: RE: RE: Surprise Baby Gift for Angelika...

Date: Apr. 10, 2017, 4:21 p.m.

    Margaret's points are well-taken. Apologies. That never occurred to me. I appreciate the "check your [ableist] privilege" moment! Thank you, Margaret.

--Isla Smythe

Lecturer, Department of Psychology

Sere Valley University

Fr: Elizabeth Wagband—e.wagband@svu.edu

To: Womyn's Scholars Group Listserv

Subject: RE: RE: RE: RE: RE: RE: RE: RE: RE: RE: RE: RE: Surprise Baby Gift...

Date: Apr. 10, 2017, 4:45 p.m.

    I've thought of a more appropriate option I'm surprised no one's mentioned yet. I think the title is something like *Nursery Rhymes for Progressives*. It was published a few years back. I *think* I read a favorable review of it in *The Guardian* at the time. It's shocking how offensive so many of the original rhymes are—racist, ableist, misogynist, fascist, etc. And they're meant for children (!). This work is a much-needed, heavily revised, and

THOUGHTFUL version of the "Mother Goose" rhymes (aside: not all geese even *want* to be mothers).

For example, "Simple Simon" (!) is reimagined as "Neuro-divergent Simon." Sadly, in the original, oppressive version, as you may recall, Simon asks to taste the wares of the "pieman" (updated to "pie-person" in the new version), and that crass merchant says, "Show me first your penny." Simon replies, "Indeed, I have not any." Presumably, Simon goes hungry. (Note: the original poem is unclear, but given Simon's implied lower socio-economic status, it is probable he lived in an urban food desert to begin with—high-sugar, low-nutrient baked goods were likely the only foods available.) In the progressive version of the rhyme, Simon politely but firmly explains to the pie merchant that proper nutrition is a human right. The merchant has a change of heart and decides to leave the pie business behind to start a community garden non-profit.

As you can see, the updated version is a great improvement over the original.

Regards,

Elizabeth

--Elizabeth Wagband

Professor, Department of English Literature

Sere Valley University

An additional 47 reply-alls were generated over the course of the week. The group did not reach a consensus on the topic of appropriate children's books for Angelika's fetus. Darlene the admin eventually interjected and suggested a gift certificate from Barnes & Noble. This was rejected by the Womyn's Scholars in favour of a gift certificate from The Best of Tomes, Sere Valley's only independent new and used bookstore. Upon calling the store, Darlene discovered that it did not sell gift certificates. The group, unfortunately, was unable to decide on an alternative by the end-of-week deadline, and so Angelika was never given a baby gift.

***

"A veritable barrage of bullshit," said Adrian at The Ranch Hand that Friday night, shaking his head in disgust as Tessa recounted the email chain debate. "How do you tolerate it?"

Tessa grunted and lifted her pilsner heavenward.

"Your liver doesn't think that's a good long-term solution."

"My liver doesn't get a vote."

Adrian chuckled. He was pleased he had convinced Tessa to emerge from her basement lair. She hadn't been out in weeks. As he had told his mother on the phone, Tessa seemed to have turned a corner and was finally getting over the Andrew split and whatever had happened to her over Reading Week in Beaconsbridge. He knew she had started seeing a counselor, and it was helping.

"What happened to Boudicca, by the way?" he asked.

"Her army was defeated and she committed suicide."

"Riiiight."

"Mark bailed on me. We only sent out one more email out after Christmas. And frankly, I didn't have the nerve to keep it up anyway."

Adrian resisted the urge to say, "Isn't that's what Andrew said?" Too soon. He waited a beat, listening to Reba on the jukebox warbling "Fancy."

"I guess you didn't have a card to play after Maia dumped him."

"The original agreement was unclear. And to be fair, it was a risky undertaking. Mark said Computing Services was getting a lot of complaints from the PFP and they were starting to suspect an inside job."

"Isn't Computing Services just that old Hans dude and a couple Support Desk serfs? They're clueless."

"Yeah, but even they were starting to put shit together."

"Oh...So how's the PD talk coming along? That's next Friday, right?"

"Yes, and you better be there for moral support. You promised."

"Oh, I'll be there. Not like I have anything better to do."

"I know."

Adrian rolled his eyes and sipped his cocktail.

"I can't believe Flamm had the nerve to ask you to do it, after they rejected you for the TT position."

"He knows I'll do a good job and he knows I need references."

"You also need an endless stream of shitty term-to-term teaching positions while you look for a full-time professorship. Those fuckers really have you over a barrel, don't they? Who got the job, anyway?"

"Some floozy Flamm has the hots for, according to Pearl...Okay, that's mean. She's an American. Around my age. From one of the Ivies—can't remember which. An SVU Ph.D. doesn't really compare to a Harvard one. And there are good reasons not to hire internally, I guess."

"But if they don't value their own degrees when it comes to hiring, aren't they tacitly admitting their own department sucks?"

"Very good, Adrian. You've cracked the code. Welcome to Canadian academia."

"It would appear to be as milquetoast and ball-less as all things Canadian."

"Toast and testicles. That's quite the mixed metaphor."

"Call me Whitman. *Walt* Whitman."

Tessa cracked a smile, noticing that Adrian's button-down shirt had a coffee stain running half the length of his chest. He had several things in common with the bohemian poet.

"So are you done writing the talk yet?" asked Adrian.

"I keep starting and then deleting everything…It's lies. All lies."

"But you've always managed your cognitive dissonance in academia so adroitly before."

"It's true. I'm conscientious that way."

"Very."

"Lately I've started to think I've gone as far as I can go with conscientious. Maybe I need to give audacious a try."

"What do you have to lose?"

"Only the last decade of my life."

"No biggie."

"Nope."

"Well, if you need an editor or an audience, I'm happy to oblige, friend."

"I know. Thanks, buddy."

The pair finished their drinks, split the tab, and took the #5 back to the townhouse together.

Chapter Seventeen: Fiddleheading

This is the forest primeval.

Deborahann only remembered the first line from the Longfellow poem. She hadn't read it since high school, but she thought of it every time she was alone in the woods, as she was that Sunday afternoon.

Tessie-Bear would love that line, she thought, always proud of her literary-minded oldest daughter.

If Tessa's realm was that of the mind, her mother's was of the earth. The happiest times in Deborahann's life were spent weeding her garden, rambling the Madawaaksis countryside in search of wildflowers, or what she was doing now, foraging for fiddlehead ferns in the backwoods. When Deborahann was indoors she felt a near-constant tightness in her chest. Sometimes it was difficult to breathe. She often felt claustrophobic. When she was outdoors, preferably with her hands in the soil, that tightness lifted.

Vic was resentful whenever his wife was not at home at his beck and call, but he hadn't been able to come up with a reason for her to stay home that afternoon. Vic himself didn't care for fiddleheads, so he didn't see the point of his wife devoting an afternoon to foraging for them. To placate him, Deborahann baked a blueberry pie for lunch. "It's not runny enough," he told her, which is what he always said. "I like 'em runny. I'm not fussy about these clumpy pies you make."

The pie, nonetheless, bought her a few blessed hours of freedom that afternoon, after church. Like every adult resident of Madawaaksis County, Deborahann had a favorite foraging spot for the April crop of fiddleheads; these spots were jealously guarded secrets. She parked the car on the shoulder of the road out of town. The Civic was at a discreet distance from her actual entry-spot into the woods—all the better to throw off busybodies.

Deborahann always thought about her father when she made her yearly fiddleheading excursion. They used to go fiddleheading together when she was a little girl; he knew all the good places. She didn't have many memories of him, but the few she had were cherished. She would take them out periodically, run them through her mind like a jeweller polishing a hoard of precious gems. Once again she felt his presence under the gently breathing canopy of the Acadian forest. As she came upon a sunlit clearing, she half-expected to see him there, in his old leather hunting vest and rubber boots, the usual wry smile on his face.

Why Jack and Ada had no children of their own was a mystery. No one discussed such things in those days, though there were whispers that Ada was barren. Deborahann worked up the courage to ask her mother once. Ada sat up straight as a bow and said, "It was God's will, Deborahann," which her daughter interpreted as infertility. She never asked again. Had he not been under the soil for 24 years, old Dr. Clifton could have told her that her mother had had eight consecutive miscarriages over five years, before giving up and turning to adoption.

Jack Case agreed to adoption, "to please Ada," he said. But he was the one who took to the blocky, solemn-eyed child, and vice-versa. Deborahann and Jack were simpatico from the start. Ada was a stickler for rules, but Jack let Deborahann play in the mud and eat cookies before supper. Her father's sudden, swift death of lung cancer when she was 10 years old marked a clear divider-line in Deborahann's life. Before he died, she was the cherished only child of the town storekeeper and his wife. After he died, she was the unprotected child of a neurotic, religious widow.

The house was paid off, but without Jack's earning power, it began to deteriorate. First, they lived off Jack's life insurance, then his small nest-egg. Then they sold the few acres of wood lots Jack had acquired over the years, and lived off that. When those wells ran dry, they lived off welfare and charity. Once the last word in modern convenience, their 1960s kitchen stayed frozen in time, from Jack's death on. Like the entire house, it grew shabbier with every passing year. Deborahann no longer had new clothes. She exclusively wore home-sewn dresses or hand-me-downs from cousins. Ada told her that real friends were interested in her, not her clothes, which was sensible enough, but of no comfort to an insecure 10 year old.

Ada had always been a religious fatalist; after Jack died, she fully accepted their reduced circumstances, and even saw them as a badge of honor: "We're not fancy," read the cross-stitch on the wall, "We're *family*"—as if financial and emotional security were mutually exclusive. Besides driving her around, Ada also relied on her brothers or charitable neighbors to fix her appliances when they needed repairs, to mow her lawn, to paint her house—and so on. She always told Deborahann, who was more worried about money than her mother was, that the Lord would provide. And He always seemed to, although in later years, Deborahann realized that it was the Canadian taxpayer, not the Lord, who did most of the providing for them.

Frowning as she tromped through the brush, Deborahann recalled one dreadful day at school, a few years after her father died. Always a plump girl, her tight, patched, third-hand pants split across the rump while she was playing at recess. Her homeroom teacher, a warm-hearted woman named Mrs. Westbrook, lent the child an extra skirt. All of this was embarrassing enough for Deborahann, but worse still was overhearing a conversation between Mrs. Westbrook and another teacher. "That's Deborahann Case in my skirt, poor thing." Her colleague, who fancied herself a wit, replied, "Charity Case, more like!" The joke burned into the firmament of Deborahann's soul. She picked at her supper that night and went to bed early. Ada wondered if the girl was coming down with something.

Deborahann remembered every detail of that day as she walked in the shadows of the woods, closer to the rushing water, where the biggest fiddleheads grew. She could hear the hissing of the brook in the distance. She tried to push the bad memories aside. There were so many good ones too.

She remembered being sent by her mother to the dirt-floor basement cold room to fetch a jar of mustard pickles for supper. She was five. Half-way back up the stairs she dropped the jar. It smashed into a thousand jagged shards everywhere. Brine, pickles and glass covered the stairs, the basement floor, and Deborahann's dress. *Mummy was going to be mad!* With a small child's clumsy fingers, she tried to gather together the broken pieces of glass and clean up the mess. It was impossible. The anxious child burst into tears.

Her father was returning home from work. Hearing sobs from the basement, he dropped his lunch-bucket, and hurried down the stairs, heart in his throat. Had she fallen? He sized up the situation in a second and swooped up the little girl before she could cut herself on the glass. "D-D-Daddy, I br-br-broke it," blubbered Deborahann, enormous crocodile tears streaking her face. Jack hugged her close. "It doesn't matter, girlie," he said. Deborahann knew instantly and with certainty that Daddy didn't care about the wasted pickles or the broken jar. She wasn't in trouble. It was going to be okay.

But it hasn't been okay since Daddy died, thought Deborahann, 42 years later, in the cool of the woods.

The sound of someone crying jarred her from her brown study. *Is that a woman or just the brook?* she wondered. It was a piteous sound, whatever it was, like someone's heart was breaking. Deborahann moved toward it with caution. As she approached, her jaw dropped. Surely that half-obscured figure on the ground by the brook was Margaret Fudge herself, the pastor's wife. She was hunched over in a fetal position. Deborahann knew that the parsonage property bordered the other side of this woods. It wasn't so strange that Margaret would be there, only strange to happen upon her like this. Deborahann stepped heavily on the brush, making an obvious rustle to alert Margaret of her presence. Margaret startled nonetheless, her body recoiling like a spring. Still crouched on her knees, her back snapped up straight.

"Margaret, it's just me, Deborahann," she called out, a few feet away.

Almost imperceptibly, Margaret's posture relaxed.

"Are you okay? What's wrong?"

Margaret's face was red and tear-streaked. She continued to sob.

This was not the closed-off, robotic woman Deborahann had known for years. This was another creature entirely, a fellow sufferer, here midst the flickering leaves, and the whisper of the brook. Deborahann walked closer and helped Margaret to her feet. She gave her a hug.

"It's okay."

The spell didn't last long, only a few seconds, then Margaret, as if suddenly coming to her senses, pulled away.

"I went for a walk…I'm not feeling well…I need to go..."

"If there's something wrong—whatever it is—you can talk to me, Margaret."

"I need to go *now*."

There was an urgency in her voice.

"Ok."

Deborahann watched Margaret as she scrambled away awkwardly, up the embankment, and out of sight. As she disappeared at the edge of the tree-line, Deborahann wondered if she had imagined the whole thing. *What on earth is the matter with Margaret?*

***

That night after supper, the tightness in Deborahann's chest was almost unbearable. She couldn't make any sense of her encounter in the woods. She felt a nameless dread. It seized upon her as soon as the sun set, growing progressively worse as the shadows lengthened. She didn't understand it and she refused to let it coalesce in her head. Instead, she tried to block it out, focusing on scrubbing off every morsel of encrusted food from the casserole dish. Deborahann could make out the unmistakable buxom shadow of Audrey MacBride at her kitchen window next door, similarly employed. Vic was in the next room, snoozing in his recliner, as usual. Deborahann felt like the last man on earth.

After she finished scrubbing the pots, she grew restless again. Vic had a pair of overalls that needed patching; she could do that. Deborahann made a mental inventory of the food available for the upcoming week's five suppers. She decided there was only enough to get them to Thursday, even with leftovers. *I'll buy a cheap cut of meat at Cuthbert's tomorrow after work. I'll marinate it overnight and it will taste as good as sirloin.* She prided herself on her ability to make tasty food on the cheap, and felt guilty when she spent money on lunch at work, instead of bringing something from home.

Deborahann felt a sudden urge to drink a tall glass of cold milk. It was a luxury she'd rarely allowed herself when the girls were still at home, reasoning that growing children needed milk more than she did. Now she reasoned that Victor needed it more than her because he did physical work, and she just "stood behind a counter all day," as he put it. She resisted pouring herself a glass. *I don't need it. There won't be enough for Vic's cereal tomorrow.*

Deborahann paced. If pressed, she would have labelled her restlessness as boredom. *I'll give the girls a ring. See what they're up to.*

Deborahann dialed Tessa's number. The time zone difference meant it was three hours earlier "Out West," making it 9:15 p.m. in Beaconsbridge, New Brunswick, and 6:15 p.m. in Sere Valley, Alberta. Like many New Brunswickers, Deborahann thought of Out West in the abstract, as that enormous, semi-civilized swath of Canadian territory, stretching from the New Brunswick-Quebec border, all the way to the Pacific. The phone rang many times, and she called repeatedly before Tessa picked up.

"Hi Tessie!" Deborahann burbled into the phone.

"What is it? Is there an emergency?"

"No, doughnut. I just wanted to hear your sweet voice."

"Mum, you called, like, 50 times in a row. I thought it was important."

"Grumpy bear! Do I need a reason to call my girls?"

Tessa sighed.

"I'm working on something."

"What?"

"The professional development talk Flamm asked me to do. It's on Friday and I won't have a chance to work on it much this week. I need to finish it tonight."

"Oh yeah?"

Deborahann was too agitated to listen. 95% of what Tessa did in academia was boring and impenetrable to her anyway.

"I just wanted to chat while I was doing the dishes. Do you have five minutes?"

"I guess."

Deborahann launched into a breezy monologue, complaining about Amber and Elinor at Sentimental Occasions. As she spoke, the anxiety ebbed, the silent things lurking in the shadows were buried under heaps of commonplace words.

"…so I said to Amber, 'Amber, I can't go behind you and re-do every arrangement. You need to listen the first time!'"

"Uh huh."

"Do you think I went too far? Your father thinks I went too far. I wasn't ignorant." (Tessa wondered, briefly, if there were other English-speaking groups around the globe who used this word in the peculiar Canadian Maritimer sense, meaning rude, not lacking knowledge.)

"I don't know, Mum."

Tessa put the phone on speaker and returned to her talk, pecking away on her laptop.

"Tessa? Tessa, are you listening?"

"Yes."

"You're on your laptop, aren't you?"

"No."

"Yes you are. I can hear you typing."

"No I'm not."

"Tessa!"

"Look, Mum, I don't have all night to listen to you bitch about Sentimental Occasions. If you don't like it, why don't you quit?"

Deborahann bristled.

"And pay the mortgage with what? Fresh air and fiddleheads?"

"You make peanuts in Beaconsbridge. Can't you just travel a little further and find some other job that pays peanuts in Moncton? You can't find another flower shop job there? Have you even tried?"

"Of *course* I've tried, young lady! D'you know how hard it is to find anything around here at my age? I'm not young and cute like you. I'm 40 pounds overweight. I'm not bilingual. You know what that means in Moncton. And I don't have a degree. It's all frigging around with computers now, and I can't do that. I have no experience other than Sentimental Occasions and staying home with you kids."

"Mum, you've been doing accounting and God-knows-what-all admin work for Dad at the garage for years. It would be underwater if it wasn't for you. You can do more than wait cash at a small town flower shop."

"Me 'waiting cash,' Tessa Anne Stevens, put food on the table and clothes on your back!"

"I know, I know. I'm appreciative," said Tessa.

"Well you sure don't act like you are."

Tessa took a deep breath and tried again.

"I'm not pooh-poohing your work, Mum. I'm just saying you're smart enough and capable enough to do more. Maybe you could take night courses in accounting or something like that. You always said you wanted to do a business degree."

"At 52 years old? It's too late for me."

"No it's not."

"I don't have the time and I don't have the money."

"Can't you guys economize for a while and let Dad hold down the fort?"

Deborahann chuckled.

"Even if we *could* afford it, which we can't, your father can't manage for an afternoon without me, let alone however long it would take for me to do a diploma in something. Besides, it would be selfish of me to take that time away from the house. Your father and I are a team."

Tessa snorted.

"Uh huh. One of the team members contributes a helluva lot more than the other one."

Deborahann let that one go.

"I just wish you would do something for yourself some time."

"I do, Tessie! I have my flowers and my painting. And the church—all that committee-work. I'm way too busy for anything else."

"Yes, you're certainly very busy."

"What's that supposed to mean?"

"I mean you certainly keep busy."

"I don't know why you're in such a snarky mood tonight, Tessa."

"You were always so busy when we were growing up that you never had a spare moment for Lilly and me—always running around like a chicken with its head cut off. Grammy Ada at least made the time to read to us and play games with us."

"Well, excuse me! Maybe I would've had as much time as your precious Grammy Ada if I decided to fold my hands once my husband died and live off welfare for years! But I wanted you girls to have more than I had growing up! I didn't want you to be beholden to anyone! That's not a fun feeling, believe you me, miss!"

"You know what, I think you *like* being busy. I think you *like* being a slave to Dad—then you can complain about being put-upon."

"*Excuse* me?"

"You heard me. I have a question for you, Mum. Listen to me for once. Is working around the clock the price you pay for your right to live?"

"I don't understand."

"You don't need to apologize to anyone for your own existence—especially Dad. You deserve to be on this earth just as much as everyone else. And you deserve breaks. And you deserve *fun*! You're not just a bloody accessory to other people's lives."

Silence. Tessa went on, hell-for-leather.

"Or is it this: do you keep yourself busy so you don't have time to think?"

"What?"

"So you don't have time to think about problems in your life? This way you don't have to make any hard decisions. You can just coast along with the current, letting Dad and everyone else boss you around, instead of taking responsibility for your own damn life."

Deborahann regulated her breathing and put on her Mom voice.

"Tessa, I called to chat, but I can see you're in one of your moods. You're not making any sense."

Tessa's voice was shrill: "Why won't you listen to me?"

"Because I don't know what you're talking about! Tessa, I'm hanging up now. I'll talk to you again in a few days."

"Oh, whatever."

"I'm hanging up now, Tessa."

"Then hang up already! I don't give a shit. You're the one who called, bugging *me* in the first place! Why don't you just leave me alone? Keep right on ruining your own life and stay out of mine!"

Deborahann's voice broke, "That's not a very nice way to speak to your mother!"

"Well, you're a shitty mother! You think Lilly and I liked listening to you and Dad scream and yell at each other every day, while we were upstairs trying to do our fucking homework! Fuck you both!"

Deborahann gasped.

"I did my best…"

"It wasn't good enough!"

"Tessa…"

Tessa dropped the call on her cell. Her head throbbed. She wanted to call back, but steeled herself not to. She returned to the PD talk on her laptop, determined to make more progress that night, but the tears in her eyes blurred the words on the screen. She finally gave up and went to bed. She thought about toddler Deborahann at the group home, with the burnt foot; she thought about what happened with Uncle Milt; she thought about all the times she heard her father tell her mother she couldn't do anything right; she thought about what happened over Reading Week. It was like watching a decades-long suicide.

Chapter Eighteen: Enter (and Exit) Athena

Five days later, Tessa was on campus, headed to her talk. It was 3:55 by the time she made it to the auditorium door. Right on time. Flamm was waiting in the corridor, greeting students on their way in. He smiled as she approached and took her aside, out of earshot of the others.

"Ahh, the good woman herself. We've quite a crowd today."

"We do? I thought no one attended these things."

"They usually don't, but I sent out a little reminder yesterday. Have you checked your email? Something along the lines of, 'We strongly recommend that you take advantage of this opportunity for professional development, etcetera, etctcetera…' Quite right, of course, and it doesn't hurt the visibility of the Department either when one of our instructors steps up to the plate like this. You don't see History jumping in. And their grad student cohort is the same size as ours—slightly larger, I believe."

"Are there many people here?"

"Oh, it's a full house. And more still coming in, I see."

Tessa let out a deep breath.

"Now, now, nothing you can't handle!"

Flamm made a motion as if to heartily pat her back, thought better of it, and returned the errant limb to his side.

"Will you be sitting in on the talk?" Tessa asked.

"'fraid not. I have, uhh, other work to attend to before Exam Week descends upon us. But I'd be delighted if you sent along the transcript."

"Ok."

Tessa looked wan.

Flamm made one final effort, befitting, he thought, a responsible department chair mentoring an apprentice-scholar.

"I have every confidence in you, Tess—err, Dr. Stevens."

"Thank you."

"Oh, yes, and when you send the transcript, pass along your attendance numbers as well, or at least an estimate, so I can keep the Dean's Office apprised."

"Sure, no problem."

Flamm smiled and departed. (Within half an hour, he was sitting on a bar stool at The Ranch Hand, complaining to a colleague about being behind on marking.)

Tessa checked her phone. 3:59. A few more students strolled in. She recognized a familiar rumpled, hulking form. Adrian was the last student to enter the room before her.

"Tessa," he whispered, eyes trained on hers.

"Burn. The motherfucker. Down."

She nodded and stood straighter, shoulders back. Tessa entered the room. 152 pairs of eyes followed the tall, slim young woman as she made her way to the lectern, clipboard notes in hand. She cleared her throat and began to speak.

Transcript of Dr. Tessa Stevens' Graduate Studies Arts and Social Sciences Professional Development Series Lecture #4

April 21, 2017

Good afternoon everyone,

Welcome to PD Talk #4. Many of you know me already. My name is Tessa Stevens. I'm an adjunct instructor here in the English Department. According to your materials, today's lecture is entitled, "Tips on Writing—and Completing!—the Dissertation." I was selected to give this talk because I finished my dissertation last fall, so it wasn't too long ago that I was doing the same thing you are now. Today I'm not doing an overhead, and I didn't bring any hand-outs [the audience looked quizzical], so please pay careful attention to what I'm about to say: my top dissertation-writing tips. The number one and most important tip is the following:

Don't do it.

Don't write your dissertation.

Instead, I would advise you to leave the teaching theater as soon as I'm done speaking. March directly to the Office of Graduate Studies before the admins leave at 4:30. Tell them you'd like to fill out a Program Withdrawal form. If you're quick, you can have all the paperwork for quitting the Ph.D. started before the weekend. You'll only have to wait on a few signatures.

[The audience shifted in their seats. Faint murmurs circulated around the room.]

You're now asking yourselves: why on earth should I quit the Ph.D. when I've only just started? When I've already devoted the last six plus years of my adult life to post-secondary education? When I've put my whole heart into the pursuit of knowledge, and I know that no other endeavour will ever be as meaningful or as beneficial to society?

The answer is simple, my friends: because the modern university is dead.

I repeat: the university is dead. She's a zombie now. And if you stay locked in her clammy grip, she'll eat what's left of your brains and zombify you too. That is, if *you manage to complete the Ph.D. at all,* and if *you manage to land an academic job after that,* and if *you manage to get tenure after that. On average, the whole process will take 12 to 15 years. Then you'll find yourself pushing 40, and you'll realize you've given the best years of your life to an institution as sick as any in the West today.*

Let's start with the raw numbers. How many of you are actually going to land tenure-track jobs in your fields? Let's not pretend we're doing years of esoteric scholarly research because we want to be technical writers. Or because we want to teach 8 classes a day to 15 year-olds at some namby-pamby private school in Toronto. Hell no. We want to be profs, 1950s-style profs, with the corduroy blazers, pipes, the early Melville editions, the corner offices with overstuffed leather armchairs—and most of all, because we're not total gits—we want the ultimate luxury of devoting our lives to discussing ideas and reading books. That's why most of us are here.

Statistically, in the humanities, half of you won't even complete the Ph.D. The lucky ones will figure out it's a scam in the first year or so. You'll waste fewer years of your lives. But many of you will hang on for as long as 7, 8 or 9 years before you quit. Do you enjoy eating box pasta three times a week, waiting for the bus in freezing weather, and having roommates in your mid-30s and beyond? Well, many of you will have that to look forward to for another 8 years or so, before you leave without those three letters tacked on behind your name.

Most of you who do finish your dissertation won't find tenure-track positions. Under 18% of you will, and that number gets worse every year. The vast majority of Ph.D. grads will be unemployed or underemployed in the academy for a while, before giving up on academia entirely and trying to find entry-level private sector or government jobs. Then you'll be competing with a bunch of bright-eyed, malleable 22 year-olds, fresh out of undergrad. Guess which group employers prefer? Good luck.

Some of you may go the post-doc road. That's 40k, maybe 45, if you're lucky, with no benefits. It will buy you time, but it usually just postpones the inevitable. Many of you, post-Ph.D., will go the sessional or "adjunct" route, or the almost equally weak-ass yearly appointment. However you slice it, contract work is temporary and poorly paid. You can't get a bank mortgage or plan a life around a work contract that changes every few months. Adjuncts make in the 5k range. Often less in the U.S. Say you cobble together two adjunct positions a term, three terms: that's 30 grand a year. You'd make more money and deal with less bullshit washing dishes. You know what that 22 year-old Computer Science grad is making? Try 100k. Not kidding. That's tech industry starting salary money.

"But adjuncting keeps my hat in the ring!" you protest. "It will eventually lead to a TT job." Not true. Another dirty little secret in our profession is that Ph.D.s go stale, so if you've been adjuncting for years as a Ph.D., and no school has snapped you up yet, it's probably not going to happen. You will never land a full-time faculty job. Adjuncts are not "part-time professors," friends. There's no such thing as a "part-time professor." Adjuncts are just pretentious itinerant wage-laborers, and in academia they're treated with the same degree of respect shown to wage-laborers anywhere, in any field: zilch. And good luck finding time for research—you know, that brilliant research that's going to earn you a TT job—when you're trying to keep your ass above water adjuncting. It usually doesn't happen.

It often takes a few years of adjuncting before it finally dawns on a person she's going nowhere fast. Then she finally gives up and quits. That's when the self-loathing and depression kick in. The former adjunct shares her tale of woe on social media or maybe even The Chronicle of Higher Education. *Much hand-wringing and absolutely no changes occur. So many people have shared their sob stories that the genre even has a name now: "Quit Lit." Cut through the* cant and it's just a simple question of supply and demand: Ph.D.s are legion, tenure-track jobs are few.

The great hypocrisy of all this is that while so many profs bitch about the "casualization of the workforce" by big, bad private industry, their own profession leads the way when it comes to treating their workers like shit. Today between 50 and 75% of profs teaching at all universities and colleges are adjuncts, and the number is rapidly growing. Were you told that the aging Baby Boomer profs would be retiring soon, and that a gazillion new jobs would soon become available? I sure was. Newsflash: when those old coots are finally dislodged from their posts, their tenured positions will disappear with them. That geezer at the top of the pay-scale, making $180k, teaching a couple courses a year and generating zero research?—well, when he's finally removed, kicking and screaming, he'll be replaced by a yearly $15k budget line commitment for adjuncts. And all this while administrators with made-up positions like "VP of Strategic Student Ass-Wiping" continue to multiply like poisonous mushrooms.

[The audience gasped. Tessa was warming to her subject.]

Now let's suppose, even after learning all this, you choose to continue: victims of hubris all, just like me! You tell yourself you will be different. Why not? You're used to being an outlier—the biggest nerd in the room, from elementary school to grad school. You'll make it to the top of the greasy pole. You'll finish the Ph.D. and land a university faculty job!

Well, the poor sons-of-bitches who manage that feat are the most royally fucked of all. Because those poor souls will be stuck in an environment that is the polar opposite of the one they've long dreamed of. How so, you ask?

When I started grad school, I was told many things. First, I was told that the university was home to free inquiry, and that it supported a diversity of ideas. That was a lie. All *indicators show that the professoriate, especially in the humanities and social sciences, has swung radically left in recent decades, while the general public has stayed the same. What does it mean for research when there's a single dominant ideological perspective in the academy? It means certain ideas are anathema, and can't be researched, or even said aloud. For example, how much research coming from the social sciences today emphasizes individual choice or group culture as key factors affecting life outcomes? Now ask yourself why. Who's running the show? Most of the right and the center has already been purged. It's no wonder so many professors are thought-policing themselves.*

When I started, I was also told that the university was home to free speech. That was a lie. Universities like Berkeley, once bastions of free speech, are now often the sites of violent student protests aiming at banning speakers—"deplatforming." Under the guise of protecting their fellow students from hate speech, protesters are now actively preventing the dissemination of ideas, while the spineless university admin let them get away with it. The way to combat bad ideas is to expose them to open criticism, not to suppress them by force. Besides, who gave the protesters the right to decide for everyone which ideas are acceptable for public consumption? Censors have no place in a free society. Bottom line: be suspicious of people trying to prevent you from hearing speech they don't like, especially if they say it's for your own "protection." That is the mark of the authoritarian.

I was also told that the university was a meritocracy, operating on egalitarian principles. That was a lie. In case you haven't noticed, the university is one of the most hierarchical of all Western institutions, a hierarchy that is often illegitimate, founded not on merit, but on politics. Intelligence, research output, teaching ability, university service—none of those things will necessarily advance your career anymore. Political affiliation might. Skin color might. Genitalia might. But is that how you want to be judged?

What's more, I was told that the university valued intellect above class. That was a lie. Look around you: how many tenured professors come from the working class? Black, white or purple, professors are drawn almost exclusively from the middle and upper-middle class. Why do we assume they have special insights into the nature of society when many of them think half of the country, the lower-middle and working-class half, is composed of idiot "deplorables?" When they talk about "equity" but can't make conversation with their plumber? When they have the nerve to say that poor people are voting against their own interests and even insinuate that they should be excluded from our democracy? If I had a dollar for every time in grad school I heard a comfy, tenured prof make a snide remark about working people like my parents, I'd have paid off my student loan already.

Finally, I was told that the university was a haven from "crass consumer culture." That was a lie. Public or private, universities are run on the consumer model, and they use all of the tools of modern marketing. Fundamentally, they're about putting bums in seats, not knowledge in minds. And is that necessarily a bad thing? Solvency is no crime, nor is profit—contrary to what's been drummed in to our skulls here. What I do object to is the hypocrisy: arts profs have a lot of gall to criticize business principles when their institutions are run on business principles, and their salaries are dependent on them.

In summary, we've all been taught by bad teachers in a bad school. Let me put it into postmodern terms for you: the grand narrative we've learned here is A LIE. The university is not the happy home of intellectual inquiry anymore, if it ever was. At its worst, the modern university—in our disciplines, at least—is a neo-totalitarian cult, worshipping at the feet of it bloody-mawed idols: their names are "Social Justice," "Equity," and "Diversity." Today I will call them by their real names: "social justice" is "social engineering," "equity" is "unfairness" and "diversity" is "uniformity of thought." It is immoral to judge people based on the amount of melanin in their skin, their genitals, their sexual preference, or any other immutable characteristics that are mere accidents of birth—and the Cult of Identity Politics is predicated on these unfair judgements. Instead, as Martin Luther King said, the only sound moral judgments are those based on the content of a person's character. We've thrown away this wisdom, to our detriment. The university has gone backwards.

Fellow seekers of truth, we are heading into uncharted territory. Our challenge going forward is to keep the world safe for the free exchange of ideas. Sadly, the university has ceased to be a place that does that anymore. It has betrayed its own mission. Perhaps the new online media platforms will serve freedom and meaningful intellectual debate; whether they yield to the censors remains to be seen. Perhaps we will need to build new platforms.

What I can tell you is that there's an entire world of ideas and thinkers out there, beyond the propaganda of the gated academic institutions. Seek them out. Know that today most of the proponents of free inquiry and the rights of the individual operate outside of the university. These people are the modern torch-bearers of the Enlightenment. How will you know who belongs to this group of heterodox thinkers? First of all, look for thinkers on the left, right and center united in the belief that only rational, open debate can solve our problems. Those who offer up excuses for limiting what can and cannot be discussed are automatically not members of this group. And keep in mind that discussing an idea is not the same thing as embracing it.

The second hallmark of these thinkers is this: HUMOR. William James said humor is common-sense dancing. How right he was! Beware of people who become enraged when their *dogmas are questioned. That's the sure sign of the cultist, religious or secular. As serious as they are about the importance of ideas, this group of free-thinkers is capable of taking a joke. Remember: there is humanity in laughter.*

I can't force anyone to make the decision to leave academia. I can only advise you based on my own experiences. Whatever you do, I urge you to consider my words today, and whatever you choose--

Reclaim your minds.

Reclaim yourselves.

Tessa exhaled and looked up from her notes at Adrian in the front row. The classroom had cleared out. Besides her roommate, only three students remained. They looked bewildered. Adrian began to clap. He was joined by one other student. It was Polly Glamorous.

***

While Tessa was giving her speech in Sere Valley, Deborahann was making bouquets at Sentimental Occasions. She was pleased with herself. The shop had been hammered by orders that day, and even though Amber, as usual, called in sick when most needed, Deborahann managed to handle the heavy work-load on her own. Thankfully Elinor hadn't been in, poking her nose around and getting in the way, so Deborahann could work at maximum efficiency. By 5:00 o'clock she had curled the last ribbon on her last bouquet, a "Springtime Promise." Springtime Promises were a fussy Elinor design of tulips, irises and daffodils, beribboned extravagantly with blue curlicues. Amber had flatly refused to learn how to make them, leaving Deborahann with the job whenever they were ordered.

That morning there had been no fewer than a dozen Springtime Promises on the order form. Deborahann worked through lunch to finish on time, chomping on an apple with one eye on the shopfront window, lest Elinor or an Elinor spy witness her transgression. Eating on the job was forbidden by the boss. ("So unprofessional, Deb'rann.") But Elinor also expected her to crank out all of the day's orders at top speed. And Vic expected her home no later than 5:15 to make his supper and attend to his various and diverse needs. Something had to give and that something was usually lunch.

Deborahann felt tired but satisfied as she surveyed the dozen perfect Springtime Promises and the other bouquets she'd made that day in the floral cooler. Work tasks complete, she only had a few more hurdles to clear before she could call it a night: Vic's supper, the dishes, two loads of laundry, and Vic's favorite boiled icing chocolate cake for Saturday. It was his 53rd birthday. She had all his presents wrapped and ready to go. She might even get a chance to putter around in the garden tonight, if she moved quickly.

At 5:03 she was buttoning up her coat, when she heard the door bells tinkle. It wasn't a late customer. It was Elinor.

The exchange that followed was brief. Elinor flipped the door sign to "Closed" and asked Deborahann if they could have a word in the back before she left for the weekend. Elinor was determined to be neither apologetic nor sheepish.

Business is business. I've done a lot for her. I'm not running a charity here. I've kept her on months longer than necessary anyway, she thought. *It's just so awkward when you see them at church all the time.*

Elinor stuttered a bit as she looked into Deborahann's questioning eyes. Her little prepared speech didn't come out as matter-of-factly as she would've liked, but she got the gist out: they couldn't afford to keep two cashiers; she had to make a difficult decision; she understood Deborahann had more seniority than Amber, but Amber was better with the new software, and improving on making the arrangements, etc., etc. She knew Deborahann would understand. Nice to give young people a chance, you know. Customers like a fresh face, you know.

Elinor concluded, "...so that gives you a whole month before you move on to something else. Plenty of time, really. And I would be *dee-lighted*, Deb'rann, to provide a reference any time you like. Just give me a ring."

Deborahann barely said a word. Elinor was relieved that there was no awkward scene or tears. She knew Deborahann was mild-mannered, but it was still wise to be careful. Robert had told her about a "perfectly nice young fella" he laid off at the mill "going psycho" on him. "You never know how they're going to take it," he had warned his wife.

"Enjoy your weekend!" Elinor said, and made her way out, leaving a cloud of rose perfume in her wake.

Deborahann soon followed, double-locking the shop door and trying the lock just to make sure, like she always did. She walked to the car in a brain fog, noticing, with clinical indifference, the rust and salt damage creeping up the side-panel. She sat down and turned the key backwards in the ignition. The dash flashed "5:32" and the Stampeders wailed, "Swee—ee—eet, sweet city woman./ I can see your face,/ I can hear your voice,/ I can almost touch you." She checked the mirror, and backed out on to Main. It was dead already. In the village on Fridays, most people stopped real work by noon, dragged ass until 4:00, then stopped even pretending to work. "Rush hour" in Beaconsbridge was 4:00 to 4:30.

Deborahann had anticipated this day for years, but now that it was here, she felt nothing. She watched her hands on the steering wheel. They seemed to belong to someone else. In a month she'd be out of a job. For a little while, she could collect Employment Insurance at a much smaller percentage of her regular pay. Then that would run out. They were barely making the mortgage and paying the bills as it was. It had taken her over a year to find her current job, eight years ago. How long would it take this time? How would they live in the meantime?

Deborahann also worried about how Vic would take the news. He would be furious, of course. He was probably already angry she was late. He would blame her for the lay-off, tell her she was to blame for being late too often. Maybe it *was* her fault. Amber was Elinor's niece, and though she was useless at the shop, she put on a good show of efficiency when Elinor was around. And it was true that Amber understood the new software better. She was definitely younger and cuter: a "fresh face" indeed. Vic had often warned her that if times got tight, naturally, Amber would stay, and she would go.

The Crossmans all stick together, she thought. *I should've known. I should've been looking around. Why am I so stupid?*

Deborahann reached the outskirts of town with no memory of driving there. Vic always complained about "that bloody hill" just past the Women's Institute Hall. Once Deborahann went over it, she was only a minute or two away from her driveway. Madawaaksis County was nothing but hills. Driving it was like sailing a choppy sea. That Friday afternoon, Deborahann drove up the blind hill. She never came down.

***

Fr: Karen Dyer Sellers—kd.sellers@svu.edu
To: Tessa Stevens—te.stevens@svu.edu

CC: Edwin Flamm—ed.flamm@svu.edu; Tabitha French—tm.french@svu.edu; Pearl Coleman—p.coleman@svu.edu

Subject: Notification of Termination of Employment

Date: April 22, 2017, 2:55 p.m.

Dr. Stevens,

    This email message is an informal notification of termination of your employment at Sere Valley University, effective April 30, 2017. It has been called to my attention that the content of your Graduate Studies Arts and Social Sciences Professional Development Lecture, on Friday, April 21, 2017, was in violation of Section 4, Article 5, Part 17 of the Faculty Code of Conduct, as outlined in the 2016-2017 Faculty Handbook: "Faculty Responsibilities Regarding the Provision and Maintenance of University Safe Spaces." The Code states that the entire university is designated as a safe space, and defines the term as follows: "a safe space is an environment in which all students are free from harassment, criticism, or other emotional or physical harm, irrespective of their sex, race, religion, sexual preference, and gender alignment." As a result of your talk, our students' right to a safe space was abrogated. We consider this to be a serious offence.

    As per your contract, please note that as an adjunct lecturer, you are not subject to university disciplinary procedures reserved for full-time faculty, and can be terminated at any time. You are also not entitled to severance pay or other compensation.

    Your two upcoming examinations next week will continue as planned. Upon submission of your final grades, your work duties at the university will be concluded.

    Dr. Flamm and Ms. French will be in contact with you presently with further information. Official notice of termination to follow by mail.

Sincerely,

Dr. Dyer Sellers

--Karen Dyer Sellers, Ph.D.

Associate Dean of Arts

Professor, Faculty of Management

Sere Valley University

Chapter Nineteen: So Long, Deborahann

A chubby, middle-aged woman lay flat on the stretcher, unconscious. Her torso was covered in bloody shreds of what had once been a blue and white polka-dotted dress. She wore one tan shoe. The other foot was shoeless, revealing a carefully applied pink home pedicure. Her face was covered by a high-flow oxygen mask. Two paramedics rode in the back of the ambulance on either side of an orange stretcher. The cardiac monitor registered an irregular heart-rate, spiking at 180 beats per minute. They were somewhere in the middle of Madawaaksis County, still 40 minutes away from the nearest hospital in Moncton. The younger of the two paramedics cursed as they went over another bump. *These damn dirt roads. Why must these people live out in the boonies?* The ambulance driver was doing his best to negotiate the twisting, tree-lined road. The clunky old ambulance should've been retired a decade ago. Deborahann was aware of none of these things. She did not know or care whether she would make it to the hospital in time.

***

I'm here again. I've had this dream a thousand times since I was a girl. I'm back at Uncle Lew and Aunt Moira's. The old grey farmhouse in the hills. But this time I'm not a little girl anymore. I'm Deborahann as I am today. The farmhouse is empty. No one's in it but me. I'm in the basement. We were never allowed to go down there. Yule and I used to dare Jimmy to go down and steal apples from the cold-room. He was afraid of the dark. Poor Jimmy.

The basement is dim. It smells like damp earth and mildew. The walls are torn down to the studs. There's no visible foundation, only water where the floor should be. I'm clinging to the house's framework, balancing on a wooden board just broader than my foot. A few other boards are floating here and there, and the odd piece of debris. I'm alone.

"Hello? Hello?" I call out.

"Mum? Aunt Moira? Jimmy? Yule?"

No reply.

I want to escape, but there's no staircase anymore—it's also vanished. And there's no way to reach the windows overhead. I'm trapped down here.

This is the part in the dream where the water begins to rise. The hem of my pants and my shoes are wet. But there's nowhere higher to go, and the water's still rising. I'm panicking.

I'm going to drown in the house with no foundation.

And this is when I wake up. Every time.

Only this time I'm not waking up.

Don't they say if you're dying in a dream and you don't wake up in time, you die in real life?

Now the water is at my shins. It's dirty and freezing cold.

I don't want to die.

Tessa.

Lilly.

"DEBORAHANN."

A voice. Someone's here!

I turn in the direction of the voice. It's coming from the northwestern corner of the basement. I notice a wooden door floating on the water. A small egress window is above it. But it's so far away. And there's no floor to walk on, only water.

"DEBORAHANN. JUMP IN THE WATER. SWIM."

I pause a few seconds more, then I obey. The shock of cold water is unbearable. The water is as sludgy and thick as chowder.

"SWIM, DEBORAHANN."

I swim the length of the basement, my damp clothes dragging me down. I reach the floating door. It's unstable.

"PULL YOURSELF UP."

I'm so cold. And tired. I cling to the half-submerged door. My arms aren't strong enough to pull myself up.

"I can't!"

I fall back into the water. I'm sinking.

They say your life flashes before your eyes when you're dying. Maybe it's different when you're dying in a dream. I don't see anything but black water. I feel relief. 52 years of struggle.

The voice of Victor reverberates in my head:

"You stupid ditz."

"You useless arse."

"Stupid."

"Useless."

No one will ever call me useless again.

No one will ever call me stupid again.

I will never struggle again.

My body keeps sinking. It's not me anymore. It's 165 pounds of wet garbage.

No father. No mother. The baby no one wanted with the burnt foot. I came from nothing and I return to nothing. The black water.

I continue to fall. 10 feet. 20 feet. 30 feet and more. Plunging fathoms and fathoms into the darkness.

"DEBORAHANN."

The voice cuts through the murmuring of the water like the blade of a hatchet.

"FIGHT."

I'm falling.

"FIGHT."

The black water.

"FIGHT."

"Why?" I scream.

The sound is muffled by the water.

I scream again.

"Who am I?"

Silence.

My heart beats once. Thud-thud.

Twice. Thud-thud.

Three times. Thud-thud.

"DEBORAHANN."

A pause.

"YOU. ARE."

A long silence.

I decide.

I am not done.

Something remains. In the core of my chest. I claw above my head like an animal, scratching bloody tracks through the water. I kick my legs. I propel myself up, inch by inch. My lungs burn. I raise my head above the water.

I haul myself up onto the door. I slowly rise from a crouch. The water level has raised the floating door so that my head almost touches the ceiling. I float alongside the egress window. It looks just big enough for me to fit through. The glass is broken and the light shines in. I pull myself through and out into the window-well on the other side. Out of the darkness. I step up out of the hollow on to the ground outside. I roll over and lay panting on the grass, flat on my back, dripping water. My chest heaves up and down. It's a sunny day. A fat, red-throated robin flies above, fluttering from one maple tree to another. The bird chirps and hops on one foot along a branch.

No. I'm not done.

Chapter Twenty: The Queen is Dead; Long Live the Queen

Tessa had never seen her mother so still before. Deborahann was usually a vital force, and now she lay before them, a lump of human clay. Her exposed skin was chalky-white or purplish where the bruises were. Her head was half-concealed by bandages. She wasn't wearing her glasses. A paramedic had found them on the dashboard, miraculously intact and unscratched. The hospital room was a small, gray rectangle, crowded with an array of beeping equipment. A poster on the wall of a plucky cartoon cookie read, "YOU'RE ONE TOUGH COOKIE."

Tessa observed for the first time that below the bruises her mother looked old and tired. She was ashamed she'd never noticed before. In her mind, her mother was perpetually in her mid-30s, her pie-baking, child-rearing prime. But the woman lying on the hospital bed looked every day of her 52 years and more. The Deborahann frozen in Tessa's mind was up to every challenge. Call her from an airport out of the blue, as Tessa had once done, saying you'd be landed in New Brunswick in two hours, and she'd be there at the appointed time to drive you home, feed you, and tuck you into a warm, freshly-laundered bed. She'd cluck and complain, but she'd be there.

You don't do things for Mum, Tessa thought, *Mum does things for you.* But the woman before her, with tubes and wires running in and out of her nose, was incapable of helping anyone. Standing by their mother's side, Tessa and Lilly felt the same fear: with Deborahann down, there was no one behind the wheel anymore. Someone else had to grab it before the car went off the road. At ages 28 and 22, they finally had to become adults.

Vic was in the hospital canteen. After he'd called Tessa early that Saturday morning, she booked the first flight east, threw some clothes in a duffel-bag, and hopped into a cab. Tessa had known something was very wrong when she answered the phone, expecting her mother, and heard her father on the other end. He had never called her before. He didn't consider it his job. No one found this strange. The pattern was set long ago: their father was physically present at home, but he was not required to talk to them or to be interested in their lives. When Tessa did speak to her father, it was to exchange logistical information.

Tessa made it back home in half a day. Vic picked her up at the airport and drove her directly to the hospital. She had read the Associate Dean's email in Toronto, while switching planes to the puddle-jumper flying to Moncton. The email's bureaucrat-ese barely penetrated the fog of her consciousness.

Only a few hours away, Lilly had borrowed her best friend's car and raced to the hospital. Since her arrival that morning, she'd barely left her mother's side. Deborahann was still unconscious, hooked up to IV painkillers. Tessa noticed how intensely Lilly was staring at their mother's face, as if willing her eyes to open.

Lilly's face was splotchy with tears. Tessa remembered the same sad face on Lilly as a baby. She recalled trying to distract her little sister from the sounds of their parents fighting downstairs. Tessa had read *I Am a Bunny* as loudly as possible, trying to drown out the scary noises. She rubbed baby Lilly's forehead until she fell asleep.

Lilly explained everything to Tessa when she arrived: the car accident on the blind hill, and the injuries. The accident itself had been a minor one. The two cars only grazed each other, and neither was travelling very fast. The other driver and her vehicle were fine, but the Civic had ended up in the ditch, knocking Deborahann out cold. The airbag inflated, but somehow Deborahann still banged her head. One of the paramedics thought her seatbelt was on too loosely. She was badly bruised, one leg was sprained, and she sustained a minor concussion.

The doctors' biggest concern, however, was her heart. After the crash, Deborahann had suffered an atrial fibrillation episode. Lilly explained to Tessa that that was an irregular heartbeat. While the medics were loading her into the ambulance, Deborahann had gone from atrial fibrillation to full cardiac arrest. They had to use a defibrillator to save her. Now no one knew if Deborahann had an underlying heart condition, or if the atrial fibrillation incident had been a one-off, triggered by the trauma of the crash. Lilly tried to pry as many answers as possible out of the doctor, when he finally made it to her mother on his rounds, but he only stayed for a few minutes, and wasn't forthcoming with information. It was a typical public hospital in the Canadian Maritimes: they were understaffed and overworked, and full of geriatric patients who wouldn't be going home. Deborahann was stable and therefore low on the priority list.

Grammy Ada had come and gone earlier that day, driven to the hospital by a solicitous neighbor. Her concern for her daughter was real, but she drove Tessa to distraction with her repeated invocations of "She's in God's hands now." Tessa was glad to see her leave. She may have imagined it, but Deborahann's brow seemed to furrow more when her mother was in the room.

There was another less-than-welcome guest. Pastor Fudge also made an appearance, called in by Victor to provide spiritual aid and emotional succour. Victor was out running his mother-in-law back to Beaconsbridge when the pastor arrived, leaving Tessa and Lilly to deal with him. Lilly was polite; Tessa was businesslike.

"Shall I pray for her?" he asked, over Deborahann's prone body.

"No," said Tessa.

It was just after 10:00. It had been a long day. Vic returned to the room from the canteen, decaf coffee in hand. He cast an eye in his wife's direction, scanning the vital signs monitor. No changes. Lilly nodded a greeting. Tessa didn't look up.

"Well, this has been some birthday for me," he said, with a sigh. "Typical. I never have any fun on my birthday."

Tessa resisted the urge to react. Lilly made the ghost of a "hmm" sound.

"No cake either," said Vic.

Tessa focussed on just breathing. She didn't look at him.

"No sense in stayin,'" Vic said. "The nurse said she's stable. I'm headin' back for the night."

"I'm staying," said Tessa.

"Me too," said Lilly.

Vic harrumphed. "You'll just tire yerselves out for no reason."

"We want to stay, Dad," said Lilly.

"We want to be here when she wakes up," Tessa said, looking him full in the face this time.

Her own face looked back at her: the same long nose, green eyes, and angular features. Here was an older, male, rustic version of Dr. Theresa Anne Stevens. Her father's eyes registered neither recognition nor empathy. They were shallow pools of muddy water.

"Suit yerselves," he replied. "Be heroes."

Vic stretched and shifted his weight, glancing at the door. Nurses kept coming in and out.

"Well. See yez tomorrow. Some of us who work for a living need our rest."

He turned his head on the way out, saying, "Let me know if she takes a turn."

He shut the door.

The girls waited a 10-count, as they'd done for decades.

"That sack of shit!" Tessa exclaimed.

Lilly's golden head collapsed into her arms and she wept.

"What the hell is wrong with him? He's thinking about his fucking birthday cake while she's lying there looking like that."

Tessa gestured at the crumpled scrap of humanity that was their mother.

"He might be in shock," whimpered Lilly.

"Shock, my ass. He just feels sorry for himself because his servant is down."

"Can we not fight right now?"

"Can you not take up for him for once in your life?"

"He's our father," said Lilly.

"More's the pity," snorted Tessa. "Listen to me, Lilly—you know as well as I do, if she doesn't come out of this, he'll have some new woman to wait on him before the body is even cold."

"That's not true."

"He doesn't give a shit about us! He never has! Or her! He's an obsessive-compulsive, narcissistic, religious fanatic *asshole*! That's our father. That's the dad we got. Wake up!"

Lilly continued to sob.

Tessa lowered her voice and kept going, deliberately: "We've closed our eyes to this for years. The way he is—it's not normal. The way he treats her is not normal. It doesn't have to be a black eye to be abuse. He's emotionally abusive. He degrades her on a daily basis. No wonder she has high blood pressure! No wonder she walks around in a daze most days! No wonder she has heart problems we didn't even know about!"

"The heart thing was from the accident! You can't blame it on him," said Lilly.

"Why did she even *get* into an accident?" asked Tessa. "She's driven over that blind hill a million times, but this time she wasn't paying attention! You told me the other driver said she was *way* over the line when she came over that hill."

"What does that have to do with Dad? He didn't cause the accident! She hates Sentimental Occasions! She was probably stressed out from work, as usual, and in her own little world," said Lilly.

"'In her own little world!' 'In her own little world!' Listen to yourself: you are repeating the same crap, word-for-word, he says! He's been manipulating our perception of our mother since the day I was born! He always makes her out to be this ditz who can't do anything right, when she manages everything for him—for all of us! That shitty garage of his would've folded years ago without her! Who does all the bookkeeping? Who does all the advertising? Who calls and settles all the accounts? And then he has the nerve to call her a ditz and we go along with it!"

"Of course she's not a ditz, Tessa. But you know Mum is spacey sometimes—always has been. She was bound to get into an accident eventually. She talks to herself, for frig sakes!"

"Maybe instead of laughing at her when she talked to herself, we should've tried talking back to her! Maybe she's 'spacey' because she has big problems and no one to talk to!"

"Problems? What problems? What are you talking about?" Lilly looked confused.

Tessa caught herself.

"Lilly. People can process normal amounts of stress when they have emotional support. She doesn't. I bet she was racing home to get his fucking supper, as usual."

"He's not to blame for this, Tessa. Calm down. Blaming him doesn't solve anything."

"I blame myself too! We all went along with his version of things. We didn't speak up when he made fun of her. But we were kids. He should've known better…The constant migraines were a wake-up call. This accident is a wake-up call. The atrial-fucking-fibrillation is a wake-up call! Does she need to die next time for all of us to see the truth?" asked Tessa.

"D'you think she's happy? Do you, Lilly?" she continued. "Do you think our mother's been happy all these years?"

Lilly had no answer.

"She's *not*! You clinging to this fantasy that we have a happy fucking family does her no good. That goes for Grammy too. How many times did we show up there in tears as kids, after another one of their big fights, and she never asked us a single question?"

"She took care of us!"

"She took care of us and she looked the other way while her daughter was suffering. God forbid she get a divorce! What would people at the church say?" said Tessa, voice drenched in sarcasm.

"She looked the other way. Everyone in Beaconsbridge looks the other way. The hell with you all."

Lilly's body shook with sobs. Tessa felt a pang.

"Listen, I don't know what's wrong with her," said Tessa, looking toward the bed again. "She needs to figure that out for herself. I'm not a psychologist. But I know damn well she's not going to get better in that house, in that sick relationship, with Dad telling her she's stupid every day of her life."

She took a deep breath. Across the room, the bulging eyes of the anthropomorphic cookie stared at them.

"That's it."

Tessa walked over, ripped it off the wall, and stuffed it into the garbage.

Lilly blew her nose and wiped her eyes.

"I've wanted to do that all day," said Tessa.

They didn't talk for the rest of the evening. Lilly spent most of it curled up in a chair by their mother's side. Tessa sat in another hospital chair at the foot of Deborahann's bed. A nurse brought in some scratchy flannel blankets and pillows, and the sisters waited out the night.

***

Around dawn, Deborahan woke up groaning. She tried to reach for something, and winced at the effort of moving her arms. Lilly was awake and standing over her in an instant, ready to help. Tessa ran to the nurse's station.

Deborahann was groggy from the painkillers. She blinked at the rays of sunshine filtering in through the venetian blinds. One ray highlighted her lumpy torso. Lilly carefully put her mother's glasses back on over the bandages. Deborahann's myopic blue eyes blinked in her direction.

"Lilly-Willy," she said slowly, with a smile.

She made out Tessa at the foot of the bed.

"Hi Mum," said Tessa, trying not to cry. "The nurse is coming."

"You flew home, Tessie," Deborahann said, still smiling. Then she frowned. "What…a waste of money."

Tessa hugged her gingerly.

"I'll phone Dad," said Lilly. "Do you want him to bring anything?"

Deborahann shook her head. Tessa held her hand.

"He's on his way," said Lilly, after calling. "Just a few errands, he said, then he'll be right here."

The nurse came in to check on Deborahann, followed by an orderly with a breakfast tray. Tessa and Lilly darted around the room, fetching Kleenexes, buttering Deborahann's toast, poking her straw into her juice-box, and otherwise making themselves busy, relieved to be able to do something, anything, at last.

Deborahann asked about the car, her purse, and if the other driver was okay. The girls smiled nonstop and gave her the most positive possible answers. They knew not to deluge her with questions. Deborahann barely ate anything and was dozing again by the time the orderly returned for the tray.

The girls tensed at a knock on the hospital door, but it wasn't their father. Yule poked his grizzled head in warily, Abby at his side. They were holding yellow roses and a big, red "GET WELL SOON!" balloon. The sisters relaxed and motioned them in, fingers to their lips, signalling silence while their mother rested. Yule winced at the sight of his cousin. "Well sir!" he whispered. Abby embraced both girls in turn. She smelled like Palmolive soap and warm bread. After a few moments, everyone stepped back out into the hall to talk.

"Aunt Ada called last night. Of course, we already knew. It's all around the village," said Yule.

Tessa nodded.

"How's she doing today?" asked Abby. Tessa and Lilly explained. Yule and Abby looked relieved.

Lilly's ears pricked up at the faint sound of Deborahann groaning in the room.

"We won't bother you any longer," Yule said. "Just wanted to pop in and check on Sissy."

Lilly whispered a "Thank you!" and hurried back inside, leaving Tessa with them.

"Give her a hug for us!" said Abby, to Lilly's back.

"Tess," said Yule, lowering his voice. "Is your father coming back soon?"

"Any minute now."

"Look, when your mother is feeling better, you tell her…I dunno what she plans to do, but tell her she's always welcome with us," said Yule.

"I will."

"We can help her move her stuff, if it needs movin'. He won't act up if we're there. I'll see to that. I'll bring the boys," said Yule, speaking quickly. "And the 12-gauge." He chuckled, but his eyes were serious.

"Thank you for always being there for Mum."

Yule grunted and made a quick, suspicious dabbing motion at his eyes. He awkwardly slapped Tessa on the back.

"Chin up!"

"It's going to be okay, honey," said Abby. She gave Tessa another hug.

Inside the room, Deborahann was still asleep. Yule and Abby had been gone only a few minutes when Vic arrived. He'd had a bad night of it. The doctor had said they needed to run some tests to learn more, once her condition improved. Vic spent much of the evening imagining himself tending to an invalid Deborahann: bringing her soup, combing her hair, emptying her bedpan. *It could go on for years*! he worried. He also imagined himself as a widower, making his own meals and going to church alone, just like Arnold Hayes, whose wife had died of breast cancer just last year. *Poor Hayes is odd man out of everything now*, thought Vic.

Vic entered the room that morning with a small bouquet of pink carnations. It was the hospital gift shop's cheapest option. He smiled at the girls. Tessa did not smile back. The girls knew carnations were their mother's least favorite flower.

"How ya' doin'?"

Vic paused, searching for a likely endearment as he stood over the bed. After three decades of marriage, they had no nicknames for one another.

"How ya' doing…old girl?" he tried.

"She's gone back to sleep. Don't wake her up," said Tessa.

"I think I can talk to my own wife!" He instantly bridled.

"The nurse said we should let her rest," said Lilly.

Vic let it go. In public, he was usually on his best behavior. Lilly changed the subject, telling him about Deborahann's awakening, and their visitors. Vic rolled his eyes at the mention of Yule and Abby, but his face brightened at Lilly's medical report. *Maybe nothing's going to change after all*, he thought.

Victor's arrival had chilled the air in the room. Tessa and Lilly struggled to talk to him without their mother mediating. It also felt odd to focus on her, the inert body in the middle of the room, instead of their father, the usual center of attention. Like the night before, the conversation lurched along in fits and starts. Vic settled on a favorite topic, his sinus head-colds.

"Couldn't sleep more than five minutes at a time last night. Woke up a million times, coughing and hacking. The mucus runs right down the back of my throat."

"Your mother, she's lucky," he continued, pointing to the pile of bandages nearby. "She never gets a cold! Just brings 'em home from work for me!"

By now Tessa was experiencing everything several removes from reality, even anger. She was tired and sweaty. She needed to go home and sleep. She was about to ask Lilly for a ride back, when the silence was broken by groans from Deborahann's direction.

Victor stood over his wife, instantly assuming the role of solicitous husband.

"Deb? Can you hear me?"

She motioned for her glasses. Lilly gently placed them back on.

"Vic...Victor?"

"How are you feelin', Deb?" he asked. "Look, I brought you flowers."

Vic pointed to the three stubby pink carnations, which he'd placed on the side-table in front of Yule and Abby's dozen yellow roses. He reached for his wife's hand, the first time he'd spontaneously held it in decades.

"Deb, I promise you, once you're better, things are gonna change. I've been thinkin'. I know yer stressed out and tired. I'm gonna help more around the house. I'm gonna take care of you."

Deborahann's eyes fluttered.

"Don't you worry, Deb. I'm doing just fine. You rest as much as you need. The girls will take care of me and the house while yer in here."

"We'll take care of everything, Mum," Lilly repeated.

"Vic...?" murmured Deborahann again.

"Are you worried, honey? What are you worried about?" he cooed.

More groans.

"Picked up my birthday cake from yer Mum's this morning," said Victor. "I got one after all, so you don't have to worry about that. But the best birthday present is just you gettin' better."

Tessa stared at her mother's face, obscured by the bandages. The bags under her eyes were enormous pouches. She wondered how long they'd been like that. They aged her by 10 years.

"Victor...?" said Deborahann, her voice barely audible.

"Yes, honey?"

Deborahann blinked twice and looked up into the eyes of her husband of 33 years, the father of her two daughters, the man who'd given her the only adult identity she'd ever known, as Mrs. Victor Stevens. It was the name she'd chosen for the return-address stickers on all her letters and Christmas cards.

"Victor, I want a divorce," she said.

The sunlight streamed through the window, bringing every wrinkle on Deborahann's battered face into sharp relief. To Tessa, she was beautiful.

Chapter Twenty-One: Happy Hour at The Ranch Hand

"I have to say, I wouldn't have guessed a safe space would take you down," said Adrian, twirling the straw in his half-priced margarita.

Adrian and Tessa were a couple drinks in to Happy Hour at The Ranch Hand. Tessa had just returned to Sere Valley that afternoon, after her traumatic week in Beaconsbridge. She and Adrian had already covered her mother's accident and had moved on to a discussion of the PD talk and its fall-out.

"The irony," Tessa replied.

"Frankly, my money was on sexual harassment."

"You thought I was going to get sexually harassed? By who? Flamm?"

"*Whom*. No, I thought *you* were going to do the sexual harassing, dear heart," said Adrian. "I've seen you eye those undergrads."

"Uh huh. Nothing's hotter than not knowing the difference between "t-h-e-i-r" and "t-h-e-r-e." I like 'em tall and illiterate."

"Oh, I know all your kinks...But seriously, what kind of bullshit is that? Who narked on you?"

"I narked on myself. I sent the text of the PD talk to Flamm—as promised."

"Whaaaat?" Adrian almost did a silent film-style spit-take.

"You couldn't prevaricate? Say you lost it or some shit? Why commit suicide like that?"

"You're the one who's been Polonius-ing me with all this 'be true to yourself' crap."

"I assumed you'd find some clever way to cover your ass."

"You assumed wrong."

"You did it on purpose, didn't you? You knew what would happen. You wanted to go out in a blaze of glory."

Tessa shrugged. "Glory. Ignominy. Doesn't matter anymore."

She took a long drink.

"So was it Flamm who got you canned?"

"No. He outright said he was going to look the other way. Chalk up my 'outburst' to job hunt stress. It really was a safe spaces complaint. Before my talk was even over, he said the Associate Dean was getting emails. Or maybe email, singular? Flamm was unclear."

"Associate Dean? Of Arts? Do you mean Dyer Sellers?" Adrian sneered. "I know her. That bitch is so stupid she can barely walk upright. Classic lickspittle over-promotion to Admin."

"Bitch, eh? Do I detect a hint of misogyny?"

"Yes, I hate women, ya whore. I hate them so much I hold them responsible for their stupidity, just like I do all humans."

"Just checking, ho-bag," said Tessa, raising her voice to be heard over the sound system. Linda Ronstadt was imploring The Ranch Hand patrons, "I've been cheated,/ Been mistreated./ When will I be loved?"

"You should've told Little Ms. Cunty McGee that the only safe space is a box under the ground," said Adrian.

"Tempting to add a perceived death threat to a dean to this fiasco, but no. I'll stick to just torpedoing my academic career and leave criminal acts to the real pros."

"So I take it based on the PD talk, you're not going to apply for other academic jobs?" asked Adrian. "You could just keep adjuncting, if not here, somewhere else, while you figure things out."

Tessa lowered her drink.

"No more adjuncting—no more whoring. If I'm going to sell myself, it won't be so cheaply."

"That's not fair, Tess. Adjuncts aren't whores. People like whores."

"I'm out of the game, babe."

"Out?" Adrian was incredulous.

"Out. Let's just say I've become a critical thinker at last."

"Right…" He trailed off. "Have you told your Mum yet?"

"Not yet."

In the distance they saw the tall, gangly figure of Mark at the bar, chatting up one of the waitresses: the new one with the Bettie Page bangs. He leaned over her conspiratorially, gesturing in wide circles with one hand. She giggled.

"Never say he's not resilient," said Tessa.

Adrian waved the idea of Mark away.

"No need to pooh-pooh. Boudicca will always consider him an ally."

"Oh, he's a 'hashtag ally' all right." Adrian smirked. "So what are you going to do now?"

"I'm going to order a Sazerac."

"Ooooh. Big girl drink. And after that?"

She paused.

"I'm here a few more weeks covering for someone at the Writing Center. The Administration wanted me gone earlier, but Flamm promised I would hold off corrupting young minds for a few more shifts."

"Then what?"

"In June I'll fly back to New Brunswick to stay with Mum, lick my wounds, and plot my next step. She'll be moved in to an apartment in Moncton by then."

"Is she doing ok on her own?"

"I guess so. She's at least financially stable for a little while—for the first time in her life—even though she lost the stupid flower shop job. You won't believe this, but Grammy Ada gave her a bunch of money."

"From what?"

"That old perv, Great-Uncle Milt, left his life insurance and estate, such as it was, to his dear sister. His wife's long dead. They had no kids. So Grammy turned around and gave every penny to Mum—every *penny*, Mum said…Grammy Ada's a lot of things, Adrian, but she's not greedy."

"I thought they didn't get along?"

"They don't."

"Then why…?"

Tessa sighed. "It's a long story. Let's just say Grammy must've thought it was the right thing to do."

"I see," said Adrian, mind swirling with gossipy possibilities. "So…you're not staying at the house when you go back? You're not going to Beaconsbridge?"

"If you're asking whether I'm going to go see my father, I hadn't planned on it, no. He can have the four bedrooms to himself. I'd rather sleep on Mum's hide-a-bed than in the same house with him anyway."

Adrian fiddled with the straw in his drink. "I'm sorry your Dad's an asshole, Tess."

Tessa was silent for a few seconds.

"He called me, you know. He never calls us. He was desperate. Wanted me to convince Mum to stay."

"What did you say?"

"I told him he'd always treated her like crap, and that I'd been trying to get her to leave him for years."

Adrian whistled. "There goes the inheritance."

"He totally lost it then. Called me a 'little bitch.' Said he always knew I 'encouraged her to act out'—like she's a four year old…Oh, and he said I stabbed him in the back."

Adrian was speechless.

"I said, 'No, I stabbed you in the front. And you had it coming."

Adrian could only mutter again, "I'm sorry, Tess."

"It's okay. Did I send you that article link? Many great men throughout history had absent or asshole dads. Lots of presidents: see Reagan and Obama. It either breaks you or it makes you resilient."

"Maybe," said Adrian, "but you said 'great men.' I assume most chicks with mean daddies go the Sylvia Plath burn-out route."

"Ahh, but don't you know I have 'the heart and stomach of a King, and of a King of England too?'"

"I have long admired your metaphorical balls, Tessa," said Adrian solemnly.

"And besides," she continued, "what doesn't kill you makes you stronger…or embitters you to the point of dysfunction. Can't remember which now."

"Well, at least your Dad just called you a bitch. I got 'fuckin' faggot.'"

"Charming."

"Wasn't it? To be fair, he was pretty wasted at the time."

"Fair enough."

They clinked glasses.

"Seriously though, being around him always made me tense, even with Mum there. It will be interesting to spend time with her without him breathing down our necks. I feel like I'm just starting to get to know her, since everything went down after the accident."

"There might just be a Deborahann Renaissance."

"I hope so. I hear it's easier to find yourself after the surgical removal of a 200-pound tumor."

Adrian snorted. "Are they selling the house?"

"Yeah. I think it's mostly paid off too."

"That'll be hard on your Mum."

"Yeah, she loved that house. And the garden. Too much. It was a millstone around her neck. It kept her in that marriage when she should've booked it years ago."

"Well, she worked so hard for the house."

"Yes. They both worked hard for it. Like most Maritimers. Like most of the world. *We're* the useless chattering class."

"At long last!" said Adrian. "Though not you anymore, my dear."

Noticing Tessa's face settling into hard lines, he redirected, "So, the overloading paid off. I'm on track to finish the MBA by the end of the summer."

"Then where?" asked Tessa. "Toronto? Vancouver?"

"Try New York or L.A. With a Fortune 500. I'm blowing this commie popsicle stand."

"Traitor!"

"Who said just because a man was born in a barn, it doesn't make him a horse?"

"I'm pretty sure that's a line stolen from an L.M. Montgomery book…So you're off to Sodom and Gomorrah?"

"Dear girl, when good Canadians die they go to America."

"Pshaw."

"I want to develop my potential, Tessa. America is still the only place on earth where a man can be his own grandfather. You can't do that in a country that still has the English Queen on its money."

"What does that have to do with anything?"

"The colonial hangover here guarantees an inferiority complex. I want to be audacious. Start my own business someday. Do new things. That means a clean break with the past."

"Good luck with that. And you do realize you don't have to live in a poky place like Beaconsbridge or Sere Valley, right? There are more cosmopolitan Canadian cities."

"Marginally. But why stay in Carthage when you can make it to Rome? Maybe you'll join me some day, when you tire of the rustic charms of the homeland."

"Or once Mum starts driving me crazy." Tessa grimaced. "I'm only staying there until I figure out what's next. A few months, tops. The Maritimes will always be home, but…you know."

"I know. I love Madawaaksis County as much as you do, but the Maritimes is 10 men fighting over a five-piece pie."

"*Mais non, mon coeur!* In New Brunswick, that's a five-piece *pâte à la viande*," she corrected.

"Right."

"You're full of shit, Adrian. No one has more of the ironic Maritimer sensibility than you do. You'll always be a Maritimer with a sprinkling of book larnin' on top. The Maritimes made you. You can't deny that."

"I do not. The question is, how do I monetize this ironic Maritimer sensibility? Sadly, one can't make money off the Maritimer sensibility *in* the Maritimes. It's a problem…Be right back."

Not bothering to ask what she wanted, Adrian went off in search of the next round. Up at the bar, Mark's waitress reluctantly pulled herself away from her suitor to take Adrian's drink order. Mark greeted Adrian with a "Bro!" and a back-slap. Adrian nodded like a marionette and grunted a reply.

Back at the table, he handed Tessa her Sazerac.

"Here. I had to explain to Lolita how to make these."

"Thanks."

They sipped their cocktails.

"I still can't believe it, Tess. What are you going to do if you're not a prof? Even a bullshit adjunct prof. I mean, I know academia's fucked up right now, but geez. You don't have a lot of options, do you? You've done nothing but teach slack-jawed undergrads and go to school yourself for the past decade. What a waste of a Ph.D."

"It was a pleasant enough way to kill time."

Adrian continued, "Your CV won't mean jack-shit to private sector employers."

"Ok, enough Adrian. Not helping."

"Sorry."

"Flamm pretty much said the same thing to me yesterday. He's been Peak Weird since my firing. I detect both horror and envy. Of course, he'll continue to complain endlessly to Pearl about SVU, the Administration, how put-upon he is, and the hick town he can never leave, and he'll never do anything about it."

"Not everyone's like us, Tessa."

"Foolhardy?"

"No. Not everyone is adamant about being who they are," said Adrian.

"Well, I hope I can be who I am and still eat."

"Uh huh."

"We're lucky, Adrian. We're single. Youngish. No kids. We have the luxury of standing for principle."

"It's not a luxury. It's a necessity."

"Maybe. And maybe, as you implied, I've fucked up my life."

Adrian rolled his eyes. "I was teasing! You'll survive, dipshit. Your folks are divorcing and you just lost your job—make that your career—so I'll let you hold a pity party right now. But the day is coming when I may have to apply said boot"—he raised an Oxford—"to yon ass."

"Thanks buddy. I guess if Mum can start over at 52, I can do it at 28."

"Any time."

Adrian glanced up at the bar and noticed that the young waitress was done her shift. She'd removed her apron and migrated to Mark's lap.

"Look at that bastard."

Tessa shook her head in wonder. "Like watching Picasso paint or Michelangelo sculpt."

"Or Mata Hari whore."

Just then one of the circulating waiters set down two more Sazeracs on the table, saying, "Enjoy folks. These are from a friend."

"Who on earth...?"

"I'm supposed to say they're for Boo...Boo...?"

"Boudicca?" Tessa prompted.

"Yeah, that's it."

The waiter departed.

"Well, I'll be damned. Who...?"

"Don't look a gift-horse in the mouth, Tess."

Adrian claimed his drink.

On the other side of the bar, Destiny Claremont kept an eye on Tessa and Adrian's table. The hint of a smile played on her face.

"Sociable?" said Tessa, lapsing back into the vernacular, as she always did when she was drinking.

They clinked glasses again and drank. Townes Van Zandt's "Waiting Around to Die" began playing. Tessa reflected that the music had changed at The Ranch Hand in recent months. It was still country and folk, but with more of an edge to it. She liked the change. Adrian thought the same thing and wondered if the bar was under new ownership, non-locals perhaps. They drank as the sun set, as the light on the prairies softened and the shadows grew. It was their last Happy Hour together at The Ranch Hand.

Epilogue: Tomorrow (Starting Over)

Fr: Deborahann Stevens—deborahannstevens@hotmail.com

To: Tessa Stevens—te.stevens88@gmail.com; Lilly Stevens—l.stevens@wc.edu

Subject: New digs!!!

Date: May 14, 2017, 10:12 p.m.

Tessie-Bear and Lilly-Willy,

Ok. I am not using capitol letters any more. You complained so much. HAPPY? Haha that was the last one.

Yule and Abby and the boys helped me do the last leg of the move Friday night with the truck. The boys lifted the couch and Grammy Ada's big armchair. You know who didn't help of course.

Lilly-I talked to Jayson and he said he only has two terms left of law school and than he was doing the apprenticeship thingy (article-ing??) and than DONE. He is very handsome now! Might be more fun to be a lawyer's wife than to teach little BRATS all day! Just a thought. Hint hint. Sorry Tessie but Matt is TAKEN. HA!

Have internet here already but no landline. Will get new cell phone tomorrow and will call you than ASAP. Here is the new address-

35 McKenna Court, Apt. # 24

Moncton, NB E4H 2K2

Have been working all weekend opening boxes. 10 o'clock now and I am POOPED. Want to make the apartment nice and cozy. Brought all the house-plants but no room here so it looks like a JUNGLE. The hoya doesn't look so hot. They are very funnylooking and exotic plants. I miss my garden but like you said Tessie, I can live without it. I guess I can.

How did the chowder turn out, Lilly-Willy? Idella's old recipe is the best!

Dr. Leblanc's office called and said ECG test and blood tests all fine. Woohoo! Going in next week to get a 24 hour heart monitor thing as FINAL test. Dr. Leblanc said it was just to be on the safe side though as she thinks I am fine. (NO WORRYING! OK?)

Tessa- can you set up Netflix when you get here next week? (We are going to have so much fun!!!)

Some Beaconsbridge gossip: Margaret left Pastor Fudge! Went back to her family in Amherst. No one knows the whole story yet.

Maybe I will watch *An Officer and a Gentleman* now before bed. You know who would not let me watch my DVDs or my shows on the big downstairs tv but now there is only one tv and only ME so I can watch it any time I want! It is nice to just sit and not have someone yelling to make him a sandwich or come get something for him. HA.

Answer your phones please tomorrow.

Trixie says Hi!

LOVE TO MY TWO SMART GIRLS!

SEE YOU NEXT WEEK, TESSIE-BEAR!

MUM

P.S. The apartment is very quiet. You know I have never lived all by myself. You girls will have to show me the ropes. I'll be all right I guess.

Made in the USA
Las Vegas, NV
18 February 2021